Total Surrender

Total Surrender

Cheryl Holt

St. Martin's

Chapter One

"My goodness!" Lady Sarah Compton murmured aloud as she sat up straight and peered out the window. "I didn't know things like that went on in the country!" Her voice resonated in the empty, elegantly appointed bedchamber to which she'd been assigned.

Down below, the grounds were immaculately tended, with walkways carved in symmetric lines through the shrubbery. Torches were flickering, and couples were strolling about, enjoying the summer evening. Far at the rear of the yard, one pair paused for a lingering kiss. Their lips melded, their arms wrapped tightly, the embrace continued on and on, and she watched, embarrassed about staring but unable to stop.

The man slipped his fingers inside the bodice of the woman's dress, tenderly caressing her voluptuous breast, and for some reason, Sarah's own breasts swelled in response. Her nipples tightened and elongated, rubbing irritatingly against her corset, making her aware of her body in a fashion she'd never been before. Uneasy with the odd sensations, she shifted about in the window seat where she'd reposed, but she couldn't get comfortable.

Eventually, the man lowered his hands to the woman's bottom, urging her closer by massaging her buttocks, and Sarah lurched forward, intrigued and amazed by the blatant spectacle, until gradually, the duo shifted away, heading into the shadows where she couldn't observe them.

Raising her fingertips to the glass, she held them against the pane, tracing in deliberate circles, her gaze lingering on the spot where they'd been. They looked so compatible, as if they unequivocally belonged together, and their display stirred in her an unbearable longing for a similar attachment with another.

Her room was cheerful and pleasant, decorated with light blue rugs, wallpapering and draperies. The furniture was serviceable, the bed large and soft, the chairs cushioned for snuggling in front of the small hearth, but it was located on the third floor in a secluded wing of the mansion, which meant that there were no guests' voices or servants' footsteps passing by in the hall.

Though it was early June, the night was cool, and one of the maids had lit a fire. The dry wood popped and sizzled, creating the only sound in the silent chamber, and she felt totally removed, as if she was the very last person on earth, so disconnected that she might have been sitting on the moon.

The twilight sky was a deep indigo fading to black, and a single star flickered on the horizon. As though she was a silly young girl, she nearly made a wish on it, but caught herself before engaging in the absurd flight of fancy.

Wishing was for fools.

Even if she still believed in such idiocy, what would she pray for anyway? A different fate? A fortune to fall upon her? A rich husband? How ludicrous! As if she'd marry on the spur of the moment just to rescue her brother, Hugh, from his current fiasco!

"What am I doing here?" she queried aloud, but no answer echoed in reply.

A sense of separation and disorientation manifested, which was out of character. Typically, she relished solitude and preferred her own company to the blathering of others. Yet, now, she found herself yearning for . . .

She wasn't quite certain what. A huge cloud of dissatisfaction hovered over and around her, and she couldn't shake it. Nothing interested her, and there appeared to be no appropriate remedy for what ailed her. Since she wasn't precisely sure of her affliction, she couldn't concoct a cure.

Until recently, she'd always been assured of her path.

Her reclusive life in the country, her management of the family's Yorkshire estate, those decisions had been easily made and the results gratifying. But no longer. Discontentment reigned supreme.

Perhaps her restlessness was due to her advancing age. At twenty-five, she was entitled to evaluate the turns in her road, to review the detours she'd selected because of her unwavering recognition of duty and responsibility. The men in her family had never shown a predilection for preserving the ancient Scarborough title or property, so she'd juggled a cumbersome burden.

In the process, she'd given up a chance for her own home and children. While in the past, she'd never thought she'd wanted them and had never obsessed over their absence, of late, the missed opportunities were weighing heavily.

Should she have wed all those years ago?

She'd actually had a Season in London, but when she'd gone at age sixteen, she'd been ungainly and socially inept. Teased and laughed at, she'd been tormented, and the butt of more than a few cruel jests. Girls had tittered behind their fans over her genuineness, her lack of sophistication. Boys had snickered over her inadequate breasts, her crimson hair, her unwillingness to hide her intellect.

She'd fled the city, vowing never to return. Despite their father's subsequent ultimatums and demands, his insistence that she marry to shore up the family's lagging finances, she'd rebuffed his attempts at wedding her to any of the cruel oafs of the aristocracy who had belittled her. A categorical spinster, she'd spent the intervening years flourishing in the country at the Yorkshire property she loved.

Since those early days, she'd blossomed and matured, and she could have selected another path for herself. If she had, her life would be so different. She'd be admired, cherished and respected, a nobleman's wife, a parent. Instead, she'd remained single, a sort of jaded nanny for her father and half brother—two adults who had no inclination to grow up, and who had thus required incessant mothering.

Somehow, someway, she'd succumbed to the insupportable existence, and she couldn't tolerate the untenable onus inflicted upon her by those she was supposed to love.

When her father had been alive, it hadn't seemed so difficult. He'd been a kindly man, with good intentions, but his judgment was perpetually routed by bad choices. His disasters had habitually left him perplexed over the size of the catastrophes he'd wrought, but with his death, Hugh had assumed the title of Earl of Scarborough, and he gambled and played as though decadent comportment was his preordained right.

In direct contrast to their departed father, Hugh never evinced any fondness for the estate or the people who depended upon its prosperity for their incomes, and he was even more apathetic now that his character had worsened. Drink and fast living had brought on strange mood swings, and he could be cruel, prone to violent outbursts and heedless conduct.

His latest gambling blunder was a perfect example of his slide to perdition, and she couldn't help but replay their horrid conversation, when they'd discussed the loss and the unknown man who'd prompted it. The words tumbled through her head like a bad refrain, flaying her with the evidence of the sorry state of her affairs.

"Was it the faro tables?" she'd asked him, as if the method of his downfall had mattered!

"No."

"But it was cards?"

"A few games of commerce is all."

"I see. How much?"

"All that's left."

"Define all."

"Whatever is not entailed to the title."

"The furniture?"

"Yes."

"The last of the farming equipment?"

"Yes."

"The clothes off my back?"

"Perhaps. I'm not sure how far he will dip into the personal possessions of the family."

"How about me?" she'd probed starkly. *"Have you wagered me away, too?"*

"He'd have no use for you," Hugh had retorted coldly. *"He typically likes his women a tad on the feminine side."*

The cut had been harsh, striking at her old insecurities, and it still hurt to think that he'd uttered it, but that was Hugh: rash, negligent, and caustic.

What she wouldn't give to throttle him! It was bad enough that he'd gambled away the last of their possessions, but the twenty thousand pounds he'd lost as well— money they didn't have and never would—was reckless beyond imagining.

When he'd visited at Yuletide, she'd given him the last three-hundred pounds from her dowry, and she'd warned him there was no more. Not that he'd listened. He'd forged ahead with his corrupt course and, while the villain holding his markers had allowed him three months to pay, there was no way they could come up with that amount of cash.

Of course, Hugh's solution was that she save him, once again, by marrying a wealthy husband as quickly as possible. The idea was absurd, yet she'd found herself agreeing to try, simply because she hated being at odds with him, but she was heartily weary of pandering to his needs, of adapting to his degeneracy, scrimping and saving, never having enough.

How she hated being poor!

Perhaps that was the real reason she'd decided to go visiting and had traveled to Bedford and Lady Carrington's house party—for it assuredly wasn't in order to snag a spouse as Hugh insisted she must.

Excessive, unrelenting poverty was so grim. Didn't she deserve a bit of fun? Hadn't she earned some frivolity and merriment?

There was so little joy in her days, no carefree, gay entertainments, no pleasurable meals or leisurely afternoons spent at capricious pursuits. There was just apprehension and despondency and gloom, and now—with Hugh's latest conundrum—there was desperation, too, but she'd been expecting the worst forever so the end was anticlimactic.

For once, she had no inclination to rescue Hugh. She'd delivered him from one debacle after the next until he'd begun to erroneously assume that she could rectify any exigency, and he obviously thought she was prepared, on this occasion, to work another miracle. Unfortunately, her patience had finally been exhausted, and her stamina for weathering another calamity had vanished.

She'd had months to brace herself for the sordid conclusion that was approaching; she'd felt it down to the marrow of her bones. All through the winter and spring, she'd kept peeking over her shoulder, as though Doom was lurking there, ready to overtake her when she least suspected it. Yet, her destiny had quietly arrived in the form of a nameless, faceless gambler.

Who was the man foolhardy enough to wager for Hugh's pitiful belongings? Down to the candle holders on the walls, it would all go. Such a meager pile! Who would want it? Who would be that greedy? Clearly, the blackguard was more addicted to gaming than Hugh. What a sorry individual he must be!

A knock sounded on the door, and she rose slowly and trudged to admit the serving maid and a quartet of burly men who carried large jugs of hot water for the bathing tub awaiting her in the adjoining dressing room. As they grappled with their task, she relaxed on a chair beside the fire, eyes closed, ears peeled, eagerly listening as the water splashed into and filled the basin.

A real bath! The maid had offered one, and Sarah had selfishly accepted the luxury. At home, she never had a full bath anymore. There were only a few elderly servants remaining, and she never had the heart to obligate any of them to lug the heavy load upstairs.

Her personal washing was done in the kitchens after supper, quick swipes with a cloth. How exotic it seemed to have the opportunity to immerse her body! The thrill she received just from thinking about it only underscored the miserably low level to which her fortunes had descended.

The men—buckets empty—departed, and Sarah had the maid unfasten her gown and corset, then she ushered the woman out. This extravagance was one she deigned to enjoy at length and privately.

With modest complications, she shed her dress and most of her undergarments. Clad only in a chemise that hung to mid-thigh, she went to the inner chamber. The room was small and cozy. A miniature brazier, the coals aflame and glowing, heated the air. A painted screen was set against one wall, and the tub hidden behind it.

Sarah approached. Steam drifted up, and she dangled her fingers, checking the temperature. On a nearby vanity lay a stack of towels, soaps, and other bathing accouterments. She opened bottles and sniffed at the contents, locating a rose-scented oil and adding it to the vaporous mixture.

Ready to begin, she almost stepped in, then paused. A sudden whim to be daring and bold ensnared her, so she reached for the hem of her chemise and pulled it over her head.

She'd bathe in the nude! She never had before, but who would know? The maid had been dismissed, she was far from home, on her own. Within reason, she could engage in any scandalous behavior without detection.

Feeling naughty and audacious, she spun about and saw her reflection in a mirror positioned next to the tub. Entranced, she realized that she couldn't remember when she'd ever inspected her nude torso.

As though taking inventory of a stranger, she tipped from side to side, searching for attributes and checking for flaws. Ultimately, she decided that she was beholding a fetching woman, slim, rounded, with stunning emerald eyes and glorious auburn hair. Her body curved appropriately—expansive at the shoulder, narrow at the waist, flared at the hips—and her slender legs made her appear taller than she was.

Shifting, she appraised her profile, but the stance highlighted her breasts in a manner that was as enticing as it was disturbing. She couldn't quit looking, and she was overcome by the disquieting notion that this was why one didn't parade about naked. Too many unsettling and unusual sensations were provoked.

Under her visual inspection, her breasts felt fuller, heavier, and her pink nipples hardened into two taut little buds—just as they had when she'd been spying on the two lovers in the yard. Curious, she rested her palm against one of the extended tips, and the action brought about a flurry of physical agitation.

Her nipples started to ache and throb. With each beat of her heart, the pulsation hammered through her chest. It progressed down her abdomen to lodge deep inside, at the core of her womb, causing it to shift and awaken. The woman's spot between her legs seemed to expand and moisten.

Unexpectedly, she was deluged by a wave of longing so intense that she nearly crumpled under its strength, and she grabbed for the rim of the tub to steady herself from the onslaught. The impression was puzzling to describe. She craved . . . though *what* she couldn't have explained.

Surprisingly, she envisioned the couple in the garden again, and she scrutinized her smooth, bare flank, remembering how the man had stroked the woman's buttocks, how he'd levered her closer. She recalled how the pair had slipped into the dark, and she speculated about what had occurred once they were in a more remote area. What sorts of mysterious things had the man done to the woman?

The proceedings were beyond the ken of a virginal spinster, but she couldn't help wondering. Apparently, her imagination was quite vivid, for the mental pictures increased her agonizing awareness of her breasts.

"Craziness," she muttered. Craziness to be alone and retired for the evening, and ruminating over lewd riddles.

Disgusted with herself, she plucked her roving hands from her body and locked them around the edges of the tub where they would stay out of trouble.

Carefully, she sank down, and she hissed out a breath

as she landed on her knees, and the blistering liquid slapped at her thighs. She proceeded with scrubbing her various parts, but much of the pleasure she'd hoped to delight in had disappeared. Every place she touched reacted. The rough nap of the washcloth aggravated her receptive flesh, so she gave up, sliding farther into the basin and reclining as much as she was able.

Struggling to relax, she balanced on her arms and tipped her head back, relishing the warmth. At some point, fatigue overwhelmed her, and she dozed. When she opened her eyes again, she'd slept for quite a while. The water had cooled, so she stood, letting it sluice off her skin, then she climbed out onto the rug and snatched one of the towels.

Commencing at her neck, she worked across her breasts, her stomach. Briefly, she rasped across the delicate cleft between her legs, but she didn't care for the stimulation it induced, so she bent over and rubbed down thigh and calf. As she straightened, movement captured her attention, and she glanced into the mirror.

A man was lounging behind her, perfectly at home, and casually viewing all! The sight was so startling that she was temporarily paralyzed, incapable of processing what she was witnessing. His appearance seemed like a dream, and she narrowed her focus at his reflection, grappling to make sense of the bizarre development.

Not an illusion, he was really and truly there.

Tall, with trimmed black hair and striking sapphire eyes, he was a ravishing man—perhaps the most handsome she'd ever encountered. He had high cheekbones, an aristocratic nose, a generous mouth. His wide shoulders tapered to a thin waist, lanky hips, long legs, and powerful, muscled thighs.

He wore only a pair of fitted trousers, no shirt or shoes, and she was tantalized by the absurd observation that she'd never before beheld a man's unclad chest. It was covered by an intriguing fur of dark hair, piled thick on top then dwindling across his flat stomach to a slim line that disappeared into the waistband of his pants. The top two buttons were undone, so she could see much farther than she ought, and the spectacle was perturbing and exhilarating in a manner she didn't comprehend.

"Lovely . . ." he murmured in an enticing baritone that skittered across her nerve endings and induced her abdomen to clench in response.

The peculiar salutation snapped her into action, and she whirled to face him. Nervously, she clutched at the towel, desperately striving to shield herself, but his probing examination slithered over her like a tangible caress, lingering on her lips, her breasts, the juncture between her thighs.

"How did you get in here?" she reproached, endeavoring to sound adamant and assertive, but the quaver in her voice communicated her uneasiness.

"Through the door." He gestured, and she noticed a second screen and a door behind it, adjoining her dressing room to the next bedchamber.

He took a step toward her, and she took a step back. "You're not welcome. Leave at once!"

"Are you sure you want me to go?"

"Absolutely!"

"But wouldn't it be more amusing if I stayed? You could climb in the tub again, and I could wash you. Or"—he glanced down at his pants that so graphically outlined his masculine form—"I could soak in the water, and you could bathe *me*. Either way, I promise the experience will be everything you desire. And more."

A man and a woman bathing? Together? Washing? Each other? A whirl of incredulous scenes flashed through her mind, and her heart raced.

His fingers went to the front of his trousers and touched the placard as though he was about to release the rest of the buttons and strip himself. Panicked, she kept her gaze bravely affixed to his. "What do you think you're doing?"

"Disrobing."

"Don't you dare!"

He chuckled, oozing charm. "I'd heard you were eager, but I don't mind prolonging things with a few games."

She had no idea what he meant and couldn't even hazard a guess. Flustered, she resorted to the type of polite disdain she regularly employed with recalcitrant underlings. "I've politely requested that you leave, and now I insist."

"Before you've had your fun?"

The question was mildly raised, his tone one of intimate promise about matters she didn't understand. There was a confidence and subdued arrogance in his demeanor that seemed to guarantee gratification.

He moved closer.

The mirror was directly behind her, the basin on one side, the vanity on the other, and he was in front. She was hemmed into the corner, unable to slip past, and it occurred to her that—discounting Hugh—this was the only instance she'd ever been closeted with an adult man. The doors were closed, the room isolated, the servants abed, and if she'd chosen to call out, no one was available to assist her.

She was totally at his mercy, and she was supposed to be scared and alarmed, yet she found herself elated by the scandalous interlude. Where the heady, ribald euphoria sprang from she couldn't have explained, because she hadn't realized she was craving a clandestine adventure.

Perhaps the man, himself, instilled the improper sentiment. He was overtly complacent about their situation, assured that he had every right to enter, confident that she would appreciate the wrongful intrusion. When he stared at her with those extraordinary eyes, she yearned to acquiesce to whatever he suggested.

Still, she couldn't permit him to remain, and she pulled herself up to her full height, which was distinctly lacking considering how he towered over her. "I'll not ask again, sir."

"I've been watching you."

He'd been watching her? From where? For how long? Had he observed her whole bath? Mortified, she clasped the towel more securely against her breasts. "How terribly vile."

"You opened the peephole." He shrugged, his offensive

shattering of polite conduct apparently being of no import. "Why wouldn't I look through?"

"What peephole?" she inquired, aghast.

"The one between our rooms." He ignored her outrage. "Your skin is so smooth. Like silk."

The simple statement disconcerted her. She'd never before received a flattering compliment from a man, especially not an attractive, virile, mostly naked one, and as she stumbled for a response, he advanced like a large cat, a graceful, predatory beast like those from the jungles of Africa that she'd seen at an exhibition in London. He was so near that the fist she'd valiantly anchored to her bosom to hold the towel was pressed against his ribs. His skin was warm, and his matting of chest hair tickled the heel of her hand.

She tilted away, but the mirror prevented evasion. Though she fought to appear staunch and in control, her dilemma had quickly spiraled beyond her ability to navigate. Anxiously, she licked her bottom lip, which instantly had him studying her mouth as though intent on devouring her.

"Sir, you're scaring me."

"How?"

"I'm not certain why you're here—"

"Aren't you?" His words were husky with a dangerous lust that even she, in her sheltered, virginal state, couldn't misconstrue.

"—or what you propose . . ."

"You know what I *propose*. I'll be very gentle if that's how you like it." With a sure finger, he traced down her cheek and across her neck, and his touch was so blistering that she felt as if she'd been burned. She flinched, and he soothed, "You don't need to be afraid."

She battled to comprehend what he was saying. It seemed that he aimed to force himself upon her, but there was no urgency in his demeanor. "If you were any kind of gentleman . . ."

"I'm no gentleman, my dear lady. Never have I professed to be."

Her pulse thudded at a higher rate. She had no notion how to interact with a man who uttered such a wild claim. If he didn't deem himself to be a gentleman, then what code governed his behavior? "If you don't depart, I'll scream."

"I don't care if you scream. I'm happy to indulge any of your whims, just as you'll get to indulge mine, so you're free to do whatever makes our rendezvous more enjoyable for you."

What? She shook her head, perplexed and becoming frightened even though he'd done nothing that was outright menacing.

"Please . . . I'm here alone, and I'm . . ." She wanted to state the obvious—that she was undressed—but she couldn't speak the word *naked* to this unknown scoundrel, and she blushed bright red, the flush originating somewhere in the vicinity of her stomach and sweeping up her breasts to her cheeks. Unduly warm, she resisted the impulse to fan herself lest she drop the towel.

"I demand that you go."

"God, you're pretty." He reached behind her head and tugged at a comb that had helped to restrain her abundant locks, and the velvety mass cascaded down her back and hung to her waist. "I love your hair. It shimmers like fire."

For one, mad instant, she thought he planned to kiss her, but instead, he ducked under her chin and nuzzled against her shoulder at the site where her pulse pounded so furiously. A shiver of excitement tore through her, and she swallowed a baffled squeal that could have been either delight or indignation.

His lips were heated and soft, and he tenderly kissed against her nape then, to her astonishment, he licked across her skin. She jumped then twirled away, only to end up facing the mirror, with him behind her, and she assessed the two of them, evaluating the differences: his tall to her short, bronzed to fair, brawn to lean.

Boldly, he settled his hands on her hips and snuggled her backside against him, and she was assailed by an array of unique anatomical impressions. As though she'd been searching for this man all her life and had finally found him, she ignited with sensation, every pore alert and animated, and her nipples tightened painfully, poking at the towel.

The knave immediately noticed how they'd peaked. "I can't wait to have my mouth on you."

The declaration kindled cryptic images, and restlessly, she scrambled to flee—from the unusual fleshly perturbation and from him—but because of their positions, he merely nestled her close and flexed against her. His groin stroked across her bottom in a manner she'd never presumed a man might attempt with a woman. There was a solid ridge along his abdomen that dug into her buttocks, and her traitorous body reacted by squirming to get nearer to it. He appreciated her participation and gripped her firmly, flexing again.

"Your breasts are so beautiful," he murmured. "Just the size I like on a woman. Not too big. Not too small." Before she knew what he was about, he'd pushed the towel aside, revealing one to his torrid gaze. He cupped it, weighing it with his palm, then he pinched the nipple, twirling and manipulating it back and forth.

The swirl of agony he instigated was like nothing she'd ever previously experienced. The torment blazed a trail that commenced at her bosom, then rushed out across her torso, to the roots of her hair and the tips of her toes, and she curled them into the rug.

"Please," she begged, but whether she was beseeching him to continue or cease was impossible to surmise. On some secret level, she surreptitiously craved what he was vigorously inflicting.

"Look at us," was his rejoinder. There was a gleam in his eye that made him appear wicked and beyond redemption. "Look at how exquisite we are with my hands on you."

His gaze met hers in the mirror, and she could only conclude that he was correct. Mesmerized, she was beguiled by the incongruous perception that she was magnificent in his arms: curvaceous, feminine, alluring. Their bodies were flawlessly reconciled, perfectly attuned, and the display titillated and disturbed. Much as she wanted to, she couldn't quit staring.

He could read her thoughts, and he smiled insolently. "You see it, too, don't you?"

"You're mistaken," she pointlessly asserted.

"Am I?"

Determined to prove her wrong, he unveiled her other breast, and she desperately grasped the towel around her waist, so it wouldn't fall to the floor and leave her uncovered. As she battled with her nude condition, he petted and fondled, squeezing the mounds and tweaking the nipples until they spasmed intolerably.

Her breathing hitched. Too much was happening too fast. The wanton episode was so inconceivable that it played out like a fantasy—except that he was really present, arousing and addictive. Her mind wailed for her to call a halt, but her body wouldn't obey.

"I'd planned to have you on your bed the first time"— his assertion brushed against her ear—"but maybe I should take you here, by the mirror, so you can see how splendid we are together."

An exotic fog may have temporarily immobilized her, but a fragment of sanity managed to seep in, and she was coherent enough to realize that her virtue was in peril, so she fought his restraint, but he scarcely noted her opposition. He lifted her and deposited her on the vanity, in a fluid move, scooting her back and positioning himself between her thighs.

They had rapidly vaulted to a different, more ominous, stage of involvement. There was an obstinate air about him; he wouldn't desist until he'd journeyed to a conclusion of which only he was cognizant.

He yanked the towel away, and she was completely ex-

posed, and he dipped to her nipple and sucked at it. The
untried crest was raw and inflamed from how his fingers
had handled it, and his mouth only increased her distress.
With a yelp of surprise, she resisted his machinations, even
as her body hastened forward toward an unfamiliar destination, and she had to combat the urge to spur him on.

So entranced was she by his concentration on her nipple
that she didn't discern how he'd shockingly traced his hand
down her stomach until he massaged across her womanly
cleft. Without warning, he delved through the springy hair
and parted the folds, then pushed a finger inside. She froze,
wondering what he contemplated, but he caressed her gently, the maneuver at odds with the tension she could sense
emanating from him. The foreign intrusion strengthened her
conviction to escape, but retreat was blocked by his hips
and thighs.

"Stop it!" she commanded, but he didn't appear to hear
her; he kept on. "Stop it, now!"

Blindly, she groped about, latched onto a heavy decanter, and swung it at his head. The blow glanced off his
crown, but it definitely got his attention. He wrenched
away, patently confused.

"Jesus," he muttered, "what the bloody hell did you do
that for?"

She swung again and caught him alongside the temple,
tearing a gash. Blood welled into the cut, and he staggered,
momentarily off balance, and she utilized his distraction to
leap away, swathing the towel about her as she went. Dashing into the bedchamber, she considered sprinting into the
hall, but she couldn't let anyone discover her predicament.

Commotion emanated from the dressing room, and she
spun around. Her adversary, a cloth jammed to his head,
had stumbled in behind her, and she cast about for a
weapon but didn't see anything useful. She still held the
bottle, so she smacked it against the marble of the fireplace,
and it shattered effectively.

"Stay away from me," she ordered, brandishing the broken glass. "Depart at once—the same way you entered— or I'll slice you to pieces like the swine you are."

The man paused for the slightest moment then, enraged as a wounded bear, he stalked toward her.

Chapter Two

Michael Stevens stopped in the doorway to the bedchamber
as the crazed woman before him smashed a decanter against
the fireplace. Glass shards flew everywhere.

"I mean it!" she repeated in threat. "Go!"

He wasn't certain what had just occurred between them
in her dressing room but, considering the aftermath he was
now viewing, he had to sincerely wonder whether she was
prone to lunacy.

What type of female invited a man to her boudoir, enticed him beyond reason, then panicked like a silly virgin?
She was fortunate he still had control of his wits, that he
wasn't the sort who would rush across the room and take
what she'd initially offered but had obviously decided she
didn't want to supply.

The woman was a menace, and he couldn't help but
wonder what Pamela Blair, Lady Carrington, was thinking,
welcoming such an unstable person to her fete. Pamela regularly opened her home to her decadent friends and acquaintances, providing them with a private and confidential
environment where they could frolic at their leisure. They
came in droves, to fornicate and debauch, both the men and
women ready to wallow in every sick, ribald, immoral fantasy imaginable, and there were plenty of men currently
visiting who wouldn't desist, despite these loud, fervent
protests.

Pamela was risking disaster by bringing such a volatile
guest onto the premises, and Michael couldn't wait to tell
her so. In the meantime, he had to figure out a method of
soothing this beautiful-but-deranged shrew before she
shouted the house down.

To think that he'd let himself be lured away from a placid, civilized game of cards for this! If he'd utilized superior judgment, he could be downstairs—winning—while safely sequestered in the company of rational men or, better yet, he could have gone to cavort with any of the other female guests who'd asked, and he could at this very moment be copulating in peace, without being banged on the head for his troubles.

Considering the numbers of gorgeous, lustful women who were flowing in and out of the property, he'd had numerous other acceptable choices. As he was the most disreputable male in their midst, the wanton ladies of the *ton* were positively dying to couple with him, and for the past few weeks, he'd impulsively obliged their despicable caprices.

The party was every man's greatest dream come true. The level of decadence guaranteed that anything and everything was permitted, the women pleasing and amenable, and rules and inhibitions abolished. Raw interaction and meaningless sex, copious, insignificant, unrefined intercourse, was not only tolerated under Pamela's roof, but absolutely encouraged, with the prerequisite being that the people partaking of her hospitality were completely predisposed to misbehavior.

So what was this woman doing in Pamela's house? What did she hope to accomplish by this maidenly display of offense?

Belowstairs, he'd stepped from the card room in order to stroll outside in the fresh air, when he'd been accosted by a buxom blonde who'd pulled him aside and whispered insistently that the auburn-haired virago standing in front of him wanted him to visit, that she was too shy to come to him later on as others would, so she sought a covert rendezvous in the privacy and sanctity of her own bedchamber.

Supposedly, she'd never previously attended one of Pamela's parties, was nervous about her participation, and therefore wished an inconspicuous orientation into the carnal routine.

When the request had been posed by her alleged friend, he hadn't given much thought to who the blonde ambassador was, or to why she was soliciting sexual congress on behalf of another, but he was definitely curious now as to her identity. Earlier, he'd presumed she was a lady's companion or perhaps her maid, so he hadn't ruminated over the entreaty or why it had been oddly made.

Already, he'd grown bored with the proceedings that Pamela had instituted and the situations she'd convinced him to try. The available lovers were as jaded as himself, and surprisingly, he missed the closeness and spark that should have come with making love, so he'd readily consented to indoctrinate this novice but, in light of the manifest level of her upset, he had to admit that something was seriously awry.

She hardly resembled a reticent, demure paramour. Instead of a lonely female awaiting a bit of subdued loveplay, she appeared overwrought, shocked, outraged, and—if the murderous gleam in her eye was any indication—ready to kill.

Typically, he disdained the bored, unhappy aristocratic noblewomen who had filled Pamela's country house to overflowing. He detested their loose morals and their lewd, lascivious lifestyles. They were pathetic in the lengths to which they would go to find diversion from their tedium.

With no conscience and no integrity, they would commit any contemptible act. They saw nothing wrong with cuckolding their husbands, with carrying on indiscreet liaisons, or fornicating with little concern as to whether they bred children not fathered by their spouses.

His aversion to them was only surpassed by his disgust for their husbands, those lazy, impotent peers of the realm who drank and wagered and debauched without regard to the consequences. They assumed they had a God-given right to inflict themselves on the rest of the world.

In London, he and his brother, James, owned a gaming

club where they pandered to and coddled the slothful lords. Those earls and barons couldn't keep their blunt in their wallets or their cocks in their trousers, and he and James catered to their base whims, which was undeniably the reason their business was so popular.

If he'd been in town at the moment, he'd have been hard at work, ensuring that there was adequate liquor and food available, so that the exalted gentlemen would be comfortable while they complacently gambled away their estates and their children's inheritances.

How he despised them all!

They were men of no principles or ethics, who would spout their accursed code of honor until they choked on it, but deep down, they were blackguards and cads with nary a scruple, so he was more than happy to have sexual relations with their willing wives, which was why he'd traveled to Bedford.

Whenever one of their spouses beckoned, he was entirely agreeable. In any manner, in any fashion, as often and savagely as they could bear it, he'd dabble with them, heedless as to the damage he might leave in his wake, because in his opinion, they deserved every bit of misery he was able to mete out.

So he wasn't exactly sure what had gone wrong this time. He'd been *invited* to the damned room. Asked to watch. Asked to fondle. Asked to fuck. And all he'd gotten for it was a cockstand so excruciating he could barely walk, and a crack on the skull that had nearly put him out. As it was, he'd probably end up with a stitch or two in his cheek before the night was through.

Bloody, wretched woman! Didn't she know better than to trifle with a precariously aroused man?

Though he'd never been the sort to raise a hand to a female, he had half a mind to take her over his knee. In his present mood, the chance to deliver a good thrashing—especially to someone as reckless and idiotic as she appeared to be—sounded like a fabulous idea.

He stepped into the room. "Would you please lower your voice before someone hears you?"

"Stay back!" she commanded again, wielding her make-shift weapon, and she lifted one of her dainty feet as if she might actually wade into the sea of broken glass surrounding her.

Marvelous! Just what he needed, both of them cut and bleeding! Perhaps he should send down to the kitchens for a physician and the thread to sew them up!

"Are you mad?" he barked, but softly. Taking into account his dubious position with these illustrious personages, he never made a public scene, and he wasn't about to start, yet she didn't seem overly concerned about the opinion of others.

Not inclined to make matters worse, he threw aside the cloth he'd pressed to his wound, then he stormed toward her until they were toe to toe. A piece of glass pierced his heel, but he was so angry that the pain barely registered. "Give me that!"

He reached for the fractured decanter and yanked it away, hurling it into the nearby hearth where it clanked undramatically against the bricks. She squealed in protest and twirled to run, but he grabbed her from behind, slipping an arm around her waist and lifting her up. As he swung her out of the pool of shards and slivers, she struggled to escape, administering a swift kick to his shin that had him wincing, but, for the most part, her efforts were ineffectual.

The only true damage was to his abused, overinflated phallus, but it wasn't physical injury he was suffering. Their awkward position had deposited her shapely ass directly against his groin, and his cock swelled further and cried out for an excuse to finish what they'd started.

God, but he wanted her!

The woman possessed no secrets. From the beginning, when she'd entered the dressing room and tested the temperature of the bathwater, he'd been spying on her through the tiny hole affixed to the wall between their rooms.

The antiquated mansion was notorious in its design, a

veritable lecher's treasure trove of concealed rooms, secluded hallways, and peepholes so that when she'd pulled
off her chemise, he'd seen all: the graceful legs, the curved
hips, the crimson hair shielding her pussy, the pert breasts
with their beaded nipples.

She was a ravishing woman, with that spectacular hair,
those cheekbones, that cute nose with its upturned tip. And
that mouth! With its wicked tongue! How he longed to
learn how adept it could be when she wasn't busy using it
to spew sass and issue orders.

As she'd deliberately and languidly stripped herself bare
then knelt in the tub, seductively scrubbing her private
places, she'd seemed an intriguing mix of innocence and
experience, wholesome yet tantalizing. Knowing he was
watching—or so he'd believed—she'd presented a sensual,
galvanizing exhibition that could only have been designed
to titillate and inflame. The interlude had been the most
erotic he'd ever witnessed in a lifetime that had been filled
with naughty sexual activity.

Remarkably, the most intriguing segment had been when
she'd lain back in the water with her head tipped against
the rim and her eyelids had fluttered closed.

While she'd slept, she'd appeared young, ingenuous, and
removed from the worries that had marred her face when
she'd first arrived. She snored, and he couldn't help chuckling at the memory, or speculating as to how indiscreet
she'd deem him to be if he mentioned it.

Unwonted emotion had tugged at his heartstrings as
she'd slumbered so serenely. What had brought her to Bedford and Pamela's indecent party? What horrid episode had
transpired that would make her presume the gathering
would rectify her woes?

She doesn't belong here.

The conviction had spiraled through his mind over and
over again, and he'd been overwhelmed by the perception
that he understood more about her than he properly ought,
that he could sense things about her he had no reason to
distinguish. Absurdly, he was desperate to keep her safe

from harm, and he'd nearly persuaded himself that he'd be doing her an enormous favor if he spirited her away.

Eventually, he'd shaken off the ludicrous notion. Spurred by unfathomable motives, the woman had summoned him upstairs, which meant she was a pampered, amoral member of the *ton* who had come to Pamela's abode of sin and vice of her own accord, and who was downright eager to enjoy the licentious amusements the lady rendered to her guests.

Pamela habitually catered to the male libertines and roués of High Society, as well as to their degenerate women, so he was inordinately familiar with this termagant's type of debased disposition, and he'd relished the idea of having her.

There was a deceptive air about her that fascinated him; she was natural yet beguiling, and he'd calculated that copulation with her would be a refreshing development, that she would bring something to his sexual intercourse that had been lacking for a long while. By doing nothing at all, she fomented a diverse jumble of sentiment that had him craving more than a heedless carnal encounter.

Perhaps his heart had not turned to stone, after all.

With a great deal of excitement and anticipation, he'd approached her, enthusiastic to dispense the sensual attention she'd requested, while anxious to obtain a nebulous, but undeniable, benefit in return. He'd silently observed as she'd awakened and dried herself, scrupulously evaluating her saucy breasts, her rounded ass, and ultimately determining that she would be a perfect partner for the ribald sorts of libidinous recreation he enjoyed.

Initially, with her exclamations of shock and insult at his appearance, he'd thought she was playacting. So many of them did, feeling the need to blunt their depravity by feigning umbrage. As they'd studied their joint reflections in the mirror, she'd been so curious, so responsive and receptive, but as he'd moved to the next level, as he'd suckled at her supple breast, he'd received the distinct impression that she was unprepared for what she'd initiated, which left him totally bewildered.

Unceremoniously, he dumped her on the bed and tossed her towel after her.

"Cover yourself."

She hastily complied, but the towel wasn't wide enough to suit her purposes, and trembling, she cowered beneath it. He glanced about until he located a green robe draped over a chair; he retrieved it, and pitched it to her.

"Put this on," he dictated, then he showed her his back while searching the walls for peepholes. Behind him, he noted her hesitation, then she hurriedly moved about on the bed. When the mattress shifted and her feet hit the floor, he spun around.

Mercy, but she was an erotic sight, with that splendid hair curling across her shoulders. She'd cinched the robe's belt at her waist, and the fabric flawlessly outlined her magnificent body, her graceful hips, her pouty breasts with those tempting nipples. Their discord had elevated her pulse and flushed her cheeks to a flattering rose color.

Their gazes linked and held. Though she was shaking like a skittish colt, she meant to stand her ground.

"Who is your husband?" he quietly demanded.

"I'm not married."

"You're a widow?"

"No. I've never wed."

"You're single?"

"Yes."

Tersely, he bit out, "Then why did you ask me here?"

"Me? Ask you?"

"If you didn't plan an assignation, why invite me to your room? Are you so naive that you don't appreciate how dangerous it is to dabble with a man when you've no intention of following through?"

"You believe that I'm the kind of woman who would . . ." Aghast, she sputtered. "That I . . . that I . . ."

Apparently, she couldn't utter the words that would describe the type of person he suspected her of being. A niggling wave of doubt swamped him. "You fancied *me*. You specifically propositioned *me*."

"You wretched bounder!" Thoroughly insulted, her stunning emerald eyes glimmered heatedly. She clutched at the lapels of her robe. "How dare you concoct such a wild story!"

Taking her measure, he carefully scrutinized her affront. He was a good judge of character and always had been. In his line of employment, he had to regularly assess veracity and temperament, and he was convinced she was telling the truth. She had neither solicited him nor procured his services.

So, who was the blond emissary who had lured him to her? And why? Clearly, someone hoped to set a carnal trap. But for him? Or for her? And to what end?

Abruptly and gravely apprehensive, he raced to the door and locked it.

"What are you doing?" she queried, but he ignored her.

A painting hung on the wall, and he lifted it off its hook. Sure enough, there was a partially hidden peephole that would have allowed a voyeur to lurk in the hall and peek inside. He flipped the artwork upside down, and the opening was effectively shielded.

After a meticulous search of that wall and another, he discovered no more holes. The third wall faced the exterior of the house and the fourth, the inner dressing room, so they couldn't possibly contain any. The only other entrance—the door to his adjoining bedchamber—was barred from within. For now, they were relatively secure. No one could fortuitously stumble upon them in a compromising situation.

Wary and determined, he confronted her, once again. "Who are you?"

"I don't wish to say, and if we should ever have the misfortune to meet a second time, I insist that you pretend you don't know who I am."

"Not bloody likely."

He stomped over to her, and she straightened, distressed

yet striving to appear brave. Angrily, he stared her down until it gradually dawned on him that a strange energy was sparking between them, their bodies extending out to one another, and he grimaced with dismay. He didn't want to be attracted to her!

As a man vastly experienced with women, he readily recognized that they shared an acute physical affinity. Whether she emitted a covert signal or radiated a particular chemistry, he couldn't explain the phenomenon, but she aroused him as no other could, and he hastily squelched the bizarre erotic realization. At present, he had bigger problems to mull than an asinine, unwarranted amorous bond.

"Do you have any idea"—his hushed tone was scathing—"what would have happened if we'd been discovered just now?"

The question startled her. Evidently, she'd been so overwhelmed that she hadn't had the opportunity to reflect upon the momentous consequences. "What do you mean? Are you suggesting that someone aimed to catch us?"

"Your name, madam. If you please." Mutinously, she returned his glare but didn't reply. "Fine. Then tell me this: Who is a blond woman in attendance? She's about your age, petite but shapely, with big blue eyes." *And fabulous breasts,* he nearly appended, but he wouldn't describe her by such a crass method.

After a lengthy hesitation while she weighed all the angles, she retorted, "Probably my cousin. Why?"

So . . . she had a family member on the premises who proposed personal mischief. Interesting and terrifying! He was an expert at ferreting out suspicious facts and histories; he did it systematically at the club where he frequently unearthed the sordid details of their customers' lives. There were many ways to untangle this debacle.

"No reason," he responded enigmatically, which caused her to bristle.

"Why did you inquire?" she decreed authoritatively as

though she spent her days expounding proclamations that were instantly obeyed.

"I shan't confess, milady." Menacingly, he towered over her. He was purposely trying to intimidate with his size, but it wasn't working. "And might I recommend that you refrain from ordering me about? I'm not one of the lowly minions in your orbit who will leap to do your bidding."

"What is your name?"

"Michael Stevens."

He braced for the predictable sign of recognition . . . but none followed. Because of his gaming establishment, and the notoriety of his parentage, he was so infamous in her circles that he was inevitably identified and gossiped about wherever he went. The fact that she was clueless as to his renown was definitely a puzzle.

His mother was the celebrated actress Angela Ford, and his ass of a father, the wealthy and illustrious Earl of Spencer, Edward Stevens. Michael and his brother had to be the two most conspicuous bastard sons ever conceived. How could she not know? Had she been raised in a cave?

"Why are you here at Lady Carrington's party?" he snapped.

"I'm on holiday." Churlishly, she added, "Not that my schedule is any of your concern."

"Madam, I just mistakenly had my mouth on your breast, and my hand up your twat. I'd say that makes everything about you my business."

"How utterly crude of you to mention what transpired!"

Irritated, and tired of whatever plot someone was hatching, he harshly retorted, "I didn't hear you complaining."

"Are you implying that I instigated this fiasco? You despicable cad!" Steam was literally shooting out of her ears as she jabbed a finger in the center of his chest. "I didn't! I told you to leave! I advised you from the first, but you wouldn't listen! How dare you insinuate otherwise!"

Although he was loath to admit it, she was correct, and he burned with chagrin. He'd thought her introductory, tepid denials had been an eccentric version of lovemaking, and despite how much he'd like to lash out, the debacle was scarcely her fault.

"You're right, of course. My apologies."

"Thank you." At her acceptance of his olive branch, her gaze united with his as she entreated, "What do we do now?"

"*Now* . . . I get the hell out of here." But he instantly atoned for his rough language. "Beggin' your pardon, milady."

"You won't discuss this with anyone, will you?"

"No."

"Swear it."

"I swear."

Her eyes were open wide, analyzing, delving far inside to the spot where his black heart beat its steady rhythm. "How can I trust you?"

"My word is my bond."

"But you said yourself that you're no gentleman."

"Nevertheless, I never make a vow unless I mean to honor it."

Gad, but when she looked at him like that, she was so exceptional. Fetching, impressionable, defenseless, she inspired a myriad of masculine instincts to protect and shelter, and he yearned to wrap his arms around her, to hold her close while whispering that everything would be all right. The urge to safeguard her was so overpowering that he was frightened by the strength of it.

He declined to feel any emotion toward her! He abhorred her kind! It was neither his affair nor his problem if she had a corrupt relative who was endeavoring to drag her into some sort of public calumny, of which he would play no part.

Shifting restlessly, he merely wanted to exit the dreadful scene. If he was extremely lucky, he'd never again have occasion to cross paths with the hapless woman!

"I must be off," he lamely communicated, "and don't worry. This incident will remain our secret. No one will ever hear of it from me."

Her attention lowered to his bared stomach and, though
he hated to acknowledge it, the sensation tickled all the way
down to his toes. He instructed his feet to move away, but
they wouldn't comply. Rooted to the floor, he let her look
her fill. For a woman who'd purportedly been traumatized
and assaulted by his male presence, she was distinctly inquisitive, and he was vain enough to admit that he liked
how her absorbed regard roved over him.

Astounding him immensely, she spoke. "Would you explain something before you go?"

"If I am able."

"When we were in the dressing room"—she stopped,
swallowed, fidgeted with her robe—"what were you striving to achieve?"

What! A damned virgin?

"Oh, Lord, spare me." He groaned and tilted his head
back, pressing a finger and thumb against the bridge of his
nose, praying for fortitude while fighting the fierce head-
ache that was forming. "Say it's not true! You can't be a
virgin!"

Silence was his answer, and he whipped his gaze to hers,
requiring that she look him in the eye, but she wouldn't.
She was excessively interested in a spot somewhere over
his shoulder, her cheeks flushed with embarrassment.
Forced to recognize how untried she actually was—she
couldn't even verbalize what had occurred between them!—
he calmed himself. "You don't have any idea what we were
about?"

"I suppose you were . . . we were . . ."

White-hot anger set in. At her. At her family. At himself
for the predicament in which he'd almost landed. How he'd
like to march downstairs and have a chat with her scheming
cousin! He never would, though, because he couldn't risk
inciting a furor over their clandestine contact.

Michael was not his brother, James. James had few res-
ervations about the upheavals he sporadically inflicted on
the members of the Quality, and if the occasional innocent
became ensnared in his wretched machinations, he didn't

care and suffered no compunction to make amends.

Not so, Michael. He'd never furnish others with reasons to compare him with his father, the Earl of Spencer. The earl had seduced Michael's mother, sired two illegitimate boys on her, then left her alone to raise them while he went on his merry way.

Michael would never commit such a callous exploit, so while he had no qualms about copulating with the degraded wives and widows of the *ton* who sought his favors, those favors never extended to their chaste daughters, because he declined to end up shackled for all eternity to one of the selfish, spoiled snivelers.

And now that he thought about it, why the hell was she quizzing *him* about prurient behavior? She was hardly a girl fresh out of the schoolroom.

"How old are you anyway?" he peevishly posed. "Twenty-four? Twenty-five?"

"What's my age got to do with anything?"

"You're too old to let yourself get involved in a mess like this!"

"I am not old!"

"For pity's sake, you're a spinster—"

"I'm not a *spinster*!"

"—prancing about this dissolute mansion, where there are nothing but rakes and rogues lurking in the halls." He indicated her curvaceous torso. "You stroll about naked, with your doors unlocked. What did you expect might happen?"

"I never go visiting! I never guessed that a man would just . . . would just . . ."

To his dismay, tears welled into her lovely eyes. He couldn't abide female histrionics! If she commenced, he couldn't guarantee what he might do. "Don't you dare cry!"

"Then stop yelling at me!"

"I'm not yelling!" he hissed rabidly.

"Yes you are! This has been an horrendous event. You're not helping by being so grouchy!"

She was plainly not prone to sentimental outbursts; one

impeccable tear tracked a charming trail down her cheek, and she glanced away. Flustered, she battled to stabilize her breathing and regain control, and he heaved a resigned sigh.

The ice around his heart began to melt. Incapable of sustaining his upset, he swiped his hand across her silky skin, capturing the warm moisture on his thumb, then he stuck it in his mouth and sucked at the salty drop. She was out of her league in this residence and with these people; a lamb led to the slaughter.

How could he leave her to her own devices?

"I was touching you," he patiently elucidated, "as a man touches his wife. They do things to one another."

"What things?"

"They kiss and caress each other. It's arousing and pleasurable."

"But we're not married."

"We don't have to be. A man always relishes a woman's passionate company, and the two participants need not be wed to practice intimate indulgence."

"If we'd continued, you'd have taken my virginity?"

"Yes."

"In what manner is the deed accomplished?"

How on God's green earth had he fallen into the middle of this conversation?

Gently, he admonished, "I hardly think I'm the one to advise you."

"No, I don't suppose you are," she agreed, after a protracted contemplation.

"What is your name?"

"Sarah."

He nodded; it suited her.

"Sarah"—he determinedly rolled it off his tongue, and it felt just right—"you can't stay here in Bedford."

"What do you mean?"

"This house, this party." He gestured around, including all that was transpiring under the mansion's taciturn roof. "I realize that you are desirous of a country holiday, but this is not the simple rural assemblage you imagine it to be. The people who have traveled from London . . ." Briefly, he considered minimizing the gravity of her circumstances. After all, she was unsophisticated and would have no idea that men and women conducted themselves in such an egregious fashion. Yet he couldn't have her discounting the perils. "The guests are not here for socializing and entertainment."

"Then why have they come?"

"To have sexual relations."

"That's the only reason?"

"Aye."

She weighed this information then, skeptical, she grinned. "I don't believe you."

Capturing her arm, he ushered her toward the wall that faced the outer hall. "Look!" He lifted the painting he'd rearranged and pointed to the peephole. "Men can prowl in the corridor and spy on you."

On tiptoe, she flattened her eye to the hole. Faced with the bald confirmation, she was less assured when she shifted back, and she dubiously folded her arms over her alluring bosom. "Why would they want to?"

"Men like to watch. It's titillating for them—especially when the woman doesn't know. It makes a man wish to sneak inside and do things he oughtn't." She shivered, and he dropped the painting back into place. "This house is teeming with these blasted holes. Never permit this picture to be shoved aside or removed. Always check it."

Still doubtful, she moved to the bed and, like a sailor drawn by a mermaid's siren song, he followed. In a mere handful of minutes, he'd been captivated by her, powerless to separate himself. It was far past time he departed, but like a smitten lad, he kept prolonging their discourse so he could linger.

"This seems so far-fetched."

"Yet it's true, Sarah. The other guests have been in the city for months, and they're bored. They're seeking distraction. I won't go into the details because they're too delicate."

"I'm not a child!" she huffed, piqued. "What do they propose?"

He'd hoped that she'd be easily shocked, and thereby easily induced to return to her own home, but clearly, she was exceedingly stubborn, so he clarified starkly. "They will tarry in each other's bedchambers where they will engage in the sorts of physical sport I attempted with you. The difference is that the women are willing."

"But they're nearly all married."

"None of their husbands are here."

"So?"

"They plan to dally with other men."

This news gave her pause, and another, more disturbing possibility presented itself. "Will *you* philander with any of them?"

"However many ask," he candidly replied.

The fact troubled her, and her brow wrinkled in consternation. "Why would you?"

The answer to her interrogatory was so long, and so complicated, that he wasn't sure he could provide an accurate rejoinder if he'd had a week to contemplate one. He couldn't rationalize the sick recreation he pursued. She would never understand, and while he'd satisfied himself that he suffered no stabs of conscience over the state of his carnal dissolution, he found that he couldn't justify his conduct to her.

He settled for, "I'm bored, too." Declining to furnish an additional excuse for an inquisition, he parried with, "Promise me that you'll go home first thing in the morning."

"Why would I? These tales you're spinning are preposterous. My very own brother suggested that I attend this party. He wouldn't implicate me in such an abominable undertaking."

"Wouldn't he?" Her denial wasn't quite as vehement as he might have predicted. Had he heard equivocation? He sidled nearer, until the sparks were flowing between them once again. Unafraid, she glared up, challenging him.

"Sarah, listen . . . I've been acquainted with Lady Carrington for many years."

"So have I. Pamela is a friend of my family."

"But you don't know everything about her, or you wouldn't be here. She has a distinctive reputation."

"What sort of reputation?"

"For hosting lewd parties, the more wicked the better. I've attended many of them, and I'm not joking; it's risky for you to stay."

Unable to resist, he laid his hand on her nape, feeling the petite, fragile bones of her shoulder. She accepted the gentle caress, a major feat after what she'd endured from him earlier. He stroked up her neck and lifted her chin with his thumb. "I don't want you swept up in any disaster. Leave! Tomorrow!"

Just then, a soft knock sounded on the door, and the knob rotated unsuccessfully, but solely because he'd possessed the foresight to secure it when he'd had the chance.

Very softly, a female called, "Sarah . . . ?"

"My cousin Rebecca," Sarah whispered, and her eyes narrowed with trepidation and a hint of indignation.

Staring her down, he dared her to form the correlation, to deduce for herself that she was in the middle of something much deeper and larger than she could handle.

He leaned in, inhaling the smell of roses that clung about her. No gentleman by any stretch of the imagination, his lips grazed the curve of her ear. "I must be away," he mouthed. "Keep your doors locked—at all times. Both the one that opens out to the hall, and the one between our rooms. And *go home* in the morning."

She turned slightly as though she might argue, and the shift brought them so close that their lips were all but joined. Only a breath separated them. Their eyes connected, and expectation hovered in the moment.

Almost against his will, he was spurred toward her, but he was neither his impulsive brother nor his incorrigible father. He was a mature, twenty-eight-year-old man, who would control his unruly, libidinous cravings.

He bestowed the lightest kiss, just because he could and she couldn't refuse, but he didn't attempt more.

"Promise me," he mouthed, once more.

Belligerently, she simply smiled, and he ached to compel her acquiescence. Undeterred, her cousin tried the knob again, and he whirled away, not permitting himself a backward glance at her seductive form.

The lass was hazardous. To his equanimity. To his well-being. To his keen drive for self-preservation. So he'd make certain there'd be no further opportunity for stolen kisses.

On nimble feet, he vanished into his room, closed and barred the door behind.

Chapter Three

Sarah tossed and turned and finally gave up any attempt at sleep. She was uncertain of the time but figured it had to be after two. The fire was out, and a glimmer of moonlight glowed in the window. The mansion was unnaturally quiet, and she lay still, listening to the beat of her heart.

After the dashing Mr. Stevens had so fleetly fled her room, she hadn't closed her eyes a single second. How could a woman possibly rest when so much new stimulation had been thrown at her?

Everything was tangled in her mind: Michael Stevens, the house, the party, her brother, her cousin. The jumble of images played over and over, and she couldn't stop contemplating what had happened and what it all meant.

Mostly, she couldn't quit thinking about Michael Stevens. Now that she'd had opportunity to ponder their meeting with a clearer head, she wasn't angry or distressed. She was curious. Their corporeal adventure had been dramatic and thrilling and, though she was loath to admit it, he had left her hungry for more.

She felt as though she'd read the initial chapters of an exciting novel, but the book had been snatched away just when she was getting to the good part, the section that would have explained the secret intricacies of the plot. Yes, it had been inappropriate for him to come into her room, and yes, it had been wrong for him to have handled her as he'd done, but regretfully, she couldn't find the temerity to be sorry, and she wished she hadn't become overwhelmed and bonked him on the noggin. If she hadn't reacted so timidly, like the spinsterish virgin he'd accused her of being, she might now be cognizant of numerous libidinous particulars about which she'd ruminated for years.

Their encounter had been amazing, breathtaking. He'd touched her in ways she'd never imagined a man might touch a woman and . . . it had been wonderful. Shocking, too, but *wonderful* was the only accurate method of describing it.

All these hours later, her body was alive and thrumming with an unfamiliar, exotic energy, as though it had been in hibernation and had just been awakened. Her nipples were alert and aroused from how he'd pinched them. Whenever she shifted about on the bed, the fabric of her nightdress irritatingly rubbed against them and made her wish he was present to fondle them again.

He'd suckled against her! With his dark hair splayed across her chest, and his lips wrapped around her breast, he'd looked so beautiful. The episode had been brief and abrupt, but the agitation he'd inflicted with his atrocious teeth and tongue still tormented.

Her womanly cleft was overly aggravated, as well, and when he'd caressed her there, she'd been outraged by the intimate penetration of his conniving hand, but not now as she reflected upon it coolly and analytically. His shrewd finger had fit exactly right, had stroked across an itch she hadn't realized needed scratching.

Retrospection about him and his indecent gestures caused her to press her thighs together, but the movement inundated her with searing sensation, and she groaned in frustration. Her tender, feminine flesh was moist and swollen, and to her consternation, she wished he was available to continue his maneuvers. Without a doubt, he would be competent to ease her physical woes.

Michael Stevens, bounder that he was, had created this abject misery, and he would be aware of the route she needed to travel to assuage her unrelenting agony. The man was a walking, talking primer of information on the female torso. He knew more about a woman's anatomy than she knew herself.

Just before he'd departed, he'd kissed her. It had been

scarcely more than a peck, but considering that it was her first kiss, she lingered over the nuances. The transient embrace had been magnificent, and her mind wandered again to the couple in the garden who'd united so ardently, and she couldn't help speculating as to what it would have been like had Mr. Stevens kissed her like that. Long and deeply and passionately.

Her nipples began to throb, once more, and she rubbed her palm over one of them, presuming she'd allay the arduous distension, but the slight palpation initiated a fresh flurry of unusual perturbation. Alarmed and flustered, she rolled onto her stomach and stretched out, but the position made matters much worse. Each of the spots Mr. Stevens had rigorously provoked was in direct contact with the mattress, and she was inflamed anew.

Appalled by her state of affliction, she jumped out of the bed as though she'd discovered snakes in it. There was a bottle of wine on the dresser, and she poured a glass and paced slowly, sipping the red liquid and trying to calm her shattered nerves.

What had happened to her?

Her body had careened out of control, making her yearn for things she couldn't have, for things she'd never guessed she desired. She'd grown daring and reckless, and if Mr. Stevens had been with her at that very instant, she'd have let him do whatever he pleased as long as he promised to terminate her infernal suffering!

She was obsessed with him. Why was he at Lady Carrington's party? Who was he? Where did he live? How did he support himself?

He was certainly refined and self-possessed enough to be a member of an aristocratic family, but he was too bold and dangerous to have sprung from such a tepid background. With the cryptic comments he'd supplied about his participation in the festivities, he'd hinted that the female guests were zealously vying for his favors. Was he some sort of sexual servant? A man who made his way by pleasuring the women in residence?

The concept—that he shared his marvelous physique with anyone who asked—was so fantastic, and so far beyond her realm of experience, that she couldn't process it. Who was he? *What* was he?

Any probable answers to her questions were too disturbing, so instead, she switched to pondering his warnings about the gathering, about her family. Critically, she strove to recall every tidbit of the conversation she'd had with Hugh that had led her to Bedford. The visit had been his idea, as had the choice of location, and other than his efforts to coerce her into rescuing him from his financial straits, she couldn't recall any untoward remarks with regard to the party or the people who would attend.

How about her cousin Rebecca? Rebecca's decision to accompany Sarah had also come about at Hugh's recommendation. Was she simply a congenial, innocuous traveling companion, or was she actually an instigator of trouble? Mr. Stevens seriously believed that Rebecca had steered him to Sarah's room, then stopped by—supposedly innocently—to check if Sarah was settled. Why? Was she anticipating that she'd catch Mr. Stevens on the premises? Could she have acted so despicably?

They were friends, relations. When Rebecca's parents had died four years earlier, Sarah had taken her in and provided food and shelter when Rebecca was out of options, when she'd had nowhere else to go. After prevailing on Sarah's generosity for so long, what could Rebecca hope to gain by sending an unknown man bent on ravishment? Had that been her aim?

Sarah refused to credit it.

And the party . . . Was it the lewd assembly Mr. Stevens insisted? How could she find out? She could hardly wander the halls and go sneaking into people's bedchambers.

Should she depart for home as he'd demanded? Did she wish to leave?

There was nothing for her in Yorkshire, no reason to rush back, and now that she'd met Michael Stevens, she was determined to stay. Distressing as it might be to chance upon him, she *had* to see him again.

Throughout her musing, her eyes had grown accustomed to the dark, and she noticed a sliver of light emanating from the dressing room. No lamps or candles were burning, so she couldn't fathom from where it emerged. She walked into the smaller room and was surprised and astonished to discover a peephole.

Intrigued, she marched over to it and stood on tiptoe, trying to peek, but the hole was too high, so she retrieved a footstool, climbed upon it, and peered inside.

A tiny room was visible. She couldn't see the entirety, just part of one wall, a chair, a table, and a narrow bed. Two candles flickered in a holder, illuminating the enclosed space.

Michael Stevens was there, alone, dressed as he had been earlier in a pair of tight-fitting trousers and naught else. He lounged negligently on the bed, his back against the wall, one ankle carelessly crossed over the other. From his rapt stare, Sarah assumed he was waiting for someone to join him. On the surface, he appeared relaxed and bored, but there was a restless energy hovering about him that piqued her interest.

Would he realize she was watching? Was she the only one? He was acquainted with the purportedly perverted workings of the manor and had intimated that there were copious peepholes, so there could be many people spying on him.

Did he know? Did he care?

Conspicuously unconcerned, he rubbed circles across the center of his chest, his fingers scratching through the mat of curly, tempting hair. Languidly, methodically, he arced lower, past the waist of his trousers, across the placard. He was swollen down below, the odd ridge of flesh prominently manifested, and he stroked the heel of his hand along it, a pained look on his face, as though he was extremely uncomfortable.

Despite the fact that she barely knew him, she sensed

many things about him—what he was thinking, what he was feeling—and she could tell he was eager, expectant, anticipating whatever was about to happen. She strained against the peephole, searching for clues.

Off to the side, a door opened, and a woman stepped into view. She was wearing a cloak, the hood pulled over her head and shielding her identity. Sarah rudely studied the goings-on, and when the pair began to talk, she pressed her ear against the hole so that she could eavesdrop on what was being said.

"What's your name?" Mr. Stevens asked, his voice husky.

The woman spoke softly, and Sarah couldn't discern her reply.

"Who is your husband?"

This response was also unintelligible, but Mr. Stevens chuckled over whatever he'd learned.

"What is it you would like to do for me?" He regarded the woman with a jaded, intense expression.

The woman gawked at her feet but didn't speak.

"You know the rules," Mr. Stevens advised sternly. "You have to say aloud what it is that you want." The woman hesitated, then leaned closer to Mr. Stevens and whispered something. "Ah . . ." he murmured, a brow rising, "one of my favorites. Are you undressed under your cloak?"

"Yes."

"Show me."

Her fingers went to the clasp at her neckline, then pushed the fabric off her shoulders but the hood remained in place. Sarah observed the woman's body in profile. She was naked, her breasts exposed. Her nipples were a brown color, elongated, and they jutted outward.

Mr. Stevens reached out and manipulated both of them with finger and thumb, inducing the woman to writhe uneasily, and Sarah's heart pounded. He was arousing the woman in the same fashion that he'd handled Sarah and, conscious of how it had felt, her own breasts reacted, tingling and hardening just from her watching. Though he was caressing someone else, it seemed as if he was touching her own bosom. Mesmerized, she was bothered and startled by how easily she was drawn in just from viewing the erotic interlude.

"Excellent . . ." he crooned seductively.

The sexy timbre of his compliment—bestowed on another lover—tickled down to her toes, and the realization confounded her terribly. The display was corrupt and deviant, and she understood that she should desist. Her behavior was improper, disquieting, and the outcome none of her affair. There was a shutter she could utilize to cover the hole, but embarrassingly, she couldn't force herself to use it.

Disgusting as it sounded, she was absolutely captivated by Michael Stevens. He was so handsome, so wholly virile, in a manner she'd never encountered before. Until they'd met, she'd had no idea there were men like him in the world, no inkling that people carried on in the shameless ways he welcomed, and a team of horses couldn't have dragged her away.

Like the worst sort of voyeur, she had to witness how the incident unfolded.

He moved behind the woman and turned her toward the opposite wall—one Sarah couldn't see—but it was clear that the couple was facing a mirror. Mr. Stevens was gazing over his lover's shoulder, just as he had with Sarah, and he cradled the weight of her breasts as he nuzzled against her throat. Whimpering with apparent ecstasy, the woman's eyes fluttered shut, her head tilted back, and he nipped against her nape.

"Do you like it when I do that?" he questioned, fiercely twirling at the woman's nipples.

"Yes." His lover was breathless, excited. "Don't stop."

"Your breasts are so beautiful," he declared, assessing the two mounds in the looking glass. "Just the size I like on a woman. Not too big. Not too small."

What!

"Maybe I should take you here in front of the mirror, so you can see how splendid we are together."

Sarah lurched away from the hole, the familiar words ringing in her ears.

"Look at us," he continued. "Look at how exquisite we are with my hands on you."

The cad! Only hours earlier, he'd uttered identical statements in her very own boudoir! How dare he lavish the same praise on another! It made their rendezvous seem so tawdry and ordinary when, on her end, she'd ultimately decided that it had been the most fascinating, enchanting event of her entire life. After reflecting at length, she'd persuaded herself that he'd been as charmed by her as she'd been by him, that he'd found her to be special as no other man ever had, that she was attractive and appealing.

Now, she simply felt like a fool.

In a temper, she whipped away from the peephole so rapidly that the stool wobbled and tipped, dispatching her to the floor with a loud thump. She landed crookedly on her rear and smacked her ankle against the vanity. Pain shot through the joint, and she moaned aloud, then clapped her hand over her mouth, wondering if the occupants in the adjoining room had heard the commotion.

If Mr. Stevens detected that she'd been snooping, she'd die of mortification!

Cautiously, she tugged herself up to a standing position. Though her ankle ached and her bottom smarted, nothing was injured but her pride. The beam of light from the hidden room was like a beacon, urging her to return to her perch on the stool, but she categorically refused to heed its beguiling call. However Michael Stevens might conclude his bizarre evening, she didn't care to know. She didn't *want* to know. Some mysteries were best left unexplored.

She hobbled out, shutting the door that separated her bedchamber from the dressing room. Confused, anxious, haunted by what she'd seen, she forced herself to bed and jerked the covers high. Eventually, after suffering through hours of wretchedness and chaos, she fell into a fitful sleep.

*   *   *

Michael heard a strange noise, as though someone had fallen, and it was followed by a restrained whimpering, but he didn't allow the sound to distract him. There were several peepholes into the Viewing Room so, no doubt, diverse people were watching, and anything could be happening just beyond the walls.

For a moment, he endeavored to conceive of who some of the spectators might be. Perhaps it was one of those eccentric men who enjoyed huddling alone and playing with himself during the proceedings, or one who became stimulated for later sexual congress by spying on others. Perchance it was one of the handful of aberrant men with baser appetites, those who were not attracted to women at all—but to himself as a potential partner. They would be impatiently waiting for a degenerate glimpse of his engorged member, an impressive sight by anyone's standards.

More likely, it was one of the women he hadn't had yet, a newcomer to the party who was wondering if she had the necessary lack of inhibition to take a turn with him. They were all so overtly titillated by the prospect.

After years of existing on the fringe of their society, he possessed a wicked reputation that was decidedly deserved, and they craved the chance to engage in carnal relations with him so that they could brag about their exploits later on. Come the morn, he would be the main topic of conversation over breakfast: who'd lain with him, how many times, in how many ways.

His own motives for participating in Pamela's lewd games weren't specifically comprehensible. It was as though he was driven to prove, over and over again, that nothing mattered. Yet his obscure purposes paled in comparison to those of the women who coupled with him. They were lonely, bored, degraded in their pursuit of entertainment, but he declined to feel sympathy toward them. Pamela had devised the rules for the tainted amusement, and they flocked to indulge, hoping that something especially nasty would occur—the naughtier the better—so that they would have more to bluster about to their friends.

He cared not. Not about their motives or their needs or wants. They could all go hang.

Even as the contemptuous thought passed through his mind, he suffered a pang of guilt, remembering the vixen named Sarah into whose room he'd been stupidly drawn. Her chamber was close by, and he was glad she had no method of watching what he was about to do.

The notion that she might stumble upon him in the midst of such corrupt conduct was unsettling and filled him with shame, and he grimly pushed her memory away. He didn't choose to consider her predicament, or what might befall her. He didn't plan to worry over her, or have her interfering with his practice of pleasure.

Already, she was plaguing his battle-scarred conscience, the one he'd carefully tucked away when he'd fled London three months earlier. His heart had been bruised and battered by those he loved, and he'd had his fill of compassion and empathy. Now, he was content to drift, indifferent to his misdeeds, so he wasn't about to countenance some red-haired witch burrowing under his skin.

If she finagled herself into his life, he'd start fussing about her and chafing over her plight. He'd revert to the type of sensitive fool he'd been before events had taken their toll. The frivolous noblewoman had managed to insert herself into the middle of treacherous intrigues that were too abundant to mention, and if he wasn't circumspect, he'd find himself checking on her, guarding her, keeping the lechers at bay, unveiling the scheme of her brother and cousin.

Dammit! The blasted woman wasn't any of his concern! How she'd been lured to Pamela's house, why she'd agreed to attend the party, what might transpire because of her family—none of it was any of his business.

He was here to fornicate and to gamble, and for no other reasons, and he wouldn't fret or fume over an imbecilic spinster who didn't have the good sense to depart when she should. The crazed woman needed a protector, but he wouldn't endeavor to assume the role.

He wouldn't care about her. He wouldn't!

Forcing his attention to the mirror, he scrutinized his current paramour. Her breasts were nicely formed, and he toyed with them overly long. He was hard, ready, willing to offer her however much she'd accept, but the woman herself did not matter.

No higher purpose lurked behind his actions. There was just the sex; vulgar and crude and risqué—just how he fancied it. The anonymous, blatant copulation fit his mood perfectly, and he intended to bury himself in this stranger until he couldn't continue, until his overeager phallus was limp, his raging sexual drive finally, but temporarily, slaked.

Gripping her hips, he deliberately flexed against her buttocks, letting her savor his enormous size, providing an indication of what was coming. Shoving the cloak off her abdomen, he eyed her pussy; it was bald and smooth as a babe's. "You've shaved yourself."

"Aye."

"Just for me?"

"Yes."

His male vanity was immensely stroked by the inane feat she'd performed for him. He cupped her, then roughly entered her with two fingers, conferring no ease, pilfering what he wanted, supplying what she craved, but as he worked against her in a fixed rhythm, another uncomfortable image of Sarah flashed, diverting his attention.

What was it about her? She'd bewitched him!

When he'd agreed to this evening of debauchery, he'd foreseen a leisurely, sating escapade with the woman in his arms, as well as with the various others who were scheduled to visit later, but intrusive thoughts of Sarah made this seem ridiculous; he was out of his element, unprepared to proceed. Suddenly, he felt unclean and profane—just when he'd resolved to feel nothing at all.

Desperate to chase Sarah away—quickly—he whispered into his lover's ear. "I'm ready now."

"Yes . . . all right." She consented haltingly, and stiffened, apprehensive about the hasty escalation.

"I'll lie down on the cot." He released her and moved to the bed, propping the pillows behind his head. She froze, either too disconcerted or too nervous to approach, but he was confident that she wouldn't leave without providing him a carnal release. Others might be watching, and she'd never embarrass herself by fleeing the scene. Her vanity wouldn't let her become a laughingstock.

"Come here," he ordered, and the terse command propelled her forward. She knelt down and fiddled with the buttons on his trousers. Her slender fingers slipped the top one through its hole. Soon, he'd be bared to her torrid gaze and able ministrations, and he braced for the rush of lust to flood over him, but it never arrived.

Dispassionately, he waited. He was incredibly hard, his cock never failing to rise for any dubious occasion and, in anticipation, his phallus swelled further. Ultimately, he was free and in her hand. She stroked him and licked him, until his hips responded of their own accord, then she leaned down and slipped her lips over the crown.

He was a big man, bigger than any of them ever supposed, and he didn't let his impressive proportions interfere with his gratification.

"Take more of me," he decreed. Reaching for the back of her neck, he eased her down, and she went without complaint, while he stared at the ceiling, focused on a crack that ran from one edge to the other.

The woman adeptly proceeded with her task, but true desire proved elusive until, without warning, Sarah once again rudely intruded into the center of the sensual exercise. He visualized her stepping out of her bath, wet and slippery and smelling like roses. He recalled the firm, taut nipples he'd suckled, the slick, tight pussy he'd fingered.

For some reason, she excessively excited him, so he closed his eyes and pretended that *she* was the woman stooped over him, that she was enticing him with her wicked mouth and tongue. Vividly, he imagined teaching her to suck at him, making her practice, encouraging her to master his favorite techniques. Adamant yet gentle, he'd be a relentless instructor, and she'd be an apt, enthusiastic pupil, set to learn what he deigned to impart.

Steadying his paramour, he held her in place, granting her as much as she could manage, urging her to take a bit more.

"Sarah . . ."

In his mind, he pictured her in all her nude, glorious splendor, and his level of desire soared to a previously unascertained height. He shuddered and let himself go.

Chapter Four

Sarah sat on the verandah, her face shielded by a bonnet, observing the other guests and enjoying the late afternoon sunshine. The fabulous summer day was quickly approaching evening, temperatures were balmy, the sky bright blue and filled with fluffy white clouds. Soon, everyone scattered about at the various tables and settees would venture inside to dress for supper, and she should have been content to relax, but disturbing ruminations kept creeping in, rendering it impossible to cherish the moment.

After her encounter with Mr. Stevens, then her subsequently stumbling upon him during his odd tryst, she was definitely in a state. He had cluttered her senses in indescribable ways, and though she screamed at her overly zealous mind to give it a rest, her active imagination wouldn't calm down. The only matter she could contemplate was him and what he'd been doing.

Surreptitiously, she scanned the long porch that wrapped around the mansion, wondering who his lover had been. She scrutinized the mannerisms of the women, evaluating how they moved, tipped their heads, and gestured, but to no avail. She couldn't tell.

During the night, she'd removed herself from the dressing room and the temptation it provided, but she'd spent interminable dark hours regretting her decision. To her ultimate dismay, she wished she'd continued on! She was frantic to learn how the rendezvous had developed and how it had ended.

Shocking as it seemed, she hoped she'd have the fortuity to watch him again before too much time had passed. There was something abominably erotic and alluring about spying. If she shut her eyes, she could pretend that *she* was the woman in the room with him, and that he was perpetrating those treacherous exploits against her own person.

What was the matter with her? Why did she find his comportment so titillating? Even as she recognized the impropriety of her conduct, and even as she exhaustively chastised herself for her wantonness, she was craving a repeat performance.

Her nocturnal reveries about him and his antics had grown cumbersome as he now commanded her entire daylight attention, as well. She couldn't stop conjecturing as to where he was and how he was spending his afternoon. Disgustingly, she was perpetually craning her neck, searching the crowd for a glimpse of him, but she'd not seen him anywhere.

While she'd never admit as much to another soul, she was fascinated by him and what she'd witnessed, and she was impatient for the chance to ask him: Why? Why did he act so decadently? Why did his physical peccadilloes hold such appeal? What was the attraction?

For some inexplicable reason, she felt as though she'd always known him and could interpret his thought processes, and she'd been left with the overwhelming impression that he hadn't actually wanted to be engaged in such depraved misdeeds. Deep down, he was a good man; she was certain of it, though why she believed so, or why she might presume to judge, was beyond her ability to explicate.

She perceived an affinity between them that she'd never had with another, and she couldn't shake the sensation that he didn't belong at the party any more than she did. Their strange assignation had so thoroughly disordered her world that she was convinced there was a larger purpose behind their meeting, and she refused to go home until she had occasion to explore what it might be.

As she fantasized about Mr. Stevens, her gaze wandered to the sloping green yard where several couples competed at an informal lawn game. They were hitting a ball across the grass with a sort of mallet and aiming for a basket that was located quite a distance away at the base of the hill. She wasn't sure of the rules, but it seemed that whichever couple landed their ball in the basket with the least amount of strokes was the winner.

Rebecca was one of the participants and, when the contest had begun, she'd invited Sarah to play, but Sarah had declined, and she was relieved that she had. On the surface, the sport seemed harmless enough, with eager contestants and innocuous jesting and wagering over the tough shots, but there were undercurrents to the verbal banter that she didn't grasp, and a great deal of unusual, intimate touching that would have been disconcerting.

She couldn't pinpoint what was making her uncomfortable. Perhaps the laughter was a little too familiar, the subtle looks between the partners a tad too prolonged, but whatever it was, there was a strain in their interacting that bothered her.

As the women leaned down and positioned their sticks, the men were constantly nearby, snuggling themselves against the women in order to abet them with their swings. After the episode with Michael Stevens, she recognized how unsettling it was for a man to press himself against a woman's buttocks. She readily recalled how he'd held her hips and flexed his groin, and she shifted uneasily, relieved that she hadn't allowed any of the men to act so familiarly.

However, she was striving to be fair about the entire event. So far, she'd witnessed nothing that she would deem downright inappropriate, and she was forced to speculate if this wasn't how adults related when they were visiting. This was unmistakably a fête for grown-ups. There were no children invited; only men and women who had plenty of leisure time and who required some means of occupying it.

Perhaps she simply didn't understand the social conventions when a crowd of such people gathered together. Obviously, the standards were a trifle lower, but casting about, she couldn't help but remember Mr. Steven's descriptions about the assemblage. He'd contended that the women wouldn't be accompanied by their husbands, and apparently, he was correct. While there were many gentlemen present, none were married to any of the ladies.

She endeavored to guess at the number of guests, but tabulation was difficult. Lady Carrington was adept at offering varied amusement, with concurrent merriment occurring, so visitors weren't convened in the same spot.

Card games were progressing in the house, gambling in some of the backrooms, where even the women were permitted to join in. Outside, there was horseback riding, meandering through the gardens, and one bunch had even commandeered several carriages for a picnic at the lake.

Just then, her hostess emerged through the French doors and blazed a trail through the guests. Sarah enviously studied her, trying not to be overly conspicuous. A beautiful woman, ten years Sarah's senior, Pamela Blair had been the fourth wife of an elderly earl, but also his favorite, and thus, upon his death, he'd graciously bequeathed several valuable properties and a significant income with which to enjoy them.

She regularly entertained huge groups, and her soirees were invariably the rage, with people begging invitations whenever she was having a particularly interesting masquerade or banquet.

Tall, blond, slender, and graceful, she murmured hellos and conversed with old friends. Eventually, she reached Sarah, and the two women chatted, while casually regarding the competitors in the yard.

As a girl of seventeen, Sarah had met Pamela during her failed debut outing, but they'd not crossed paths since that dreadful debacle. Pamela had been twenty-seven years old, already a widow, and Sarah much younger, so they'd not formed a confidential association. Nevertheless, Sarah had discovered her to be direct and forthright, which had been refreshing in view of how ghastly her brief excursion had been, and she retained fond memories of the woman who'd never been judgmental or cruel during a period when Sarah had been so terribly out of her element.

Pamela was amiable but detached, welcoming but not inordinately so, absorbed but not acutely. There was a coolness that kept others at a distance, especially someone like Sarah who had never made friends effortlessly, yet Sarah trusted the older woman and suspected that the fickle members of High Society preferred her fellowship for the same reason. She had a reputation for being loyal, reliable, and discreet, admirable qualities in a small, elite community where everyone attended to everyone else's business.

Pamela inquired after Sarah's family, her brother, their Yorkshire estate. As Sarah was uninformed as to Pamela's private life, she had difficulty making chitchat in return, so she stuck to flattering observations about the weather, the festivities, the company.

When Pamela quizzed her about the adequacy of her accommodations, Sarah finally found the opening for which she'd been waiting.

"Do you happen to know who's been assigned the suite next to mine?"

"Why?" Pamela laughed softly. "Were they keeping you awake?"

"No, nothing like that. I just noted a gentleman when he exited." She was dying to simply speak the name Michael Stevens aloud, but she was a horrid liar, and she couldn't fabricate an acceptable story as to how they might have met. "I recognized him from somewhere, but I wasn't positive of his identity."

"Hmmm . . ." Pamela brooded, pondering the arrangements of the sprawling mansion. "I didn't realize there was anyone in that room. Once Hugh advised me that you were coming, I intentionally gave you a quiet chamber away from the gaiety. Some of my companions can be . . . rambunctious . . . in the night, so I figured you'd relish the additional privacy."

"I do," Sarah agreed, while theorizing as to the woman's definition of *rambunctious*. "Thank you."

"What did this mystery man look like?"

"Handsome. Broad shouldered. Dark haired." More

wistfully than she intended, she added, "He has the most spectacular blue eyes."

"Well . . . that would *have* to be Michael Stevens. He definitely has eyes that prompt a woman to fantasize about things she oughtn't." Pamela chuckled, then leaned over and patted Sarah's hand. "I wasn't aware that I'd situated him near you, but trust me, dear, you're not acquainted with him. Nor should you be."

"Now I'm absolutely intrigued."

"To put it bluntly, Sarah"—Pamela stared out at the yard for a lengthy interval, carefully choosing her words—"he wouldn't be a fitting prospect for you, so there's no excuse to amble down that road." At Sarah's raised brow, Pamela hastily supplied, "Pardon me if I sound unduly harsh, and please don't misconstrue. Michael is a great friend of mine, but he's not at all what you're seeking."

Sarah blushed to the tips of her toes. Did Pamela suppose she was husband-hunting? Did everyone? What indiscreet statements had Hugh used to explain Sarah's attendance? Flustered, she glanced around. Were the other guests stealthily assessing her, eager to behold more of her inept forays into the matrimonial quagmire performed by the aristocracy?

"I'm not searching for a man," she felt obligated to clarify.

Pamela bent closer still, and Sarah was frightfully glad that they were sequestered. If a single utterance of their conversation was overheard, she'd expire from humiliation. "Let me be frank, Sarah. I know why you're here—"

"No you don't," she interrupted. "Not if you think I'm stalking after a husband."

"But Hugh said—"

"Hugh was wrong."

"Oh, my apologies." Confused, Pamela queried, "So, why exactly *are* you here?"

"I'm not sure," Sarah replied with such candor that Pamela laughed aloud. "I was just so tired of being at home. It's been . . ." She paused. Though she liked Pamela very

much, and the woman inspired confidences, Sarah wasn't
ready to confess how dire were the circumstances, so she
finished with, "It's been hard. I was anxious for a change
of scene, and it's been terribly long since I've gone visiting."

"Too true," Pamela concurred. "This is so embarrassing.
Hugh told me that you were set to wed, and he requested
that I facilitate matters by introducing you to any gentlemen
who might suit. I've been racking my brain and luring some
of them out to the country. Hugh insisted you were disposed."

"That rat! I'll kill him."

"Don't waste your energy, dear," Pamela succinctly asserted. "Hugh can manage to *kill* himself without any assistance from you."

Because the proclamation was so agonizingly accurate,
Sarah didn't respond. Hugh was in a descending spiral that
couldn't have a satisfactory conclusion, but she'd deduced
ages ago that there was nothing she could do but persevere
while preparing for the worst. "Hugh presumes I'm in pursuit of a husband," she grumbled, "but really, I just came
to get away from all the pressure."

"As you should have"—Pamela smiled conspiratorially—
"and I'm honored that you selected my party for your holiday. How long will you stay?"

"How about three weeks?"

"Marvelous. We'll fill your time with engaging recreation, then send you home refreshed and primed to face
whatever is approaching."

From Pamela's shrewd expression, Sarah suspected that
the other woman had learned much more about Hugh's affairs than she was willing to divulge, but then, it was ru-
mored that there were few secrets Pamela Blair hadn't
uncovered.

Sarah affirmed, "The rest will be vastly appreciated."

"Then *rest* you shall. And who can say? Maybe my
machinations won't be for naught. Perhaps some dashing
beau will catch your attention."

"I doubt it," Sarah griped, which caused Pamela to laugh again.

"An innocent flirtation might be just the ticket." Ready to move on, she stood. "If I can do anything to make your visit more pleasant, please notify me." She turned to go, hesitated, then whispered, "And at all costs, avoid Michael Stevens. You don't need a complication like that in your life."

With a wink, she sauntered down the terrace, and Sarah jealously critiqued how she mingled with the crowd, how readily she belonged in any situation. The ability to fraternize was never a gift Sarah had possessed, and she suddenly felt all alone even though she was surrounded by dozens of people. She hated being so detached, and she yearned to fit in, so when Rebecca waylaid her a second time and urged her to attempt the game of balls, she grudgingly acquiesced.

As she walked down the steps and onto the grass, a man got up and followed her, and if Rebecca looked as though she'd beckoned him into action with an urgent tip of her head, Sarah chose not to heed her ruse.

What did she care if Rebecca was soliciting gentlemen to court attention on her? Their courtesy and civility didn't have to portend anything more than Sarah wanted it to. She was adept at the art of putting imprudent men in their places; she'd had a lifetime of practice with her father and Hugh, so she wasn't worried that one of them might take unfair advantage on Pamela's lawn.

Besides, she would be carrying a rather large mallet. If any of the men became exceedingly fresh, she wasn't averse to rendering a deserving smack!

Another contest was about to commence, and there were ten couples geared to shepherd their various balls down the grass. Sarah and two other ladies were new to the sport, so everyone chattered jovially about the necessary techniques. Bets and boasts were affably bandied about as the first pair took their turn. The woman always began, with her male cohort positioned behind and guiding her through the motions.

Sarah's partner had been introduced to her by Rebecca as George Wilson, a gangly, balding man with bad teeth and body odor. He'd bowed politely over her hand, but when he'd risen, she could smell alcohol on his breath, and there was a disquieting gleam in his eye. Evidently, he was sizing her up with dubious intent, and though he struggled valiantly to lock his gaze on hers, it kept dipping to her cleavage, so she faced the yard and the line of players, but the maneuver provided him with a profile of her breasts, and his stare was blatant and incessant.

The couple ahead of her hit their ball, then trailed after it, leaving her with George, and he gallantly offered her their stick, gesturing magnanimously. "After you, Lady Sarah."

As she stepped to the ball, he converged on her from behind. In a low whisper, revolting in its intimacy, he declared, "Allow me to show you how it's done."

Despondency had prompted her into the rash diversion, but reality had rapidly settled in, and she thought she might die if he laid a hand on her. She dithered, trying to conceive of a gracious retreat, just as a familiar voice spoke.

"Hello, Wilson." Michael Stevens casually strutted up as though his entrance was the most ordinary of occurrences, when it obviously wasn't. His interjection of himself into the proceedings had heads swinging from all directions. He called several people by name—he knew many of the male guests—and they grumbled their welcomes in return. No one was glad to see him but, almost as if they were fearful of insulting him, they couldn't show their displeasure too openly.

Surprised and thrilled, Sarah jerked around to face him, only to confront his resigned stare that seemed to say: *I knew I'd find you in the middle of a calamity.*

He was more dynamic than she recollected, his dark hair shimmering in the bright sunshine, and his piercing sapphire eyes silently scolding until he had her squirming under his meticulous assessment.

With his generous height and wide-shouldered physique, he towered over everyone, and the entire group appeared to be furtively analyzing him, while flagrantly pretending not to have taken excessive note of his arrival.

He exuded an energy and intensity that had the men discreetly checking him out, hoping to ascertain how he carried himself so effectively. The women were more impertinent in their evaluation, boldly examining him as one might a rare jewel or extraordinary painting.

Dressed as the finest gentleman, his light blue coat and tan trousers precisely outlined his muscled form. His black boots sparkled, the white of his shirt blinded, his cravat was expertly tied, and he was frowning at her with a severity that stole her breath.

When she'd fantasized about the subsequent appointments they might share, she assuredly hadn't dreamed of anything like this. Why had he put in an appearance? What did he contemplate?

"My apologies, Wilson," he was stating to her partner, "but her first game was promised to me long ago." He glowered at her, challenging her to contradict him. "Isn't that right?"

The onlookers were spellbound by the fascinating display. Not wanting to cause a scene, she lied affably. "I'd given up on you, Mr. Stevens, and decided you weren't coming. How kind of you to finally join me."

"I was detained." He ushered her away, efficiently dismissing George. "Perhaps you can have a subsequent match with her, Wilson, although I doubt she'll be inclined. Once she's had the best, it will be hard for her to lower her standards."

Sarah didn't exactly comprehend the implications of his remark, but she was astute enough to perceive that it had been uttered at her expense. Several men snickered, a woman briskly fanned herself, and Sarah's cheeks blushed bright red as dozens of meddlesome eyes fixed on her.

For a brief instant, George vacillated as if he might protest Mr. Stevens's usurpation, but Rebecca shot a quelling glare that had him scurrying off.

Fuming, Sarah used the distraction caused by his departure to lean over and whisper, "What did you mean by that?"

"Keep smiling," he whispered in reply. "Everyone's looking."

"At you!" she hissed. "I was perfectly anonymous until you abducted me!"

His lips grazed her earlobe—deliberately, she was sure—his hand rested on the small of her back, and she was overwhelmed by having him so near. With all the attention leveled their way, they were awkwardly conspicuous in a fashion she hated, so she deigned to act as normally as possible. She gripped the mallet, but just when she would have attempted her initial swing, Mr. Stevens reached around her, effectively trapping her in the circle of his arms.

"Permit me to instruct you," he said, and chills sped down her spine. "The game goes like this."

Warm and magnetic, the entire front of his body was flattened against the back of hers, and she could feel the solid plane of his chest, the curve of his abdomen as he arched over her, the strength of his legs as he balanced her between them. His groin was directly against her posterior, and the sensation produced an exhilarating swirl of butterflies that cascaded through her stomach.

Wrapping her small hands in his large ones, he controlled the arc of the stick as it landed with a firm thump, and their ball careened down the hillside.

"Very nice," he murmured, though she was quite sure he wasn't referring to the ball or the swing at all.

They straightened, and their gazes met and locked. Lord, but it was sinful for a man to be so pleasing to behold. He retrieved her arm, then gallantly steered her across the yard. The nosy spectators still evaluated them, but at least they were traveling away from all those perked ears.

As he'd advised, her smile was firmly in place, and when

they'd covered enough ground to initiate a candid conversation, she asked, "What were you implying about me?"

"Simply that you and I are acquainted."

"It was more than that!"

"Aye, it was."

"You intentionally made it sound as if we're . . . we're involved." Her stomach tickled at the delicious sentiment, but she easily feigned pique.

"Cross your fingers that everyone thought so."

"But it's a lie!"

"One that I trust will keep your sorry hide out of trouble."

"Of all the nerve . . ."

"Though why I should bother is beyond me." He sighed heavily, a man with the weight of the world on his shoulders. "You seem determined to plague me with your tribulations."

"The only *tribulations* I've sustained"—she attempted to pull to a halt, but he tugged on her arm, maintaining a slow and casual pace as they paraded down the lawn— "have been with you, Mr. Stevens. Now, I'm just trying to enjoy a peaceful game of ball."

"You're so oblivious"—he made a derisive sound low in his throat—"you don't even realize how badly you need my assistance."

She chuckled, treasuring this chance to engage in capricious repartee. "You're too rude and domineering to be of much help."

"That's what you think." He tucked her arm more tightly into his own and reassuringly caressed her hand; goose bumps shot up her arm. "Stick close, and perhaps the lechers and perverts will keep their distance."

Glancing around, she had to concede that those in viewing range were tediously normal, with nary a reprobate among them. "How will you contrive to restrain them?"

"I'll scare them off." He wiggled his brows. "I'm good at it."

"They *do* look afraid of you."

"They are."

"Are you a brute?"

"I can be."

"You certainly frighten me with little difficulty." From various positions across the grass, the other players continued to furtively spy on them, and she couldn't help but report, "They're watching you as though you might do something nefarious."

"They merely can't believe I've joined the game," he explained. "It's common knowledge how much I loathe your kind."

"My kind!" What was that supposed to mean? He was at a gathering full of the nobility! "There's an insult buried in there somewhere."

"Absolutely." He stopped their momentum while they waited for the couple ahead of them to swipe at their ball. "Ignore them like I do," he insisted, once the pair had moved off, shrugging them all away as inconsequential. "I've uncovered too many of their dirty little secrets, and they're simply embarrassed by what I've learned."

How interesting! What a mysterious man, and how wonderful that they'd met! Her musings were a jumble of possessive impulses and absurd longings that she couldn't set aside. She suffered from an insane urge to inquire as to where he'd been all day, but she hadn't a clue how to frame her question, because she'd never discerned how to engage in the coquettish flirtations at which other females excelled.

"If you abhor us all so much, why are you here?" Sarcastically, she batted her lashes. "What possessed you to grace us with your stupendous presence?"

"Would you rather I'd stayed upstairs and let Wilson fondle your pretty bottom?" He peered over her shoulder, baldly scanning her backside, and her knees weakened at the decidedly salacious gleam of approval he flashed once he'd finished. "While I admit it's quite lovely, I'd thought you'd applaud my intervention, but if you'd like me to go . . ."

"No, you bounder." Recalling how disgusted she'd been

by Mr. Wilson's advance, she gripped his hand more firmly than she should have, and he rewarded her by snuggling her a bit closer than was proper. "Don't you dare leave my side."

"What's the matter with your foot?"

The change of topic made her dizzy. "My foot?"

"You're limping."

Her ankle still throbbed from her ignominious fall off the stool, but she wasn't about to reveal any details regarding her mishap!

"I tripped."

"But you're all right?"

"Yes."

"You look very fetching"—her breath hitched at the unexpected compliment, and she peeked up at him from under the rim of her bonnet, when he appended—"with your clothes on."

"Oh, you horrid man!" she reproached as a dimple creased his cheek, making him appear wicked and irresistible. His words induced a swarm of recollection, both wonderful and horrid, and a blush started to rise again, somewhere above her ankles, and it swept up her body, heating her chest and face.

"Too fetching, in fact," he went on. He was distinctly flustered that he'd noted her comeliness, downright perplexed by their flourishing entanglement. "You can't go prancing about, looking so *fetching* at this party."

"My apologies for getting dressed," she retorted facetiously.

"Why are you still here, anyway?" he inquired cantankerously. "You swore to me that you would go home this morning."

"I made no such vow." She dug in her heels, ready to argue the point, but he serenely continued on as though they weren't having a bodily tug-of-war in the middle of the yard.

"I expected you to heed my advice, but perhaps I should

have stayed on the verandah, and let Wilson have his way with you."

"Ooh! You're an absolute cad to allude to such crude behavior."

"Of course, I've seen what you have to offer, so I can't blame him for trying."

She was amazed that two adults, who scarcely knew each other, could carry on such a shameless conversation. Still, she wouldn't have ended it for the world. Primly, she rebuked, "You, sir, are no gentleman."

"We've already established that fact."

They approached their ball, and she stepped next to it, then froze. He was staring at her so intently that she was completely mesmerized by the magnificence of his blue eyes. Up close, they were sharp and clear, cool as shards of ice, and she could have stood there all day, studying them, for they made her absurdly, recklessly glad that he *wasn't* a gentleman.

He pressed himself against her, and as they swung at the ball together, those idiotic butterflies swarmed anew, but she refused to chase them away. She was situated so that her backside was shielded from the prying eyes of their audience, and astonishingly, he indelicately stroked his palm across her flank.

"You have the most shapely ass."

"Desist!"

She whipped to a vertical position and nailed him with the penetrating glower that regularly turned Hugh in a bumbling, prevaricating idiot, but the practiced look was wasted on Michael Stevens. Belligerently, he met it, then his focus dropped to her lips and lingered, as tangible as the kiss he'd bestowed the previous night. He was much better at intimidation than she'd ever conceived of being, and she bravely strove to rival his hot stare, but could only persevere for a moment.

Irritated by her lack of fortitude where he was concerned, she whirled away, but he matched her stride for stride, moderating their progress so it seemed friendly and methodical.

Calmly, tenaciously, he propounded, "That's what they're all contemplating."

"What?"

"They're inspecting your bottom and your bust, and they're imagining how arousing it would be to catch you by yourself." They'd reached their ball, and she waved toward it so that he might strike at it alone.

"Be my guest," she said.

"Rules of the game, darling"—the endearment rolled off his tongue as though he'd spoken it to hundreds of women in his life—"we have to hit the ball together. It is specifically designed to provide the men with infinite opportunities to be naughty in public."

She peered about, cogitating as to whether he was telling the truth, because if he was, then the guests would infer that he'd come out onto the yard in order to touch her improperly, and with his disposition and posturing, he'd done nothing to squelch the notion. Plainly, they'd created a maelstrom of supposition, with the spectators patently curious as to why he'd sought her out.

The women regarded her jealously, wishing they'd secured similar prurient courtesy for themselves, but the men had a heightened awareness of her, as though—if Stevens was attracted—there must be something provocative they'd missed.

Were they all leering at her with indecent purpose? Or were Mr. Stevens's admonitions inciting paranoia?

"If what you say is factual, then your conduct has made matters worse. Not better!"

"Hardly. Don't forget that I'm the one who prevented Wilson from groping you."

More cautious now, she let him slip his arms around her, and she liked how she tingled when his body made contact with her own. The surroundings were more extreme, the grass greener, the sky clearer, the air fresher. When his hands encompassed hers, and they mutually batted with the stick, she relished the unadulterated power of his torso. He moved with a fluid grace, inducing a myriad of lurid images. Of his naked chest and brawny shoulders. Of his adept fingers and seeking tongue.

Of the naked woman with whom he'd cavorted in the small, dimly lit room.

Gad! She must never discount his natural proclivities!

The ball glided off, and she shifted away. "For some reason, you want to alarm me, but it's not working."

"He'll try to sneak into your room."

"What?"

"In the night, Wilson will strive to gain entry. I succeeded with little difficulty, so he'll be able to prevail if he's obstinate enough. Which he is."

"You're mad."

"He will," Mr. Stevens announced with such conviction that she shuddered involuntarily. "How will you protect yourself once he's there?"

Desirous of knocking the arrogant oaf down a peg or two, but not sure how, she caustically stated, "I guess you'll have to crash through our adjoining door and rush to my rescue."

"What if I'm not about when it occurs?" He scowled at her, patently puzzled by his burgeoning involvement in her affairs. "I'm not joking," he reiterated. "You're not safe here. Please go. First thing tomorrow." She glared at him but said nothing, so he added irascibly, "Promise me you will!"

"Mr. Stevens"—she was categorically exasperated by his caution—"why does it matter to you whether I remain or depart?"

For a single second—just one—she thought he would answer honestly. Stark worry and bleak concern were evident, and she braced to hear a heartwarming comment that would confound her common sense. Then, as though a screen fell into place, his emotions were deliberately masked.

"I can't tolerate insipid women, Sarah, and you don't

seem stupid. You must realize that dawdling here is fool-ish."

Idiot! she chided herself. As if this flinty scoundrel would have professed a kind sentiment!

The remark was issued just as they approached the end of the lawn, which precluded further discussion. All of the contestants' balls were in the basket but theirs, and Mr. Stevens administered a quick swipe that spun it into the middle of the pile. His overbearing demeanor precluded any gay jesting with the other couples. Not dallying to sociably tally with the rest of the group while they established the winner, he briskly escorted her toward the verandah.

Once they were out of earshot, she scolded, "You are the most discourteous person I've ever met."

"Yes, I am."

"You go out of your way to be uncivil."

"I thrive on it."

"I can't abide such churlish behavior."

"I don't care."

In two more strides, they were at the porch, and it dawned on her that she'd been given the perfect excuse to probe him for personal details, and she'd squandered it. He addled her wits as though she was still an awkward ado-lescent girl, dazzled by a dapper male.

She climbed onto the lowest stair, while he resided on the grass, and the extra height put them eye to eye. Re-garding him painstakingly, she'd have been perfectly con-tent to tarry, daydreaming and seeking to understand him, but others were tracking their every move.

"Thank you for the game, Mr. Stevens."

"My pleasure." He bowed appropriately over her hand. "Have a pleasant evening."

Brushing past her, he disappeared into the massive house without a backward glance, while she stood like a simple-ton, reflecting on how terrible it would be if she never saw him again. For all his contemptuous manners and crude, imperious ways, she'd never hitherto encountered anyone like him, and she was undeniably enthralled.

At his departure, people gawked at her as if she'd sprouted a second head, and she yearned for privacy, but she couldn't retire so early. Casually, she strolled into the residence, rambling about, until she deposited herself in the music salon where two women were performing duets on the pianoforte. She reclined on one of the couches and listened, the music washing over her and calming her racing heart.

On the mantel, the clock ticked aggravatingly, and she silently calculated how long it would be before she could plead fatigue and escape for the night, and even as she marked the slow passage of the minutes, she pondered whether Mr. Stevens would later visit the secret room, if he would cavort with another lover.

Sarah had no intention of forgoing the lewd distraction Pamela had so obligingly furnished. She planned to watch all; every riveting, disturbing, glorious aspect of Michael Stevens's indiscreet exhibition.

Rebecca Monroe scrutinized her cousin from across the lawn. She had always liked Sarah in the abstract, though she was envious of her, too. Sarah was all that Rebecca was not. Strong-willed, determined, and headstrong while Rebecca imagined herself to be the opposite: inept, wavering, and inefficient. Plus, Sarah had the unfair advantage of being the daughter of an earl, while Rebecca had emerged from the indigent side of the family, the only child of a severe, incompetent merchant who'd died drunk and penniless.

For many years, Rebecca had soothed herself with the perception that she'd bested Sarah in looks and comportment, the only commodities that held any value for a woman. Rebecca had been born pretty, and Sarah had been gauche and plain. While growing up, Rebecca had seen Sarah on a handful of occasions, and she could vividly recall how people used to privately despair over how she would mature. Yet Sarah had blossomed, and her current state of loveliness irritated Rebecca to no end.

Still, she struggled not to be petty or bitter over all the blessings that had been conferred on Sarah and that she perpetually took for granted. After all, Sarah had offered her shelter at a desperate time, and because of her generosity, Rebecca had managed to gain Hugh's regard. If Sarah hadn't asked her to live at the estate, Rebecca would never have had a chance at Hugh's affection.

Considering all that Sarah had done for her, she tried not to be resentful, yet she was irked that Sarah refused to utilize her assets to help Hugh. Through the simple step of marrying—which was unconditionally required for a woman of her class and station—she could fix so many problems.

That's why Rebecca had concocted her scheme to see Sarah expeditiously wed. Rebecca wanted Sarah gone from Scarborough, plus she wanted to make Hugh proud. He never was, always claiming she was useless and ineffectual.

Despite the three Seasons she'd joined him in town, acting as his hostess and more, he was never satisfied with how she carried out her tasks. But she'd show him!

For a long while, she'd been reflecting on how she could force Sarah into marriage. Sarah seemed in no hurry to accomplish the deed, so Rebecca merely intended to give her a little shove in the right direction.

When the invitation had come from Lady Carrington, Rebecca had instantly mulled the possibilities and decided it would be the ideal method of achieving her goal. Since he knew how ribald the party would be, it had been easy to convince Hugh that Sarah should attend. The opportunity to have her completely compromised was simply too good to pass up, and Rebecca wasn't about to be thwarted.

She'd invested too much energy, and endured too much of Hugh's distasteful conduct, to admit defeat. If Rebecca had anything to say about it, Sarah's reign at Scarborough was about to conclude, because Rebecca had other motives, more personal ones, for wanting Sarah gone from Yorkshire. She didn't dwell upon them, because she hated to seem exceedingly covetous, but once Sarah wed and went to live with her husband, Rebecca would finally get to marry Hugh, just as he'd promised from the first time she'd shared his bed.

She'd become the mistress of Scarborough.

And wasn't that a glorious notion? How she'd lord it over all those slothful servants who perpetually treated her like a dreaded poor relation! Once she was their countess, they'd snap to when she passed! She'd dreamed about it at length and often, and the fantasy was about to change into reality.

So . . . though she liked Sarah well enough, she also believed that—sometimes—you had to lend fate a hand. Sarah would marry eventually, and Rebecca pictured herself as simply hurrying matters along, and she wasn't unduly bothered about the identity of the prospective bridegroom. As far as she was concerned, men were all alike. Any of them would be acceptable so long as they had money. Lots and lots of money to bail Hugh out of his latest misfortune.

There were a half-dozen suitable prospects already on the premises and, upon perusing Sarah, each had expressed an interest in what they presumed would be a tiny taste of her abundant delights, although with Rebecca's solicitous facilitation, a *taste* would develop into the full meal. She'd do anything to become Hugh's wife, and like it or no, one of the blasted fellows would be betrothed to Sarah in the impending fortnight.

She peeked over her shoulder, stealthily appraising Michael Stevens as he walked Sarah up the hill toward the manor, and she couldn't help but notice how the two of them were whispering as though they were fondly acquainted. Sarah was captivated by the notorious gambler and ladies' man—just as Rebecca had suspected she would be.

Now, all Rebecca need do was work on the timing. She thought she'd had it arranged the prior evening but, for some reason, Stevens hadn't followed through as Rebecca had postulated he would. He hadn't been in Sarah's room when she'd *happened* to stop by, but clearly, something had occurred between them.

"Oh, well"—she reminded herself of the adage—"good things come to those who wait," and she was extremely patient.

How could Sarah resist the man's precarious charms? And if, at the conclusion, Sarah's husband turned out to be Michael Stevens, wouldn't that be the most apt resolution for all concerned?

Chapter Five

From somewhere distant, a clock chimed the midnight
hour, and Sarah slipped from her bed and crept to the peephole in her dressing chamber. After retiring, she'd lounged
and walked the floor, occasionally checking to see if anyone occupied the hidden room, but so far, it had been
empty, and her apprehension and anticipation grew.

Michael Stevens completely absorbed her thoughts.
Their nude encounter the previous evening, followed by
their brief chat on the lawn that afternoon, had her head
spinning. She'd kept tiptoeing to the door that separated
their suites and pressing her ear to the wood, yearning to
detect him moving about, but her attempts had been greeted
by silence. No one appeared to be there.

Once, she'd even firmly and carefully turned the knob,
though she wasn't certain of her intent should the loathsome thing have swung open. Almost with relief, she'd
discovered it locked from his side, precluding any decision
about how she'd progress, or there was no telling what
heedless act she might have perpetrated.

Would she have brazenly entered? Searched his personal
papers or read his diary? Hoping to find what?

Though she hated to admit it, she was desperate to
breathe the air he inhaled, to inhabit the territory where he
roamed, to handle his belongings, to rifle through his shirts,
and examine his cuff links. Thank goodness he'd had the
foresight to secure his door, thus preventing any such foolishness on her part!

Cursing her sorry, disordered mental state, she climbed
onto the footstool and, silent as a mouse, adjusted her eye
to the peephole. She froze; her heart pounded. The event

for which she'd been waiting all day was about to commence.

Michael Stevens rested against the pillows and sipped red wine from a stemmed goblet. His steady gaze remained fixed on the entrance.

He was once again wearing only a pair of trousers, chest bared, and the sight was extremely arousing. All that naked male flesh, all that dark, swirled hair, was unsettling and thrilling. She longed to run her fingers through the matted pile, to rub her nose against it, while she traced over sinew and bone.

With a slow hand, he stroked the bottom of his chalice against his torso, arcing down in circles to his stomach, then lower, to the ridge in his trousers. The motion induced him to stir uncomfortably, and his groin flexed.

Just then, a woman joined him, another cloak shielding her identity, but she wasn't the same lover Sarah had spied upon the night before. She moved differently, and she was shorter and broader across the shoulders and buttocks.

Mr. Stevens rose up off the cot and stalked toward her like a predatory beast, all elegance and smooth, menacing purpose. His whole torso seemed to glimmer with an undefinable emotion that reached out to Sarah, billowing across her nerve endings, tickling her abdomen and breasts. A wall separated them, yet he beguiled her, and she couldn't prevent herself from wishing that his enticing regard was focused in her direction.

How she'd adore the chance to become the female enclosed with him! To stand next to him, to bask in his presence, to have those stunning blue eyes searching her own. If she was ever lucky enough to acquire a subsequent opportunity at being sequestered with him, she wouldn't be so quick to send him packing!

Mr. Stevens began with the same question he had the prior night. "What's your name?"

The woman spoke softly and, as before, Sarah couldn't detect her answer.

"Who is your husband?" There was a telling silence, a

muttered comment, then Michael's sarcastic grin, and Sarah would have given all she possessed to behold the woman's expression. Finally, he asked, "What is it you would like to do for me?"

After a lengthy hesitation, the woman leaned forward and whispered in his ear, hovering close. He'd cocked his head, listening, and Sarah suffered a strange flash of envy and jealousy at noting their nearness, but she impelled herself to remain calm. To watch. To study. No matter how disturbing, she had to ascertain what they were contemplating.

"Ah . . . *I* get to choose . . ." he mused. "Have you been informed about what I like best?"

The woman nodded and said something, but the only word Sarah could decipher was *mouth*, and, upon hearing whatever she was suggesting, Mr. Stevens's eyes glittered with triumph. What was it that he liked *best*? There seemed to be a cryptic code to these assignations that everyone could interpret but herself, and not understanding the intricate meanings was the worst sort of torture.

"And you're still inclined to proceed?"

Another nod.

"I'm a big man. Bigger than most."

"Aye," the woman murmured, "so I've been told."

"Once you've started, you have to finish. You might find it unpalatable."

"I'm sure you're wrong. I expect it will be *very* pleasant." The woman was obviously regarding him speculatively, appraising his marvelous physique. "I wouldn't have scheduled an appointment if I wasn't disposed to continue to the end."

For what precisely was he contracting? Sarah wondered. How many ways could a man and woman delight in each other's physical company? Plainly, there were many clandestine behaviors about which she was unaware, though Mr. Stevens had hinted at some of them during his abridged visit.

Eagerly, she eavesdropped, anxious to learn more.

"Are you undressed under your cloak?" Mr. Stevens inquired.

"Yes."

"Show me."

Coming up behind her, he trapped her in the corner, and she stiffened at the sudden contact. His hands fell to her waist, and the muscles across his back tensed and bulged as he pulled her against him. She unfastened the clasp, and he dictated, "Push it off your shoulders."

She complied, but the hood stayed on, so her face was still hidden, and Sarah's view included the woman's arm and back. Mr. Stevens's questing fingers lifted to cradle her breasts and, although Sarah couldn't see the maneuver, she sensed his ministrations.

He was trifling with the woman's nipples, twisting and twirling them as he had Sarah's own, and she observed, stimulated and agog. He rocked his front against his lover's backside, and he dallied, his searching hands never still, until he had her squirming. The woman groaned, as though in misery, but Mr. Stevens only gripped her tighter.

"Does your husband touch you like this?" he queried.

"No, never."

"How about like this?"

"No," the woman repeated, gasping and writhing, and Sarah received the distinct impression that he was smirking and preening.

Men! She'd never comprehend their thinking or their motives!

She strained against the peephole, but she couldn't discern exactly what he was affecting. He was caressing the woman, but how? How was he provoking her to dissemble so dramatically?

His paramour was definitely relishing his thoroughness. Guttural moans issued from her throat, a fist wrestled against the leg of his trouser, grappling for purchase against the taut fabric. In visible ecstasy, her head tipped back, and Mr. Stevens kissed and bit against her nape.

He rotated her, until they were facing the mirror, and

the moment became too personal for Sarah, because she
recalled only too well how he'd positioned *her* when he'd
been in her dressing room, how he'd cupped her breasts
and toyed with her nipples. She could still vividly recall
the heat and scent of his skin, the strength of his resolve.

Her nipples began to ache. With each beat of her heart,
her pulse pounded through them. They cried out for a type
of relief she couldn't describe and, hoping to ease their
distress, she covered one of them with her palm. The contact set off a maelstrom of agitation that rolled through her
chest and rushed down her stomach, centering between her
legs.

Her womanly cleft dampened, the flesh swelled. In agony, she grazed down her abdomen to her wet core. Even
through the fabric of her nightrail, she could feel the radi-
ating warmth. Her total being pleaded for a release that was
outside her realm of experience, and a frantic longing
seemed about to sweep her away. Without a doubt, the
novel, strange appetites were stirred by what she was perusing.

Stop watching! she ordered herself. *This isn't right or
proper.* But she could no more quit than she could halt the
sun from rising on the morrow. She was mesmerized by
the sight of his bronzed fingers on the woman's pale breast.
The display incited unnatural cravings and kindled formerly
shrouded desires, desires that she had no means of quelling.

Although she should have felt ashamed or—at least—
confused, she simply became more and more curious.

Unrepentant, she pressed against the peephole, braced
for more.

Mr. Stevens's arm was draped across the woman's torso
and spread low where Sarah couldn't investigate its performance. Presumably, he was fondling her cleft as he had
Sarah's, and the woman zealously luxuriated in his intimate
treatment. Their bodies rode together in an adapted rhythm,
the woman making pitiful, begging noises.

"Look at us," Mr. Stevens commanded. "Look at what
I'm doing to you, and say my name."

"Michael Stevens," she replied.

"Louder." She uttered it distinctly, and he appeared exultant. His hips ceased their perpetual movement. "I'll have you now," he declared. "On the bed."

Where the minute before, he'd been amorously attuned and greedy for her, he'd instantly changed, strutting away as though he hadn't a care, as though it didn't matter if the woman followed.

Sarah held her breath as he relaxed and arranged a pillow. What did he propose? What would he require?

She couldn't see enough of the room to know!

Frustrated, she attempted to alter her location on the stool, peering up and down, seeking a wider panorama, but to no avail. The peephole offered only limited access. Mr. Stevens's head and chest were discernible, but not his waist or anything lower.

His lover approached, and it appeared as if she knelt over him, but Sarah couldn't be sure, and evidently, she hesitated overly long, because he decreed, "The top button, madam!" A moment passed, then another, and he ordered, "The next one, if you please."

She was opening his trousers! To what end?

Sarah wanted to bang her forehead against the wall. How cruel to have been led down the carnal path only to have her journey obstructed at the last bend. For years, she'd ruminated and stewed about what men and women did when they were alone. Improbably, she'd stumbled upon a private, confidential method of determining the particulars, the mysteries of the world were about to unravel, but she couldn't observe the details!

How grossly unfair! Whoever had designed the spot had poorly planned the result. What was the point of contriving a peephole that didn't furnish a full vista? She hadn't wanted to witness some; she wanted to witness all!

"You're larger than I imagined," the woman remarked, uneasy.

"Yes, but you were advised at the outset," Mr. Stevens explained indifferently. "Take me at once. I'm ready."

Heeding his command, the woman did something that induced him to exhale in a slow hiss. His entire body tensed.

What? Sarah longed to shout. *What are you about?* But instead, she whirled away. Remembering her inglorious plunge the previous evening, she gingerly descended, then paced. A tangle of erotic images had her body throbbing and vibrating in places she'd never noticed before, and she strolled back and forth, scrambling to soothe her riotous breathing and thundering heart.

What were they striving so frenetically to accomplish? Unfortunately, her background and upbringing provided no mechanism for solving the riddle. She simply couldn't conceive of where their actions were leading, or why they would persist in the manner upon which they both seemed so intent.

At a loss, she sneaked back to the stool and quietly clambered to her perch. To her consternation, whatever adventure had kept the pair involved had been rapidly concluded. It was over. The woman's cloaked back was to Sarah, and Mr. Stevens faced her, looking apathetic. They were silent, unmoving.

Finally, the woman sputtered, "Did you enjoy yourself?"

"Yes." He was cold, devoid of emotion.

She wavered, then petitioned, "May I meet with you again?"

"As you wish."

The woman's shoulders sagged as though he'd just bestowed a great benediction, but Sarah could have sworn his tone was one of bored acquiescence. If he never saw the woman a second time, he wouldn't care.

The woman dawdled, clearly yearning to discuss what had just happened, but Mr. Stevens's lack of interest precluded her speaking further. Eventually, with a slight shrug, she departed.

Mr. Stevens paused for a lengthy interlude, apparently listening to ensure she'd actually gone. Then, mollified, he leaned against the wall and smoothed a weary hand over his brow. He looked more ominously handsome than she'd yet seen him. Rumpled and mussed and fatigued, he yawned and scratched across his stomach.

Unaware of her avid assessment, he turned so that he was directly situated for analysis, and his expression was one of despair and discouragement. His melancholia was so manifest that she wished there were no barriers separating them, that she could be by his side, resting her palm against his cheek, while she gently reassured him that everything would be all right.

Heaving a labored sigh, he blew out the candles and exited, shutting the door with a sharp click.

Stirred, stunned, distraught, and overwhelmed, Sarah peered into the darkened room long after his footsteps faded.

Michael stared at nothing.

The enclosed space was permeated with the odors of raucous sex, sweat, and candle smoke. The ambiance was stuffy and suffocating, and he had an urgent need for a cooling, invigorating breath of fresh air. From the strident sexual intercourse, perspiration had wetted and snarled his chest hair, and he swabbed across it, striving to wipe away the stench.

He could smell the woman on his skin and taste her on his tongue. She'd adequately tended to his ever-present lust, but he'd not been attracted to her in the slightest, and now that he was sated, her lingering essence was nauseating, and he forced down a wave of repugnance.

Disheveled and unkempt, he gazed at himself in the mirror that hung on the opposite wall. The man reflected back was in a sorry condition. His cock had been meticulously serviced, and it hung useless and limp against his leg, but he'd gained only temporary gratification. While most men would have reveled in the chance to engage in such an indecent, debauched oral ejaculation with an anonymous partner, he was not one of them. Try as he might to pretend otherwise, he was sickened by the corrupt level to which his conduct had fallen.

Pamela had concocted the offensive amusement, readily grasping how it would appeal to his sense of the absurd, how it would fan the fires of his enmity toward the aristocracy. When she'd urged him to participate, he'd agreed, thinking himself so detached that he could fornicate freely and without restraint. In past years, he'd sporadically and gladly acceded to her bizarre offers of carnal recreation, but to his surprise, at this current party his misdeeds only increased his despondency, further ravaging his anguished mind and troubled heart.

The women with whom he consorted were so willing to debase themselves, and he abhorred them for it, but he detested himself even more. As though a stranger had inhabited his body, he was lashing out at them, with his words and careless attitude, abusing them—and thus their husbands—with his cuckolding, but despite how often he copulated, he was never going to find genuine contentment, because the animosity he fostered wasn't for any of them specifically, or for the nobility in general.

He wasn't fooling himself: the actual object of his anger was his father, Edward Stevens, the Earl of Spencer.

Of late, memories of his father—and what he'd brought about all those years ago—were floating on the surface, and Michael could no longer push them down. Wherever he went, he seemed bent on wreaking paths of destruction in his efforts to run from the disturbing reminiscences that constantly cropped up.

His father, the king of all bounders, the epitome of all cads, was the catalyst behind his raging. The esteemed nobleman had been a thorn throughout Michael's life, jabbing and poking at his unstable existence at the most inopportune moments.

As a lad, Michael had loved Edward, had worshiped him with a godlike awe, but Edward was only a mortal man, comprised of human vice and bad behavior. When Michael was just three, his father had deserted their small family, had abandoned Michael's mother, Angela, and her two young boys in order to do his duty to his earldom by marrying a girl of the *ton.*

Angela had never recovered from his callous, contemptible act. James and Michael had suffered, as well, as they'd struggled to overcome the inexplicable loss of their father. They'd grown up to be undisciplined, impetuous boys, had matured into brutal, dispassionate men who did not trust or love, who never formed emotional connections, who never allowed anyone close.

Michael had neither forgotten nor forgiven those ancient sins that had been so casually and remorselessly committed. When his newly widowed father had dared to show himself in their peaceful, happy home—the one they'd created with no assistance from his illustrious self—and had lorded it over them by playing on Angela's interminable affections and seducing her anew, the resulting scene had been horrid.

Michael had felt betrayed. By his beloved mother. By his incorrigible, obstinate father. By his brother, James, who had placidly watched the debacle unfold but who hadn't done anything to stop what was occurring.

Edward had mistreated Angela for over three decades, yet she still loved the aging roué. There was no accounting for it, no understanding to be had for the affairs of the heart that propelled people to such insane attachment.

He'd fled London that day and, shortly after, Edward and Angela had eloped, tying the knot as they'd insisted they should have when they were young and foolish and less circumspect. Their marriage had completely numbed him, and he simply couldn't locate the fortitude he needed to carry on as though nothing had changed—when, in fact, everything familiar had been destroyed.

In response, he could only manage to wander, to gamble, to fuck and denigrate the immoral women who came to him, but deep down, he recognized that he could never vent the wrath he harbored for Edward. There were not enough hours in the day to totally unleash his malice, so why keep on? Why did he persevere?

Unbidden, an image of Sarah popped into his head, and he shuddered with disgust at himself. What he wouldn't give to laze in her virtue, to frolic in her untainted company. He felt unclean and impure, and his spirit begged for deliverance from the burdens that prodded him to comport himself so imprudently.

Earlier in the afternoon, when he'd glanced down into the yard from one of the upstairs windows, he'd been shocked to find her still in attendance. He'd been so positive that she would heed his frightening advice and go home. Then, when he'd seen that libertine George Wilson about to touch her inappropriately, outrage had compelled him to intervene. Against his will, she'd awakened his protective instincts and caused his forsaken chivalry to rear its ugly head. Like a magnet, she tugged at his resistant impulses to safeguard and cherish.

She was so original, so unsullied, and he couldn't abide the idea of her being tarnished in any fashion. In his current state, among these vile people, she seemed to represent the only good thing still thriving in his universe, and he shook away his thoughts of her. In such a foul atmosphere, it was wrong to contemplate her.

Scratching across his stomach, he could smell himself and the woman's cloying perfume. He reeked. The sticky residue from his seed had dried on his phallus. He was sickened by his degeneracy, and he desperately craved a bath to wash away the evidence of his degradation.

Initially, he'd told Pamela that he'd have carnal relations with two other women before the night was over. Usually, he accommodated her whims and caprices, but his desire to oblige her had waned, and he couldn't go through with it.

He blew out the candles and walked out to the secret stairwell, destined for his bedchamber. In the shadowed hall, a vision of Sarah flashed through his mind again, and he flinched.

What would she think if she ever discovered the depth of his depravity?

Chapter Six

Pamela Blair reclined on her sofa, her negligee loosely tied and widely parted to reveal bare cleavage and a smooth, waxed leg. Across her sitting room, Michael Stevens brooded and stewed and, as usual when he was near, he took up too much space. Such a virile, vital person, he was so different from the diverse gentlemen of her acquaintance who were watered-down versions of the male animal.

He exhibited none of the fluff or posturing, none of the pretension or swaggering, that the others practiced ad nauseum, but then, he didn't need to preen or pose. With that invincible combination of attitude, demeanor, and temperament, rivals could only jealously envy him. And he was so bloody good-looking. An amazing body, coupled with a comely face and those mesmerizing sapphire eyes, ensured that he cut a swath wherever he went. Heads turned, women coveted, men begrudged. It almost wasn't fair to the members of his sex that he possessed so much, while the rest of them had been graced with so little.

His dynamism came from his mother, she knew. Angela Ford, the flamboyant actress, had set society on its ear thirty years earlier through her notorious affair with the Earl of Spencer. She was now in her mid-fifties but remained a stunning, enchanting beauty, acclaimed for her keen wit, outlandish dress, and direct manner.

While his father, Edward Stevens, was a handsome, intelligent, and vibrant man, Angela's allure was responsible for Michael's constitution. He had inherited her fabulous traits, yet he incessantly carried himself as though he had no idea of his staggering impact.

She'd known him for over a decade, and had initially

become friends through his older brother, James, who was Michael's duplicate in sexy dispensation and bold demeanor. They had just returned to London after living in Paris for fifteen years. Angela had raised them there, out of the hurtful glare of the Quality's lofty snobbery. But once the boys were grown, she'd brought them to London, and Pamela chuckled whenever she recalled how introduction of the two Stevens sons had stirred the staid lives of so many.

What a commotion they had caused!

Wealthy, elegant, disreputable in their appetites, they had been rash, careless, out of control, eager to embrace any untoward behavior. Mothers had swooned at the very mention of their names. Fathers had wrung their hands over the potential disasters they might instigate. Girls had chased after them in a heedless rush.

Pamela, herself, had considered dabbling with one or both—how could a woman resist?—but as her dear husband had been alive at the time, she wouldn't have risked jeopardizing her cordial relationship with him, not even for a tumble with a luscious partner like Michael Stevens. Although that's not to say that she hadn't sampled his delectable charms on numerous occasions after her spouse had passed on.

He stood before her now, showing her his back. Restless, jaded, potent, he'd matured, and thus calmed some of his excessive conduct, but he wasn't averse to sporadically participating in periodic extravagant immoderation.

Sipping a glass of the strong Scots whisky he favored, he was ignoring her and gazing out into the yard, and as she studied him, she couldn't help wondering what had plagued him the past few months. Ordinarily, she had no problem ferreting out lurid details, but despite all her inquiries, she hadn't been able to uncover what had driven him from the city. And Michael assuredly wasn't providing any clues. He could be as tight-lipped as a jar of sealed preserves when the situation called for it.

Some disturbing circumstance had sent him into a bizarre downward spiral that was distinctly out of character. Instead of administering his duties at the famous gentlemen's club he owned with James, he'd been attending country parties, one after the next. He couldn't abide rubbing elbows with the exalted slackers and louts who also visited, frequently explaining that he was forced to put up with them at his establishment, but not in his private hours.

So . . . what was he doing at her house?

Gambling impulsively, for incredibly high stakes, he no longer appeared to care how much he won or lost. Nor was he concerned over who was damaged in the process, even though he invariably harbored a reputation as deliberate in his games of chance. He'd witnessed too much of the havoc produced by wagering, so he seldom indulged more than the smallest bets, yet now, he was bent on destruction.

While she wouldn't have been surprised by such outrageous behavior from his brother, Michael had perpetually been the more reticent of the two, and more likely to refrain from excess.

His sport with the female guests was typical of the recent changes. While he wasn't averse to partaking in lewd entertainment, he wasn't usually the first in line to volunteer, either. Yet when she'd suggested her latest visual amusement, which allowed her to take full advantage of the manor's less savory attributes, he'd promptly agreed.

The lady party-goers were begging to couple with him, and the news that he was present and available had them scurrying from London. Though her fetes were constantly well attended, his appearance had made the gathering an absolute priority for many. She hadn't managed to generate such enthusiasm since the time his brother, James, had done much the same.

The silly ninnies of the *ton* were scared of Michael Stevens, and they weren't sure how to interpret his commanding personality. With his curt comments and fuck-me-or-don't attitude, the women were lining up in droves, greedy to experience his rough brand of illicit sexual intercourse and, though none of them would admit it, each slyly yearned to be the unique paramour who cracked through his hard shell.

Plus, he was just so damned pretty. There wasn't a woman in the kingdom who had the fortitude to deny herself such pleasure when it was freely offered.

"Let's engage in some loveplay," she stated baldly, wishing he'd acquiesce but figuring he wouldn't. She'd invited him upstairs for a tryst, but he'd yet to indicate any interest.

Further opening the lapels of her robe, she granted him an abundant view of her rounded breasts—if he'd ever deign to look in her direction—then she stroked with her hand and squeezed the nipple, effortlessly arousing herself as she thought about how agile he was with that wicked tongue of his.

"I don't think so."

"You cad!" she grumbled, though she was smiling. They'd not been lovers for an eternity, and she missed him, enough so that she'd lured him into her private salon in the middle of the day. He was a man with whom she could flagrantly trifle and not worry about an unwanted pregnancy. Michael was extremely careful and would never provoke a conclusion that might lead to disaster. "Don't you dare say you're not in the mood!"

"I won't," he concurred, and she was fairly confident he was smiling, too.

"I've undressed and everything!"

"Sorry."

"You can be positively lethal to a woman's pride!"

"I try my best."

"You bounder. Now that you've been so cruel, I don't think I'll share the dreadful news I've received from London." She playfully pouted, suspecting that her reference to the city would pique his curiosity, and she was correct. He glanced at her over his shoulder.

"I don't care to be apprised of anything that is occurring in town."

"Aren't you a fine friend! You won't fornicate with me, and you won't listen to my woes, either."

"I loathe your gossip."

"Men!" she chided. "Why do I keep any of you around?"

He sighed, trying to sound put-upon but failing. "What is it?"

"My stepson, Harold"—she exaggerated the appellation of her late husband's son, an ass who was ten years her junior, a boor whom she despised—"has resolved to marry. I'm about to become a dowager!"

The tidbit had the desired effect. He chuckled. "You? A dowager?"

"Yes, can you believe it!"

Mischievously, he regarded her scantily covered torso, inspecting the swell of her bosom. "Well," he mused casually, "you *are* starting to sag a tad here and there."

"Oh! You horrid wretch!" She laughed and grabbed a pillow, flinging it at him. "If the term *dowager* ever springs from your lips, I'll wring your neck!"

"Yes, ma'am," he avowed sternly, pretending to be thoroughly chastised. "Is he busy having the dower house cleaned and equipped so he can hide you away?"

"I'd kill the little worm if he tried."

"Yes," he asserted, "I suppose you would."

Her feud with the callow boy was protracted and had begun the day his elderly father had selected a youthful bride. "I'm fortunate my dear, departed Charles provided for me so well." If he hadn't, she'd have very likely found herself out on the streets about now, beseeching old friends for food and shelter. Early on, she'd learned how to survive; she was proficient at chasing after what she wanted— and retaining it once she had it.

"You'll be all right?" he prompted.

"Absolutely. My financial affairs are suitably arranged; he can't touch any of my properties or my money."

"You'll advise me if you need assistance? Because Harold owes me a fortune. I could fend him off quite easily."

His overture was typical. While he customarily displayed an inflexible front, the handful of people who knew him intimately recognized the soft heart that beat beneath the steel exterior. "I'd come to you and James, straight-away."

"I should hope so."

He poured himself another whisky, and the silence lingered as she indulged herself by assessing his marvelous anatomy. She couldn't wait to gauge his reaction to the next, so she delayed until he was completely comfortable once again. "I have other tidings from town—"

"And I told you that I've no desire to listen to—"

"James wrote to me." He seemed to cringe slightly as if hearing of James was rather like receiving a physical blow, but the impression passed so quickly that she was certain she must have imagined it.

He shrugged. "So?"

"He inquires as to whether you're here with me."

"You may inform him that I am."

"You don't mind?"

"Why would I?"

"You tell me." She raised a brow. "Are you two fighting?"

"Hardly. I don't *fight* with my brother."

That wasn't true, but she let it slide. "He writes that he hasn't received any correspondence from your parents, so he assumes that they're well and enjoying their honeymoon in Italy."

Michael was so unaffected by her pronouncement that she felt as if she'd mumbled in a foreign language. Two months after it had ensued, the hasty, unanticipated elopement of his parents was still the hottest topic of discussion in London. Michael hadn't uttered a word about it, but the incident had to be the reason he was raging and alone.

After a while, he remarked, "Bully for them."

"There's more."

"What?" He couldn't prevent the question from slipping out, for try as he might to pretend he didn't care, he did. Too much.

"James himself has married."

In light of the dramatic and shocking nature of her disclosure, she wasn't entirely positive what she'd expected, but not this overwhelming, imposing quiet. She rose and stepped to her desk, retrieving the letter and tendering it to him, but he didn't reach for it, so she dropped it to her side.

"To whom?" he ultimately inquired.

"Lady Abigail Weston."

"Of course . . ." he murmured.

"She's the Earl of Marbleton's sister.

"Yes, I'm aware of that fact."

Pamela was perplexed that the information invoked no rejoinder. James had already suffered through one horrid marriage to a *ton* princess, and taking into account Michael's entrenched dislike of the aristocracy, she had predicted a biting response. She—as well as everyone else in London—was dying to discover how James had involved himself with the beautiful, reclusive spinster.

"What the bloody hell is wrong with you?" she inevitably blurted out. "Aren't you curious about any of this?"

"Not really."

She rested a consoling hand on his shoulder. "What is it, Michael? You can confide in me. Your secrets will never leave this room. I swear it." He merely stared at her with those glacial, detached blue eyes that gave nothing away. More gently, she added, "I detest seeing you like this."

"I'm fine."

"Liar." He shrugged again, and she stifled the urge to shake him. "He wants you to come home."

"Not likely." *Especially now* resonated clearly, though he didn't speak the sentiment aloud.

"He's been searching everywhere for you; he was anxious to locate you before the wedding so you could be his best man."

"Well . . . that's one affair I'm glad I missed."

"He's worried about you, darling. What may I divulge to him?"

"Whatever tickles your fancy. It matters not to me."

Abruptly, he stood, momentarily towering over her, the masculine closeness of his body and the appealing scent of his skin making her light-headed. He slipped his fingers inside her robe, affording her breast a naughty caress, then he moved to the window, displaying his back once more.

"You're impossible." She sulked, retiring to the sofa and lounging as he gulped the last of his whisky and persisted in contemplating whatever was keeping him so fascinated down on the lawns. "I hate it when you don't pay attention to me. If you're not careful, you'll destroy my self-confidence."

"I doubt that," he muttered, laughing softly. Eventually, he queried, "Who is the fetching woman who's visiting? She has the most striking auburn hair. Her name is Sarah."

"Oh, no . . ." Groaning, she proceeded to pour herself a drink. First, Sarah was asking about him; now he was asking about Sarah. This was bad. Very, very bad. "I presume you're talking about *Lady* Sarah."

"Who is her family?"

"Compton."

He spun around, his fierce gaze on hers. "She's Scarborough's sister?"

"Aye."

"They look nothing alike."

"Different mothers."

"What's she doing in Bedford?"

"*He* maintains she's determined to marry and is hunting for a husband, but *she* insists she's just taking a holiday."

"But why here? For Christ's sake, she's a virgin!"

"How would you know that?" For once in her life, she actually had the opportunity to observe Michael blushing. Would miracles never cease? Two bright spots of color marred his cheeks.

"I can tell," he said lamely.

"What? Can you smell chastity or something?" Irritated, she approached, clutching the decanter, and refilling his libation while she peeked out the window. Below in the yard, Sarah was pointedly visible, sitting on a bench while surveying the other guests and relaxing in the afternoon sun.

"Stay away from her, Michael."

"I have no idea what you mean."

"She's had difficult times lately, and there are even more ahead. She scarcely needs you as a complication."

"I'd never involve myself with one such as she."

"She's a wonderful woman. I like her very much."

"Then send her home. Today. She doesn't belong with this crowd; she's like a sheep among the wolves."

Pamela was regularly privy to confidential knowledge about the clandestine intrigues of others, so she deemed herself to be an expert at deduction. Obviously, these two had done more than pass each other in the hall. Michael seemed totally smitten, with Sarah in no better condition.

"She's delighted to be here," Pamela noted, "and I'm glad she is. I won't demand that she depart."

"Do it because she's your friend. Protect her."

"She's safe enough." He shot her a penetrating glare that said he didn't credit her denial, and she was affronted. Yes, she hosted ribald parties, but her male guests had never violated any of the females. There were too many convenient, willing women.

"You appreciate how Hugh acts," she admonished. "You can't begin to understand the kinds of unpleasantness she's had to endure by being related to him. She's entitled to this break from her obligations."

"What she *needs* is a stern scolding. A swift kick in the rear wouldn't hurt, either."

She bristled with dread. They were already dangerously attached. How had this happened? "Michael, heed me: If Hugh is spewing the truth, for once, and she *has* settled on marriage, she deserves to find an appropriate mate."

"Absolutely."

"It can't be you."

"As if I'd ever want it to be me." He snorted crudely. "I can't believe you feel you have to warn me off."

Disgusted with the sudden tenor of the conversation, he set his drink on the table and prepared to stomp off in a huff, and she took hold of his arm, halting him in mid-stride. "Don't be upset."

"I'm not," he finally remarked, and he acknowledged her expression of regret by wrapping a strand of her long hair around his finger and using it to draw her near.

"Will you play the game tonight?"

After pondering for a lengthy moment, he replied, "Oh, hell . . . why not?"

"Excellent. The ladies will be elated."

"I'll bet."

"And if you decide you'd like to dally"—on tiptoes, she brushed a kiss across his unresponsive mouth—"just knock. I'm still interested."

"I won't change my mind."

With that, he walked out, and she tied her robe and locked the door behind. Clucking in dismay over this newest turn of events, she went into her bathing chamber to wash. When she exited some minutes later, she peered outside again. There, bold as brass, was Michael Stevens sharing a garden settee with Sarah Compton.

"Bastard . . ." she grumbled, though not unkindly. Sarah was lovely, and Pamela couldn't blame Michael for being tempted. Yet, for all his impetuous disposition, and though he continually and zealously disputed her opinion, Michael was a gentleman. He was gravely cognizant of his status where a woman such as Sarah was concerned, and he wouldn't forget it.

Still, as she covertly watched the pair, their eyes sparking fire, their torsos sloped toward one another, a great wave of unease swept over her. They were attuned as only the most intimate of lovers could ever be. Their attraction was so blatant that she couldn't help speculating as to whether an innocent flirtation with Michael might be beneficial for Sarah. The adventure would definitely boost her lagging spirits before she traveled to Yorkshire to confront the future.

What's the worst that could transpire? she mused.

The dozens of frightening, sinister answers that rushed

to the fore were so distressing that she declined to reflect on any of them. She strolled from the window, refusing to prolong her spying.

Whatever Michael was about, she didn't want to know.

Chapter Seven

Michael was certain he'd lost his mind. Assuredly, he was deranged. Perhaps a wicked spell had been cast over him, or he'd been bewitched with a charm. Whatever the impetus, he was rashly and stupidly advancing toward Sarah Compton. Though she hadn't glanced in his direction, and didn't realize he was imminent, she was luring him in as firmly and methodically as if he was a fish impaled on a hook, and he couldn't arrest the progress of his feet. With each step, he marched to his doom.

When he'd answered the summons to Pamela's room, he'd gone with the unmitigated aim of coupling with her. They were highly compatible and, as he'd not partaken of her delights in many months, an assignation would have been an entertaining, amiable way to pass a boring afternoon. But when he'd gazed out her window and had seen Sarah sitting in the garden, on a cloistered bench where anything might happen, he'd lost his ability to concentrate. Suddenly, his plan for an uncomplicated sexual encounter with Pamela had vanished, only to be replaced with unwonted apprehension about Lady Sarah Compton.

Why was she still tarrying in Bedford? How could he persuade her to leave? What words could he utilize so that she'd go home where she'd be safe?

With all the dreadful news that continued to pour out of London, following him and unsettling him wherever he went, he was frantic to regain some semblance of control over his private affairs. As a man who cherished his independence, and his ability to direct his own course, he was frustrated and baffled by the swirl of events into which he'd been thrust. For once, he couldn't manipulate the conclusion according to his instructions.

He was desperate for one happy ending, and for reasons that were utterly unfathomable, he'd concentrated his attention on Lady Sarah, daftly assuming that hers could be the fitting resolution he so rigorously sought. If he could just get her to agree that departure was imperative!

Ludicrous and strange as his motives seemed, he craved the opportunity to have her reliably sheltered so that she would never be adversely affected by this harsh, unforgiving world in which they were both enmeshed. If he had to toss her over his shoulder and drag her off, that's exactly what he was prepared to do.

She must listen to him!

Quietly, he converged on the bench, and as he drew near, he was struck anew by how exquisite she was. Her spectacular auburn locks were pulled up, and a few ringlets dangled to tickle and glide across her nape. Distinctly, he recalled how soft her hair was, how thick and heavy, how silky.

Keenly and astutely, she surveyed the surroundings, her comely face puzzled, her pert brow quirked. Her lips pursed in an enticing pout. Moist, ripe, inviting, her mouth was the kind that had a man disposed to more than kissing. There were so many delicious diversions for which she could be trained that would put it to beneficial use.

The dark green gown she wore, with its scooped neckline, stretched tightly across her bosom and outlined her magnificent breasts. They were high and rounded, and he recalled how eager he'd been when he'd cupped them, when he'd sucked on those two taut nipples, and the graphic recollection set his male urges afire. Attracted to her as he'd been to no other before, he was incorrigibly titillated and aroused. Though his enchantment was unsuitable and could never be acted upon, he lusted after her with a foolhardiness that was frightening.

He wanted to have her and exploit her in every manner a man could possibly covet a woman. The sentiments she inspired were feral, animalistic, ungovernable, an irrepressible compulsion that was beyond his cognition or command. He couldn't fight the restless impulses she inspired nor was he inclined to; he simply desired her with a negligent impetuosity that was manic in its intensity.

The lowest of scoundrels, he'd invaded her boudoir, yet he wouldn't pretend to be repentant. Offered the least provocation, he'd intrude a second time, and very likely, he wouldn't depart when she ordered him out.

With a careless urgency, he yearned to hold her down, to fuck her until his passion was sated and his cock was limp. In the process, though it was lunacy to presume so, he imagined that by precipitously spilling his seed, he would finally find some peace!

Compelling himself onward, intent on shattering her serenity, he breathed her scent, and their exotic chemistry began to spark. Abruptly invigorated and enervated, he felt vibrant and exuberant; the colors brighter, the air purer, the sunshine more concentrated, just from lingering in her proximity.

The response she engendered in him was relentless and unyielding, beyond his ken. The only conceivable interpretation for his affliction was that they shared an incomprehensible affinity. However, his body needed no rationalization. His robust, unruly phallus sprang to attention and filled his trousers, causing him to ache intolerably. It was reacting as though he was, once again, a lad of fourteen and sneaking out to visit the French whores with James.

How could a woman incite such torment by doing nothing at all? Just by sitting there, looking so damned winsome, she ignited a flame that caused him to burn for her with an unremitting ardor.

Without requesting permission, he joined her on the bench. Obviously, she'd not discerned his approach, and his unforeseen move made her jump.

"Mr. Stevens!"

"Lady Sarah."

"You startled me." Distrustful, she scowled at him. "I suppose it would have been too much to expect that you could announce yourself like any other civilized man."

"There's nothing *civilized* about me."

"I enthusiastically concur!"

She shifted so that she was facing him and, because the bench was small, with an arm on each end, space was limited, so her torso was forced into closer contact with his. Suddenly, their shoulders were touching, her stomach curved against his side, her hip leaned into his thigh. Most delectably, a breast—the nipple pointed and easily apparent—brushed against him and, in shock at the suggestive impact, she reared back but encountered no means of escape.

He was behaving like an imbecile and a knave, yet he pressed his advantage. Employing only his greater size, by bending near and hovering, he worked her into the corner. A passer-by wouldn't have noted untoward conduct, but they were so confined that she couldn't flee. As it was, her hand instinctively rose, an ineffectual barrier, and she situated it in the middle of his chest where his pulse reverberated under her palm.

"Do you mind?" she queried.

A special musk wafted about her. If he'd been blindfolded and locked in a room with a hundred women, he could have picked her out by her distinct fragrance. The heady aroma called to his basest instincts, attracting and tempting him to experience her extraordinary charms.

"Not a bit."

"Oh, you are insufferable!" But she was laughing, her voice low and seductive and urging him on.

In the past, he'd never spent time with females of her station, because he hadn't the patience to weather their prattling, but oddly, he found Lady Sarah to be outrageously sexy and absorbing, and he hung on every word that popped out of her desirable mouth.

Her expressive green eyes flashed with what appeared to be delight at his nearness and, hoping to provoke her to chatter, he said, "I've provided you with sufficient admonitions about this party."

"Yes, you've been an unequivocal boor about it."

"Then why are you dawdling about out here?"

"It's really none of your business."

"You're incorrect. Since you're plainly bound to get into trouble, someone must watch out for you."

"And you've appointed yourself my guardian?" A contemptuous snort rumbled low in her throat. "Is that why you've stumbled along?"

"You're lucky it was I and not one of the other blackguards at this gathering."

"As if you're more honorable than another!" She sniffed contemptuously, turning up her saucy little nose. "You forget, Mr. Stevens, that I've previously witnessed the type of calamity that can arise when I'm in your company."

"I quit when you asked me to, milady," he reminded her quietly, even as he secretly wished he was the sort who could have proceeded despite her protests. Perhaps if he'd carried on, he wouldn't still be so intrigued. "Most men wouldn't have halted."

"Most men wouldn't have entered in the first place!"

Her glare could have melted lead, and it was so thoroughly mocking that he supposed she stood in front of a mirror and practiced to perfect it. With a brother like Hugh Compton, she probably had to bestow it often, but he rather enjoyed seeing her in a temper. The emotions that swept over her pretty features were interesting and pleasing to behold.

"You haven't answered my question," he reminded her. "Why are you here? I'd assumed you'd be traveling home by now."

"I am utterly fascinated as to why you conceive that you're in a position to order me about."

"Somebody should."

"I'll let you know when I'm ready for it to be you."

She kept pushing at his chest but with no success, because he didn't prefer to be shoved away. Crazily, he

yearned to lean in, to capture her lips with his own. He
focused on the hand that was touching him, and he even
engaged in a transient flight of fancy where his avid imagination painted them secluded and alone. Those long, slender fingers would stroke across him, down his stomach and
lower.

The very idea impelled him to grow hard as stone.

What marvelous sensations she invoked! She felt them,
too. Her eyes widened in surprise, her nostrils flared, and
she calmed, terminating her efforts to propel him away. He
could almost see the wheels spinning as her mind struggled
furiously, striving to process her body's devastating response.

There was no explanation. They enjoyed a physical
bond. It was no more simple or complex than that.

The rendezvous became intimate, extremely so, and he
was stunned by the compulsion he suffered to fully understand this woman, which induced him to suspect that he
was losing his grip on reality. There was no other intelligent
rationale for the sentiments she inspired.

"I saw you from the house," he absurdly mentioned.

"You were spying on me?" She smiled, enlivened by his
disclosure.

"Yes, that's why I came down."

"You were worried about me. Again."

Though their conversation had evolved to a juncture
where confidential remarks might be bandied about, he
couldn't bring himself to acknowledge as much, so he
chided, "Do you have any idea how isolated this spot is?
Anyone might have blundered by."

"But no one did."

"Lady Sarah—"

"Sarah. And . . . may I call you Michael?"

"Certainly." He received a huge jolt of satisfaction from
knowing that she wanted to call him by his name.

Slipping his hand under hers, he linked their fingers,
then dropped them to his lap. Lazily, he caressed his thumb
across the center, and he'd expected her to withdraw, but

astonishingly, she seemed mesmerized by his bold gesture.

She studied their united hands, inquiringly noting the dissimilarities—of fragility and daintiness compared to his own broad proportions—and for an attenuated interval, they tarried under her silent, acute scrutiny. A gentle breeze rustled through the trees; a bee buzzed past in the flower beds.

When she lifted her gaze to his, once more, she was staring at him with such frank, visible veneration, that he determined he might be able to dissuade her from her incautious path. He had to persevere until he prevailed on her to depart!

He reiterated, "Tell me why you're out here by yourself."

"Since you demand a confession, I admit that I was searching for you."

The proclamation stopped him in his tracks. "For me?"

"Yes."

"Whatever for?"

"I've been waiting for you to wander by for the past two days, but you've been terribly uncooperative. You never join in any of Lady Carrington's entertainments, and you never appear at supper like a normal person."

The insult made him chuckle. "No, I don't."

"And I've been dying to talk with you."

"Why?"

The vexing noblewoman longed for a discussion? On what topic? She hardly seemed the type to simper over tea about her hair or clothes or any other tedious subject. They had no communal background, one mutual friend, and limited interaction, yet he couldn't tamp down the flair of excitement that had him mulling why she was considering him at all, or why she'd be dallying in the garden and anticipating that he might saunter by.

Out of the blue, she inquired, "Are you happy that you're here?"

"What?"

Shifting uncomfortably, he was disconcerted by her assessment. She peered far into the core of his black heart and made him wish he'd never been so idiotic as to seek her out.

"You keep imploring me to go home, but I must concede that I could say the same to you." She squeezed his fingers encouragingly. "You don't belong in Bedford any more than I. You're so discontent."

How had she noticed? How could she be so unerringly perceptive? "I'm not *discontent*," he was compelled to assert, "just bored."

"No. You're distressed—and dismayed because of it."

"For a woman who's scarcely acquainted with me, you're categorically convinced of your opinions."

"It is peculiar, but I comprehend much more about you than I ought. Why is that? Can you explain it to me?"

Nervously, he brooded over why she was able to glean so much. The enhanced awareness that drew them together defied all logic, and he hated that she felt confident enough to delve and pry. He'd never confirm her excessively accurate appraisal of his condition, so he didn't corroborate or deny her judgment, but still, she gazed at him with a genuine admiration that threw him off guard.

Wanting to lessen her impact, he grasped her arm. "Let's take a walk, shall we?" If they were strolling side by side, he'd not have to directly confront her during her annoying examination, and if he was clever in the route selected, he could maneuver her back to the house before she guessed what he was about.

"No, I'd rather not," she replied infuriatingly. "I'm quite cozy where I am."

Did she move just a tad bit closer? His hand was now unacceptably pressed to her side, and his naughty fingers—despite his strict command that they remain stationary—massaged against her tiny waist in a slow circle. However, his impropriety met with no complaint, so he didn't desist.

For an untried woman whom he'd nearly ravished two days prior, she'd become inordinately complacent! What had transpired to bring about this transformation?

"I don't think"—he fought to sound stern—"that it would be fitting for others to observe you loafing on this bench with me."

"Your reputation must be horrendous," she reflected, composed as you please, as though she'd been thoroughly apprised of his disgraceful notoriety and was wholly indifferent.

"It is." Amazingly, he was blushing. With the exception of his mother, he'd never cared what females thought of his character, yet he was ashamed that Sarah might have uncovered some of the less savory aspects of his constitution.

"I've never before been introduced to a despicable cad," she said lightly, "so I shall consider our meeting to be an adventure. It will be a learning experience; perhaps I'll finally ascertain why women are so regularly beguiled by a scandalous figure."

A definite twinkle glimmered in her eye. The impertinent woman was laughing at him! "You're evidently not bothered about appearances when you should be."

"Why don't you leave this place?" she queried softly, cutting off further dissection of his distinction or disrepute. "What is troubling you so?"

When had he become so bloody transparent? "There's nothing *troubling* me."

"You're upset. Has something happened?"

Before he could check himself, the words spewed forth as though bubbling from a fountain. "Well, I've always lived with my mother and my older brother, but my mother recently married a man I can't abide."

"That would be difficult."

"And a few minutes ago, I was informed that my brother has also wed someone whom I don't particularly like."

"Are you and your brother close?"

"We were."

"I'm sorry for you."

Bewildered by his folly, he endeavored to grasp why he'd divulge so much to this virtual stranger. He exhaustively shielded his privacy, yet he'd blurted out exceedingly personal details to her with barely any contemplation of the consequences.

Striving to mitigate the admission, he declared, "The matter is of no great import."

"You miss him."

He shook his head against her penetrating deduction. "No, I don't."

"Not true, Michael."

As she spoke his name for the first time, his heart hammered with an unaccustomed gladness, and with an unwavering conviction, he yearned to hear her murmuring it over and over again.

"So," she mused, "if you left this party, you'd have nowhere to go, would you? Is that why you stay?"

Instantly, she'd homed in on the very conundrum that had been driving him these many months. Life—as he described it—had ended when his mother had wed Edward. He had no home. No family. He was drifting because of it, and couldn't seem to find any good reasons to go back to London.

"I *stay* because this is precisely where I belong." He thought of the decadent women, the lewd couplings in which he engaged, the sick, ribald sport he instigated in his meager attempts to relieve his doldrums through sexual satiation.

Now, it seemed his entire existence was one, lengthy episode of debauchery and vice with nary a pleasant intervening interlude. He'd fallen so far into the abyss of corruption that he couldn't locate the road that would return him to a sane system of carrying on. There was no reality for him but these perpetual days—and nights—of dissolution and iniquity, and even if he determined to switch his course and tread a more virtuous path, he wasn't sure how to alter his direction.

"We've a lot in common, you and I," she contended.

He sniggered disdainfully. "Stuff and nonsense."

"Why would you say so? I don't really have a home,

either. Everything I've held dear is being taken from me. Perhaps that's why I feel this incredible association with you; we've both been cut off from all that's familiar."

A hideous stab of unbidden guilt slithered through him, but he quashed it ere it could flourish. "Kindred spirits?"

"Exactly."

"That's ridiculous."

Boldly, she set her hand on his chest a second time. Her steady gaze slid to his mouth and fixated on his lips, inducing him to crave and remember things that were best ignored.

She prompted, "Do you ever think about that night you came to my room?"

"No," he lied. "Never."

"I do. Constantly."

His thundering heart skipped several beats. She'd been reflecting upon their tryst? About their truncated foray into pleasure? About how they'd touched, kissed, connected? "Why would you?"

"I've just been speculating as to what might have occurred if I hadn't said no."

The earth seemed to stop spinning on its axis. On a thousand occasions since that despicable event, he'd pondered the same. If they'd forged ahead, if they'd coalesced in sexual ecstasy, would he now be languishing so wretchedly? Why was he so inanely positive that physical knowledge of her body would be a cure for so much of what ailed him?

"You've taken leave of your senses," he muttered, and he removed her hand. With it floating so near to his heart, it created the queerest sensation that she was massaging his woes. "It's this house that's making you contemplate such wicked subjects. All the better that you depart."

"But if I left, I'd never see you again."

"There isn't any reason you should want to," he stated, though the identical notion had crossed his mind. Somehow, she'd niggled into his consciousness, and he'd never be fully shed of her. With the information that Pamela had imparted—that Sarah's brother was Scarborough—any man who possessed a shred of integrity couldn't help but fret over her future.

"I can't account for why, but it just seems so . . . so *vital* that we spend time together."

"For what purpose?"

She deliberated, vexation wrinkling her smooth brow, her incessant attention captivated by his mouth. A weighty supposition clearly engrossed her, for she couldn't look away. The pink tip of her tongue flicked out, wetting her bottom lip, making it glisten, and the sight made him dream about the fabulous games she could be taught to play. That he could be her tutor!

A flush darkened her cheeks, her pulse elevated and pounded at the base of her neck. She probed far inside his being, examining his shallow depths, hunting for emotion that was long absent, and finally, she wrenched her torrid gaze to his own.

Humbly, fantastically, she requested, "Would you kiss me?"

He nearly fell over. "What did you say?"

"You heard me." She blushed a bright scarlet and stared at her lap. "It was difficult enough to ask. Don't be so crude as to insist that I repeat myself."

"I *heard* you, all right. I simply can't believe my ears."

A rush of images swamped him as he recalled his previous fleet effort at seduction: her slender body, impertinent nipples, and taut pussy. When her cascade of crimson hair was hanging loose, it shimmered and swirled about her hips.

Astoundingly, he could picture her in his bedchamber in London, a site where he'd welcomed no other paramour. He'd lay her back, sample and savor, have her until she was begging and pleading for him to cease, then he'd begin anew. He'd continue until he was drained, satisfied, replete.

Vividly, he recalled their one and only brief kiss. How delectable it had been! How undone he'd been afterward! And for so many hours! He'd craved so much more from her. More than she could ever give. More than he should ever receive.

"No, I will not."

"But why? You've come to dabble with the female guests. Why not with me?"

He'd been curious as to where her solicitation was leading, and now he had his answer: His innocent companion was intrigued, hankering for a few love lessons with an adept partner. He couldn't decide if he was angry or amused. "Because, milady, you are a virgin."

She flinched as if he'd slapped her. "What has that to do with anything?"

"I'm conversant with what you may have deduced about my character"—he fumed at the image of her eavesdropping while his indecent antics were dissected by some of the guests—"but I am not in the habit of debauching untried women."

"I didn't invite you to defile me. I merely requested a kiss!" A spark of temper flickered into full view, and he treasured the spectacle. "I may be unschooled, but I don't believe they're similar!"

The volume of their voices had risen, so he bent nearer and hissed, "Have you gone mad?"

"Perhaps!"

"It seems as if you're anxious to be ruined!"

"What if I am?" She haughtily threw out the potentiality, almost as if it was a dare. "It's no concern of yours!"

"That, my dear, is where you are wrong!"

"If you won't accommodate me, I'll just have to ask someone else. I'm sure I can locate another who won't deem the idea to be as unappealing as you obviously do."

The thought of some other man kissing her was so disturbing that he was forced to admit he was . . . was . . . jealous! How absolutely bizarre!

Perchance if he'd been born to different parents, if his childhood had been contrary to what it actually was, if his life wasn't occupied with immorality and vice, she might have been the sort of woman he'd have chosen as a bride.

She was good and kind and precious—the total antithesis of himself.

For her to wheedle and feign fondness, to tantalize and entice with a promise of unattainable possibilities, was beyond the limits of what he could tolerate. He was resolved to show her, once and for all, just how incredibly imbecilic she was acting. The insipid ninny was enmeshed in a perilous pursuit, but she was too foolish to realize it.

Glancing around, gaining his bearings, he saw a small gardener's shed at the fork in the walkway, discreetly hidden behind a row of hedges and sheltering oak limbs. He rose, seized her elbow and brought her to her feet, spurring her along as though she weighed no more than a feather.

"Come!" he ordered.

"Where to?"

"You're about to learn why we can't sneak about *kissing* each other."

With a hasty peek down the footpath, he could distinguish that no one was in sight, so he yanked at the shed door and crept inside, dragging her in behind. Turning the wooden latch, he secured them from detection. There was a window up high that allowed air to flow. Dust and sunlight danced through it.

He stared at her, then rudely and inappropriately advanced, so that her breasts brushed against him, and his abused phallus was cushioned by her abdomen. To her credit, she didn't shy away. She straightened, unafraid of whatever he proposed.

All beauty, temperament, and allure, she was splendid.

"You want a kiss? Fine! I'll give you a kiss." He grazed his thumb across her bottom lip, loitering, conscious of a gale of stimulation that extended to his extremities. "Close your eyes."

"Why?"

"Just do it," he scolded, exasperated.

Carefully, she studied him, then her eyelids fluttered shut, and without hesitating to debate the wisdom of his decision, he pressed his mouth to hers. Confounded, she stiffened but didn't pull away, not hindering him in the least, so he pretended that her placidity was acquiescence.

Holding only the back of her neck, he didn't deepen the embrace, nor did he caress her or flex against her. He simply merged with her and, as he'd suspected, he was immediately overwhelmed.

This is what heaven must be like. The transient concept drifted past, then evaporated.

Sweetly, almost chastely, he discovered her best-kept secrets, using scant pressure and bare coercion. With a feeling approximating joy, he teased and trifled.

Her reaction was just as instantaneous and staggering as his own. Her breasts swelled, her nipples beaded and buffeted against her corset, imploring their release from confinement. Her pulse escalated, her skin heated. Losing her balance, and needing to steady herself, she clasped his waist, her fingers kneading into the fabric of his coat.

A moan—one of bliss and awe—escaped, and he wasn't sure from whom it had emanated. Mayhap, it had been a mutual recognition of their collective exhilaration.

He couldn't have guessed how long he stood, deliberately luxuriating with her. Time had slowed, reality had no meaning. There was only her and the drab shed, and the divine impressions that swept over him.

When they finally separated, he was shaky, perplexed, and agitated—just as he'd known he'd be. His pulse was racing, his body ablaze, and his cockstand so painful that he wasn't sure how he'd walk inconspicuously to the house.

Gradually, he distanced himself, readjusting to being two distinct people when, for a transitory moment, they'd been a single entity unto themselves.

She breathed a soft sigh of regret, then her eyes opened, and she regarded him with artless candor and, if he wasn't mistaken, an extremely misplaced amount of tenderness.

He was a villain. A bounder. An undisciplined rogue with no morals or scruples, the fact that he'd now twice used her badly being the unequivocal proof.

"Oh, my . . ." Her confusion and wonderment were manifest. She held her fingertips to her lips, as though containing the blistering commotion.

"That, Lady Sarah," he stridently professed, "is precisely why I won't kiss you. Don't ask ever again."

Though he was desperate to continue, to keep on until he hadn't the power or inclination to halt, he went to the door, freed the hook, and peeked out. No one was about.

He peered over his shoulder. She was bathed in shadows, a lovely, sheltered, exquisite gem inexplicably dropped into his sordid world, and he wanted her with an unrelenting, reckless abandon.

"Good day, milady." He bowed stiffly. "Don't wait for me in the gardens or anywhere else. I shan't stop by."

With that, he departed, leaving her to her own devices, returning to the manor and the privacy of his rooms where he could contemplate the long, depressing hours till evening and the depraved night yet to come.

Chapter Eight

Sarah paced furiously from one end of her room to the other. She couldn't quit thinking about Michael Stevens, about their rendezvous in the yard, or their furtive trip to the gardener's shed. The kiss they'd shared had been the most thrilling, intriguing event in what she deemed to be her extremely eventless life.

He'd done nothing but lightly touch his mouth to hers, so how was it possible that such a simple gesture could be so riveting? All these hours later, long after he'd departed in a huff, and she'd returned to the house alone and more frustrated than ever, her body was completely disconcerted by the sensations the tender interlude had invoked.

She'd become uncomfortably conscious of her condition as a woman, a spinster, a virgin who was quite sure she didn't want to be one much longer. Yearning for his company, she was now eager to while away her time in wanton pursuits that she'd have previously considered patently ridiculous.

From the moment she'd first laid eyes upon him, she'd been drawn into his sordid realm, until she couldn't imagine an occurrence more lovely than the opportunity to revel in his sweet version of erotic excess.

How and why did he fascinate her so? What was it about him that overwhelmed her common sense, that had her mooning about the mansion, hoping to catch a glimpse of him? It was as though she'd reverted in age to a love-struck adolescent who was teeming with youthful, unrequited reveries which, given the state of their acquaintance, was absurd.

Three days prior, she'd met him in a shocking fashion,

but since then, she hadn't learned any detail of consequence about him. He was purportedly a cad and a bounder, a man of horrendous reputation. But what else?

He had a mother and brother about whom he cared deeply, he was marvelous at kissing, and he would commit any foul escapade with a woman. That was the extent of her knowledge.

Craving an in-depth interview, she'd spent her entire daylight hours wandering about in search of him. In the breakfast room. At the card tables. Out by the stables. She'd walked the grounds, peeking through hedges and selecting provident viewing locations where she might spy on the entrances to the manor. Yet she'd had no luck at chancing upon him, which had only induced her to stew about where he was, what he was doing, and with whom.

When he'd finally surfaced, it seemed as if she'd conjured him up, but once she'd had him within her purview, she hadn't discovered any useful tidbits. In his magnificent presence, she could concentrate on nothing but the physical: how he carried himself, the husky timbre of his voice, the dangerous glitter in his eye. The fact that he was fully clothed and looked superb.

Like a thunderstruck dolt, she'd pondered his corporeal attributes and conduct, while privately wishing that he might visit her clandestinely, once again, and reveal more of his sensual secrets. In too short an interval, she'd developed a strange and unexplainable attachment to him, and she didn't appreciate the notion of him bestowing his favors on his various paramours. If he was going to dabble in carnal indiscretion, she was prepared to insist that he seek out her and no other.

The impetuous decision had been so strong and pervasive that she'd even deigned to knock on the door that separated their suites, urging him to open, so that she could declare herself, but annoyingly, he'd not been there. Or, if he had been, he'd refused to answer her summons.

His absence had driven her crazy with anxiety as to his whereabouts. She'd impatiently prowled, hunting for him, so she could tell him not to visit the hidden room that evening, that he should allow her to be the one to bring him comfort and relief. He could teach her, then let her practice her new techniques on his fabulous anatomy.

Despite how he'd scoffed at her assertion that they were kindred spirits, she felt linked to him as she'd never been with another, and her impression of closeness caused her to worry and fret. About him. About his family situation. About his dissatisfaction with life and his place in it.

Her peculiar enlightenment as to his personal problems plagued her with an extraordinary level of concern for his welfare. She was convinced that he shouldn't be cavorting with the female guests. The lewd behavior was out of character for him, and she intended that he desist. At once. That he regroup and renounce his reckless conduct. Their kiss had been phenomenal, splendid, and she simply couldn't abide to learn that he didn't possess a similar sentiment about the whole affair. After their heated, bonding embrace, he absolutely couldn't go around making love with others!

The hour was late, the manor settled and quiet, and she contemplated whether she should endeavor to locate the stairway that led to the hidden room so she could stop him before he entered. For a good part of the day, she'd tried to ferret out the mode of access, but she'd been unsuccessful at deciphering its position, so she doubted if she could stumble upon it in the dark.

Baffled and apprehensive, she went to her dressing room, sneaked to the peephole, and stealthily climbed onto the footstool. To her dismay, Michael Stevens had magically appeared and was sequestered inside. He lounged, negligent as ever. Bored and delectable, he waited for another anonymous lover to join him.

Though she longed to pound on the wall and call his name, she restrained herself. She watched—as she always did. She couldn't tear herself away from his beautiful face, his furred chest, his tight trousers. As usual, the top buttons were unfastened, and her gaze was held captive by the male mysteries buried below.

How she craved to see him in the altogether! To run her hands across that marvelous torso! To massage and caress as he permitted his other paramours to indulge themselves on a regular basis!

From off to the side, the door opened. A woman stepped into sight, cloaked and concealed, and Michael straightened.

"Don't do this," Sarah implored, but silently. "Michael, please . . ."

Hating to observe, but unable to discontinue, she kept her eyes glued to the pair, bracing for what was coming, aware of the sick amusement in which they would engage, but she couldn't stop herself.

The titillation was extreme, the arousal disturbing and impossible to resist. Disgusted with herself and her motives, disgusted with Michael and his, she pressed her eye to the hole just as Michael rose to his feet.

"What's your name?" he inquired, and at the woman's casual response, he chuckled. Whoever was under the cape was a person Michael knew well, an associate whose company he relished. He stared at her with a bemused expression, and he chided her lightly, a hint of familiarity and admiration in his question. "Why are you here? You don't like showing off."

"You've been neglecting me, darling," the woman pouted. "You declined to oblige me this afternoon."

Sarah's mind swirled in panic. He'd been with this woman during the afternoon? When? Before or after her own assignation with him? Could he have kissed her so amorously, so passionately, then casually moved on to another? The concept didn't bear contemplating.

"I wasn't in the mood," Michael said somewhat petulantly, which caused his companion to laugh aloud.

"Well, you'd best be now," she scolded, though impishly. "Surely you wouldn't begrudge me a bit of a frolic."

Michael was clearly intrigued that the woman had visited, and he was ready to humor her whim with a friendliness and sincerity that Sarah had not noted in him before.

To her consternation, this novel attitude of his was more disconcerting than ever. It had been painful enough to scrutinize him as he'd manhandled his partners with a calculated, unshakable disregard, but it was so much worse to see him dallying with someone for whom he sustained an evident fondness.

A powerful, unaccustomed jealousy roared through her, and she cursed him and his lover. The affectionate tone and genuine regard were excruciating to endure. She abhorred witnessing the couples' amiable connection, but she'd already enmeshed herself so far in Michael's activities that she couldn't withdraw.

They were conversing, and Sarah struggled to hear.

Mockingly, Michael queried, "What's your pleasure, milady?"

"You shouldn't have to ask."

"And you know the rules," he advised. "You have to state your preference."

"Blast the rules!" she asserted, but she was laughing again.

Their bodies were melded, her hands massaging through the luscious matting of hair on his chest, then lower. Sarah couldn't distinguish the exact maneuver, but the woman seemed to be stroking his abdomen, rubbing across the protrusion in his pants. She huddled near and whispered her predilection in his ear.

"A pleasure to service you, milady," he intoned.

"You scoundrel! I'm perfectly willing to beg—if that's the only way I can garner your attention."

"Are you naked under your cloak?"

"Yes! How indelicate of you to mention it!"

"Let me see."

With a flourish, she whipped the cape off her shoulders and preened before him, nude and insolent. Her hair was wrapped in a white turban, supplying no clue as to its color, and her face was discreetly covered with an intricate purple mask, rimmed with feathers and golden sparkles, so her identity remained disguised.

"What do you think, darling?" She squared her shoulders
and thrust her bust forward.

"Very nice . . . as always."

He reverently stroked a plump, rounded breast, and
Sarah wanted to die! How could he worship at another
woman's bosom when he'd so recently showered *her* with
tenderness? She loathed the patent admiration that he showered on his lover, because she remembered all too well how
it had felt when he'd gazed similarly at her.

Leaning down, he suckled at a nipple, gently and obligingly tasting the rosy nub. Enthralled, the woman smiled
down on him, then shivered with delight as she ran her
fingers through his glorious black hair.

Sarah's heart pounded, her womb stirred. As usual, it
seemed as if he was manipulating her own breast. Her nipples throbbed and ached, and she squeezed one of them,
hoping only to alleviate the furious pang of agitation, but
pinching the distressed tip proved dangerously exciting.

She forced her hand away and focused her concentration
on the duo, determined that she wouldn't miss a single second of their sortie, despite how difficult or stimulating it
might become.

Michael fell to his knees and, whatever he was accomplishing, his companion's eyes glittered, her back stiffened.
She bit against her lip, her breath coming in fast respira-
tions, and her fingers gripping his shoulders.

"God, you are so good at that," she muttered.

"We aim to please."

"I'll be sure to recommend you to all my friends."

"I'm humbled."

Sarcasm dripped from his words, and Sarah strained
against the peephole, desperate to discern precisely what
had his visitor so preoccupied, but she couldn't identify the
procedure.

The episode resumed, the woman increasingly distraught, her body exhibiting more tension. Then, for some
inexplicable reason, she stepped away from him.

"Not just yet."

From his position on the floor, he glared up at her. "I'm not finished."

"Neither am I."

Winking playfully, she scooted to the bed and giggled when he grabbed for her. He climbed behind her, centering himself, and it looked as if he was unbuttoning his pants. The woman wiggled against his groin, and she was merrily preventing him from achieving whatever he intended.

"Behave!" the woman scolded as Michael bit against her neck, and she shrugged him off. "I advised you of my choice. And it's not this! You must honor my request."

They tumbled about, kissing and cuddling, until Michael was lying on his back, the woman on top. Down toward the bodily regions Sarah couldn't perceive, the woman's hands were busy stroking him in a fashion he greatly treasured, but Sarah couldn't begin to speculate as to their task.

"You are so hard for me," she asserted.

Apparently, she was proud of what her efforts had attained, and she brushed a chaste kiss across his lips. "Close your eyes, darling, and I can be anyone you want me to be." Mischievously, she added, "You can even pretend I have green eyes and auburn hair; I won't mind."

"Witch," he grumbled as the woman committed an exploit that caused them both to gasp with a sort of reciprocal anguish. Then . . . they were moving conjointly, much as one would when riding a horse. The motion went on and on, the lovers more involved, more intense in their enterprise. The woman adjusted herself so that her breasts dangled over Michael's zealous mouth. He pressured, milked, and suckled.

Sarah watched to the end, repelled, captivated, discomfited, wanting them to cease immediately, while at the same juncture, never wanting the torrid exhibition to conclude. They reached a mutual goal, a pinnacle, both crying out with a strangled elation, and she felt ashamed and sickened to have witnessed the intense emotion that flared between them, yet she was glad she had.

Their pace slackened, the tension abated, the pair relaxed, and Michael rubbed the woman's back.

Arrogant and satisfied with himself, he murmured, "Feeling better?"

"Oh, Lord . . . but you utterly kill me when you do that."

Balanced on her haunches, she studied him with a possessive smugness, and they shared a charged moment awash with cryptic meaning, and Sarah's heart twisted at having to acknowledge how closely acquainted they were.

Was she his mistress? His true love? She couldn't stand the thought that he might belong to another before she'd ever had the occasion to win him for herself.

Without speaking, they dressed and prepared to exit. The woman donned her cloak, then delayed to carefully inspect him.

"Will you be all right?" she gently interrogated.

"Of course."

"You have another appointment scheduled at two. Will you keep it?"

"I'm not sure. I'll need to think about it."

Evidently cognizant of his dark secrets, she assessed him scrupulously, then ultimately admitted, "I hate seeing you like this."

"I'm fine."

"You could come to me later."

"I won't."

"My door will be unlocked. Just in case." Sighing, she brushed another kiss across his lips, then swirled away and was gone.

Michael sat on the edge of the bed, his head down, arms on his thighs. Regret weighed heavily; Sarah could sense it as clearly as if he was articulating aloud.

Whatever foul incident had driven him to Bedford, with its hidden room, and the decadent females with whom he philandered, he found no solace. Not even the present encounter, and a lover he obviously cherished, brought contentment.

Sarah spied on him for as long as she could tolerate the scene, when it dawned on her that she had to find him. She

couldn't allow him to debase himself with another paramour. He had to abandon his plans for a subsequent tryst.

Without pausing to reflect, or to heed his warnings about
the nocturnal proceedings in the house, she grabbed a cloak
and a candle, then crept to the door and peeked out. The
corridor was dim and deserted, and she tiptoed away.

She was going to locate that accursed secret room if she
had to tear the mansion apart brick by brick!

At the end of her own hallway, she commenced her investigation by feeling along the walls, the floorboards. She
even tugged at a window and poked her head out, wondering if there was an exterior stairwell, but no entrance
was discovered. Retreating to the stairs, she descended to
the second floor.

As she started down, she thought she might have heard
a door shutting, and she glanced over her shoulder, but
there was no one behind her.

Hesitating, she was overcome by the strongest sensation
that someone had been lurking and awaiting the moment
she would leave her room. Which was nonsense. She'd only
been at the party for a limited time, had hardly met any of
the guests, and it was after midnight. Who would expect
that she might be up? That she might be roaming about?

Still, with those devious musings swirling, the shadows
seemed inordinately sinister. Hurrying to the next landing,
she was certain a footfall sounded behind her, and she tarried again, listening, but no one approached.

Chastising herself for being foolish, she went directly to
the rear of the passageway and persisted with her examination. As she passed bedchambers, no light emanated, yet
in one, a woman moaned. In another, a man was groaning
as if in repressed pain. The noises were unnatural, and made
her flinch nervously.

It's just the dark, playing tricks.

She'd always detested the dark. The fear had blossomed
after her mother's funeral, when she'd been a tiny girl.
Night terrors had originated and had never completely dis-

appeared but, as she was now an adult, she refused to have the old dread ruling her behavior.

Noticing no dubious signs that she had company, she returned to the landing, determined to proceed to the first floor, just as a man emerged out of the stairwell, impeding her progress. Fleetingly, she conjectured that it might be Michael but, as he neared, she could instantly ascertain that it wasn't he. The interloper was shorter, wider across the middle, and he smelled different.

Wary, she moved back, and her heart pounded as he moved with her. She narrowed her eyes, seeking evidence that might help her distinguish who he was, but nothing about him seemed familiar.

"Good evening, Lady Sarah," he crooned softly.

A chill ran down her spine. Her hood was in place. But for her candle, the area was black as pitch. How had he guessed her identity?

"You've mistaken me for another, sir." She ventured to elude him by shifting toward the steps, but he effectively blocked her escape either up or down.

"I've been waiting for you." His words seemed full of furtive significance and purpose. "Ever since you arrived, I've been waiting."

"I have no idea to what you refer. Now, if you'll excuse me . . ." Struggling to seem brave and in control of the situation, she shoved at him, but he was large and immovable.

"So . . . that's your game." He chuckled menacingly. "You act the innocent most credibly. Well, I enjoy it, too. We'll have some enormous fun, you and I."

Abruptly, he pinned her against the wall, circling her waist and binding her arms at her sides, and her candle dropped and flickered out. Their positions were angled so that her body was stretched out, her breasts mashed to his. Disgustingly, he'd insinuated his thigh between her own, and he pressed at her core, rocking toward her in a foul rhythm.

"Release me, or I'll scream."

He pushed her hood off her head and jerked his fingers

through her hair. "I don't mind a little commotion."

"I'll call for help," she threatened.

"But you shouldn't expect anyone to come to your aid. Should others happen by, I'm quite sure they'll delight in the spectacle. There are several here who'd love to watch while I give it to Scarborough's little sister."

His vulgar breath swept over her cheek, and he covered her mouth, muzzling her, as he reached under her wrap and fondled her breast. Wildly, she battled against his abominable groping, but he was too big, and she was obstructed by his excessive bulk.

"Such a pretty, pretty girl." His fingers fumbled with her skirts and began inching them up.

Sarah bit him as hard as she could, but she didn't have sufficient leverage to inflict significant damage. Still, he momentarily loosened his hold.

"Help!" she shouted just as he gagged her, again. He leaned nearer, his mouth at her ear, his hand laboring to insinuate itself between her legs.

"You like it rough, do you? Excellent."

Chapter Nine

Michael stepped through the secret door and into the pantry. A candle had been left in a holder for him, and he thought about lighting it but, after glancing out into the kitchens, he deemed it unnecessary. The moon was high, shining in the windows, and he could easily make his way.

He commenced down the lengthy corridor, leaving the serving facilities and proceeding toward the more social sections of the house. Passing the library, he paused and observed—unnoticed and unseen—the decadent revelry going on inside.

Pamela contributed the site for all of them to act out their lewd fantasies, but she never joined in, and he wondered if she realized the undignified level to which her parties sank in the dark of night. Early in the morning, her competent, efficient staff cleaned and tidied, affording no clue that anything indecorous had occurred. Perhaps she wasn't aware of how rashly events were wont to spiral.

Heavy, pungent smoke from a Chinese pipe swirled through the room, painting a grotesque, unreal scene. Two women were naked and embracing on one of the sofas while several gentlemen watched. The men were in a state of half-dress, and one of them walked over and began fondling, then fucking, the woman who was on top. Another man rose and mixed with the trio, taking the second woman in her mouth. Roughly, he proffered more of his cock than she could tolerate, but she was inebriated, lethargic, and thus compliant to his demands.

Michael stared, as did the others, as though it was the most common of sights. The four lovers were degenerately displayed, a ribald tableau of sex and sin that appealed to the onlookers' base desires.

How had his life sunk to such an appalling low? He'd exposed himself to degradation for so long that his moral compass was broken.

When had he become this callous and detached? He—who had formerly carried on with such fierce enthusiasm—could only scrutinize with an abstract, isolated disinterest.

The man came in the woman's mouth, holding her down until she swallowed, then he removed his wilting phallus and straightened his trousers while his companion continued to saw away between the thighs of the other woman. The male audience was laughing, spewing crude remarks, as a third man decided to sample of the orifice that had just been filled to overflowing, and Michael departed, unable to further bear the spectacle.

At the main foyer, he climbed the grand staircase, feeling unclean, sullied, and craving a bath. From past experience, he appreciated that the hot water would wash the taint on his body, but it would do little to cleanse the stains on his soul.

He was just about to reach the landing on the second floor, when he was jolted by a woman's soft cry of alarm. Her plea was cut off before the word *help* could be completely uttered.

Crude and harsh, a man's voice followed. "You like it rough, do you? Excellent."

A couple was struggling, their clothing in stark outline against the white of the wall. He could smell the odor of strong drink on the man's breath, and an earthy, familiar, unmistakable scent emanating from the woman. A sensation of inevitable destiny surged over him, and he sighed, then rushed to the pair, grabbed the man and, with hardly any effort, flung him aside.

"What the devil!" the scoundrel muttered as he stumbled to his knees.

Shielding Sarah from the man's furious regard, Michael inserted himself between them and glared at the cowering nobleman, recognizing him as one of the scores of debauched rakes of the *ton* who enjoyed the excuse to inflict himself on unsuspecting women.

"Good evening, Brigham," he menacingly articulated.

"Stevens!" Brigham griped. "I might have guessed." Wobbling, he rose to his feet, striving for bravado as he spat out, "Bastard!"

"Careful now," Michael cautioned. "Don't forget how much money you owe me. I might decide to call in your markers." He moved closer. "You've upset the lady. Apologize."

Brigham scoffed as if Sarah was a whore. "Bloody asshole, why don't you mind your own damned business?"

Brigham was a coward and a bully, so if he'd exhibit any sort of bluster, he was abundantly foxed. Michael clutched the front of his shirt and yanked him up, showering him with a close-up view of blazing temper.

"Last chance," he threatened.

Despite Brigham's level of intoxication, he possessed enough of his wits to recall Michael's pugilistic abilities, and he grasped that Michael was ready to tear him to pieces. Tentatively, he eased back, hastily shedding his confrontational mien.

"I apologize, milady."

The supplication was lukewarm, and he didn't so much as glance in Sarah's direction, but Michael let the slight pass. Later on, he'd deal with the contemptible swine. For now, he had to get Sarah back to the safety of her room.

"I'm positive you mistook her for another. Isn't that right?"

"Absolutely," Brigham concurred.

"You've got exactly five seconds to disappear." Michael hurled Brigham toward the stairs. "One . . . two . . ."

Michael's skills as a brawler were renowned, so Brigham needed no second warning. He scurried away like the rat he was. Michael waited until he'd vanished, then he turned, the voluminous force of his concentration falling on Sarah.

Brigham was notable in his reputation for violent and obscene fornications, and Michael shuddered at what might have happened. Why was the insane female wandering the halls? Did she think he was joking in his admonitions?

"Who was that loathsome individual?" she inquired, possessing a mere inkling of her usual vigor. She was trembling and distressed, but blessedly, appeared uninjured.

"Be silent!" he tersely counseled, as he tucked her hood over her auburn curls and clutched her arm. "Let's get the hell out of here."

Lest they encounter other guests, he spurred her along, scanning alcoves and doorways, but no one witnessed their passing. Briskly, he wound them through the maze of corridors until they arrived at their own secluded wing of the mansion, and he ushered her to her door, his lips pressed to her ear. "Go inside and secure the lock. I'll be with you momentarily."

Without affording her the opportunity for debate or dissent, he pushed her through the portal and shut it behind. Pausing until the lock clicked, he shook his head in dismay over the predicament in which she'd deposited them.

Didn't she comprehend that he'd have to call Brigham to account for his behavior?

He prowled around the corner and entered his own bedchamber, advancing to the door that separated their suites. Since his initial foray into her territory, he'd kept it barred, a signal to himself that he dare not submit to another rendezvous with the exotic meddler. Jerking it open, he sped through to her main sleeping chamber, first taking a quick inventory to assure himself that the peephole he'd previously blocked remained covered, then he marched over to her in the center of the room.

"What were you thinking, being unescorted like that?" He quizzed her softly, in case anyone was strolling by.

The hood of her cloak was down, and she quavered slightly. She looked young, confused, lost.

"He knew who I was." She was baffled and perplexed by the information. "He followed me."

"Of course he did!" He seized her by the shoulders, but handling her was a mistake. As if he'd burned his hands, he instantly dropped them. "Haven't you listened to a word I've said? About this gathering? About these people?"

"He wanted to have his way with me; because of my brother."

Michael could barely force the question past his clenched teeth. "Did he hurt you?"

"No. There wasn't time."

She shivered with distaste and, to his horror, tears welled into her pretty eyes. In his ragged state, he'd failed to reflect on how overwhelmed she'd be. He'd only contemplated his own frenzied reaction. Not hers. Very likely, she was stunned to the core, yet he was reproaching and scolding her as though she was a child. It seemed a madman had invaded his body, but he'd just been so upset at witnessing her abuse.

What if he hadn't chanced by? What then?

An alluring tear fell and slid down her cheek, and she swiped it away. "He scared me."

A low grumble—whether of disgust or resignation, he wasn't sure—erupted, and he snuggled her against his chest. The top of her head tucked neatly under his chin. Her rounded breasts, the two beaded nipples erect and alert, poked into his ribs. Her stomach gently cradled his phallus. Despite his recent exploits with Pamela, his body sizzled to attention, wild to dabble with a new partner.

He was a wretched excuse for a man! A detestable human being! She'd been tossed about, violated, and, even as he smelled of the sex he'd just had with another, he could only ponder what a precious carnal haven she would be.

At a previous time in his life, he could have promptly curbed his libidinous proclivities, but no longer. He was out of control, incapable of curbing his conduct, and he was afraid of what he might initiate. Not willing to risk alarming her further, or accomplishing something he oughtn't, he set her away, putting plenty of space between them.

Not comprehending why he'd declined to render consolation, she gazed up at him, making him yearn to comfort and soothe, which was terrifying.

Never before had he been compelled to offer solace to a distraught female. The women with whom he typically consorted didn't generate concern for their predicaments or woes. In contrast, he recognized Sarah as a dangerous adversary, for she instigated all manner of appalling sentiment, until he yearned to protect and revere, to treasure and nurture.

He didn't want to be ensnared by her dilemma or problems, yet here he stood, rabid for the slightest excuse to furnish assistance.

What a precarious path he'd trod!

"It is the middle of the night." He fought to remain calm. "Why were you out in the hall?" Lord help her if she'd been sneaking to an assignation with a lover. He really wasn't certain what he might do if that was her response.

"I was looking for you."

"Me?" *Again? Why on earth . . .* He bit off a curse. "I apprised you of the hazards of this house. Why didn't you heed me?"

His temper flared, but he effectively reined himself in. Not intending to be acrimonious. Not planning to lambaste her with his furious comments. He'd just been so . . . so . . . bloody *frightened* when he'd seen the mess into which she'd stumbled, and he'd been deliriously and foolishly anxious to charge to her rescue.

"I didn't mean to cause any bother," she quietly declared. "I simply had to find you."

"With all the blackguards residing under this roof!" He repressed a quiver of abhorrence. "What was so idiotically consequential?"

Glancing at her feet, she was suddenly shy and embarrassed. "I didn't want you to keep your appointment."

"What appointment?"

"The one scheduled for two o'clock in the hidden room where you . . . where you . . . dally with those women while others spy on you." Avoiding him, she went to the corner, untying her cloak and hanging it on a hook. Her back to him, her shoulders sagged. "I couldn't stand for you to meet with another lover tonight. It seems terribly wrong. When you behave so, I fear for you; I really do. I had to stop you."

He couldn't move. He couldn't speak. She knew about the Viewing Room? Frantically, he tried to recollect his current misdeeds. In the preceding days, he'd cavorted there on at least a dozen occasions. Had she beheld every episode?

"How . . ." he sputtered.

"There's a peephole. In my dressing room."

Feeling ill, treading like an automated machine he'd once viewed at a museum, he walked to the smaller chamber, casting about to get his bearings. Then he noticed the footstool, the visible dark hole with its shaft of light shining through.

As opposed to Sarah who was shorter, he didn't need the stool, and he toed it away, then flattened his eye against the opening. The room was empty, but a lamp still burned, the wick turned down. Barely breathing, he surveyed, letting the sordid surroundings register, remembering how he'd performed with the women who'd deigned to frolic.

The vista was tawdry, sleazy. What must Sarah have thought? He felt soiled, impure, unworthy to be in her company, yet in a daze, he blundered to her bedchamber. She was perched on the edge of the bed, patiently awaiting him, and though he'd resolved to keep his distance, declining to approach and sully her further, he couldn't stay apart. He loitered at the foot of the bed, using one of the frame's carved poles for balance.

What could he say to justify his actions? Why was an interpretation necessary? She was a stranger, an irritation, who'd been nothing but trouble from the minute he'd met her, so where did this overpowering desire spring from to mitigate and account?

He swallowed. Swallowed again. "How many times?"

"Three."

"Oh, God . . ." He leaned against the bedpost and stared
at the floor. Flushing, he felt the wave of heat flash in his
nether extremities and fling upward. His cheeks were tinged
red with unaccustomed chagrin and something else. Shame,
perhaps. Or guilt. "I'm sorry you saw."

"I'm sorry you were there!"

"You don't understand."

"No, I don't, and you could never rationalize it for me."

"I wouldn't even try."

He heard her arise, and he wished he could simply va-
porize. Then she was directly confronting him, her skirts
twirling about his legs, her body leaning into his. "Don't
go again. Promise me!"

"Sarah . . ."

"Is it a manly wanting? Is that the reason?"

"No . . . no . . ."

"Then, why?"

"I couldn't begin to explain." His focus flitted to the
wall, the ceiling. Anywhere but into those shrewd, verdant
eyes.

"You're searching, and I'm not sure for what, but you
won't discover it in that room."

"I'm not *searching* for anything." He was just fervid to
achieve some peace!

"Come to me, instead. Let me be the one to love you."

Her unruffled entreaty obliged him to meet her gaze, and
the intensity with which she regarded him was acute. "I've
advised you before that there can never be a relationship
between us. We've a strong physical attraction, you and I,
and—"

"More than just physical."

"Perhaps," he ultimately allowed, the indications of their
ardent connection too clear to deny. "But we dare not act
on our impulses. We would be reckless to pursue such a
passionate course."

Her hand was on his chest, and he couldn't locate the
strength required to remove it. He was tempted to hug her

tightly, once more, but Pamela's scent hovered over him, the evidence of his doomed moral character hanging about him like a damning cloud.

"You won't be intimate with me. Why? Is it that you think you're not respectable or reputable enough?"

"Yes, that's exactly what I think."

Detecting what he hoped was a safe harbor, he gripped her waist, and she responded warmly, wrapping her arms around his back and distending herself so that their bodies melded. He cherished having her so near, even as he ordered himself to ignore her marvelous presence. "You are so fine, so rare, and what am I? A man without honor or scruple. You observed my true nature."

"That's not who you really are. I'll never believe it."

Then, she did the very worst thing he could possibly imagine. She tenderly kissed the middle of his chest, over the spot where his heart ached so intolerably, and he lurched away, her affectionate position agonizing to endure. Accusingly, she stared up at him.

"The scent of a woman is on me," he mentioned baldly, constrained to display the extent of his failings. "I've just lain with another; I've just come from bedding her."

"I don't care."

"I do."

"Then wash yourself; return to me."

Oh, that he could obey her command! That he could have her in all the ways a man covets a woman! To his very marrow, he cried out to redeem himself in her arms, but how could he befoul her with his attentions when he thought her so extraordinary?

"I can't."

"Can't or won't?"

"Won't." His rejection of her overture pricked painfully, like a stab from a sharp knife.

"You'll dally with the others at the drop of a hat. Why not with me?"

"It is different with them."

"*Different* how?" A hint of ire flared.

"They don't matter. Not in the least."

Skeptical, she chuckled disdainfully. "And you're saying I'm important to you as they are not?"

"Aye."

His admission shocked them both. He was fascinated and surprised that he'd reveal so much. She was dubious, distrusting of his motives, and she released him and slipped away. Immediately bereft without her, he was impelled to hasten after her, to hold her close where she definitely seemed to belong, but he restrained himself.

She went to the window and studied the night sky, and he fought the urge to talk, to join her. He suffered the strangest compulsion to beg her forgiveness for being the man he was, for not being more suitable or more worthy, but he couldn't confess what was in his heart. Silenced by impossibilities and remorse, he was transfixed, powerless to make amends, incompetent to alter events. He could only impotently watch as she grappled with the quagmire in which his irresponsible conduct had landed them.

"I'm twenty-five years old," she finally said. "I've never had a beau. Never been kissed, or strolled in the moonlight with a handsome swain. My family's situation is a mess, so my future is very unsettled; I don't know what the impending months will bring."

At the veiled reference to her brother, he shifted uncomfortably but offered no comment. There was nothing to be gained by reviewing her wayward sibling.

"What are you implying?" he queried instead. "That your personal life is a muddle so you'd like to complicate it further by consorting with me?"

"No." She turned to face him. "I'm saying that I'll be here for two more weeks, and then I journey home to odious alternatives and extreme choices"—she stalwartly mastered a wave of emotion that made her eyes glitter with what he suspected were unshed tears—". . . and I am so desperately unhappy."

"Oh, Sarah . . ." He couldn't stand to hear her tragic disclosure, or to witness her anguish, but he had little remedy to contribute.

"But you're here, and I'm here, and something remarkable could ensue in the next fortnight. I feel it in my bones."

She was correct, yet he lied. "Nothing good could ever come from a liaison between the two of us."

"You're only fooling yourself, Michael," she unwaveringly asserted. "This affinity"—she gestured, indicating what couldn't be put into words—"you sense it, too."

"But I'm a grown man," he indicated, "and just because I lust after you doesn't mean I have to act upon it."

"It is more than mere lust, and you know it." She left the window and cautiously moved in his direction. "My entire blasted life, I've done precisely what was required of me, so this once, I'd like to reach out and seize some joy. I truly, truly would."

"You won't find any *joy* with me."

Scrupulously, she assessed him. "You're afraid to determine what it could be like."

"No, not at all."

"What is it, then?" She was growing angry, defensive.

"We're drawn to one another, so I grasp how it would be. There are physical ways in which I would use your body." Doggedly, he chided, "What I would take are gifts you should save for your husband."

"But I never intend to marry," she declared with a ringing finality. "So where does that leave me? Should I never learn of these secrets that transpire between a man and a woman? I admit that I'm selfish, and I crave some of your mysterious bodily titillation for myself. Should I deny myself this contentment?"

Michael was in agony. What man had ever been presented such an enticing feast? She was a mature virgin, primed and ready for sexual initiation. If he acceded, he could excite and stimulate her, teach and disclose to her the sexual methods he enjoyed. A devoted, zealous pupil, she would wield her distinct skills with lethal precision for his exclusive benefit and delectation.

His weary spirit wept in anticipation of how much succor he would obtain. His cock swelled from conjecturing how it would be. Still, he valued her too much, treasured her too much.

"The fact remains that you are a maid." He was reminding her—and himself.

"Your lovers"—she blushed, her chaste condition profusely apparent as she courageously forged ahead to discuss inappropriate carnal proceedings—"they do things to you with their hands and their mouths. You could instruct me."

Peeking down at her slender, adept fingers, then back up to those lush, moist lips, he could conceive of her kneeling before him, stroking and cupping him, while her tongue imparted dazzling pleasure.

"I touched you in a forbidden manner, once before," he pointed out. "You didn't like it."

"You're mistaken. I loved it; I was simply overwhelmed."

They'd gradually migrated across the floor until they were, once again, toe to toe. Her gown twisted around his legs, his boots dipped under the hem. Their frank conversation had elevated her pulse, her breathing was labored, her breasts toiled against her corset, the outline of her nipples conspicuous against the bodice.

Vividly, he remembered every detail of those two breasts, the shape, the size, the color of the solid tips. How firm they'd been! How sweet they'd tasted! With a flick of his wrist, he could have her bared to suckle and play, taunt and tease. He could introduce her to sensual gratification and, in the process, seek his own, but he simply couldn't behave so badly toward her.

He couldn't commit a despicable offense against her. As an untried woman, she didn't fathom the full implications of her proposition. If she was to bestow her virtue on some lucky fellow, he should hardly be the one. Practically any

other gentleman of her acquaintance would be more deserving.

"You are curious. You've seen much that has your body
eager and your mind intrigued." He slipped his hands into
hers, and he felt as if he was holding her protected and
safe. "But this is not the place, and I am not the man with
whom you should indulge these whims."

"It is not a *whim*." She linked their fingers, the maneuver
bringing them closer still. "Can't you feel it?" Her eyes
were wide with delight, her smile brimming with wonder.
"Can't you feel what happens when you're near?"

The sensation was genuine and profound, and perhaps
that was the real reason he refused to dally. If he bought
into her mad scheme and seduced her, where would she be
at the affair's conclusion?

In a brief interval, their fates would illicitly entwine, and
she couldn't possibly realize how thoroughly they would
become embroiled. Nor could she comprehend that his level
of involvement would be so much different from hers.

At an early age, from the period when his father had
abandoned their family, he'd learned that it was perilous to
love. So he didn't. Never forming sentimental bonds with
his paramours, he sought out a woman's company for sexual alleviation and no other purpose.

Gad, but he wasn't confident he could ardently devote
himself to a woman. The very idea seemed so asinine that
he couldn't picture himself in such a negligent venture.

Briefly, he would share her life and her bed and—without a doubt—they would have fabulous sex, but that was
all, and when she ascertained what she'd surrendered, she'd
rail and hate, and he couldn't abide the notion of creating
so much havoc, or of causing such wrenching tribulation.

He didn't want to discuss their association, or demon-
strative shackles, or mutual dependence. Her feminine daydreams, her romantic hopes for ruination, only increased
his longing for too many things that could never be.

Still, he was so terribly lonely. What did it signify if he
looted just a bit more of her innocence? The kiss they'd

Cheryl Holt

relished earlier in the gardener's shack had been distracting
him for hours. The lusciousness of the moment, the strength
of the sentiments it generated, had him eager to repeat his
folly until he was far beyond rational consideration or action.

"You are so lovely," he proclaimed. "Too lovely for the
likes of me."

His statement puzzled her, and he took advantage of her
consternation, catching her and seizing her mouth before
he could change his mind—or she could change hers.

He nipped and reveled, toyed and tarried, thinking that
her flavor was so infernally superb, like peppermint and
spice. Needing more, he insinuated his tongue between her
ruby lips. Beseeching. Persuading. As though she'd kissed
him a thousand times before, she opened and welcomed
him inside.

There was no hesitation, no inhibition; she joined in the
vivacious kiss with a gladness and ebullience he'd never
encountered with the scores of jaded lovers who littered his
past. He worked against her, teaching her the tempo, and
she met him stroke for stroke, sparring with him in a fervid
dance.

His hands gripped her lush bottom, and he lifted her off
the floor, until her feet were dangling, her perfect torso
stretched out the length of his. Her breasts were crushed to
his chest, her nipples jabbing like shards of glass. Stom-
achs, thighs, calves, they were forged fast.

Though he'd spilled his seed not an hour prior, his phallus was enlarged and alert, pleading for freedom from cap-
tivity. He felt like a robust, strapping lad of fourteen, ready
to come at the snap of her fingers.

Not willing to deny himself a modest sample of the shattering excess, he spun her and propped her against the bedpost. Her thighs were spread wide and, though many layers
of fabric separated them, his cock was wedged against her
mound, her searing heat coaxing him, urging him on and
in. Matching the thrust of his tongue, he flexed against her,
slowly and meticulously, letting her savor his aroused con-

dition, allowing her to distinguish his decadent invitation.

With a virulent obsession that confounded and amazed, he yearned to rip at her dress, to feast on her breasts, to wrench at her skirts and impale himself between her virginal thighs. She'd be tight, scalding, her maiden's blood charging him to erupt at will.

He never finished his orgasm in a woman's cleft, because the concept of planting a babe was preposterous, but with a glaring urgency, Sarah incited him to spurt his blistering emission across her womb, and he was so deliriously aroused that he deliberated whether to empty himself in his pants like an unseasoned boy.

Pulling away, he checked himself, quelling his appetite as much as he was able, even though he couldn't bring himself to completely disengage. Not just yet. Her feet touched the rug, and he rubbed her back as he trailed light kisses across her cheek, her brow.

"Why were you doing that?" She was short of breath, exhilarated. "You were pressing against me. Why?"

"It's the rhythm of mating. I want you ... as a man wants a woman." He dipped below her chin and licked where her pulse throbbed at the base of her neck. Her skin was hot and salty. "My body is aflame, demanding that I make love with you."

"Then take me," she whispered against his mouth. "Touch me as you did when you were here that first night. Show me how it can be."

Poised on the brink of a drastic cliff, he was geared to jump off into a void from which he could never return. He desired her beyond wisdom or sense, but as with so much in his life, he simply couldn't have her.

Confused, reluctant, reeling, he removed himself from temptation by stepping back and permitting the chilly air of the room to swirl betwixt their heated torsos. Instantly, he felt deprived and forlorn, and he grieved the loss of her mollifying presence.

"Don't stop," she appealed, her gaze expectant and trusting. "I want you to be the one."

"I can't, Sarah."

"I feel as though I've been waiting for you all my life."

"You ask for too much," he insisted. "More than I am. More than I could ever be."

"No, I hardly ask for anything." Her hand rose and massaged his chest in a lazy circle, consoling him, recognizing how he craved her brand of comfort. "I request only these few days. This scant increment of time."

"The stakes are too high. If we were detected . . ."

"No one will ever know; I swear it." Her eyes probed his. "I'll never seek another boon from you; I'll never contact you again after I leave here. Please . . ."

Oh, that he could relent and appease them both in a fleeting erotic liaison. Her solicitation was outrageous, thrilling. Such ecstasy was meant to be acknowledged, but he simply, unconditionally, could not partake of what she was proposing.

"No," he said resolutely, while disgracefully pilfering a last kiss but, as he'd already stolen so much, what was one thing more? "Good night."

"Michael . . ."

He departed, not looking over his shoulder lest he see her lovely face and be dissuaded.

Into his own bedchamber he strode, shutting and securing the door. A servant had left water, though it had cooled. Stripping swiftly, he washed, lagging, the cold cloth soothing his torrid skin. Then, he crawled into his bed, naked and alone, determined not to think, not to recollect, not to care.

Chapter Ten

Sarah sat at a table on the verandah, admiring the grounds. The distinctive porch wrapped around the side and back of the house, and various guests surrounded her, sipping beverages and prattling amicably. The day had bloomed sunny and warm. The sky was blue, the lawns spectacularly green, and a few horses grazed in a far-off pasture.

A carriage wound through the idyllic scene, traveling up the lane leading to the manor. A quartet of gaily clad women chattered as they approached, their journey from London almost at an end. Numerous guests promenaded arm-in-arm along the meticulously groomed pathways of the gardens, serene and content to savor the lazy afternoon.

She watched all with a jaded detachment. The gathering appeared to be just another country party, attended by the bored members of the *ton,* but time, distance, and events had made her more wise.

A half-dozen couples competed at a licentious game of ball down on the grass, and she wasn't foolish enough to let loneliness or dissatisfaction lead her to join in. She pretended to be enthralled, but she really wasn't, not caring in the least who frolicked naughtily in plain sight.

Beside her, Rebecca gabbed convivially about the varied amusements in which she'd partaken. Two women wandered by, and they talked to her about London and a theatrical performance they'd all seen. Rebecca was in her element, fraternizing in a manner at which Sarah had never excelled.

For the past three years, Rebecca had accompanied Hugh to town for the Season, acting as his hostess, so she was familiar with many of Lady Carrington's visitors as

Sarah was not. Though Sarah had planned to be more friendly, to establish new relationships, she couldn't concentrate on the social intricacies of the situation.

The only topic she could mull was which of the women might have been with Michael in the hidden room. The pair before her laughed and joked, as Sarah methodically stripped them, searching for clues that would reveal if she'd viewed them unclothed.

Quietly, she inspected, politely expounding when necessary, but mostly appraising how they tipped their heads or squared their shoulders. Ultimately, she decided that neither had partnered with Michael, so she lost interest in the remainder of the discussion.

As she scanned the yard, her mind was in a whirl, her thoughts jumbled with images of Michael. He was so dashing, so handsome, so unlike anyone she'd ever known, and against her will and better judgment, she was drawn to him, to his life of debauchery and excess, to his powerful presence and dynamic allure.

Captivated, concerned, and worried about him, she was also physically infatuated as she'd never imagined herself being. They'd shared much that was inappropriate—kisses, caresses, words—yet she suffered no guilt over her lapses.

She simply craved some privacy!

What she wouldn't give to have the blasted man all to herself. To be away from prying scrutiny and nosy gawking! Oh, that they could be swept away to a deserted island, like lovers in the fanciful romantic novels she infrequently read!

Were they alone, and no one about to witness their misconduct, would he think differently? Would he act differently?

Just being in his company incited all sorts of magic, and she could only concentrate on the kiss he'd dispensed the previous night in her room. By picking her up and pressing himself against her, he'd ignited a searing fire of desire that hadn't waned in the least. If anything, it seemed to be spiraling hotter and brighter.

There was definitely an earthy, lusty facet to her personality that she'd never acknowledged before, because she wanted things from him that she couldn't even begin to describe, although why she'd allowed herself to become smitten by a scoundrel who had a veritable harem of women falling at his feet was a mystery.

After what she'd witnessed of his antics, she ought to have more sense than to be pining away after the cad, yet she couldn't desist. Like a moth to the flame, she was attracted to him with a tumultuous, unrelenting ardor that she couldn't explain or defend. When she closed her eyes, she didn't see any of his other paramours, but herself, cherished in the cradle of his arms. *She* developed into the lover he teased, seduced, aroused. *She* was the one fortuitous enough to enjoy his phenomenal attention.

With an almost oppressive longing, she recalled the turbaned woman who'd managed to break through his walls in order to garner his gentler style of affection. Sarah's goal was to reap some of the same tender courtesy, but she had absolutely no idea how to get him to agree to furnish it.

They could be so good together! She was convinced of it, and she couldn't fathom going home without sampling some of his enigmatic delights. With a yearning that was indescribable, she needed him to fill a void she hadn't recognized to exist before they'd crossed paths.

She was amenable and enthused to give herself to him in any fashion he might require, yet the prior night, without a backward glance, he'd left her lonesome and forlorn, in the middle of her room. The sound of him turning his lock had merely underscored the strength of his resolve that they not associate. His refusal to acquiesce in her mad scheme had irritated her so much that she'd very nearly stormed across the floor and pounded on his door to demand admittance.

Only the realization of how irrational she'd sound, of how completely she would debase herself, had kept her rooted to her spot. Numb with consternation, she'd prepared for her slumber by stripping to her chemise and stockings, then crawling under the cold, impersonal blankets. She'd attempted sleep, but instead, she'd tossed and turned as she'd pictured him lying in his own bed just a few feet away.

Foreign notions had kept her busy as she'd wondered what was beneath his sheets: how he looked, what he wore, how his body was formed. The unusual, outlandish ruminations made her own body tingle and burn.

Rebecca's voice intruded into her daydreams, engendering her to discover that the two women had departed. She and Rebecca were cloistered, once again, but Sarah had been so distracted by her carnal musings over Michael Stevens that she hadn't noticed.

"Honestly, Sarah," Rebecca reproached, "you can be so rude."

"I'm sorry. I was woolgathering." Sarah transferred her gaze from the horizon to her cousin. "You were saying . . . ?"

"You are impossible!" Clearly miffed, Rebecca leaned nearer as she tugged at the brim of her bonnet to protect her face from the sunshine. "There are many in the assembled company who would like to meet you—several of the gentlemen, especially—yet you set yourself apart. Just like always. I thought you were here for a holiday."

"I'm having a holiday. A very pleasant one."

"You could have fooled me." Rebecca harumphed, then stuck her dainty nose in the air.

Her pretty cousin effortlessly negotiated the daylight mingling and evening amusements. With her fair countenance, voluptuous figure, and polished comportment, she was a typical English lady. If their birth circumstances had been reversed, she could have readily been the daughter of an earl. Inordinately suited to the position, she adored the preening, the soirees and fetes, and she thrived on her months in the city with Hugh, always returning with exciting stories about the galas she'd attended, and the people she'd befriended.

"What have I done that's so appalling?" Though she

inquired politely, Sarah wasn't overly inquisitive as to Rebecca's opinion for she couldn't help recalling Michael's assertion that Rebecca was up to mischief. As he'd been correct about so many matters, she felt inclined to regard her relative with a jaundiced eye.

"You never participate in any of the entertainments that Lady Carrington has devised." Rebecca counted off Sarah's sins, one by one, on her fingers. "You rise early and have breakfast before anyone else. You spend your afternoons in the garden, preoccupied with your reflections. You dress for supper, come down at the last minute just as the meal is announced, then you eat in silence, rarely conversing with your companions. After, you retire to your rooms, and no one sees you again until morning."

"A perfect vacation."

"Everyone's whispering about you."

"Alleging what?"

"That you're a virtual stick-in-the-mud!"

"I always have been; that's hardly news."

"But how are you to make friends?"

"Maybe I won't." Glancing about warily, she grumbled, "Not with this crowd, at any rate."

"What about the gentlemen who are here? How are any of them to . . ."

There was a significant hesitation as Sarah stared her down, her shrewd gaze working as well on Rebecca as it always had on Hugh. Sharply, Sarah demanded, "To what?"

"Well, silly . . . to get to know you, of course. Hugh confided that you were hoping for a few introductions, and—"

Sarah cut her off. "I wouldn't put too much stock in what Hugh said if I were you."

"What do you mean?"

"I *mean* that I'm here to relax. Nothing more. Nothing less."

For the briefest instant, she was certain Rebecca scowled at her with an unobstructed amount of loathing, but as quickly as the sensation emerged, it vanished. She was her customary, affable self.

Sarah didn't intend to immediately worry about what the disturbing impression might portend, but she tucked it away for later. At the moment, she was too absorbed with Michael Stevens and her novel carnal quest. With her concentration so engrossed, Rebecca was like a bothersome fly, buzzing about on the edge of her consciousness, and she felt like swatting at her.

"Speaking of Hugh," Rebecca mentioned, smiling and nodding to a gentleman down on the lawn, "I received a note. He's bored in town and thinking about stopping by for a visit."

"How nice," Sarah murmured, though she was actually contemplating that his arrival would be utterly horrid. She had no desire to run into Hugh, or have him hovering about and trying to manipulate her. When she relocated to Scarborough, there'd be plenty of opportunity to worry about him and his recent fiasco. His irksome presence would ruin her blissful respite.

She pushed back her chair and rose. "I believe I'll take a walk."

"There! You've proven my point!" Rebecca complained. "A gentleman has been asking about you, and he has a friend whose companionship I enjoy. The four of us could play in the next game of ball."

"I don't think so." As she strolled away, she discreetly masked her disgust at the repugnant notion.

At loose ends, restless, she left the terrace and rambled out into the yard, roaming aimlessly until she found the bench where she and Michael had tarried. She soaked in the tranquillity, surveying, watching the house, peering at the gardener's shack where he'd lured her and kissed her so splendidly.

Where was he? What was he doing? Who was he with?

Behind her, a pair of gossiping women were gliding by. Sarah was separated from them by a thick, trimmed hedge so she could listen to them, but not distinguish who they were.

"Yes," one of them whispered, "it was Brigham and Stevens."

Suddenly frantic, her ears perked, Sarah bolted upright. Brigham was the knave who'd accosted her!

"No doubt about it?" the other prompted.

"George insists it's true," the first said. "Brigham was leaving for London, but Stevens caught him out behind the stables. Beat him to a pulp! Broke his nose, some ribs, perhaps an arm . . ."

"I'd like to have seen that." The woman giggled inappropriately. "How long ago?"

"An hour or two."

"Any idea as to the cause?"

"Well, George contends it was over an insult to a woman, but with Stevens, and his pride, who can tell? It might have been any slight."

"I can't imagine there's a female alive who could incite him to defend her honor."

"Not anyone here, certainly."

Their voices drifted off as they sauntered away.

"What's happening now?" The query drifted over the bushes.

"Brigham was destined for town, with a bloody cloth pressed to his face, and Stevens is . . ."

Sarah couldn't discern the remainder. The women had wandered too far down the footpath. She sat immobile, chaotically striving to come to grips with what she'd just learned.

Michael was fighting? With that libertine, Brigham? Was he insane? Wrestling in the barnyard like a ruffian! She couldn't decide if she was more alarmed or angry. Then, like a slow-wit, the truth dawned on her: She'd been the catalyst!

Where is he? This time, the question had a desperate edge to it. Was he injured? Did he need assistance?

She had to speak with him so as to ascertain his condition for herself. Jumping to her feet, she was eager to run for the mansion, but years of excellent breeding kicked in, and she slowed her step, lest others note her hurrying by. She was too intent on her destination to have anyone identifying her, interrupting her for a chat, or remarking on her haste.

Like the nonentity she was among the verbal, exuberant crowd, she flowed through the garden, up the verandah steps, and into the house without a single person nodding hello. Inside, she casually strode to the grand staircase that led to the upper floors. Luckily, no one was about as she ascended, and she climbed regally but determinedly.

Where else might he be but in his private quarters? She would check, and if he wasn't there, she wasn't positive of her next course of action. She couldn't plan that far in advance. He had to be in residence!

Seeming bored but firm, she slipped into her own apartment and barred the door. Shucking off her bonnet and gloves, she marched through the dressing room and knocked at his adjoining suite. If someone answered— someone other than Michael Stevens, that is—she hadn't thought about what excuse she'd render. She simply forged ahead, but no one responded, no footsteps trod toward her, so she rapped again, then reached for the knob and turned.

The two previous times, when she'd been impetuous and tested the knob, the entrance had been locked. Yet on this third attempt, to her immense astonishment, it opened. Almost disbelieving, she watched it swing back. In a matter of seconds, she stood facing his bedchamber, and she didn't have to hunt far to find him.

As though he'd been expecting her, he lurked on the other side of the room, frowning intently at her door, almost willing her appearance simply by peering at the wood. He didn't seem at all surprised to have conjured her up.

A bath had been delivered, and he was soaking—naked, she assumed—in a large tub brimming with steamy water. Leaned against the back, his knees were raised and spread. Though it was a pleasant day outside, a small fire had been laid in the hearth, and it cast his wet skin in shades of bronze. A table was next to the tub, and bathing accessories were stacked on it. A dark green robe had been casually thrown on the floor.

With his right hand, he held a glass of amber-colored liquor from which he vigilantly sipped, not taking his eyes off her as he did so. The hand was bandaged with a cloth. A second cloth had been folded over and was pressed against a bleeding cut on his brow.

Nervously, she stepped across the threshold, and she experienced the strangest sensation that she was traveling from one dimension to another, leaving her old life, her old disposition behind, as she moved forward to embrace his world and whatever she might eventually encounter within it.

"May I come in?"

He motioned with his libation. "Yes."

Compelling herself to be the assertive person she usually was, she crossed to him, refusing to be cowed by his nudity, by his maleness, or by their secluded environment. For once, she had him just where she wanted him: all to herself.

As she approached, he glowered up at her. There was a strange look about him, daring her to draw nigh, chafing to discover if she had the temerity, but she had no intention of disappointing him. She neared, bravely advancing until her thighs abutted the rim.

"I just heard," she mentioned, and she gestured toward the pad that was compressed above his eye. "Is it bad?"

He didn't answer but proceeded to stare and, when she might have vacillated or fled, she forced herself nearer still, bending and balancing her hip on the edge. She breathed in the scent of the sandalwood soap he'd used, and the pungent, healing bath salts that had been dumped into the water.

Without waiting for an invitation, she covered his hand with her own and removed the cloth from his head. The gash wasn't deep or long, but red and oozing, and it probably ached terribly. Tentatively, she traced along it. "How did you get this?"

He was silent for so long that she concluded he wasn't going to reply, then he conceded, "I'm not generally so clumsy, but I wasn't concentrating, and one of his coachmen blindsided me"—pausing, he shifted away from her questing finger—"or I might not have stopped."

His report painted distressing images of the altercation, of its brutality and violence. "And Brigham?"

"He'll live."

The admission disturbed her. He was so passionate and intense. How was a mere woman to deal with such potency? And if she tried, how could she emerge unscathed?

"Are you in pain?" A stupid interrogatory, since she knew he was, but she was struggling for something to say, which was odd. She was never tongue-tied around him; the man habitually induced her to jabber incessantly.

"A little." He shrugged. "I'll mend."

Ere she could deviate from her chosen route, she braced herself against the basin, bent over and placed a tender kiss on his forehead, just above the laceration. Lingering with her lips on his skin, his eyelids fluttered shut as he accepted the sweet ministration.

As she straightened, and his sapphire gaze captured hers once more, they were separated by only a few inches. He was incomparable, magnificently virile, and wonderfully masculine, and he smelled so fine. His hot, slippery body beckoned, and she couldn't resist touching him, so she massaged comfortingly against his shoulder.

"Why?" She had to understand. No one had ever defended her before, never rushed to her aid, or taken her side. Emotions warred; she was confused, furious, frightened, but in the same instant, enchanted that he would risk so much.

After a prolonged, charged moment, he retorted flippantly, "Why not?"

"But he didn't harm me or—"

"He *tried*. That was sufficient." Obviously, he consid-

ered the matter closed, his motives and behavior beyond
debate or dissection.

She took the beverage from him, setting it on the table,
then she loosened the bandage that bound his knuckles.
They were bruised and swollen, flinty evidence of the
thrashing he'd inflicted, and she suspected that they
throbbed unmercifully. Blood was caked between his fingers, so she grabbed a clean cloth, dipped it in the bathwater, and sponged away the mess.

Observing, but offering no comment, he was silent and
ponderous. When she'd finished, she kindly kissed across
his fist, then cradled his hand in both of her own, hoping
that by holding him in the simple fashion, she could provide
ease for his afflictions.

"We need something cold for this swelling."

"There's special water in that pitcher."

He pointed to one of the dressers, and she rose and went
to it, pouring some into a bowl. Indeed, its temperature was
frigid—several ice chunks were floating—then she returned
to him and applied the chilly covering. For a few minutes,
she clamped it in place until his tension slackened, then she
chanced another glance at him.

"Better?" she queried, but he didn't respond directly.

Instead, he narrowed his focus. "Why are you here?"

This was one of those occasions when she supposed she
should simper and coo as a more accomplished female
might, but babbling inanely had never been her style. Plus,
she appreciated that he was watching her carefully, assessing her for a greater purpose, that she now had a chance to
prove herself, to elevate their relationship to another level.

"I was worried about you, and I had to see for myself
that you weren't seriously wounded." A tad scolding, she
added, "I came upstairs the moment I learned of what had
happened. It's a good thing I found you so easily, too, or
I'd have torn the house apart, chasing you down."

"I've ended up in worse condition."

His casual dismissal made her wonder if sparring wasn't
a typical diversion for him. What a wild, marvelous notion!

She'd never known another like him; certainly not the staid, stodgy gentlemen of the *ton*. None of them would act so impulsively, so outrageously. From birth, their sensibilities were quashed to where they hardly felt anything at all. He was an extreme individual, and she'd had some of his formidable personality aimed in her own direction, so she pitied the person who enraged him enough to provoke conflict. Michael didn't look as if he lost very often.

The frigid dressing on his battered knuckles had heated through, so she went over to douse the cloth, then gingerly swathe him again. He continued to study her, and there was a peculiar air about him, his stillness like that of a viper or other ferocious animal, and she wished she fathomed more about him so that she could properly deal with whatever was troubling him.

Struggling for levity, she smiled. "I didn't realize you were a brawler, Mr. Stevens."

"There are many things you don't *realize* about me, Sarah."

"Do you regularly engage in fisticuffs?"

"When the situation calls for it."

He shrugged again, so unforthcoming that she longed to box his ears. She was so curious about him. Yet their assignations had been so odd, and so accursedly condensed, that she never uncovered any relevant information.

What drove him? Why had he been so affronted on her account? What part of his character had urged him to act as her defender?

Needing more revelations, she probed, "When was the last time?"

"A few months ago. I had to drag James out of a dockside tavern."

"James is your brother?"

"Aye."

"And he didn't wish to depart?"

"No."

With the modest revelation, a thousand questions popped up, but she seemed unable to voice any of them. His gaze had dropped to her mouth and stayed there. He was endeavoring to intimidate her, though she wasn't sure why, but whatever his incentive, he was in for a shock, because she wasn't about to shy away.

"I don't want to talk about my brother," he finally said. As before, the pronouncement made it indisputable that it would be fruitless to pursue the topic. "In fact," he proclaimed, "I don't want to talk at all."

Her heart sank. While she deemed that she belonged with him, and was ecstatic to offer comfort when he was suffering, perhaps he didn't feel the same. His dictum constrained her to suggest, "Would you like me to go?"

He shook his head, and she repressed a shiver of relief. A drowning woman thrown a rope!

"I'm glad you came," he admitted. "I'm glad you're here."

The disclosure severely astounded her, and apparently, him, as well. He scowled, pondering why he'd affirmed so much.

"So am I." Boldly, she reached out and rifled her fingers through his hair as she'd been itching to do. It was thick and silky and damp.

He seized her wrist, shifting her so he could kiss her lightly, almost chastely. When he pulled away, there was a suspicious sheen in his eyes that *couldn't* be tears. Yet she perceived that the frightful combat he'd waged on her behalf had gravely overwhelmed him, had loosened some compass that guided him. He was hovering on a cliff of despair and wretchedness over which he could leap. Or not.

She melted. For reasons she couldn't define, the man called to her, intrigued and amazed, daunted and exhilarated, and she couldn't bear his agony. Mothering instincts, to protect and hold dear, surged to the fore.

"Thank you." She cupped his cheek with her palm and bestowed a chaste kiss of her own. "For what you did today."

"You're welcome," he solemnly declared. Brooding and quiescent, he persevered in analyzing her when, more than anything, she yearned to be whisked into his arms and treasured in all the ways of which he was so capable.

But he did nothing. He said nothing.

There was so much she aspired to tell him. That she was in awe, thunderstruck, and very likely falling ridiculously and senselessly in love, yet she dared not share any silly ardent outbursts. With ominous certitude, she grasped that he wouldn't approve of a sentimental overture.

Still, she couldn't prevent herself from stating, "I hate that you're hurting. How can I help you?"

His focus sank to her mouth again, then lower, to her breasts. He caressed them meticulously with his eyes until the nipples peaked and rubbed against her corset, and she had to resist the impulse to squirm.

"If I requested that you disrobe"—his torrid examination slid up her torso—"and lie down with me on the bed, would you?"

There was a challenge in his solicitation. Evidently, he expected her to decline or feign offense. If he thought she'd retreat, he'd miscalculated, but then, he wasn't the first man who'd underestimated her, and he wouldn't be the last.

"Yes, I would," she rejoined, calm as you please. "I would undress, and after, I would happily do whatever you ask of me."

"That is what I want." His puzzling attitude intensified. "That is the one thing you can do that will make me feel better."

"Then, my precious champion"—she tipped her head, evaluating him, taking his measure, letting him see that she was unafraid of his shameless proposal—"that is what you shall have."

Chapter Eleven

Michael shifted against the edge of the tub, putting space between them, wanting Sarah to have plenty of time to come to terms with her brazen decision, but she didn't seem to have the good sense to be anxious or frightened. The look she was giving him had him utterly unnerved.

Across the room, his large bed beckoned, urging him to carry her to its pliant mattress, to lay her down, to obtain some comfort. Hovering below, shielded by the soapy water, was his fierce cockstand, his phallus painfully begging to be assuaged between her heavenly thighs.

Though she didn't grasp it as yet, once he stepped out of the bath, there would be no going back. His resolution was wrong, outrageous, idiotic, but he meant to indulge. Today and tomorrow and the next day and the next after that. For as long as Pamela deigned to impart her hospitality—though in view of her pique over his latest exploit, his stay might be cut short—he would contrive to debauch and defile Sarah in every despicable way.

Starting gradually, he would initiate and enlighten, tease and tutor, until her fabulous, compliant body was attuned and burning for his type of prurient excess. He would thrill, delight, enchant, supplying all the delectation she could possibly tolerate and, in the process, he would garner some satisfaction of his own. If it killed him, if it took every ounce of his resolve and strength, if he spilled himself a thousand times in order to achieve satiation, he was determined to eventually attain contentment.

Recent events had unleashed something inside him, something voracious and feral that scared him, because it was so powerful. He couldn't quit thinking about her. Her

. . . in the stairwell, accosted by Brigham. Her . . . in her bedchamber, admitting that she'd spied on him while he'd fornicated with other women. Her . . . begging him to seduce her, to ruin her.

Pacing and cursing, he'd passed the night, unable to rest, helpless to cease his ruminating, his yearning. With morning, he'd been like a wild animal, unruly, unpredictable. Perched at his window, waiting for Brigham to emerge, he'd known the coward would strive to slip away like the dog he was.

The fracas had been welcome, vicious, malevolent, and he'd thrived on each punch thrown, on each smack of bone on bone, each spatter of blood that flew across the ground. In every muscle and pore, he ached—his ribs, his head, his hands—but he wasn't repentant. Not over any of it, and he was so savagely delighted that he'd had the chance to vent his fury so meticulously. He felt as if he was coming back to life, reawakening after a lengthy slumber. But with the conclusion of the melee, a staggering emptiness had enveloped him and, as he'd soaked in his bath, he'd progressively deduced how to allay his troubled condition: He wanted Sarah Compton. Without limitation, without constraint.

When she'd appeared—as if his hulking thoughts had summoned her—he'd recognized, then and there, that the course he'd chosen was inevitable. He was ready to fuck and defile, to sate and purge himself; to finesse, beguile, and abuse her in every conceivable fashion, and he didn't intend to be penitent for whatever he might perpetuate.

"For the remaining days that we are here," he explained, "we will have a sexual relationship."

"I've been hoping," the insane woman freely assented.

"I will demonstrate the methods of loving, and you will practice on me until you grow proficient."

"Very well."

"You will do whatever I say."

"Within reason."

"No," he interrupted, quashing her bit of bravado. There

would be no restrictions. "I will select the path. You will follow it. I will create the games; you will play. Enthusiastically and completely. Or not at all."

She stared him down, biting against her cheek, obviously deliberating refusal. His Sarah was tough and proud; she wasn't used to having a man tell her how to act, but then, as she'd issued from a family of men like Hugh Compton, what could he expect?

Half of his enjoyment would be attained from eroding her inhibitions, from her bowing to his stipulations, from her pleas for more. She *would* become complacent to his demands.

"Well?"

"If I don't agree?"

"We won't begin."

Her dilemma was enormous. Just out of principle, she considered declining. She didn't like him mandating her behavior, yet she craved the opportunity to experience what he was offering. She sought an affair on her own terms but, by his very disposition, their *amour* could never develop in such a lame manner. He was the type of man who would set the tone and pace. Surely, she comprehended that about him?

"Fine," she ultimately said.

He had to prevent himself from shaking his fist in triumph. She would be his premium conquest. "I will require conduct of you that you've never dreamed possible."

"I realize that."

"You can't be timid or shy. You must be mentally prepared to attempt whatever I suggest, and you shouldn't be apprehensive or bothered by our conduct. Whatever transpires is allowed."

"I'm not afraid." She chuckled. "Or shy!"

"Your purpose will be to please me through the carnal acts that I teach you. In return, you will receive your own gratification. The sins of the flesh will overwhelm you; you'll wonder why you've never committed them until now." Shrewdly, he regarded her. "Do you still wish to proceed?"

"Aye."

"First, you must make one promise to me."

"If I'm able."

"You must promise me that you'll never be sorry. That you'll never harbor any remorse."

He didn't deem it feasible. In fact, he was quite convinced that the aftermath would be brimming with regrets, but perhaps if he instilled the concept at the outset, he might mitigate some of her later lamentation. "Swear it to me," he insisted.

"I swear it. I'll never regret what occurs between us." She smiled. "I never could."

He nodded, accepting her vow, pondering if she'd truly keep it. She was a woman of her word, but some transgressions—such as the ones he was about to perpetrate against her—were too serious to be forgiven.

"Have you ever seen a naked man?" he asked.

"When would I have?"

"Turn around."

Puzzled by his request, she didn't budge, so he clarified, "I'm going to climb out of the bath. I certainly don't mind if you watch, but I hardly suppose you're prepared for the sight."

Her eyes widened with comprehension. He'd managed to shock her, and she leapt to her feet, geared to bolt.

"Stop!" he commanded to her retreating back, and she slid to a halt as he suppressed a wave of male vanity at how promptly she'd complied. What an interesting seduction this would be!

He exited the tub, the water lapping against the rim, and she vigilantly listened to every sound. Her torso was ramrod straight, her fists clenched at her sides, her head cocked. Reaching for a towel, he approached until he was directly behind her.

"I'm drying myself," he declared. "I'll have my robe on momentarily."

"All . . . all right."

Commencing at his hair, he fluffed at the dampness, then he moved down, to his neck, chest, buttocks, and legs. But for their labored breathing, and the intermittent crackling of the log in the fire, the room was deathly quiet, and she tensed as the towel scratched across his bodily bumps and crevasses.

Leaning down, he intentionally let the towel brush along her hemline, and she jumped whenever he encroached. Eventually, he tired of his petty amusement, and he donned his robe, stuffing his arms in the sleeves and binding the cord at the waist.

"I am finished."

At the news, she endeavored to face him, but he prohibited the movement by wrapping himself around her and trapping her backside along his front. The sparse robe was the only garment covering him so, as he pressed his scantily clad form against her, it was as if he was wearing nothing at all.

In agony, he hardened to an obscene length.

Spreading his fingers wide across her pliable belly, he clutched at her and pulled her bottom against his groin. She had the most mesmerizing ass, perfectly forged for a man's appreciation. He flexed into her skirts, sensing her figure, her cleft. To his relief, she didn't shirk away from the intimacy, so he held her tighter and whispered in her ear.

"Do you have any idea what transpires when a man and a woman are alone?"

"No. I learned some from observing your behavior, but . . ."

He couldn't abide her talking about what she'd beheld of himself and the other female guests. His plans for her included nothing similar to those decadent diversions, and he didn't care to be reminded of how he'd debased himself and his partners. Impatient to brusquely silence her, he bit against her nape, and the sensation had the desired effect. With the unfamiliar impact, she sucked in a huge breath of air.

Their liaison would have nothing in common with the previous, lewd dalliances she'd witnessed. Her sensual fate was sealed. He wanted her; he would have her. But the journey would be languid and pleasant.

"A man and a woman," he continued, "like to kiss and embrace. To fondle one another. They undress, so that their bodies can connect"—he nuzzled along her shoulder, and goose bumps prickled down her arms—"bare skin to bare skin."

"Why?"

"A woman's nudity incites a man to physical passion. He's then eager to mate."

"Do you want to . . ."—she swallowed, swallowed again, her head tipped to the side, exposing more for him to sample—"to *mate* with me now?"

"Yes, very much."

"It's the middle of the day."

"You'll have no secrets from me."

"But we're not married."

"We don't need to be."

"I don't understand."

"All in good time, my little virgin." He laughed softly, and swept his palms up her stomach to just below her breasts, not caressing them but drawing so near. She braced for the higher level of involvement, and was frustrated when it didn't arrive. "How many pieces of clothing are hidden under your gown?"

An adorable blush crept from deep inside and colored her cheeks. She seemed incapable of responding, so he asked, "Petticoats?" She nodded, and he queried, "Corset?" though he knew the reply.

The stiff contraption hemmed her in and, with her respiration elevated by the stirrings of desire, she struggled against confinement, and he couldn't wait to pull at the laces and whisk it away. Avidly, he recalled the size and shape of her breasts, and he couldn't wait to view them free and unencumbered.

"How about drawers?" he queried, referring to the new-fangled undergarment.

"Yes."

Infrequently, he discovered them on his lovers, but he never cared. The novel contraption was simply one more item meant to conceal and titillate, one more article to peel away and discard before he reached his destination.

"I'm going to remove your dress." He stroked her heated flesh, brushing her breasts in passing, bringing his hands to rest on her shoulders. "And your petticoats. I'll strip you—"

"Till I'm . . ."

She couldn't speak the word *naked* aloud, and he almost took pity on her, but he refrained. He wanted her fidgety, uneasy, off balance. "To your chemise. No further for now."

Frantically, her mind whirled. Her wishes were about to be granted, and she was terrified by the prospect, yet she didn't disappoint. "I believe"—she trembled slightly—"I would like it if you did."

With a few snaps of his wrist, her bodice was loose, and she reflexively grabbed to keep it clasped to her bosom.

"Put your arms at your sides," he ordered, and she obeyed as he pushed the gown past her waist and hips, and soon it was pooled about her feet. He lifted her out of the pile of silk and lace, setting her on the floor, once again then, quick as a wink, he undid her corset and flung it away, mollified when her lungs adequately expanded.

Her chemise was delicate, cream-colored, with a dainty floral pattern stitched on the borders. It fell to mid-thigh, and he glanced down, noting a hint of bare leg, garter, and stocking.

"Face me."

He allowed her to spin around. The fabric of the shift was thin and transparent, and he could see her breasts, navel, and woman's hair. His erection inflated further, and absently, he rubbed across it, bidding it to recede, but to no avail. The image of her, nearly nude and calmly anticipating his ensuing imprudence, was too enticing.

Already, he'd pushed her awfully far, but she courageously passed each test he meted out, though she wasn't
currently looking him in the eye, and she was careful not
to permit her attention to wander to his lower regions where
he continued to fondle himself.

Kneeling before her, he absorbed her essence, her sweat,
the musk of her sex. He tugged off her shoes, untied her
garters, and rolled down her stockings. More goose bumps
flourished, and he massaged up and down her calves, cuddling her, warming her.

He stole one, fleet kiss against her stomach, one deep
inhale of the tang on her abdomen, of the cushion of hair
surrounding her pussy, then he stood, regarding her exact-
ingly, curious as to how she'd survived the ordeal, but he
needn't have worried. She was unaffected, her shoulders
squared, and she didn't recoil in the slightest as his gaze
roamed across her, hot and potent as his hands might have
been.

"Take down your hair."

Obediently, she set about pulling at the combs and pins.
In seconds, the heavy mass swung downward, encasing her
in a stream of auburn and gold. It fell to her waist, a shimmering ribbon of crimson designed to inflame and corrupt.

"Run your fingers through it." She acceded, as he decreed, "Whenever you visit me, you'll have it unbound and
brushed out."

"As you wish." He advanced until his chest grazed her
nipples, his thighs encircled her own, but she didn't hesitate. "What now?"

"We'll lie on the bed. You'll learn to touch me." He
flicked his thumb across her bottom lip. Full, moist, red as
a ripe cherry, he stole a kiss then, twirling her in a circle,
they sank onto the mattress, with him on his back and her
stretched out on top.

She was a vision to behold. The strap of her chemise
had slid off her shoulder, a succulent breast was partly bare,
her hair cascading about. Beautiful, arousing, she was de-

sire incarnate, and for the moment, she was his—and his alone—to do with as he pleased. He could barely stand the suspense, the marvelous sense of expectation, yet he deigned to go forth deliberately, to savor and relish every delicious instant of her downfall.

Adjusting her legs, he opened her thighs so that she straddled him. Her pussy was directly over his cock, instinctively recognizing the appropriate sensual route, and she spread and slumped further, dramatically increasing the explicit contact.

Tugging at the belt at his waist, he loosened it, and pushed at the lapels of his robe, exposing only his chest.

"Touch me," he said and, when she vacillated, he gripped her hand and laid it over his heart, then rasped it in a slow circle. "Like this."

He should have seized control of the assignation and tormented her until she was writhing and pleading for more, but truth be told, he was exhausted after his vigorous combat.

As a bastard son, who had been shamelessly disavowed by his rich and noble father, he often engaged in altercations. Offensive comments—usually aimed at his mother—were regularly hurled, and he vented his wrath at any imbecile foolish enough to make an untoward remark, so his entering into a dispute was nothing new.

A skilled, seasoned opponent, he could hurl a punch as well as take one. However, the frantic display he'd delivered to Brigham had exploded with a ferocity he'd not exhibited before, and the intensity had left him thoroughly drained. He needed Sarah's sweet courtesy, was desperate to suffer through her virginal oohs and aahs, to bask in her fascination. The feel of her smooth hands, with those slender, questing fingers roving over him, was like a healing salve to his battered body and spirit.

She amused herself with his chest, rifling through the springy hair, exploring the ridges and valleys until her maneuvers felt as natural as breathing, as though she'd touched him just so a hundred times before.

Braver, she dipped lower, across the knobs of his rib cage, but he'd secured a grueling blow to his side and, before he could warn her to be cautious, she patted across the bruising, and he flinched and winced.

She froze. "You're hurt."

"Not badly."

"Let me see." She relocated, her lush pussy easing off his phallus as she shoved more of the robe apart. The spot on his ribs was inflamed, the abrasion ghastly, and she studied and inspected, then bent over and kissed it as she had the wounds to his temple and fist.

When she straightened, she flashed a stern look. "I don't like you fighting."

"It's occasionally necessary."

"But I can't bear it that you've been injured." Gently, she traced across the damage. "Promise you won't do it again," and she graced him with a tender kiss against his mouth. "Please?"

It had been a very long while since anyone had evidenced concern for his safety or welfare. In response, he could only offer a small concession. "I'll try."

"That's worth something, I guess."

The exchange concluded, the banter lagged, the quiet magnified. She focused on him with such penetrating, abiding affection that he couldn't stand to perceive it, so he said, "Touch me again."

Steadying her hips, he centered her so that she was, once more, lingering over his erection. How he longed to thrust against her! He was so hard, he ached. His balls wrenched and cried out, but he restrained himself. This was her first encounter with male nudity, and there would be abundant excuses in the impending days to rush toward total fulfillment, but not just yet.

More sure of herself, she now confidently nestled into his matting of chest hair, burrowing her nose, sniffing at his skin, and he caught her chin and steered her to his breast.

"Kiss me here," he dictated, and his brown nipple pebbled into a compact bud as her superb lips painstakingly submitted. "Suck me into your mouth."

An adept pupil, she instantly acquiesced, nibbling and toying until he could barely remain stationary. When her teeth nipped at the tiny nub, he couldn't block the groan that escaped.

She grinned up at him. "You like that, do you?"

"Very much."

"You did it to me . . . that night in my room."

"Yes. A woman's nipples are incredibly sensitive. When a man dabbles with them, he accentuates her titillation, and she is excited and relaxed. The stimulation prepares her for what is to come."

"And what is that?"

"Soon, milady, all your questions will be answered."

He ushered her hands to both his nipples, revealing the suitable pressure, the appropriate manipulation. She trifled and played, her eyes glued to his so that she could judge his reaction.

The minx! She was a natural! Too astute. Too disposed to attempt any risqué procedure.

Her unwavering concentration was extremely disconcerting, so he guided her mouth to his other breast, easing her to the nipple. His cock was throbbing, the crown oozing with his sexual juice. He stabilized her and partook of an unhurried flex against her cleft.

As though she'd been poked with a pin, she jerked upright. "Why do you keep doing that?"

"Doing what?" He pretended innocence, flattening her against his erection, and feasting with another leisurely flex.

"That thrusting motion. It just feels so . . . so . . . ."

"Extraordinary?"

"Yes. But naughty, too. And forbidden." She wedged herself more fully along the crest of his phallus. "My body seems to fathom what you propose, when I've no notion myself."

"Absolutely." His wanton fingers slipped under the hem of her chemise and petted the smooth skin of her thighs.

"You are so ready for me to be your lover."

"How can you tell?"

"Even though you are a woman, you need sensual animation just like a man."

"I was told differently."

"You were told wrong."

The veracity of his statement sank in, and she acceded to the inevitable, initiating some flexing of her own, driving herself forward, using her knees and toes. Joyous, she smiled as though she was a child who'd just found a unique flavor of candy. "Do you feel it?"

"Aye, lass, I do." He gritted his teeth, speculating as to how he'd persevere at a sluggish pace, how he'd take minimal steps, when his entire being was spurring him to skip to the finale without delay.

Eliminating temptation, abandoning paradise, he levered her away. "You've never seen a naked man," he reminded her. "How about a boy?"

"I've bathed a few male children in my day."

"Then you're aware of how we vary."

Her brow furrowed, then realization dawned. "In our private parts." She peeked down, to what was concealed by his robe, but the solid vertex of flesh couldn't be missed. "I've always wondered why."

"It's for coupling. So that we fit together."

"How is it accomplished?"

"My cock swells, and by flexing, my seed is lured to the tip and rushes out the end."

"What does your *seed* look like?"

"White. Creamy."

"Where does it go?"

"Into the chasm between your legs. In the site from where your monthly blood flows." He rested his hand on her abdomen, his thumb pressing at her mound, but she wasn't equipped to handle more, so he didn't move downward.

At the mention of her menses, she flushed, but the delicate subject wasn't inordinately disturbing to her, which he took as an excellent sign. Before the afternoon was through, they would discuss many more distressing topics.

"And a babe is conceived in this fashion?"

"It could be. If the timing is right."

"Is this dangerous, then? I hadn't thought that we might create a child."

"We won't. I'll be circumspect."

She shook her head. "I say it again: I don't understand what we're about."

"There are techniques for dallying without proceeding to marital copulation. That is what I contemplate."

"But why would you simply want to . . ."—she searched for a term, but couldn't pick one of her own, so she employed his—"to *dally*?"

"For pleasure, Sarah." The mode in which *pleasure* rolled off his tongue caused her to stir, her loins descended, instinctively extending out to him. "A man derives great satisfaction from spilling himself. It is an activity he seeks above all others."

"So . . . *pleasure* will be our goal?"

"Yes. Our only one."

"What do I need to do?"

"You'll stroke me. With your hands and your mouth. I'll show you."

He placed her fingers on top of his bulging erection. Adding tension, he demonstrated the rhythm, but he abruptly realized that he could settle for nothing less than her bared flesh applied to his own.

He untied the knot at his waist. "Open my robe. All the way."

Chapter Twelve

Sarah didn't hesitate. She was trembling, not with fear or trepidation, but with anticipation, so she prudently masked her excitement, not wanting to give the impression that she'd become a coward at this late juncture.

By all accounts, he'd hardly done anything to her. He'd talked, he'd eliminated most of her clothing, he'd flexed against her through several layers of fabric. Yet her body was on fire, her nipples contracted so that they hurt, her skin stretched so tightly that it didn't seem to fit her bone structure.

He'd slackened the belt at his waist but, daring her to proceed, he hadn't untied it. As if she'd back down! Without being conscious of it, she'd craved this moment forever.

Carefully, she controlled her shaking fingers and unraveled the knot. Deliberately, prolonging her discovery, she drew the lapels of his robe aside, sequentially revealing his navel, then the arrow of hair that shot down his belly.

Her eyes dropped imperceptibly, and she encountered all. Like a supplicant before a shrine, she pushed at the remaining material, baring him inch by glorious inch, until he was totally naked, and the reality was like nothing she'd imagined.

At viewing the male accessory on small boys, she'd never postulated that it would enlarge, that it could mature to being so bold and manifest. Looking angry and alive, the attachment was red and distended, with a bulbous head and purple, ropy veins. It protruded from a nest of his dark hair, two sacs dangling beneath, and her visual assessment made it extend out toward her in entreaty.

She hazarded a glance at him, and he lay silent and still,

studying her with an impersonal, glacial intensity.

Had he planned to shock her? To have her tearful and swooning? To send her stumbling from the room in offense and alarm?

He was motivated by deep, unfathomable issues that she couldn't hope to understand. The chances were great that he'd merely instigated this as a bizarre diversion in order to gain a response from her, but if the man thought she was some prim, squeamish miss, he obviously didn't know her very well. She was fascinated, enthralled, and ardent to explore.

"It's larger than I supposed."

"I'm aroused."

"It changes size?" Her eyes widened with astonishment, and he chuckled at her naïveté.

"Usually, it's flaccid and harmless." Tensing his stomach muscles, the extraordinary appendage inflated even more. "But not when I'm here with you like this. I'm so hard for you. I ache with my desire."

There was a husky tone in his voice, a desperation that plucked at her common sense, leaving her reckless and rash, and just then, she'd have performed any impulsive feat he requested.

"What do you call it?"

"My cock."

She struggled for terminology, but her innocent background hindered descriptive dialogue, so she gestured over his erect body part. "Are all of these . . . these cocks so large?"

"Mine is bigger than most." He directed, "Touch me."

Tentatively, she reached out and traced a line from the base to the apex. The sheltering layer of skin was hot and smooth, pliant and malleable, but the timid contact didn't satisfy him, and he clasped her hand in his, and wrapped them together around his heated staff, so that she could adjust to handling him so privately. Then, he commenced moving them conjointly, showing her the most effective maneuvers.

"The tip is the most sensitive," he pointed out. "Try to run over it with each stroke."

"Like this?" she asked, drawing back the yielding skin, unveiling the crown.

"Yes," he muttered through clenched teeth. "I'll obtain the most gratification that way."

As she was an avid, enthusiastic pupil, he readily left her to her own devices. Fastidiously, she investigated, learning his shape, awed by the variations of velvet over steel. She pampered and played, altering the pressure, the speed, the length of her caress. Amazingly, with the slightest modification, he reacted accordingly.

What power she held over him! What marvelous authority! If she wielded this much dominance when she was unskilled, she'd be a holy terror after a few hours of practice, after a few days.

Her nerves galloped at the realization.

"What are these?" She cupped the sacs between his legs.

"My balls."

"What are they for?"

"They shelter my seed, and they're very tender." But she'd already surmised as much, and she'd decided to withdraw when, sounding afflicted, he interrupted her. "Don't stop. Just be gentle."

Cradling the precious pile, she scooted down his thighs so that she had more space to observe and manipulate. The new position brought her over his stomach, and her sudden comprehension startled her.

She remembered the lover she'd witnessed, the woman who had been bent over him, but Sarah hadn't been able to discern her activity, and she'd been so blasted curious. *Could it be?*

A inexplicable tingle rushed through her fingers, up her arms, and she was jolted by her keen insight. She gazed up his broad expanse of abdomen and chest. The pillows were braced behind his head, and he regarded her dispassionately, his sapphire eyes glittering.

"They put their mouths on you, don't they?"

"Who?"

"Your . . . your women. That's what you require of them, isn't it?" She rose onto her haunches. "They take you into their mouths."

"Yes."

"Why?"

"*Why* do I prefer it? Or *why* do they go down on me?"

"Both."

"I fancy it because it's erotic and naughty, and they do it so that they can brag to their friends that they've sucked me off."

Her brow furled. "What does that mean?"

"It's a crude phrase." He shrugged, but didn't appear repentant for having recited it. "It refers to when a man thrusts his cock into a woman's mouth. He continues until the friction is unbearable, then he discharges his seed into his lover's throat."

"You really do this?"

"Yes."

"Often?"

"Well, I wouldn't say *often*." He seemed amused. "Whenever a woman volunteers."

"Your partners swallow it?"

"Aye."

"What is its taste?"

"It doesn't actually have one. It's heat and salt."

"Your very essence," she murmured.

He shrugged again.

"This deed . . . does it have a name?"

"A French kiss."

"It's enjoyable for you?"

"Beyond measure. I relish the opportunity to spill myself between a woman's legs, but I never do, because I might create a child. So I'm obliged to any female who renders such a stunning delectation."

"You always agree?"

"I'm not in the habit of denying myself. I have a strong

sexual drive, and I accept what is freely offered."

He could baldly analyze his scandalous conduct. Most likely, he'd reveled in so much lewdness in his life that discussion of his untoward behaviors was extremely easy. How could she break through that unruffled façade?

Her heart was racing, her body afire, her womanly places pleading for his intricate manual attention. She was anxious to bring him to the same drastic condition, to where he was out of control, his guise of ennui shattered.

"Open yourself to me." He nodded toward his groin. "Take me into your mouth."

"I'm not certain that I—"

"You are."

"You're demanding too much, too soon."

"No I'm not."

Once again, he arranged her hand on his pulsating member, leading her in a languid motion, and she stared into those mesmerizing eyes. They were sublime, reassuring, and they made her crazy to blindly effect his every command. As though enchanted, she found herself leaning forward, leaning down.

"Will you finish inside me?"

"Not today."

"Why not?"

"You're geared for some. Not all."

"When, then?"

"After you've had more indoctrination."

Still, she vacillated. What had she gotten herself into? She professed, "I guess I'm apprehensive."

"About what?"

"About what I don't know."

"I won't hurt you; I never could."

The strength of his avowal was encouraging. "I grasp that. I just . . ."

Just what?

Their rendezvous was so devoid of care or concern, and he was so indifferent. It seemed wrong to proceed in such a disjointed fashion. The somber, aloof stranger lying before her wasn't the man of passion to whom she was devoted. The *real* Michael was in hiding, but she wasn't positive how to draw him out. Perhaps if she complied with his proposition, she could melt the barriers he'd erected. She was eager to please him, yet she was skeptical of his motives and fretting over her own.

"I want you, Sarah. I need you now."

His declaration soothed her turmoil, urging her on, and she couldn't deny him. Starting at the bottom, she flicked with her tongue, by degrees working up his length until she was licking at the oozing crown. When she arrived at the blunt apex, she eased him betwixt her lips.

The sensation was indescribable, his nature and spirit embedded in the turgid, obstinate extremity. Inhaling slowly, she was surrounded by his masculinity, his virility, his potency.

His hand went to the back of her head, holding her, guiding her. He shifted to his side, rotating her, as well. With his leg, he steadied her, pinning her close, and she opened further, procuring more of him than she'd previously believed possible.

As he scrupulously thrust, the physicality was amazing. The indiscretion, the impropriety, titillated her, leaving her wild and hungry for more. She basked in the lengthy, ribald interlude while he overindulged and, as she adjusted to his movements, she became cognizant of his rising ardor. Then, with very little warning, he pulled away, and she instantly regretted the loss.

Her lips were sore, chapped and stretched as they'd never been, yet she wished he'd kept on. She sensed that the procedure could have grown particularly raucous, and that he was restraining himself on her account.

"Are we finished?"

"No, love, we're not."

The endearment rolled off his tongue to slither into her confused mind, raising innumerable questions: Did he appreciate what he'd said? Was it unintentional? Intentional?

If he was aware of what he'd uttered, what had been his true purpose?

Thrown off balance, she hardly regrouped before he was hauling her up into his arms. He was smiling at her, the blaze of it so stupendous that she was glad she was lying down when it fell upon her.

He covered her with his body, his weight pressing her into the mattress, and having him on top of her was a thoroughly primal experience. He was so welcome, and he fit so perfectly—flat where she was rounded, rough where she was soft—and she couldn't prevent herself from enveloping him, her limbs spreading so that she could lovingly cuddle him. Cautiously, almost gratefully, he settled himself between her thighs, his cock heavy and wedged against her leg.

He hovered over her, his fingers at the hem of her chemise, and with no hesitation, he tugged it up her hips, disposed to remove it.

At seeing her rapid panic, he explained, "I'm terribly aroused; I'm going to come against your stomach."

"Will it hurt?"

"Only me"—he chortled over matters she didn't comprehend—"and only in a good way."

"My breasts will be bared to you."

"Again."

"Yes, and I'm nervous that—"

"They're so magnificent."

Through the fabric, he caressed her erect nipple and, like a puppet on a string, she immediately acquiesced, hoisting her lower torso, then her shoulders, so he could yank her chemise up and over her head.

How was it that he so easily routed her ingrained propriety? He but complimented her, and she jumped to do his bidding. Was she so starved for affection? So greedy for flattery and adulation? Apparently, the answer was yes.

By spewing a few laudatory words, he could prevail upon her to commit any depraved act—even those that were completely foreign to her character. Yet, she yearned to make him happy, to prompt that rare smile.

She was an unmitigated fool!

Her body was now shielded only by a skimpy pair of bright-red pantalets.

The most recent whimsy from Paris, Rebecca had noted when she'd brought them home from London.

The gift—six pairs of silky, frivolous underdrawers—had enchanted Sarah. She had so few nice garments, and no money for new. The wardrobe her father had purchased years prior for her debut was either too small or threadbare, so she'd cheerfully embraced the scanty unmentionables. They made her feel pretty and feminine, and she liked how they brushed against her beneath her clothes.

But when she'd donned them that morning, it had never occurred to her that Michael Stevens would be evaluating them that afternoon. She blushed furiously.

"Why, Sarah"—he was amused and surprised, as though womanly attire was the last thing he'd expected from her—"you're wearing French underwear."

The knave was so familiar with women that he was well versed in the modern style of intimate apparel!

The assignation had become too oppressive. What was she striving to attain? Why was she allowing him to tease her? She never tolerated men's jesting, having learned the hard way how an uncouth comment could wound, and, needing to flee, she wrenched away, trying to scoot off the bed, but he held her down.

"Let me go," she decreed, focusing on the ceiling.

"No."

Odious cad!

His hand slithered under the crimson waistband and tangled in her secret hair, then traveled on to where she was wet and swollen, and she was embarrassed that he'd detected the unusual moisture—especially when he felt compelled to preen over his discovery.

"God . . . you are so ready for me," he asserted, as two questing fingers slipped inside her.

He'd touched her in the same manner once before but,

at the time, she'd been too astonished to pay attention. Now, she moaned, clutching and weeping into his palm as he stroked deliberately, entering then retreating. The abominable machination stirred an acute appetite for more than the simple massage. She wanted things she couldn't begin to enumerate.

"Michael . . . please . . ."

"Yes, beg me. I love it when you do."

With a tap of his thumb, he sent a wave of stimulation up her abdomen to her breasts, and she whimpered.

How mortifying! She wasn't a *whimperer*. Yet, how was she to comport herself rationally and routinely when she was splayed wide and being fondled by such an arrogant rogue?

He was in pure agony, as well, as if palpating her was painful and, as he hung his head over her chest, she couldn't get past the impression that he hadn't been so unmoved, after all. Throughout, he'd seemed to be a sort of unaffected bystander, and his calm detachment had been so frustrating. She'd longed for him to endure some of the same jubilation and upheaval she was suffering.

Evidently, he hadn't been so apathetic. He was seething with unreleased turmoil.

"I have to come," he said, and he bent down and licked at her nipple. "I can't wait."

"Tell me what to do."

"Just hold me tight. Don't let go."

She snuggled him against her bosom, and his cock dilated to an enormous proportion. Insistent and relentless, he impatiently thrust it against her.

"Fuck me with your hand." And he ushered her to his shaft, once again.

She took on the erogenous chore, and her firm grip was magic. In a half-dozen lunges, he tensed and emitted a haunting groan. Hot liquid spurted across her abdomen and fingertips, purging him, then he shuddered and sank onto her, collapsing fully.

His breathing was labored, heavy and erratic, his heartbeat thundering against his ribs, beating furiously with her own. He didn't speak—perhaps he couldn't—and for once, she was glad of the silence. Words failed her.

Nothing had prepared her for how personal the moment would be. She felt he'd bared his soul, that he'd exposed himself as he never could with another, and she held him close. Eventually, he mellowed, but he was motionless, his forehead pressed to her breasts.

Abruptly, he sat up and moved to the edge of the bed, showing her his back.

His legs were unsteady, and he fortified himself then proceeded to the tub, dipping a washing cloth in the water and returning to her side. He avoided her gaze as he conscientiously cleansed his seed away, then threw the cloth on the floor. When he faced her again, in an unguarded moment, she witnessed vulnerability and loneliness.

A wave of protectiveness flowed over her, and she needed to provide comfort, emotionally as well as physically. She opened her arms in welcome, and he joined her willingly, resting in the crook of her neck. Much as one might a young child who'd been scared or injured, she nurtured him and, as she rifled her fingers through his thick mane of hair, she couldn't help thinking that this was where she wanted to always be, where she belonged.

Gradually, she noticed that he was developing another erection, and shortly, his cock was stubborn and intractable against her belly. He started kissing against her nape, sending chills down her spine, then he abandoned his safe perch, trailing down her chest, to a breast, and her breath whooshed out when he closed over the extended crest. Like a babe, he suckled against her. Gently at first, then more fervently, he increased the tension, until he had her writhing and squirming.

"What are you trying to accomplish?" she managed to gasp.

"I'm pleasuring you."

"It doesn't feel *pleasurable*."

"It will. Trust me," he commented encouragingly. "The

sensations are new, so they seem foreign to you, but they're customary."

"I don't know what to do." She hated that he was in charge.

"You don't have to *do* anything," he contended, laughing softly. "Just relax while I dally."

Relax? Was he mad? How could she relax when a man the likes of Michael Stevens was on top of her and nursing at her breast?

He kissed across her cleavage to her other nipple, and he toyed ruthlessly until it was raw and irritated. His hand idly trailed down her stomach. In a pattern of agonizing circles, he descended lower and lower, never falling quite far enough.

Finally, he sneaked inside her drawers and honed in on the spot his thumb had located earlier. At the same time, two fingers glided into her cleft, and momentarily, he had her hips flexing in an infuriating rhythm. She strained toward an unknown goal—if the cad would just point her in the proper direction, the journey would be so much easier—and she teetered on a ledge of desire, needing to leap off but not confident of when or where.

"What's happening?" she spat out, scarcely able to find the air necessary for communication.

"Have you never touched yourself like this? In the night? When you're alone?"

"No . . . never . . ." The information delighted him, and she could sense that he was grinning. The presumptuous rogue!

"You're going toward a peak of pleasure. As I did." He delayed the tempo, just when she was burning for it to multiply, and, cognizant of the havoc he was wreaking, he chuckled again. "The first time can be scary. But I promise that it will also be wonderful."

"I don't know . . . how . . ." She couldn't elucidate, couldn't implore, couldn't talk.

Oh, when would this torment cease?

"Your body knows." As though supplying confirmation,

he rubbed where all sensation seemed to be centered, and she arched up and would have flown off the bed if he hadn't been hindering her escape. "Close your eyes, and I'll take you where you want to go."

"I'm afraid," she whispered.

"Don't be. I'm here with you."

"Michael . . ."

He paused. "Say my name again."

"Michael!" she wailed, on the brink, frightened.

The cliff beckoned and, when he latched onto her breast and suckled adamantly, she jumped, sending herself into freefall. She was shattered, undone, and careening through the universe. A voice called out, with an extraordinary kind of ecstasy, and she vaguely recognized that it was her own, then his lips were on hers, silencing her by capturing her wild cry of joy.

The frenzy persisted for an eternity until, sequentially, she commenced to reassemble. Sanity and reality returned, and she was in Michael's bed, in Michael's arms.

She dared a peek at him, and he lingered over her with a look that could only be tenderness. There was a hint of male pride there, as well, at having reduced her to such a wanton circumstance.

"Much better," he murmured, and he kissed her cheek.

"Yes." She endeavored to shift away but didn't get far. His weight still pressed her down. "What was that?"

"An orgasm. The French refer to it as the *petit mort*, the little death."

"Well . . . they've surely got the right of it." She lifted a hand and let it fall with a heavy thud. "My bones have melted. I can't move."

"You don't have to. Just rest for a bit."

"Then, what?"

"We'll do it again."

"You're joking!"

"I'm not."

"My heart would quit beating."

He kissed her once more. "It will get better."

"More intense?"

"Absolutely. And quicker to achieve the more you're with me."

"I'll never survive."

"Perhaps not."

He urged her over so that her back was spooned against his front. One arm lay under her head, a muscled, intriguing pillow. The other was over her torso, his fingers making lazy loops on her stomach and hip.

Her perception was heightened—the bristle of his bodily hair, the heat of his cock on her bottom, the smell of their mingled sweat and sex—and everything appeared more extreme and profound.

A yawn emerged; she was too tired to hide it, and he drew a blanket over them, sealing them in a snug cocoon.

What next? The vexing interrogatory flitted by, but she was elated, exhausted, and too fatigued to dwell on the future.

She slept.

When she awoke, she brooked only a minor instant of alarm while she sought to recall where she was, but the episode swiftly passed, and the scandalous memories flooded in.

Where he was concerned, she'd developed an elevated awareness, and she could sense him in the room, studying her. A light aroma of tobacco tickled her nose. He was smoking—a tidbit to tuck away in her limited collection of the Michael trivialities she'd gleaned. Her eyes fluttered open, even as she pondered how they would interact now that their sexual escapade was terminated.

He was in a chair by the window, but as distant as if he'd been all the way beyond the ocean in America. He was dressed only in a pair of trousers, his hair was swept off his forehead, accenting the cut over his eye, and he watched her impassively. A half-empty glass of brandy sat on the table, and he was holding a cheroot, the butt aglow, the smoke curling upward. Behind him, she could see outside. The shadows had lengthened and much of the day had passed away.

On seeing her stir, he snuffed out the cigar, but he didn't say anything.

She came up on one elbow, her cascade of auburn hair tumbling over her shoulder. The blanket drooped, baring a breast, and his brow rose in nonchalant disinterest. Their bedplay had been engaging and exotic when he'd been participating, but now, as he frigidly stared with no deference displayed on his beautiful face, she felt absurd.

Clutching at the quilt, she posed the only query that seemed to matter. "What time is it?"

"Almost five."

Unnerved, she speculated as to whether he'd napped at all, or if he'd enigmatically assessed her, wishing she'd rise and retire, but not quite rude enough to wake her and insist.

From her perspective, the romp had been the most resplendent, fabulous ever; from his, nothing out of the ordinary. In all likelihood, he regularly wasted his days in sexual frolic, and she'd merely been lumped in with the scores of loose women with whom he cavorted.

Troubled by her musings, she strove for levity. "I guess you wore me out."

"*Fucking* will do that to a person." He nodded toward the bed. "I fetched your robe."

"Thank you."

It was draped on the bedding, and she couldn't stifle a thrilling rush at the thought that he'd visited her bedchamber. For some reason, the notion of him invading her boudoir, searching through her armoire and examining her belongings, was fascinating.

"You're going to miss tea," he remarked casually, "so you need to bathe, then go down for supper. We've been here for quite a spell, so it's important that you put in an appearance."

So, he *was* eager for her to depart. How disappointing!

"I doubt if anyone will miss me," she was compelled to

report. "I'm not any more of a social butterfly than you are."

"Your cousin knocked a while ago."

His look was filled with inquisition and accusation, and she could picture him standing in the middle of her room, robe in hand, with Rebecca on the other side of the door. They'd been so close to detection! While she should have been frantic and appalled, she was exhilarated by the danger in which she'd deposited herself—and him.

What had come over her? The woman she'd been before she'd arrived, before she'd met Michael Stevens, had vanished.

"Did she try the knob?"

"Of course." He stared her down. "She's awfully determined to catch you in a compromising position. Why do you suppose that is?"

"I've no idea," she responded blandly, adopting his reticence. She had no desire to discuss Rebecca, to permit the outside world, her other life—her real life—to intrude on this flight of fancy.

Keeping the covers flattened against her bosom, she battled to don her robe, not granting him a view of her nakedness. While the state had seemed normal when they'd been making love, with him imperturbably glaring at her, she was embarrassed by her nudity, and she simply felt inappropriately undressed.

She scooted to the edge of the bed, but she couldn't take the necessary steps to leave. She was terrified that once she departed, they'd never cross paths again.

He was treating her just as he did his other lovers, as if the event hadn't had any effect on him, and she despised his composed, nonchalant disposition. His cool reserve and taciturnity were warning her off and away. Yet, she wasn't timid; she declined to surrender without a fight, because she craved a loving relationship with him.

"Would you like me to return after supper?"

His reply was the very worst. "As you wish."

The aggravating response, the one he habitually utilized

to chase off his paramours, set a spark to her temper. She wasn't some doxy! Not a woman of loose morals with whom he could randomly trifle! She was a chaste, upstanding female, who'd chosen him—scoundrel though he was—and favored him with a part of herself she never proposed to bestow on another, and she wouldn't have her boon discarded as if she was of no import.

Stomping across the floor, she halted at his chair, their knees tangled, their feet overlapping, and he was surprised by her audacious move. Let him be!

"Stop it!" she dictated.

"Stop what?" He was plainly uncomfortable with her directness.

"Quit pretending that this afternoon was of no consequence."

He fidgeted. "I never said that."

"But that's how you're acting." Didn't he realize how special this was to her? "Our meeting held little significance to you, but it meant a great deal to me." Quietly, she added, "Don't ruin it."

He scrutinized her, then tipped his head in acknowledgment. "I didn't intend to discount what happened. I just assumed you'd want to be about your business."

"That I've had my *fun,* and now I'm finished with you?"

"Aye."

"Hear me, Michael Stevens: It will take a bit more than your bad attitude and rude manners to make me conclude that we're through."

"I see that." One corner of his exquisite mouth hinted at a smile.

She figured that was as close as she'd ever get to an apology. There were many things about him she didn't understand, but many things that were clear, as well. When he let his guard down, he could be tender and unselfish, though he resisted her attempts at closeness, and it dawned on her that perhaps he never became amorously attached to any female, so he'd built protective walls.

While he hoped to diminish the magnitude of their affinity, she had other plans. He wanted her to visit him again; she just knew he did! And she would force him to say so if she had to literally drag the admission from his lips.

"Don't treat me with the disregard you exhibit to your other lovers."

"I wasn't," he lied.

"You could have fooled me." He had the grace to blush. Without a doubt, he'd been pushing her away, but she'd spoiled his scheme by refusing to go peacefully.

"I'm confused, Sarah," he ultimately confessed. "About you. About us."

"So am I," she agreed, "but I won't deny our connection, and I won't let you deny it, either. This is too vital to me." She laid her hand on his shoulder. "I ask you again: Would you like me to return later?"

"I believe I would."

Her relief was so immense that her knees sagged, and she yearned to confide so much more—to tell him how meaningful the interlude had been, how she'd been transformed—but words failed her.

She turned and walked to the door that connected their rooms, and she stepped through but, unable to resist, she stole a peek at him, grimly desperate for a final glimpse.

Bathed in the fading light, he was handsome, dynamic, dissolute. His solitude and isolation called out to her, swayed her, and beseeched her for recognition, for help, and a sustenance that she longed to confer.

The sensations he invoked—to love, to cherish, to esteem—were so poignant that she couldn't remain. He was so alone and apart, and she required seclusion and distance to mentally prepare for their next encounter.

Impelling herself away from the perilous, heartrending sight of him, she hastened into her dressing room and shut the door.

Chapter Thirteen

Michael tiptoed down the hall. The hour was late, and he was glad his room was at the rear of the house where he could come and go without meeting any guests. He passed Sarah's chamber, then proceeded to his own. When he reached it, he slipped the key into the lock, then paused.

Would she be waiting?

At the same juncture, he hoped she was and wasn't.

Deliberately, he'd absented himself from the premises, avoiding the lure of the Viewing Room and any of the wild schemes Pamela might have hatched for the evening. Most of all, he'd made an adamant decision to insulate himself from Sarah and the provocation she rendered.

The afternoon he'd passed with her had been a slice of heaven. When they'd finished, and she'd fallen asleep in his arms, he'd felt much as he might had an angel flown down for a frolic.

The fight with Brigham had unleashed an emotional torrent he'd not endured in ages. After, he'd been weary and battered, and feeling every one of his advanced twenty-eight years. He'd craved solace and comfort as he'd never craved anything before, which was saying a great deal.

Over the nearly three decades of his life, he'd hungered mightily, seeking respect and admiration from acquaintances, love and affection from his family. The worst times had been as a child, when his mother had moved them to France. Although he would never concede as much to another soul, he'd pined away seemingly forever, expecting that his father would travel to Paris and fetch them home.

Whenever a knock had sounded on the door of their small flat, his heart had skipped a beat, certain that it was the day Edward had finally arrived. But it had never happened and, as he'd grown, his father's abandonment had lain like a heavy yoke, a burden he'd never quite been able to cast off. On occasion, the pain of that early loss still wreaked damage as though the wound was recently inflicted. The old injury propelled him to indecent acts, as evidenced by how he'd thrashed Brigham to a pulp and left him in a gory heap in Pamela's stableyard.

Lest she hear the sordid tale from another, he'd immediately visited her to confess his transgression, and he'd stoically persevered through the tongue-lashing she'd meted out, knowing she was entitled to her fury. Her censure had chafed and nettled, but some of the sting from her harsh comments was deflected by the hot bath she'd instantly sent.

As he'd chased the servants away, then lowered himself into the steaming cauldron, he couldn't remember when he'd been so isolated or detached. His personality and upbringing being what they were, he'd always considered himself a solitary man, yet as he'd relaxed in the tub, eager for some bit of mortal contact, he'd gradually fixated on Sarah.

He'd wanted succor and consolation, and no anonymous stranger would have sufficed; he'd yearned for Sarah—with her soft hands and soothing words. Sarah cared for him as no one else did, and he'd needed her ambrosial regard as he'd needed food or water.

When she'd brazenly joined him, when she'd kissed away his hurts, he'd quit fighting his impulses, determined to have her in the only way that counted. He'd behaved crudely—more so than usual—and he shouldn't have forced her into their liaison, but he'd forged ahead anyway. For reasons that had nothing to do with his birth status, he'd regularly been called a bastard and, with his treatment of her, he'd once again proved how utterly ruthless he could be.

Despicably, he'd used her, coercing her to perform acts he wouldn't have required of a whore, and she'd amiably and favorably acquiesced to every sordid exploit he'd proposed. Yet, he wasn't sorry. Their tryst had been stupendous, blissful, amazing.

After all of his erotic play, beginning when he'd been no more than a child in a man's body, he'd never so much as dozed off with a woman. Even the two short occasions when he'd kept mistresses, he'd never succumbed. There was something about *sleeping* that disturbed him with its intimacy.

Sexual congress was his only objective for visiting a lover's bed, because any other goal would likely send a faulty message as to his intentions. He dallied, he fucked, he left. Any female silly enough to demand more never saw him again. While slumbering was an innocent occupation, habit hampered him from lessening his guard sufficiently to where he was comfortable in such an awkward position.

Yet, he'd snuggled next to Sarah with nary a thought to the consequences, and he'd been magnificently surprised at how it had refreshed him to cuddle with her. Just by having her near, he'd felt connected, less separate, so he'd actually rested, but once he'd calmed adequately, prudence had prevailed, and he'd slipped out of bed, putting distance between them.

For over two hours, he'd studied her, marveling at how deeply she reposed. Fool that she was, her level of trust was out of proportion to what it should have been, given their odd acquaintance. Her body and spirit were at peace with the notion that nothing vile would befall her while he was there to watch over her.

And watch he had. She'd looked pretty, young, innocent. He couldn't take his eyes off her, and the manner in which she'd bewitched him filled him with unease. What was his aim, trifling with a virginal woman of the Quality? Scarborough's sister, no less! He didn't like her kind, or what she represented, so his motives were definitely suspect. Perhaps he and his brother, James, had more in common than he cared to acknowledge!

James had been enthralled by the members of the *ton*,

inflicting himself into their domain and vying for their undivided attention—most of it never good—at every possible turn. Michael had never shared James's fascination, convinced that he was the wiser for not being seduced by their wretched world, but apparently he'd only been deluding himself.

Sarah was a striking example of how he'd misjudged his own disinterest. At a time when his defenses were depleted, she'd developed into an obsession, and he couldn't prevent himself from chasing after her. He shouldn't even speak with her, let alone instigate a libidinous association. What benefit could he attain? Why did he persist?

Their romance would last no longer than the handful of days he'd offered her before he'd stepped out of his bath. He had numerous personal flaws; he'd never fall in love with her, never ask her to marry, never strive toward any sort of continuing affiliation. While she was convenient and available, he'd enjoy her company, then he'd leave Pamela's decadent house and travel to another country party, then another, until he finally became so bored that he retired to London.

Sarah Compton would never cross his mind again.

So why this fascination? Why this unrelenting urgency to be with her?

As the minutes had ticked agonizingly by, a horrid concept had wormed itself into his musings: Was this how his father had started out with his mother? Had Edward too suffered these unyielding, unmerciful longings that didn't abate or wane? Had he been powerless to resist Angela's allure?

Rumors had constantly abounded that Edward Stevens's relationship with Angela hadn't been a juvenile indiscretion, but an intense *affaire d'amour*. Considering how Edward had come panting after Angela and wed her shortly after his lawful, aristocratic wife had died, Michael couldn't discount the stories that had been bandied about town.

As a youth, Edward had been totally captivated by Angela, incapable of, or unwilling to, avoid the attraction she generated—just as Michael, himself, was currently unable to avert the disaster he was courting by pursuing Sarah. Perhaps he was more like his father than he dared to admit!

The opinion was unpleasant and irksome, and had been disturbing him when she'd awakened from her nap, appearing lush and well loved. He'd tried to be brusque, to push her away, but she was eminently proficient at getting under his skin and poking at his vulnerabilities. She infuriated and intrigued; he wanted her gone, he wanted her to stay.

With his ruminations in this bizarre jumble, he entered his room. Their adjoining door was ajar, and a lamp burned on the dresser. The flame was nearly expired, composing eerie shadows on the wall.

Suffering a twinge of both relief and dismay, he promptly noted that she'd fallen asleep on his bed. His initial inclination was to rush over, to ease down and shower her with kisses, but his ingrained sense of self-preservation kicked in. He locked his own door, then went to her bedchamber and checked hers, as well, assuring himself that they'd have no uninvited callers. Then, he returned to her and approached the bed.

For their prurient encounter, she'd worn a lightweight summer nightgown of pristine white with shortened sleeves and embroidered flowers around the scooped neckline. A pink ribbon tied at the front, and the luxurious fabric fell in soft folds against her torso, delineating each delicious curve and valley. Her hair was down and brushed out, and it lay in scattered disarray, a crimson stain against the bedcoverings. Her cheeks were rosy-red, her lips pouted, and her eyes fluttering with the dream she was having.

Enticing and devastating, she caused his blood to boil through his veins. His fingers tingled, his cock throbbed viciously, nearly doubling him over as his vivid imagination kicked in, painting scenes of what he would procure from her, how he would allay her fears, how he would instruct and satisfy her, while lustily and improperly fulfilling his every deviant fantasy. Yet he hardly cared. She'd begged for the chance to attend him again, and she was a grown woman who knew her own proclivities. Whatever transpired was no more than she'd sought.

Silently observing her, his concentration never straying from her captivating anatomy, he disrobed. Briefly, he pondered prolonging the prelude by obliging her to undress him, but he hastily decided against it. There would be no delay. He was aroused and prepared for the impending hours of ecstasy. His cock jutted out, proud and defiant, and he wrapped a fist around the heavy flesh.

Oh, how he wished he could spill himself in her mouth! Or between her legs! How tight that virginal cleft would be! How welcome the alleviation!

But she wasn't ready for such an event, and neither was he. Though his moral constitution was at its lowest level, he wasn't cad enough to terminate her maidenhood. Despite his extensive, incautious prior sensual amusement, he'd never stooped to stealing a woman's virtue, so he wasn't about to start. Still, the idea was so bloody tempting. *She* was so bloody tempting. How could he decline such inducement? Especially when her copious charms were freely and graciously extended.

Not wanting to frighten her, he carefully slipped onto the mattress and stretched out. She was on her side, so he scooted over and rolled her to her back, pinning her by resting an arm over her chest and a leg over her thigh.

"Sarah . . ." he murmured softly, never tiring of the opportunity to speak her name. He bestowed a chaste kiss that confused her. The reverie in which she'd been ensnared abruptly ended, and she awoke.

"Michael . . . ?"

Momentarily disoriented, she gazed up at him, genuine delight spreading through her, and he resolved that no matter what occurred between them, no matter how inappropriate his conduct, or how indecorous his actions, his folly was worth it to see her smiling at him with such unfeigned devotion. The empty spot in the center of his chest, where his heart used to beat, stirred and ached as though jolted into operation after a lengthy respite.

"Hello." An imbecilic grin crept across his own face.

"I was sleeping so hard." Mussed but adorable, she appeared confounded and abashed to have been caught unawares.

"Yes, you were."

"I tried to wait up for you."

How wonderful that she had! "I'm glad."

"Is it very late?"

"Aye."

She sifted her fingers through his hair, then lovingly placed her palm against his beard-stubbled cheek, and the move was so familiar and dear that his breath hitched in his lungs.

Why had he let his personal demons impel him out into the night? Why had he spent so much time wandering and carousing? He could have been sequestered with her and basking in her tender disposition. Kicking himself, cursing himself for his asinine tendencies, he would stop spurning the relief he garnered in her presence. For as long as they remained in Bedford, he would overindulge in her delectable refuge.

Suddenly, reality was seeping in, and her brow furrowed with concern. "Where have you been?"

Without a doubt, his whereabouts were none of her business, and she had no right to question him as to his activities. In the past, any prying female would have received an austere warning, but instead, he bit down on his sharp retort.

Sarah Compton provoked him in new and different ways, and he had to grow accustomed to their peculiar style of association. He liked that she cared enough to inquire, to needle, and he yearned to have her understand the issues that were motivating him, and the devils that were nipping at his heels.

Gad, but if she kept staring at him as she was, there'd be no stifling his negligent tongue. He'd babble away, spilling his sorrows and woes on the bed like a bottle of spilt ink.

"I was out walking," he professed honestly, "and I went clear to the village, thinking to have an ale, then I stayed for a game of cards."

"But you knew I'd be here."

From another, the statement might have sounded like an accusation, but from her, there was only bafflement.

How long had it been since a woman had missed him or prayed that he would hurry home?

"I was puzzled," he shocked himself by disclosing. "After this afternoon."

"So you concluded it was best to avoid me?" Even her censure was gently tossed.

"I wasn't going to return, at all."

"Why?" she reproached kindly.

"I like having you here." The revelation stunned him, even as he privately chastised himself for expressing the sentimental drivel.

"What a sweet comment."

Stupidity! Why encourage the woman's flights of fancy? The manner in which she was regarding him—as though he was smart, benevolent, and extraordinary—terrified him. He appreciated how women viewed carnal dealings, how they processed intercourse. They read *love* into it where naught but lust existed.

Lest he create a mire from which they couldn't extricate themselves, he had to exercise circumspection. Despite how attracted he was to her physically, he had no intention of allowing any sort of idiotic emotion for Sarah to flourish.

"What we're doing . . ." He started prudently, not anxious to hurt her with the truth. "It's not right."

She set a finger to his lips, quelling any further voicing of regret. "Whatever ensues between us could never be wrong. And I won't listen to your saying so. This is a special time we've grabbed for ourselves. Let's just be content with what *is*."

Nodding, he accepted the sagacity of her statement, for

wasn't that exactly what he'd deduced, as well? He planned to seize the moment.

"May I make love to you again?" He kissed the tips of her fingers.

"That depends." She moved her hand down his neck, to his chest, where she rubbed in slow circles. "Have you been with another woman since we separated this afternoon?"

"No," he was relieved to respond. He hadn't even *spoken* to a female since then.

"You haven't been to the secret room?"

"No," he repeated.

"Because I have to admit, I was frantic that you might have." She blushed a flattering shade of pink. "When you weren't here, I looked through the peephole, but someone had covered it so I can't see inside."

"I'm the culprit. I didn't like that you've been observing what goes on."

"I'm a grown woman," she felt compelled to indicate.

"Yes, you are," he acceded, "but that doesn't mean you should be exposed to the lewdness in this house."

"The only *lewdness* I witnessed was your shenanigans."

"And I'm exceedingly embarrassed by that fact."

"Really?"

"Aye."

Startling him, she chuckled. "So . . . you've—once again—appointed yourself as the guardian of my virtue?"

"I suppose," he grumbled.

His rigid phallus nudged against her thigh, his naked legs tangled with hers, and the ludicrousness of their situation shook them. They laughed together, then it died away to a companionable silence.

"When you didn't return," she stated, "I was so worried."

"You needn't have fretted." But oh, how splendid to discover that she had! He was inordinately pleased.

"I wasn't sure how to find you and, after last night, I was afraid to search."

"Good," he remarked. "Perhaps I've finally talked some sense into that thick head of yours."

"Perhaps," she agreed, and the quiet played out, once more. Almost shyly, she announced, "I was terrified that you were visiting a lover."

"Is it so important to you that I not?"

"Extremely so."

The implication flustered him. She was pleading with him for a pledge of fidelity! Her request was so far-fetched that he could scarcely grasp it. Monogamy connoted fealty, a promise he could never make because he could never begin to keep it.

He didn't believe in the ridiculous kinds of everlasting Grand Passion espoused by the poets. Even if he was stupid enough to become romantically entrapped, he'd never let it happen over such a fine, upstanding woman as Sarah, because he could never be the man she supposed him to be, and if they wound up together, she'd suffer eternal disappointment.

Reality was a bitter tonic to swallow, and he didn't intend that she ever detect how divergent her illusions were from the actualities of his circumstances.

Clearly, she'd developed erroneous assumptions about the type of person he was. Probably, she'd credited him with assorted asinine attributes that were merely fantasy, but he'd revel in her daydreams. Just this once, he would pretend to be whatever she wanted him to be.

She was hunting for a hero, and he didn't aim to disavow her of her perceptions. He had no desire to inform her that he thought faithfulness impossible, loyalty absurd, and long-term commitment nonsense. He couldn't fuck and love conjointly, and he never misconstrued the two. Sex was a method of assuaging his erect cock, and he fornicated in order to achieve mitigation for his masculine drives, but she didn't need to be apprised of his convictions.

Her thinking that he was a better man, a different man, was positively enchanting. What could it hurt to humor her? If it bothered her that he might carry on with his licentious distraction in the Viewing Room, it was simple to placate her. Appeasement justified the consolation it brought.

"I won't go again." Not while she was in residence anyway, but he figured he wouldn't advise her of all his awful truths. A few lies were permissible between lovers, weren't they?

"It would break my heart if you did."

When had anyone ever cared about him so much, admired him so much? They were barely acquainted, yet she was so assured that virtuous character lurked deep within him.

That he could be the man she visualized! Instead, to his shame and consternation, he was without scruple or restraint, beyond redemption, a ne'er-do-well who used women for his own despicable purposes. Didn't she see? Didn't she recognize him for who and what he was?

The agony of confronting his faults, of having them so distinctly displayed, was too excruciating. She dredged up his imperfections and failings without even mentioning them. Just by lingering in her presence, he found himself questioning his entire mode of living, focusing on his individual defects as though they could be corrected or transformed.

He didn't have the patience for perpetual self-assessment. His pride couldn't take the immutable recrimination and evaluation, yet since he'd met her, he'd been besieged by old memories, forgotten grief, foibles and fiascoes, and he wasn't going to waste any effort contemplating the varied paths he might have chosen. This quagmire of indecision and perplexity in which he was enmeshed was pointless, and he had to shift them back to a realm he comprehended.

Hoping to accomplish only one thing—that being carnal pleasure—he sought out women to grace his bed. A gifted, skilled lover, he could dally to maximum effect, and women flocked to copulate with him because of his seductive abilities. Sarah was the same as all the others. She'd chased after him, seeking an erotic relationship that she presumed—with misguided design—would turn emotional, but she was too inexperienced to realize the improbability.

By debauching her, once again, he could bring their rendezvous back to safer ground, to where he would be honed in on the only important goal: satiation. If he was lucky, perhaps he'd be so involved in his quest that he'd manage to slake his infernal preoccupation with her before it drove him mad.

Innocently, he brushed against her lips, not tarrying as he'd love to do, but refraining as was most wise. Kissing her was dangerous. Better, saner, to employ his mouth in more fruitful, innocuous endeavors.

He declared, "I thought about you all evening."

"And I, you."

"Did you enjoy our afternoon encounter?"

"Every second of it." She winked wickedly. "I came back for more, didn't I?"

"So you did."

Feeling grand, he laughed and flipped them so that she was on top. Spreading her thighs, he adjusted her till her tantalizing pussy was directly over his cock, then he braced his hands on her hips and painstakingly flexed along her cleft.

"I've been so hard for you ever since we parted." He nodded toward her body. "Remove your nightgown. Show me what you learned today."

Chapter Fourteen

Sarah glared at him, dismayed by his cool command. In her naïveté, she'd fantasized that they'd forged a new understanding and would now come together with kisses and professions of devotion.

One corner of her mouth twitched with a smile, and she bit it back. How imbecilic of her, assuming that a simple afternoon romp would have altered their relationship. He wasn't the sort prone to poetic prose or flowery welcome. He was who he was. A complex man, he'd never cuddle or coo, but then, his rough edges and belligerent attitude were what attracted her so desperately.

As usual, he was being crude and demanding, but surprisingly, she realized that she could easily tolerate his high-handed manner. While she might have bristled had they been elsewhere, in this secluded situation, poised on the brink of sexual ecstasy, she was thrilled by how he ordered her about.

Regularly, he sought out women who were predisposed to decadency. By his own admission, he had strong manly drives that demanded routine alleviation. Though he'd favored her for his partner, he hadn't ascribed any specific significance to the selection, but she wasn't about to consider his lack of deference an indication of defeat. He'd returned—after incessantly debating as to whether he should—which she would take as a sign of progress.

She harbored no illusions about why he hadn't been overly enthused about dallying with her, once again. No doubt, due to her inexperience, she'd failed to fully satisfy him. Yes, he'd spilled his seed, but as far as she could discern, she'd had very little to do with it. She'd simply been present and available. He'd toyed with her, and his ardor had spiked, but he might have engaged in the behavior with anyone, be it she or another. Given his wanton habits, any naked female would have sent him over that climactic precipice.

Yet despite his professed confusion, he'd come back to her. He'd kindly conceded that he'd enjoyed their interaction, but she was acutely aware that their tryst had been limited in quantity and quality—a circumstance she proposed to rectify as soon as she was able.

She was eager to please him in every fashion, for him to view their assignations as magical and enchanted, but perhaps she was expecting too much. For the time being, she needed to be glad that he'd arrived, when she'd been so worried that he wouldn't.

After leaving his room earlier, she'd scarcely made it through the interminable evening of socializing without dissembling. When she'd pleaded fatigue and sped up the stairs, she'd burst into his room, confident that he'd be waiting, as impatient as she for what lay ahead. Initially, the fact that he hadn't been pining away had been an incredible disappointment, but after she'd shrugged off her fit of pique, she'd stood in the middle of his bedchamber and chuckled aloud.

Of course, Michael Stevens would have better things to do! What had she been thinking! She'd calmed herself, then agonizingly paced. Each creak of the old house, every crack of the smoldering logs in the grate, the infrequent footstep in the hall, had set her heart to racing.

As the hour had grown late, and he still hadn't appeared, her self-assurance had flown out the window. She'd envisioned the places he might have gone and what he might be doing. When she'd braved a glance at the peephole, and discovered it shuttered, she'd sagged with defeat, certain he was on the other side of the wall with an anonymous lover. All her scheming and planning had been for naught!

Disheartened, but incapable of remaining in her lonely, solitary bed, she'd proceeded to his chamber and lain on his pillow, instantly pacified by his smell. Drifting between despair and sleep, she'd stayed, resolved to hash it out. He could protest and complain and deny, but they shared a destiny, and he belonged with her—at least for the next few days.

After that, what might transpire was anybody's guess, but she'd always been an optimist. Any marvelous occurrence was conceivable.

Physical intimacy would bring them closer than words ever could, so she reached for her nightrail, yanked it up and over, and pitched it on the mattress. She straddled his lap, naked but for a pair of the exotic French underdrawers that amused him. His eyes locked on her bare chest, and her nipples responded, the tips constricting.

"Your body is so fabulous."

Irreverently, he pinched one of the elongated nubs between thumb and finger. The move had her squirming as did the comment, and her cheeks flushed She wasn't accustomed to compliments, especially such indiscreet ones. Spurring her hips, he tipped her forward, and her hands steadied on either side of his head, her nipples dangling over his enthusiastic mouth.

"I'm going to make love to your breasts."

"Yes . . ." she gasped on a rush of air as he sucked at the enlarged crest. "Whatever you want."

"I'll keep at it until you can't stand any more. Until you're begging me to stop."

"No, never. I'll never ask you to stop."

"Until you're crying out my name."

Now that was a definite possibility!

Pinning her to him, he worked atrociously, and he suckled till she was raw and distended, then he detached and shifted to the other, rummaging across her bosom like a nursing babe. He located the delectable morsel, taking it with his searching, zealous lips.

Below, his cock was rudely insinuated between her legs, and his hands descended to her bottom, squeezing and manipulating the rounded globes, and utilizing them as leverage to stroke his aroused member. His hot flesh tantalized her silky undergarment, pushing it into the heated cleft, causing her body to weep.

His hands were at her thighs, spreading her so that her swollen mound was titillated by his slightest movement. Exhaustively, his cock massaged her, every delicious inch, so that when he fumbled with the tie on her drawers, when he glided inside with those resourceful fingers, her entire being was adjusted for the pleasure she now fathomed to be winging in her direction.

With a few flicks of his devious thumb, he led her to the yawning crevasse and shoved her over. Cognizant of the pending tumult, she freely leapt into the void, the jubilant anguish staggering. He swallowed her cry of delight, kissing her thoroughly to consume some of her rapture as she soared to the heavens then floated back to earth.

As he'd invariably seemed reluctant to kiss her, she'd thought he would end it abruptly, but for once, he didn't. He treasured and sampled, and she relished the attention he'd suddenly decided to lavish on her. This was *kissing* as she'd always visualized it, at its most magnificent and exciting. Their breath mingled, their hearts beat in unison, his very essence flowed through her. The embrace went on and on, and she savored the display, letting him feast for as long as he was inclined.

Gradually, the interlude spiraled to a conclusion, and their lips separated. He gazed at her with such an intense, dangerous expression that she was completely unnerved.

Struggling for levity, she smiled and queried, "How do you do that to me so easily?"

"I take it milady was . . . *satisfied*?"

"Yes, you bounder," she grumbled. "Don't look so damned pleased."

Unrepentant and overconfident, he was positively lethal to someone of her limited ability, and she heartily wished she'd steeled herself against his onslaught. A mere woman could never successfully contend with such potency.

He chuckled, then stole another stormy kiss. "I adore

how I make you come," he said impudently. "You call out for me . . . right at the end."

"I can't abide such arrogance in a man!"

"Get used to it, love."

Once again, he'd tossed out the endearment as if it was of no import. Handsome as the devil himself, his sapphire eyes blazed with desire, an abominably alluring dimple creased his cheek, and she pondered how she'd let her poor heart get into this fix. After she left for home, she would never be the same.

"You are horrid. I don't know why I permit you to abuse me."

"Because I'm irresistible?"

"Too true," she retorted. "More's the pity."

"Oh, Sarah . . ."—he chuckled again—"you are so good for me."

"Am I?"

"Absolutely."

The air was charged as before a lightning storm, full of promise and foreboding. Powerful emotions roiled through her, and she was unable to ferret out a suitable rejoinder.

"I am so hard for you," he ultimately said.

He pressed his phallus against her, and it dawned on her that whenever their verbal repartee became too intimate, he reverted to talk of the sexual. She didn't mind, though, because she wielded the most authority over him when they were naked. The more he lusted, the greater her chances to lure him toward the bond she hoped would eventually develop.

She partook of a slow flex of her own. "I like feeling you close, but it's not enough."

"No."

"Why?"

"The normal conclusion for your orgasm would be for me to penetrate you." He cupped her, fondling the silk crotch of her pantalets, then a finger slid underneath the hem, easing into her animated cleft. Sounding pained, he huskily noted, "You're so tight."

"Will you . . . ?" She didn't possess the necessary vocabulary to interrogate him as to whether he would make love to her there. Now that he'd explained her emptiness, she recognized that her body was anxious to be relieved of its virginal condition.

"Not today. Maybe not ever," he asserted. "I don't know . . ." Appearing baffled and bewildered by his reticence, he let his voice trail off as he rolled her onto her back. "I'm going to put my mouth on you."

"What?" He caressed her moist pantalets, leaving no doubt as to his purpose, and her eyes widened in shock.

"When I come, I want to have the taste of your sex on my tongue."

"You're not serious."

"Oh, but I am."

Before she could prevent it, he was tugging her drawers down her thighs, and he had them over her toes and on the floor. He dropped down and centered himself, geared to advance, and she squirmed, flustered by his bizarre request.

"Michael!"

"When you say my name like that, you sound like an expensive whore."

The odd compliment grated; she didn't care for the coarse comparison, at all. "Whatever you're up to . . . I'm not ready for . . . for . . ."

The tip of his tongue dipped into her navel, and she writhed with trepidation, and he halted. He wrenched his torrid gaze up her torso, his blatant assessment calculated to remind her of her previous acquiescence, of how promptly she'd succumbed, of how overwhelmed she'd been.

"You trust me, don't you?" he asked.

"No, I don't!" She didn't trust him any further than she could throw him.

He had the audacity to laugh at her candor, then he continued with his ministrations. Lower, past her navel, to her feminine hair. He nuzzled his cheek in it, rubbed his nose in it, rooting and sniffing as though implanting her scent in his consciousness.

"Michael . . ." she tried again, "this is too personal."

"I told you"—he lifted up from his precarious perch—"that nothing is forbidden. *Nothing,* Sarah."

"But I had no idea you'd contrive something so . . . so . . ."

"Depraved? Outlandish? Improper?"

"Precisely."

He merely shrugged. "Having you in this manner will make me happy. Isn't that why you're here?"

As he was unerringly correct, protest seemed futile.

Somehow, despite her objection, he'd managed to inflict himself betwixt her legs, and he settled her thighs over his shoulders. When he spread the mysterious folds, she arched up, seeking escape, but he was holding her down, and she couldn't get free.

"Relax," he murmured soothingly. "Close your eyes and just feel."

"I don't like it."

"You will," he insisted, cheeky knave that he was.

Baldly, he scrutinized every aspect of her feminine opening. Then . . . his tongue. There and meddling and invasive, and she flung an arm over her face, hiding, longing to disappear. She felt humiliated, ravished, yet strangely intrigued by his thrust and parry.

He kissed her leisurely as he had her mouth, piercing her in an unremitting rhythm, and the unyielding seduction began to take its toll. Her thighs parted further, offering him more space in which to perform his devious, tricky assault. Try as she might not to enjoy the maneuver, she couldn't resist being drawn in. Her traitorous body reacted until she was straining against him—not in an attempt to get away, but in another skirmish toward carnal release.

"No, I can't," she wailed, when she detected where he was leading her. "It's too soon."

"It's never too soon. Do it again. Just for me."

The invidious rogue! He acted as if she was doing *him* a courtesy by finding sensual gratification.

His fingers were at her breasts, furiously kneading her ravaged nipples, as his tongue focused on the sensitive protuberance that he finessed with such devastating effect. With minimal effort, he—once again—hurled her over the ledge of desire.

As the stimulation abated, he was towering above her, imperious cock in hand, and he guided the ample crown across her cleft. "Can you imagine how it would be if I entered you now? I would ride you so hard."

For the longest time, he didn't move, poised on the brink of a terrible impasse, and she bit against her lip, incited, prepared for the next, but it never ensued.

Sweat pooled on his brow, and he meticulously fondled her, her bodily moisture wetting the tip, then ever so slightly, he inserted himself. Vividly foreseeing what could transpire, he stared at the spot where they were barely connected. She looked down, too, agitated and aching, contemplating that his presence seemed so appropriate.

Her hips clenched, and he jumped back as though burned, but he'd been forced beyond his limits of restraint, and he demanded immediate satiation. He clutched her to his chest and stroked his cock against her, twice, thrice, then he spewed himself on her stomach and leg, the fiery liquid blanketing her, its pungent aroma filling the air.

"Oh, Sarah . . ."

Moaning, he collapsed on her, and he held himself motionless as his breathing and pulse slowed to tractable levels. Finished, he strove to slip away, but she wouldn't let him, snuggling him to her bosom, his beautiful face nestled between her breasts.

The act of mating created such a unique serenity, and she wanted to sustain the moment, but unfortunately, the lull provided plenty of opportunity for reflection about subjects best forgotten—like a home and family of her own. She'd perpetually insisted she didn't require either, but now, with the smell of his sex in the air, and the sweet

sound of her name reverberating off the walls, it was per-
plexing to remember why she'd shunned her chances for
such contentment.

How had it resulted that she was twenty-five and so
alone? Why had she settled for a pittance? She always believed her existence was eventful and consequential, and it
had never occurred to her that she was lonely, or that she
would like to live happily ever after with the man of her
dreams—that man having a suspicious resemblance to Michael Stevens.

Shutting out reality, she wished for all the things that
could never be, but concluded that she wanted them anyway. What was the harm?

Then, she kissed the top of his head, and he stretched
and groaned languidly.

"Are you married, Michael?" The interrogatory popped
out before she could snatch it back.

"No, why?" He peeked up at her. "Are you worried
about my character?"

"I'm unequivocally *worried* about your character, you
cad," she remarked, "but not because you might be cheating
on your wife. You have many more severe flaws."

"You're right about that."

"I'm just relieved that marital infidelity is not among
them." She said it lightly and, from the way he grinned,
he'd taken it as a jest, but she sincerely meant it.

"I was just curious; I know nothing about you." And in
the pause that followed, the rat didn't supply any information, though she'd presented the perfect excuse. She
sighed. "Do you ever think about getting married?"

Her heart skipped several frantic beats. Where had that
come from? If only the mattress would swallow her up so
she could vanish! What a ninny he must deem her to be!
A few tumbles in his bed, a few lessons in carnality, and
she was babbling about matrimony! After she'd waxed on
for days prior, feigning sophistication in affairs beyond her
ken and supplicating for a meaningless fling!

"No, I never do," he answered more gently than she

deserved. He kissed the underside of her breast, then he balanced himself on an elbow. His seed was drying, and he toweled it away with her nightgown. "Is that what you're hoping might happen between us?"

There was no censure or rebuke in his tone, so perhaps if she was prudent, she could worm herself out of this debacle before she made an even bigger fool of herself. "I'm just beginning to grasp that I missed much by not marrying."

"It's only natural. Sex stirs many new and strange emotions. Particularly in a woman."

"But not in a man?"

"No. Women confuse sex with love, when they really have nothing to do with one another. For a man, fornication is simply a physical discharge."

"Is that how you see it?"

"Yes." The truth hurt her, and he added, "I'm sorry to be so blunt."

"That explains why a man can have different lovers."

"Yes."

"Why a man can purportedly love his wife, but keep a mistress."

"Exactly."

"Why you can go to the hidden room and cavort with women you don't know."

He stirred uncomfortably. "Aye."

She'd totally positioned herself to weather the frank statements, staring into his blue eyes and showing as little interest as he in the laborious topic. "Was this just *physical discharge* for you?"

"It was a good deal more," he puzzled her by acceding, "but that doesn't mean we'll wed when we're through." He ran a finger across her cheekbone, her chin, her lips. "Be careful where you allow your heart to wander," he declared tenderly but firmly. "Guard it well, for I will assuredly break it if you lose it to me."

"As if I would!" she commented dryly, nudging him in the ribs. "I'd like to think I have better sense."

"I would be a very bad mistake."

"You don't have to remind me."

She was lying horridly, but he had the decency to pretend that he didn't know it, and when she held out her arms, she was immensely gratified that he burrowed himself into them without hesitation. They lay together, his leg draped over her thigh, his wrist on her waist, and he scrutinized her as if committing her to memory.

"Why have you never married?" he queried, and his examination was as startling and as peculiar as when she'd posed hers.

How wonderful that he would inquire! Schooling her features, she affected a bored demeanor, even though she was dying to confess so much.

"I always supposed I would. I even had a Season in London."

"Really?"

"When I was seventeen, but it was quite terrible."

"Why?"

"Let's just be kind and say that, back then, I wasn't a beauty."

"I find that very difficult to believe."

The compliment was as welcome as it was astonishing. As he was not given to flattery, especially over something as nebulous as a woman's comeliness, she grabbed onto his words as though they were a merciful benediction. He kissed the tip of her nose, but the soft touch dipped down to her very core where so much of her past heartbreak lingered. The sentiment sank far inside, comforting her, and she yearned for his sympathy and approval for the woman into which she'd matured. The old torments were pieces of the whole.

"Back then," she offered, "I was all gangly limbs and red hair, and I was so unprepared for what London would be like. They ate me alive."

"Your peers can be a vicious lot," he concurred wholeheartedly.

"Yes, they can." God, but she loved him for agreeing!

"And my father was pressuring me to choose one of the boys, but they were all so unacceptable. I couldn't decide."

"You wouldn't let him pick for you?"

"No!"

"So you refused them all?" The twinkle in his eye was genuine. "You defied your father?"

"I can be extremely stubborn."

"I've noticed that about you."

She could have lain there forever, hugging, and laughing and trading jibes, and she was struck anew by how much she'd lost out on by denying herself this closeness with a man, just as she appreciated that this was the sole occasion she'd ever have to endure such bliss.

Michael Stevens was a unique individual, and after this interval was terminated, she'd never experience anything similar. This singular, rare encounter would have to take her through her intermediate years and further, the constant memories of their abbreviated liaison stark and distinct.

Sadness engulfed her at the conviction that she'd never again sustain this quiet joy, and she shoved it away. She refused to be unhappy! Not while she was here with him like this. There would be many, many days down the road when she could bemoan her fate and lament over what might have been. For now, she would be content with what *was*.

"And what about you?" She was desperate to learn more and, as she'd formerly deduced, gleaning tidbits from him was like pulling teeth. "Divulge something embarrassingly scandalous that will leave me aghast."

"You've uncovered all my worst secrets."

"Then, what about something personal?" She wouldn't let him avoid a few meaningful disclosures. "How do you earn your income?"

"I own a gentlemen's club with my brother, James."

A straight answer! Encouraged, she fired off a second round. "Where?"

"In London."

"You live in the city?"

"Yes. In the theater district."

"With your mother and brother?"

"I'm not sure."

"How can you not be *sure*?"

"With their recent marriages, I don't know the arrangements now."

"You haven't been back since their weddings?"

"No."

For once, his cool detachment was markedly absent, and she trod cautiously, aware that these were sore spots. "Who is your family?"

"My mother is Angela Ford. She's quite a renowned actress."

"Really?" Amazed, she sat up.

If she'd been advised to guess his antecedents, she'd have said he was a third or fourth son of a wealthy nobleman, the bane of his family's existence, the black sheep. But the son of an actress! She'd never been acquainted with anyone quite so disreputable. "How fascinating. I saw her once on the stage when I was in town. She's legendary."

"She is at that."

Sarah recalled the dynamic woman. She'd exuded a charisma that even Sarah, with her rural underpinnings, couldn't fail to note. That the notorious celebrity had birthed Michael didn't surprise her in the least.

"Who is your father?"

He gaped. Then . . . he laughed. Loudly. At her, and what he plainly considered a ridiculous question. "Sarah, I could swear you were raised by wolves in the forest."

He was teasing her, and she was thrilled that he liked her enough to expend the energy. "Why do you say that?"

"I just never meet anyone who isn't exhaustively versed as to all my gory details."

"Well, I'm not."

"Obviously."

He chortled merrily, enjoying himself at her expense, but she didn't mind. As long as he resumed his accounting! "Are there many? *Gory details,* I mean."

"Enough to fill a book."

"Oh . . ." Just how did one reply to such a statement? No advantageous retort cropped up, and silence reigned, once again, as he regarded her with an honest affection, evidently cherishing the verbal banter as much as she.

Finally, he stated, "My father is Edward Stevens."

She had to ponder for a moment before she placed the appellation. "The Earl of Spencer?"

"Yes, but I don't claim him, and he doesn't claim me."

His admission was so quietly pronounced that she almost didn't hear it, and she studied him thoughtfully. This was a seeping wound, one that had never entirely healed. "You're not joking."

"No, I'm not."

He rotated to his back, hugging her so that she was stretched out along his side, relieved that they'd shifted positions, because she could look somewhere besides into those astute blue eyes while she weighed his background.

His paternal parentage explained a great deal: his regal bearing, his haughty attitude, his imperious demeanor. She'd convinced herself that he was an aristocrat's offspring, someone of her social standing, yet he was an illegitimate bastard. Even if by some quirk of the wildest fate he determined he loved her, they could never marry.

How was it that she could so acutely grieve the loss of something that had never been feasible to begin with?

Striving to appear blasé, she countered with, "Now that you've confessed the identity of your father, I understand why you are so incurably arrogant."

"I can't believe you didn't know."

"I probably did"—fragments of an ancient gossip rumbled but not enough for her to recall any fine points—"but I would never have connected him to you."

"Does it make a difference?"

She was now more attuned to his style, so she recognized that his was not an innocent query. It was a test, an analysis of the type of person she was, and he braced, anticipating repudiation, and she couldn't help speculating as to why he sought her affirmation.

Unless he cares more than he's willing to admit.

The idea came unbidden, loudly and clearly refusing to be muted, so she acknowledged it for the superb concept it was, even as she wished that everything could be contrary to the reality with which she was now confronted.

"No," she lied deliberately, "it doesn't signify. Not in the slightest."

The evident pleasure he received from her fabrication was impossible to calculate or describe, and she was delighted that she'd provided the petty deception. For what did her opinion matter anyway?

He'd warned her not to become attached and with valid reason! No outcome was probable save heartbreak, so there was no use indulging fantasies.

Still, as his lips found hers, as he moved over her and commenced to suckle at her breast, as his cock extended against her thigh, she couldn't recollect why this was so improper. She'd never felt so alive, so gay or fulfilled.

"I want you," he avowed.

"Again?" And she was overjoyed that he did.

"Yes." He was confounded by his burgeoning need for her. "Already. Always."

"I'm glad."

And as he escorted her on that extraordinary journey, down the path that he so expertly traveled, she didn't regret any of her choices. The *future,* such as it was, would arrive soon enough, and for now, she didn't intend to fret about what it would hold.

Chapter Fifteen

Sarah rushed into her bedchamber, hastily stripping off her gloves, ready to make a mad dash to Michael and the ecstasy that awaited. First though, cognizant of his extreme caution, she checked the lock on the door—twice—but her fingers trembled with such apprehension for the impending libidinous event that she could scarcely manipulate the mechanism.

He wouldn't appreciate any overzealousness on her part, so she struggled for calm. Walking to the mirror, taking several deep breaths, she evaluated herself, distractedly straightening her coiffure. Not that her hair needed rearranging, but the fussing gave her a few extra minutes to compose herself after flying up the stairs in such a dither.

Despite what was actually transpiring, Michael sternly contended that theirs was simply a meaningless fling, so she had to appear cool and serene, which was what he expected of her. Through his subtle demeanor and fatiguing persistence, he'd clearly indicated that they would interact in an indifferent fashion. They would fully vent their shared lust and rising ardor, but any recognition of emotional connection, or profound affinity, was forbidden and had to be discounted and ignored.

With scant difficulty, he evinced equanimity. Except in the depths of excessive passion, Michael exuded a reticence that was distinctly upsetting. When he was naked and lying in her arms, they were as close as two people could ever hope to be, but once he donned his clothes, he reverted to being reserved and aloof. Assuredly, he was a polite and interesting associate, but he'd erected a wall between them that he would not let her scale, despite how fervently she tried.

Unlike him, she had her problems with the enforced apathy, and she had to compel herself to remain remote and uninvolved, when all she really wanted was to confess how much she cherished their furtive, stolen interludes. She endured solely for those glorious moments when she strolled in and his admiring gaze fell upon her. There was nothing quite so marvelous as having his undivided attention, seeing him smile, or knowing he'd been impatient for her arrival.

With each passing hour, it was growing more arduous to feign distance. He'd filled her life to overflowing, had given it meaning and purpose: that being to wallow in his splendid presence.

Why, oh, why had she denied herself such pleasure for so long? And now that she'd experienced his special brand of revelry, how could she return to Yorkshire and persevere as though nothing had happened?

The woman who'd efficiently and exhaustively tended the estate for so many tiresome years had disappeared, replaced by a woman for whom only sex—with Michael Stevens—mattered. Where once she'd treasured her placid, unchanging rural existence, she now couldn't imagine herself in that monotonous, boring world. She'd expire in such a tedious environment!

As a plant needed air and water, so she needed Michael in order to flourish. The idea of suffering through a day—or a night—without touching him, talking to him, kissing or holding him, was a torture beyond contemplation, yet when they were together, she was supposed to act nonchalant, and she wasn't having much luck at maintaining the ruse.

Her anticipation of imminent bliss was all-consuming and meant that she couldn't socialize at the gathering. While she'd never been much for fraternization, when Michael was waiting for her, she couldn't tolerate the inane prattle, the innocuous topics, or the frivolous substance of the other guests.

Braving a meal or an entertainment was so distasteful

that she could hardly descend the stairs, yet she forced her-self to go, bowing to the necessity of putting in an appear-ance. She'd much rather stay sequestered and allow Michael to continue his proficient, thorough instruction in the carnal arts.

Just as Michael had predicted, she'd become enmeshed in the sordid dissipations he preferred, and she couldn't figure out how she'd avoided seduction until the ripe old age of twenty-five. Of course, she hadn't previously met Michael, either. Without a doubt, her attraction to him had melted some internal bastion of propriety, for she was now enthusiastic and willing to commit any lewd, indecent ex-ploit he suggested—the more ribald the better. Total sur-render—to him and the games he instigated—was her singular aim and goal.

In fact, she was wild for the debauchery to commence so that she could discover just how naughty he would ask her to be. How could she have guessed that underneath her proper, demure shell resided the soul of a complete wanton? All these years, her true proclivities had been so carefully hidden! What a joy—and a relief—to set them free!

With a final glance in the mirror, she adjudged that she was composed enough to head for his room. Fixing a pleas-ant smile on her face, she stubbornly endeavored to shield any untoward longing. There was no reason whatsoever to let him surmise that she was pining away, that she was already floundering as she fretted over how she'd carry on after they parted.

Since she was the one who'd insisted on an affair, and she'd quite verbally contended that she could participate with no strings attached, she wasn't about to admit a grave mistake in her reckoning: Detachment was impossible. He was too handsome, too thrilling, too dynamic, and there wasn't a woman in the kingdom who could avert a bur-geoning infatuation after spending so much uninterrupted time with him.

She was no exception. If anything, she was more sus-ceptible to his charm and wicked ways than another, and she incessantly pondered how she'd bear up once she left in two weeks, but she could never tell him so. They seemed to have adopted a secret pact not to mention the future; they dallied but neither spoke of, nor alluded to, that nebulous by-and-by when they would separate.

Their circumspection lent a recklessness to the assignations. The *dénouement* was drawing nigh much too quickly, so every encounter held a special semblance of finality. As though they were destined for the gallows come the morn, each rendezvous was more intense than the last, with both of them desperate to wring every speck of passion out of their communal experience.

This one, she was positive, would exceed the prior ones in excess, excitement, and satisfaction, and she would do everything in her power to ensure that the evening was merry and gay. When it ended, she wanted Michael to be ever so glad he'd passed his leisure hours with her rather than another.

Knocking softly, she opened the door without pausing for a response. They were so comfortable—like an old, married couple—that polite comportment was superfluous. She came and went, never hesitating to intrude on his individual quarters. Even if he wasn't about, she'd make herself at home, and those were the occasions she liked best. With his absence, she could snoop and pry among his belongings. Rifling through the wardrobe where he hung his shirts, or sifting through his tray of cuff links on the dresser, was enervatingly erotic.

And, of course, the dearest moments of all occurred when she fell asleep on his bed—a dreadful invasion of his privacy—and he arrived later, awakening her with kisses and more. The memory of those luscious appointments was too potent, so she steeled herself against their onslaught and walked in.

As usual, he was reclined in his chair by the window, a glowing cheroot dangling from his fingers. He lounged negligently, like a carefree prince or an Arabian sheik whose harem was about to fawn all over him. But as she'd learned early on, with Michael Stevens, appearances were deceiving.

From the manner in which he immediately examined her, from how he rose to greet her, she suspected that he wasn't nearly as unruffled as he strove to pretend. Magnetic, preposterously virile, he crossed to her. He was all grace and smooth motion, and there was a tension emanating from him that dispelled the affectation of ennui he labored so valiantly to sustain.

She buried a smile; he'd been missing her, at least a little, and she hugged the phenomenal notion close to her heart for subsequent dissection and contemplation.

He'd dressed for supper, even though he never went down, and she admired the superb sight. Rarely did she behold him primped and preened. By the time they had a few solitary minutes for themselves, he was ordinarily naked or, if he deigned to cover himself, he sported a robe.

She acutely appreciated this side of him, this civilized coating over the rough core. In the middle of a London ballroom, surrounded by the *beau monde,* he'd be spectacular. With his refinement and arrogance, he'd fit right in, his aristocratic Stevens bloodlines keenly apparent.

The fabulous dark blue of his velvet coat set off the vividness of his spectacular eyes, eyes that were focused on her with a dazzling potency. Without a polite word of welcome, he turned her and nibbled at her nape—a spot he particularly relished—and goose bumps slithered down her arms.

"Where've you been?" He was chafing, restless, lusting for her. His cock firm and obstinate against her bottom, he gripped her waist, pulling her closer. "I thought you'd be here an hour ago."

"I couldn't leave until that blasted soprano finished her aria." And what a hideous delay it had been! When the concert had begun, she hadn't been paying much attention to her surroundings, distracted as she was by her musings of Michael, and she'd permitted herself to be seated near the front, making it impossible to slip away undetected.

"You're here now."

"So I am." She tipped her head, granting him more space to sample.

"Are you hungry?"

"Famished." And hoping he was geared to indulge in a prurient feast.

"Good."

Gradually, her vision sharpened to encompass more of the room, and she saw that he'd had an intimate supper for two delivered. A square table, covered with a pristine white cloth and immaculate china and silver, had been placed by the fire. Candles glimmered romantically in the center, and the crystal stemware gleamed, reflecting the flames in the hearth.

"What's this?"

"Supper, milady."

"What a sweet idea."

He kissed up her neck, toying with her ear. "Will you join me?"

"Absolutely."

As though parading her into a grand dining room, he slipped her hand into the crook of his arm and escorted her across the floor, gallantly holding out a chair.

Scarcely capable of breathing in her elated state, she glided into it, clinging to every second of the unexpected, impulsive surprise. Up until now, she'd persuaded herself that—from his perspective—their trysts were purely sexual, that he'd prevailed with his objective of downplaying their significance, but evidently, she'd been mistaken. For him to have initiated this nonlibidinous activity was the most precious, most dangerous, eventuality he could have concocted.

Sharing a repast was a wholesome diversion, the sort of enterprise friends might undertake, and made it seem that they were companions and confidants, rather than two strangers who'd more or less bumped into each other and who were illicitly dallying after a succinct acquaintance.

"What brought this on?" she couldn't help inquiring, peeking up at him over her shoulder.

As if they regularly met for supper, he kissed her, then casually rounded the table, seating himself across from her and pouring the wine. "I decided that I wanted to have one memory of you with your clothes on."

"Beast," she chuckled. "If you wished to see me dressed, you only had to request it."

"Plus, it's so fun to remove everything"—he stared at her over the rim of his stemmed goblet—"piece by piece."

"Would you like to start straightaway?" Deliberately, she leaned forward, and the low-cut neckline of her evening gown provided him with an arresting exhibition of creamy flesh.

"Momentarily," he murmured, transfixed by her bosom. "Let me enjoy the view for a bit."

"Certainly." She adjusted herself so that he had an unobstructed display of cleavage.

His brow rose. "Are you flirting with me, madam?"

"Naturally."

"A hazardous business, considering my state of enamoredness with your copious charms."

"I'll risk it."

Vigilantly, he studied her. While he'd always been an intense man, suddenly he seemed vastly altered, as though he'd reached an intricate resolution, as though he had confessions to make, tales to tell, feelings to recount.

But instead of relating the introspections that plagued him, he shifted back. "Are you really hungry?"

"Ravenous. I left the party before the buffet was presented."

"Let's eat, then." He stood and went to the dresser where an array of covered dishes had been arranged. After filling several plates, he carried them back, situating them before her with a grand gesture. *"Voilà!"*

"Thank you."

Fleetingly, he looked abashed. "Sorry about the lack of servants, but we're fending for ourselves."

ought about engaging one of the footmen, but
they're such tattlers that I couldn't have offered a bribe
large enough to keep them from spilling all to Lady Carrington." Braced for her to object to the isolation, to the
informality, he gazed at her across the table.

Was he mad?

She was euphoric that they were alone, and categorically
enchanted that he'd gone to so much trouble. There was
fish and fowl, vegetables and fruits, cheeses and breads.
Everything was perfectly prepared, eye-catching, and when
he stabbed a miniature carrot with his fork and held it out
for her to taste, she was spellbound by how effortlessly he
wended his magic.

"This is the main course," he declared. "Later, I'll provide dessert."

From the salacious gleam in his eye, she understood that
he wasn't referring to food. "Do I get to pick my favorite?"

"With my avid assistance."

She nibbled, taking the tiniest possible morsels, drawing
out the delectation. In the process, she learned—with no
small amount of surprise—that it was abominably romantic
to have a man feed her. He rendered various delicacies, and
she eagerly participated, feeding him, as well. Lingering,
delaying, savoring, they puttered with the cuisine, and it
was fascinating to watch him perform such elementary feats
as chewing and swallowing.

Inevitably, she was full to bursting, and she pushed her
plate away, laughing when he coerced her into one bite,
then another. She had difficulty refusing him, even over so
trivial a subject as how much he wanted her to eat.

While he cleared the table, she loafed like a pampered
princess. He tidied until there were only the wineglasses
and the candles he'd shoved off to the side. When he sat
across from her, once again, she was balanced on her forearms, and he assumed the same pose, the position bringing
him so near that she could make out the gold flecks inter-

mingled in the blue of his pupils, the mark where his razor had nicked under his chin.

His left eye was slightly blackened underneath, from a blow he'd sustained in his fight with Brigham, and she reached out and traced a finger across the wound, never tiring of the excuse to touch him.

"Where will you go when you leave here?" he queried, taking her hand, linking their fingers. "Back to Scarborough?"

"Yes." She was relieved that he'd thrown the prohibited topic of *the future* out into the open, but as delighted as she was that he'd raised it, she also regretted that he had. His interrogatory reminded her that the time for separating was very close indeed, and she had to prod her next comment past the lump in her throat.

"How about you?"

"I'm not sure. Another party, I suppose."

The thought of him persisting with his licentious habits was disturbing, and she couldn't bear to conceive of him whiling away at cards, women, drink, and other senseless pursuits.

"Why don't *you* go home? I wish you would."

"I will eventually. I can't just now."

"Why did you leave in the first place?"

"I was angry at my mother. I walked in on her and my father when they were . . ." His cheeks flamed with color; apparently, he couldn't describe what he'd caught them doing.

"They're married?"

"They weren't then, which made me angry; they tied the knot a month or two ago."

"You're not close to your father, are you?"

"No, not at all. He was horrid to my mother over the years, and I've never forgiven him for his bad behavior."

"It must have been quite shocking for you to stumble on them together."

"It was, and I behaved like an ass." He chuckled, but

without mirth. "At the time, it seemed appropriate to be furious . . ."

His voice trailed off, and he couldn't explain why he'd fled or why he couldn't go back. Gently, she nudged, "You can't deduce how to return?"

"After making such a monumental fool of myself in front of my entire family, I find it's easier to wander." Shrugging, he gulped at his wine and deftly changed the subject. "I'll try to picture you in Yorkshire."

"Then get a 'picture' of something very dull, very mundane, very sedate." He laughed, which warmed her. With her eyes, she added, *And 'picture' me missing you. Every second. Every minute. Every day.*

The silence stretched, jarred, and she boldly suggested, "You could visit me. If you were in the north."

Meticulously, he scrutinized her and, after a good deal of painful deliberation, he ultimately pronounced, "I never would."

Nodding, she stoically accepted his rejection. Probably, she should have been hurt but, as he'd rebuffed her proposition, he looked so forlorn that she couldn't be aggrieved.

A stronger woman might have argued or begged for a different response, but she couldn't elicit a single lure she could utilize to induce him to travel so far. Besides, if she believed he might actually come, she'd very likely spend the rest of her life gazing down the road, moping and hoping that it would be the day he'd show his sorry face. She repeated, "You should go home."

"I know."

"I hate to imagine the calamities you'll create if you trot off to another party. You've been an utter terror at this one."

"I didn't mean to be. Pamela proposed various diversions, and I agreed, and then—"

She interrupted. "You're blaming Pamela?"

"No, I just . . ." He languished again, the color on his cheeks heightening, his chagrin conspicuous. "Come here," he interjected, and he tugged on her hand, guiding her around the table till she was sitting on his lap.

Dipping under her chin, he nipped against her neck, causing her to giggle and writhe. "I don't want to talk about me," he asserted. "I want to talk about *you,* and how rapidly I can have you out of these clothes."

Whenever she probed into his affairs, he adroitly steered her away from further review of his dubious character by reverting to sexual banter but, for once, she wasn't irritated by his evasive action. She was as anxious as he to move the assignation to the physical realm where they connected so naturally.

"I'll ring for the maid."

"We don't need the maid."

"You'll aid me?"

"I'm renowned for my ability with corset strings."

"And you are a cad to mention such a disreputable skill," she teased, but she abhorred having him refer to his other women, those scores who'd come before her and who'd come after, but she cast off her dolor. He was determined to warn her that she must never get too close, must never crave too much, or desire too badly. It was but a component of the odd game they played. Their meetings were vital to her subsistence and peace of mind, but he was bent on acting as if they were trivial and inconsequential.

He squired her to the dressing room. She carried the candelabra and held it while he lit the lamp, and she perched herself on the stool in front of the vanity. Silently and expertly, he took down her hair, combed it out, then worked at the tiny buttons on her dress. With great interest, she observed, loving how he tarried to brush his lips in just the correct spot, how his hands loitered, or his fingertips explored and searched while he seemed to be innocently proceeding with his tasks.

The haphazard touching wasn't any such thing, and by the time she was stripped down to drawers and chemise, her body was thrumming, her feminine parts on fire, so that when he was done and urged her to her feet, she zealously spun into his arms, ready for a blistering kiss, but she was graced with a tender one, instead.

"Thank you," he said, his breath warm on her cheek as he pulled away.

"For what?"

"For humoring me." He fluffed her hair about her shoulders and back. "This was another memory I fancied."

"Of you undressing me?"

His manifest sentimentality had him overtly perplexed, and he could only mumble, "Well . . ."

"I'm delighted. It was wonderful."

"Yes, it was," he managed to express. "I'm *delighted* that I had the opportunity."

Stark emotion, on which he'd never expound, was visible in his beautiful eyes, and she dared to take a chance, pointing out what was so onerous to discuss. "We don't have many days left."

"No."

The heat in his gaze seared her, and she was convinced that he would finally profess how much he'd valued their time together, or how much he'd miss her after, but he merely stared, then stared some more, committing the interval to his budding store of reminiscence.

"I'm glad we did this—" she started.

But he cut her off before she could wend the conversation in a direction he was bound and determined it wouldn't go. "I want to love you all night."

"I'd like that."

"In your bed, for a change."

"I'd like that, too."

He blew out the lamp, then clasped her hand in order to lead her out into the other room. In the abrupt darkness, a glow penetrated the shadows, and she glanced up, amazed to discover the peephole shining like a flare.

She stopped.

"What is it?" Michael inquired, and she pressed a finger to her lips, signaling for quiet.

"Someone's in the hidden room." Turning, she went

back, grabbing the footstool and positioning it below the hole, then climbing up on it.

"What are you doing?"

She peered at him over her shoulder. In the past hour, he'd shed his coat, but nothing else, and he surveyed her with his arms folded across his chest, a bemused expression on his face.

"I want to see who's in there."

"You have become an unmitigated voyeur."

"Without a doubt."

"A wench. A wanton. A hussy."

"Yes."

"Get down at once," he soundly ordered, but he was chuckling.

"Ssh . . ." she cautioned dramatically. "Not till I find out what's happening."

He approached from behind and playfully whacked her on the rear. "I've been told that you can be struck blind from witnessing so much vice."

She chortled jovially. "I'll try to pace myself."

"Trollop," he muttered, and she swatted at him while he ducked.

Jamming her eye to the hole, she peeked in. The sordid scene was exactly the same, although it wasn't quite as thrilling since Michael wasn't the main attraction. Still, the unknown man within was handsome and appealing, so she was intrigued to examine his antics. A fetching brunette, with long, straight hair and big brown eyes, frolicked with him, but Sarah had never previously seen the woman, either.

During the occasions she'd spied on Michael, she'd thought she was drawn to the decadent viewing because *he* was involved in the debasing exposition. However, she was compelled to realize that lovers could furnish a stirring display, whether she was acquainted with them or not. The carnal scene before her was disgustingly titillating. The nudity, the malfeasance, the inappropriateness—both of the couple's conduct and of her watching them—made it difficult to desist.

The man was good-looking—not as comely as Michael, of course—but he was blond, so comparison wasn't exactly fair. He had a fabulous male body, which she could readily deduce since he was naked, though all she could behold was his backside. With a cherubic countenance that promised innocence, he appeared to be an angel who'd fallen into the wrong room, but he was definitely a devil.

"I wish he'd turn around," she grumbled. She had an atrocious inclination to inspect his cock. She'd only perused one in her life and, while she was sure it was a magnificent specimen, she wasn't averse to covertly analyzing another.

"Why?"

"Because all I can see is his buttocks."

"Would you get down?" he hissed.

"Oh, my goodness!"

Clucking her tongue, she couldn't believe the spectacle into which she'd blundered. This was certainly more lewdness than she'd counted upon. Such a thing had never occurred to her! Was there no end to the eccentric, depraved behavior in which these guests would engage?

"What?" he grouched. When she didn't reply, he recited an aggravated, "What!"

At first, there'd only been the one woman, but a second female was in the room, and they were statuesque, buxom twins. The man had been facing one and kissing her, his tongue in her mouth and his fingers pressuring her nipple, when the other loomed in from behind. Rubbing her breasts over his back, she wrapped her arms around his waist and commenced fondling him.

He was wedged between the pair, and obviously in a state of bliss. The women were happy, too. They were kissing and cooing, never stationary, their lips and hands busy and adept.

Sarah couldn't look away. Shamefully, her nipples stiffened, her pulse accelerated. Perhaps Michael was correct,

and her moral constitution had sunk beyond redemption—
just like his own.

"Twins?" Incredulous, she shook her head and scowled
down at him. "Really, Michael, how do they—"

Before she could complete her query, he lifted her off
the stool and deposited her on the floor. Flattening his eye
to the hole, he glared into the room.

"Oh, for pity's sake!" he growled when he recognized
the erotic trio. "I might have known. John Clayton . . ."

"The viscount . . . ?" In a whisper, she started to inquire
as to the man's title, but Michael slapped the covering over
the peephole.

"Don't close it," she admonished somewhat petulantly.
"I'm not finished."

"Yes you are."

Prepared to scramble back up, she headed toward the
stool, but he swooped her up and tossed her over his shoulder like an unwieldy sack of flour.

"Brute!" She pounded him on his back, but she was
laughing too hard to have any effect. "Put me down!"

"No."

"Were those women twins?"

"Yes."

"Who are they?"

"His mistresses."

"Plural?"

"Aye."

"How do the three of them fornicate together? You
didn't answer my question."

"And I'm not about to, so quit asking." He smacked her
on the rear. "I swear, tomorrow I'll have that bloody thing
nailed shut. Now, be quiet!"

Marching out to her bedchamber, he ungraciously
dumped her on her bed. Then, he followed her down and,
within moments, her curiosity about the threesome had vanished. She didn't need to ponder how others were trysting
in the next room, for she was thoroughly overwhelmed by
how *she* was accomplishing it in her own.

Chapter Sixteen

Pamela stared across the small table in her breakfast salon, and she wished that she'd had the formal dining room set. By its very nature, a country party meant that guests would arise at varying hours, so it was more convenient for them to grab a quick bite in the intimate room. However, with Hugh Compton occupying the space with her, she'd relish the excuse to observe him down a long expanse of oak—the longer the better.

She hadn't seen him in months, so she was surprised by how his dissolute lifestyle had recently ravaged his appearance. A blond-haired, blue-eyed, thirty-two-year-old dandy, he'd always been handsome, but intemperance and immoderation had wreaked havoc. His skin was now lined and sallow, his torso inordinately thin and sagging, his face aged and wrinkled.

The prior night of drink and revelry was taking its toll. His eyes were bloodshot, his fingers shook, and she couldn't help but suspect that his worsened condition was due to his current addiction to an exotic pipe an acquaintance had brought back from India and presented to him as a gift.

On a frequent basis, he experimented with forbidden Chinese opiates. Liquid courage, in the form of stiff whisky, was also habitually ingested. He constantly over-imbibed on an abundant mixture of foreign herbs and alcohol.

A slight odor of smoke, spirits, and sex hovered about him and, in the mirror on the far wall, disapproval and dismay were reflected in her penetrating gaze, so she shielded her disgust.

She couldn't tolerate Hugh, with his weaknesses and complaints, and she couldn't stand having him visit, yet she could hardly ask him to leave. An open invitation had been issued in London to those who might be interested and, as Hugh was one of the most perverted, lewd members of the *ton,* she couldn't gripe when he showed up, expecting hospitality.

As an earl, he was highly esteemed, and she couldn't fathom why, but then, she'd married into the aristocracy and, as an outsider, it was frequently puzzling to grasp the reasoning of those with whom he shared his blue blood. His peers, despite his particular flaws, liked and accepted him, so she had no option but to keep a smile pasted on her face and pretend she was glad he'd come.

It irked that he'd had so many advantages, that he'd been coddled and cosseted, and what did he have to show for it? A gambling habit that had bankrupted him, and a control problem that induced him to gluttony, be it with women, intoxicating drink, or any other vice.

Though she could sanction much in the way of decadence, she wasn't excited about the type of iniquity he would bring to the assemblage, which was definitely saying a lot. The evenings were already spent in behavior that even she—in her jaded condition—deemed disgusting, and Hugh would lower the offered amusements to new and despicable levels.

Then, there was Michael with which to contend. What if Hugh and Michael ran into one another? Michael rarely inflicted himself into the gathering, but he was wont to roam at night, watching and randomly participating, and she could imagine the uproar that would develop if their two paths happened to collide. It would be an unqualified disaster.

While Michael was a great friend, and she delighted in his presence, his personal problems were growing intolerable. She was happy to extend a refuge when he obviously needed one, however he'd become too unpredictable. His temper was at flash point. Evidence his thrashing of Brigham.

She didn't much care for Brigham, either, but regardless of what he'd done, she couldn't have Michael lurking in her stables, trouncing her various male guests when they displeased him. He'd never been the sort to suffer fools silently, and Hugh Compton was the biggest *fool* Michael had encountered in a long while. She was sitting on a powder keg that could blow at any moment.

With a regretful sigh, she determined that she'd have to ask Michael to depart. Given his prevalent volatile state, he would view her decision in the worst possible light, so the odds were high that she'd damage their eccentric camaraderie.

What a detestable turn of events, that she could only allow one of them to stay, and the choice had to be Hugh!

"So"—Hugh dug into a pile of eggs—"how's my sister?"

"She's well; she's enjoying herself."

"Good, good." Imperiously, he held out his cup, not deigning to glance toward the servant who poured for him. The retainer was well trained and, if he had any opinion about the fact that he was serving brandy-laced coffee as Hugh's morning beverage, he gave no sign. "Any progress on the introductions we discussed?"

"Actually, no." She was disturbed by the conspicuous ingenuousness infused into his inquiry, and thus, absolutely on guard.

Looking at her plate, she stirred her breakfast around and around but didn't eat anything. Her mind whirred, striving to make sense of Hugh and his schemes. Without a doubt, he'd concocted some mischief concerning his sister, but Pamela didn't aim to augment the plot.

After her discourse with Sarah, she'd left Sarah in peace to treasure her holiday, and Pamela couldn't help wondering if Hugh hoped that she, Pamela, would spur things along by urging Sarah into a compromising position from which she couldn't extricate herself. Then, whatever transpired, the end result would be Pamela's fault. Hugh, as was his tendency, would remain innocent of any malfeasance.

He drained his refreshment then tendered the cup for refilling. "I allowed her to call upon you for the exclusive purpose of meeting with different gentlemen."

"Yes, but she hasn't seemed inclined to socialize." Pamela carefully sipped her chocolate, locking onto Hugh's glare with a guileless one of her own.

The pompous ass really believed that he had a say in Sarah's comings and goings! As if he could have *allowed* her to visit or not! Sarah was an adult woman and, at her advanced age, no longer under Hugh's thumb. She could do as she pleased. Hugh, with his customary dearth of acuity, hadn't realized that fact, but Pamela wasn't about to disillusion him. She liked Sarah very much, and she wasn't about to further Hugh's conspiracy—whatever it was.

As though their dialogue had conjured her up, Sarah entered, and Pamela peeked at the clock on the mantel. The hour was fast approaching noon, and she could barely prevent herself from clucking in dismay. From the first, Sarah had been the earliest of risers, yet in the past few days, something had caused a drastic alteration in her rigid schedule.

Pamela endeavored to detect as much as she could about her guests, so her proficient staff—spies all—meticulously tracked Sarah's movements. Luckily, there'd been very little to report.

For the most part, she ate her meals at off times, strolled the gardens for sun and relaxation, read in the library, and rested in her room. She appeared to be having the tranquil, restorative respite on which she'd planned, and Pamela would have been positively ecstatic had she not also been apprised that the adjoining door between Sarah's and Michael's chambers had been discovered ajar on two separate occasions. That the maid who serviced Sarah had thrice been rebuffed, with Sarah insisting through a barred door that she didn't require morning assistance. That a footman who'd been sent to fetch Michael's bathing tub, when Michael was purportedly absent from the premises, swore he heard Michael talking in Sarah's room.

Then, of course, there was the mysterious supper à *deux* Michael had had delivered to his room, yet despite her dogged persistence, she'd been unable to surmise even a clue as to the identity of the woman he'd invited when, considering the sorts of females on the premises, his special *guest* ought to have been crowing about her conquest.

Not damning by any means, but enough to have Pamela kicking herself for placing the pair in such proximity. The instant Sarah had inquired about him that day on the verandah, Pamela should have removed him to another section of the house, but forcing Michael to other quarters would have been so awkward. With the mood he was in, he would have bristled at the mandate, and she couldn't bear the idea of upsetting him more than he already had been by others.

Besides, it truly hadn't occurred to her to worry, because she couldn't picture Michael permitting himself to be drawn into a jeopardizing predicament with the stunning beauty. His brother James, yes, but *not* solid, dependable Michael. He had more scruples and conscience than James, and he'd always exercised more restraint, but apparently in this case, lust had won out.

Sarah was mature enough to have known better, but Pamela wasn't about to chastise her. Michael was the kind of man who women couldn't resist, and Pamela—with her own unwarranted physical attraction to the rogue—comprehended his allure more readily than anyone. When he deigned to focus his attention, there wasn't a female alive who could refuse him. Worldly women regularly scrambled to be the object of his dubious affection, so a person of Sarah's limited experience would have no defense against his substantial charms or expert lovemaking.

Plainly, she'd succumbed, though just how far down the road of passion she'd ventured was still in dispute. Taking into account Michael's sexual proclivities, Sarah was very likely beyond redemption, and Pamela laid the blame, such as it was, squarely at Michael's feet.

In light of his relationship with Hugh, his actions were reprehensible. Hugh notwithstanding, Michael was aware that, because of her stature and rank, he couldn't dally with Sarah, but Sarah—with her rural, unpretentious background—didn't recognize the dangers.

Pamela frowned, speculating as to how this would end, even as she was chastising herself for handling their budding romance so badly. The merest hint of intervention would have averted the entire, probable debacle.

She beheld Sarah before Hugh did, and she concluded that she ought to warn her or at least run interference. With a burst of feminine intuition, she was consumed by the notion that Sarah wouldn't be pleased to see him.

As Sarah stepped over the threshold, Pamela sneaked a hasty assessment: hair neatly combed, gown appropriate, demeanor perfectly poised. Yet, the sparkle in her eye and the glow in her cheeks removed all supposition. Sarah had unquestionably spent the night basking in multitudinous episodes of carnal bliss.

She's in love with the bounder, Pamela swiftly deduced, shaking her head at their folly.

"Surprise, Sarah," she welcomed a tad too heartily, "look who's joined us."

Sarah halted in her tracks, deep in thought, or perhaps, lost in her memories. Almost in a trance, she seemed confused by the brisk greeting and, with Pamela's indicatory gesture, she honed in on her incorrigible brother.

"What are you doing here?" she asked irascibly.

"Always a pleasure, *dear* sister," Hugh snarled, then smiled—for Pamela's benefit, she was sure—although she received the distinct impression that he'd throttle Sarah as soon as he had the chance.

Upon his oration, Hugh's company fully registered, and Sarah's countenance transformed. She'd been daydreaming, and the sight of her sibling had rudely awakened her to reality. Her spine straightened, and the glow that had preceded her disappeared.

"My apologies, Hugh. I've just risen. I guess I'm not quite myself." The corners of her lips turned up in a smile, but the salutation didn't reach her eyes, and she sounded deferential, but not very. "Rebecca had mentioned that you might be coming. How delightful that you've finally decided to attend."

Pamela studied the two of them. When they'd both been younger, and in London for Sarah's debut, their father had been alive to act as a buffer, so Pamela hadn't been able to gauge their feelings for one another, but she had no trouble now.

From the taciturn manner in which Sarah watched him, there was no love lost, but from what Sarah had endured due to his recklessness, her disregard was completely understandable. On his best day, Hugh was difficult, and whatever deference Sarah might previously have possessed had vanished. As was typical of his type of highborn male, Hugh didn't notice his sister's disdain. He would simply never assume that he wasn't liked or, at the least, greatly respected.

The siblings clearly had no knack for idle prattle, which meant that tarrying with them would be unpleasant. She desired no knowledge of, or participation in, whatever conversation might follow.

Momentarily, she pondered if she should abandon Sarah, but one glance assured her that the other woman was equipped to manage Hugh. Sarah was filling a plate, seating herself, and nibbling on a scone, very much behaving as if Hugh was no more than a pet in the corner, admitted but ignored.

"Well"—Pamela chose the coward's avenue of retreat—"I'm sure you two have lots to catch up on. I'll leave you to your chat." She rose and went to the door, but not before pausing to peek over her shoulder at Sarah, and she was certain she spotted a love bite on her neck, though it was mostly shielded by a scarf. "I have a guest who must depart.

Today," she emphasized, but neither Sarah nor Hugh was
listening. "I'm off to tell him good-bye."

Without delay, she headed for Michael's room.

Hugh lay on his bed and fluffed the pillows, the quarrel
he'd just had with Sarah replaying in his mind.

The blasted woman! Arguing with him. Laughing at
him. Why . . . she had the audacity to treat him as if he was
still a lad in short pants! With whom did she think she was
dealing?

Though he was technically her legal guardian, the arrangement wasn't taken seriously by either of them, because Sarah wasn't the type of female a man could rule.
She was too quick-witted, too self-assured, and too stubborn to be ordered about; she could make a man cower and
vacillate, induce him to distrust his purpose and objective.
Even their dear, departed father hadn't known how to control her. To the dismay of both of them, she'd always behaved exactly as she pleased but, for once, he wouldn't
permit her to call the shots.

"Not this time, little sister," he muttered.

His father's heir in every respect, his life was in London
where pleasant diversions were available. He hated the
country and always had, and he declined to waste his energy on any of the boring tasks that kept Sarah so enthralled. In his mind, it was sensible that they both aspire
to occupations they enjoyed—his being gambling, debauchery, and vice.

Sarah refused to understand his position, but he was a
man, an earl, a peer of the realm, so he need not justify
himself to her. Theirs were separate worlds but, as she was
about to brutally discover, her personal happiness and well-
being were uniquely dependent on his, and her tranquil rural odyssey was about to come to a smashing conclusion.
He was her brother, her master—her lord, by God!—and
she would not trifle with him when there was so much at
stake.

Against his better judgment, he'd left Scarborough and returned to town, graciously granting her the first opportunity to select a suitable match. Sarah was at her best when she was helping others and untangling their problems, and he'd wrongly presumed that she'd rectify this mess, too, as she typically had in the past.

With a confused rationality, he'd planned it all out: He'd facilitate an advantageous marriage for her, to a rich husband. As part of the settlement, her spouse would pay off Hugh's debt. If he was extremely shrewd, perhaps he'd even negotiate a quarterly allowance into the deal. Sarah's precious home would be preserved and restored, Hugh could go about his business in London, and they'd all carry on as before.

He'd been so desperately assured of the result! She was skilled at taking command and being in charge, and her efforts precluded him having to expend any of his own.

But he'd erred in acquiescing. She'd never intended to search for a husband, and he'd been played for a fool. All along, she'd simply thought her trip to Bedford was for recreation and relaxation. For weeks now, he'd gadded about town, stupidly believing that she was toiling toward a resolution, only to discover that she'd never meant to faithfully do her part!

How dare she circumvent his wishes!

Based on his expectations of her success, he'd ordered several new sets of clothes, checked out a team of horses for the coach he planned to purchase as soon as the marital contracts were drawn up, bid on a painting at an auction, and directed the housekeeper at the town house to have the furniture recovered—furniture that would be confiscated shortly, along with the property itself, if a financial rescue wasn't finalized.

The commoners who flitted around on the fringes of his life wouldn't confess as much to his face, but they were nervous about accepting his credit. Word of his arrearage had circulated, and everyone was convinced that he would loose all, so he was having a devil of a time making purchases or hiring workers. He'd flat out promised numerous people that he was about to have an infusion of cash, but they had the gall not to believe him, a low blow that perpetually chafed.

Indigence was the worst sort of torture!

Now, with Sarah's clever thwarting of his manipulations, he had to acknowledge that he shouldn't have deposited such an important outcome in her hands. The accursed female hadn't a clue as to how a woman attracted a man, and she was thoroughly incompetent at any situation that involved amorous matters, her failed *entrée* into society being the most striking evidence of her deficiencies in that arena. He should have recollected as much from the commencement, but he'd been so eager to have Sarah supervise the details of her betrothal.

Well, there were methods for obtaining what he wanted. In this, he would not be denied or dissuaded. He'd given her her chance, he'd trusted her, but she'd wasted it, and she was going to be shocked when she learned just how determined he was for a beneficial ending.

The door opened, and Rebecca rushed in. At age twenty-four, Rebecca was a year younger than Sarah, but different as night from day. A blond, voluptuous beauty, with features as perfect as a porcelain doll, she'd resided with them for the prior three years, after having survived a lifetime of excessive poverty inflicted on her by her profligate father. Never badgering, never complaining, never wailing over their pitiful lot, she appreciated—as Sarah never had—that affairs could be much worse.

While Sarah was likely in her room lamenting over the latest debacle, Rebecca was looking ahead to an auspicious conclusion. Sarah's appearance at Lady Carrington's gala had been her idea. Hugh could never have arrived at such a marvelous solution all on his own.

He studied her, his disapproval unequivocal. When she'd broached the asinine concept of luring Sarah to Pamela's party, she'd contended that she could execute the required eventuality in a handful of days, that she could rapidly have

Sarah totally ruined, but Sarah was proving too elusive for even the generally effective Rebecca's machinations.

Hugh was furious with her for her blunders. He'd sent Rebecca to Bedford with Sarah, thinking that their cousin would lend legitimacy to the finale. There was the additional benefit that Sarah considered Rebecca a friend, and Sarah would never suppose the other woman to be involved in any nefarious plot.

Sarah's fiasco would seem utterly forthright, and she would never have guessed his role or his maneuvering. Even if she had a subsequent inkling, there would be nothing she could do to change the outcome, but regardless of whether Sarah ultimately ascertained who had precipitated her downfall, he should have journeyed directly to Bedford to set the proceedings in motion. Matters had become too grave, and she would wed if he had to tie her down and force the seduction, himself.

He was tired of being poor, tired of having others thumbing their noses at him, tired of being spurned at his favorite clubs, gambling houses, and brothels.

He would have his way!

"Did you find a key?"

"Yes," Rebecca answered, approaching the bed, "although it was difficult without any help from the staff. Lady Carrington's people are so dreadfully loyal."

"Imagine that," he muttered sarcastically.

"When I suggested their assistance, they gawked at me as if I was speaking in tongues."

"But you acquired one?"

"I've tested it in six different doors." She held it out for his inspection. "It catches, but with some jiggling, it's fine. I filched it from a rack in the kitchens."

"Honestly, Becky, how common."

"It's not as if any of the employees would abet me. I felt like a wretched pickpocket." As she imparted a withering glare, she tossed the key, and it bounced on his lap. "I stole it for you. You might at least try to be a bit gracious."

"You'll see my gratitude when we've accomplished our goal."

"You'd better mean it, Hugh. If you're lying . . ."

He couldn't abide her flip attitude, and he'd had his fill of her whining and evasions. Since she'd been in Bedford, she'd penned three separate letters, defending her mistakes, and justifying her lack of success. He'd had to endure her continual bungling, so he didn't need to suffer through a feminine mood, as well.

"Are you threatening me?" he queried quietly. "*Me*, Rebecca?" His stern tone caused her to blanch, and she backed down immediately, once again the meek, solicitous female he demanded she be.

"No, Hugh," she said. "I apologize."

"As you should. You prevail upon our relationship too much. It makes you forget yourself." He patted the bed, urging her closer, and she obeyed. She might pout and brood, but she never stayed angry. "Did you locate any of the Chinese herbs I like?"

"Yes. In the library. Lady Carrington keeps a box for the guests. I took what was left. Here."

She rendered a neatly wrapped parcel and, as though it was the rarest of jewels, he wildly clutched at it. In London, his supplier had been out, as had his various friends, so he'd been frantic, and he was horridly relieved that Rebecca had stumbled upon a stash.

Apprehensive and irritable, he struggled to curb his obdurate craving. Realizing that the anticipation would be worth it when he finally imbibed, he laid the packet on the table, compelling himself back to his task, to his strategy for Sarah, and how it was likely to unfold.

He dictated, "Tell me again why you infer it is Stevens with whom she's dallying."

"From how they were acting when I witnessed them together. They have a much deeper acquaintance than anyone suspects. It's the manner in which she looks at him."

"How is that?"

"She's in love. It's the only explanation."

"Sarah? In love? Bah . . ." He waved away her deduction. "You're mad."

"No, a woman knows these things."

God, how he wanted her to be correct! And if it was Michael Stevens! The revenge would be so sweet!

"Did you ever ask him about that first night? When you sent him up to her room?"

"No, a second overture would have sounded suspicious. When I made the initial proposition, I'm sure he thought I was a servant, and I didn't want to disavow him of the impression."

"You needn't have fretted," he mused, recalling Stevens's history with beautiful women. "If he saw you again, he'd never remember you." He was too self-absorbed to notice the hurt that came over her, and he perked up. "Well, then, we'll pay a call on her this evening. Not too late. How about an hour or two after she retires?"

"She won't be hurt, will she, Hugh?"

How ludicrous for Rebecca to be experiencing a belated stab of conscience! "Where's the injury in her marrying a wealthy, successful businessman? By having the chance for a home and children of her own? That's what all women crave, isn't it? Now . . . be a dear and fetch me another brandy."

Without argument or condemnation of his bad habits, she proceeded to the sideboard, retrieved the decanter, and filled his glass.

"There's a good lass." He tossed it down in a single swallow as she hovered over him, seeing to his comfort, and he was struck again by how pretty she was. With that lavish blond hair, and those magnificent breasts squeezed into that fiercely laced corset, she was an arousing spectacle. In her glorious sapphire eyes, he could read the bald—but idiotic—affection she harbored for him and, after the arduous interview with Sarah, her fondness was soothing.

While Sarah was content to wallow away in the country, Rebecca periodically accompanied him to London where she acted as his hostess—and more when the occasion presented itself. He'd never admit to another soul that he lusted after his cousin, but she was so bloody accommodating. So bloody convenient. How could a man spurn what was so graciously offered?

"What if she's alone when we barge in?" Rebecca inquired. "What will we say?"

"We'll simply invite her down to the party—as though that was our sole purpose."

He'd worked it out in his head, in his disordered state, satisfied that he was making flawless decisions. Rebecca cheerfully assented as he'd predicted she would. She wouldn't question him, not after she'd created such a mess when left to her own devices.

"And if we don't catch her with Stevens," he pointed out, "we'll opt for another fellow. We'll unlock the damned door and shove someone inside—if that's what it takes."

"Too bad about Brigham," Rebecca noted.

"Too bad, indeed."

Rebecca had discreetly orchestrated Brigham's interest in Sarah and, with his fortune and title, he'd have been an excellent choice as her husband. Yet, nothing had progressed properly. Not only had the man *not* crept into Sarah's room, he'd been forcibly removed from possible consideration by his run-in with Michael Stevens.

No one had unveiled the basis for their violent disagreement, and Hugh shuddered over the pummeling Brigham had received. The nerve of Stevens, handling a peer as he'd done! The talk was all over town, though nothing would come of it. The man was a raving lunatic who ought to be hanged, or at the very least, transported at the earliest juncture.

Only Stevens's father, the Earl of Spencer, stood in the way of the contemptible scoundrel getting what he truly deserved. With his connection to Spencer, Stevens was untouchable.

Factor in the number of markers he owned, and the damning, confidential secrets he'd unearthed, and who was safe from the bastard's wrath? He was a menace, one that Hugh would be delighted to destroy.

All in good time, he counseled. Stevens would get his due, but for the moment, Hugh wasn't going to fuss about him. He was exhausted from traveling, and the constant trepidation induced by his fiscal dilemma, and he was geared up for some entertainment.

While he was anxious to retrieve his pipe from his bag, he pushed his impatience aside. Once he partook of the herbs, he wouldn't be able to adequately savor Rebecca's ample charms. After he'd debauched her a time or two, he'd indulge in his favorite pastime.

Obscurely, it occurred to him that sex had previously been his *favorite* diversion. When had that changed? And why? But the sentiment was fleeting as were so many. Recurrently, concentration proved elusive.

As he contemplated Rebecca, a welcomed stirring tickled betwixt his legs, and he almost wept with relief. Sporadically, with all the liquor and herbs he consumed, he was unable to perform his manly duties, and the incidents were beginning to frighten him. His inability to generate a cockstand had advanced into a recurring problem, and he was increasingly concerned that his aptness might vanish forever.

"Come here," he ordered.

More and more, women failed to spur his male urges. Even the most disgusting, unconstrained whores had no rousing effect on his limp manhood, so when he felt another prickle of desire in his nether regions, he was deluged with optimism and abruptly ablaze.

"Really, Hugh," she huffed, affronted. "Since you arrived, you've done naught but chastise me, and now you presume that I'll just blindly do whatever you require." Her pert nose went up. "Well, you've just pushed me too far."

"Come here," he repeated more forcefully.

"I won't, I tell you!"

"You will," he crooned softly, "or I'll be extremely angry."

"For once, I don't care."

The bitch spun away, as though she'd march out in a snit! Who did she think she was, putting on airs? For the first time in months, he could fornicate without any disconcerting obstacles, and by the heavens, she would oblige. Just the notion that she had the temerity to reject him inspired him to a fierce cockstand.

Embarrassingly, there were many available women at the party besides his cousin, but he couldn't seek out any of them for fear of being incapable of maintaining an erection. So far, Rebecca was the only person who'd been with him when the worst had ensued, so Hugh never had to brook any discomfiting rationalizations or humiliating elucidations. She was in no position to discuss their sexual relationship with others, and she hadn't sufficient carnal enlightenment to grasp what was amiss.

She couldn't depart; he wouldn't allow her to.

Exhibiting uncommon agility, he leapt to the floor, grabbed her, and whipped her around. "Get back in bed."

"Hugh, stop it," she sniveled as he urged her toward the mattress. She attempted to stare him down, but her defiance waned—as always—when confronted by his firm insistence. "You're hurting my arm."

"I won't be denied, Rebecca."

In a visible rage, she lay down, and he fell on top of her. He bared her breasts and suckled, but she was unmoving as a corpse, declining to participate as he'd repeatedly instructed. He thought about slapping a response out of her, but didn't. At the moment, he was unconcerned by her deficient cooperation.

Stimulated by the fierceness of her insubordination, he spread her legs and feasted. Elated that he was able, he climaxed in haste, then pulled out and collapsed on his side. She scooted away, scurrying to right herself.

"Don't leave," he decreed. "I'll have another go at you in a few minutes. As soon as I've rested." But the haze from his orgasm was clouding his deluded brain, and he faded into a disturbed slumber.

Chapter Seventeen

Michael was resting impatiently on his bed when he heard Sarah's arrival in her room. Though the hour wasn't overly late, he'd been waiting an eternity for her to return from supper. She'd begged him to join her, but he'd rebuffed her invitation—not out of his customary disdain for fraternizing with the other guests, but because of their diverse positions.

They wouldn't have been able to converse in the parlor before the meal was announced and, due to their disparate statuses, they'd have been seated at opposite ends of the table. He couldn't conceive of watching from afar, pretending they weren't intimate, as she chatted and mingled. If she was in proximity, he couldn't feign disinterest.

How he wished he could have accompanied her downstairs! That he could have proudly stood with her, her arm slipped through his. That he could have escorted her into the dining room, held out her chair, whispered in her ear throughout the banquet.

Astoundingly, he was chomping at the bit, hating the elite restrictions that kept them from acknowledging one another in public. While usually he could have cared less about the constraints upon him, for once, he was keenly feeling the divisions that his dubious parentage had engendered.

Over the years, he'd ridiculed James for his fascination with the members of the *ton*. Michael had always assumed that he had more sense, but since meeting Sarah and becoming involved with her, he recognized that he wasn't immune to the enticement of her world.

In Paris, with his mother a lauded, sought-after celebrity, his paternity hadn't seemed important. He'd been welcomed into the looser French society, befriended by the noble sons of the wealthy families, eyed for future marriage by the daughters of the prosperous merchants. His ancestry hadn't had any effect on his behavior, so he hadn't worried about fitting in.

But in London, where lineage was everything, he'd been slapped in the face with reality. A trespasser, he'd fluttered on the fringes of their exclusive domain, an interloper simply because his father and mother—two dynamic, charismatic, selfish individuals—had never wed.

Edward Stevens had four adult children—three daughters and a son—who were legitimately born to him during his lengthy marriage, and it had been painful to discover how differently they were viewed. Michael and James were Edward's shameful indiscretion, and despite how much they looked like Edward, or acted like him, how much they postured and strutted, they could never be anything but his bastards.

The inequity had been harrowing, and he'd eventually accepted their situation, but not James. Though to be fair, James had suffered more due to the fact that he'd been older when they'd moved away. His recollections of their father were precise and ingrained, so his loss had been greater. He was the firstborn son of the prominent aristocrat, but he could never hold his rightful place, and he had yearned for approval, while Michael had perpetually conjectured that he was beyond those youthful daydreams of assimilation.

Then, Sarah had bewitched him. From the start, he'd been infatuated with her, even though attraction was pointless. When he should have run fast and furiously in the opposite direction, he'd acceded to her bold petition for an affair, and as a result, they'd instituted some of the most lusty, ribald sex he'd ever encountered.

Interspersed with the erotic sessions were tender words, quiet interludes, and gentle sharing that had left him enchanted, enraptured, and utterly immersed in the liaison until he couldn't eat or sleep. His entire life now revolved around the handful of stolen moments when he could tarry in her arms. The past had disappeared; the future had no meaning. He existed solely for their episodes of carnal bliss.

Thoroughly besotted, he never tired of watching her, never wearied of her company, of her pretty face or lush body. Considering his enchantment, he couldn't have gone to supper with her, because he would have spent the repast gazing longingly down the large table like a lovesick boy.

He listened to the muffled noises she made, and he could picture her perched on the stool at her vanity. As the maid unbuttoned her gown and unlaced her corset. As she washed, then slipped into her nightrail and robe.

Amazingly, he visualized himself—instead of the serving girl—assisting her, once again, with her private ablutions, and the notion was unsettling. The desire to aid her was irresistible, and he'd previously given in to it on that one occasion when they'd dined together, but he'd carefully prevented himself from doing something so idiotic a second time.

Never before had he been prone to dawdle in a woman's boudoir. With all the lovers he'd had, nary a one had inspired him to loiter. He'd never cared how they undressed, how they bathed, or readied themselves for slumber, but with Sarah, his beguilement had flared, early on, and he couldn't seem to get enough of her mundane details.

How unfortunate that this remarkable relationship would terminate before it had begun. There would be insufficient opportunity to explore these strange and wondrous sensations, and he sighed regretfully. What would Sarah think when she learned that he was packing his bags? Would she be upset or, more likely, would she be relieved that their *amour* had been so easily concluded?

Though he hated to admit it, Pamela had done them both a favor by forcing him to depart, and the request hadn't been a surprise. After the incident with Brigham, he'd been expecting it. She'd been courteous and compassionate; he'd appreciated her tact and, bearing in mind that Hugh Compton had arrived, she could hardly have acted in any other fashion.

But how to disengage from Sarah?

When he'd rashly initiated their romance, it had never occurred to him that it would be difficult to end it. He'd always been a competent, shrewd fellow, who examined every angle and option before proceeding, yet he'd permitted this slip of a woman—whom he barely knew and with whom he had so little in common—to totally inflict herself into his life and heart. He couldn't predict where he'd travel next, because he couldn't envision being separated from her.

What a foolish, foolish man he was!

The adjoining door opened, and she peeked in, smiling when she saw him. As he ached over the dreams that would never come true, he was confronted with the ample depth of his folly.

How could he endure losing her?

"I asked to have a bath delivered," she said. "Would you wash me?"

"I'd like that."

His cock hardened at the idea of touching her when she was wet and slippery, and she immediately noticed. Her delighted appraisal lagged on the bulge she'd produced in his trousers.

"Then, when you're finished, we'll switch, and *I* will bathe *you*."

The gleam in her eye was lecherous, and he chuckled. "I've created a monster."

"Yes, you have. Are you sorry?"

"Not a whit."

"I didn't think so."

A servant rapped on her door, and she motioned him to silence, then vanished in order to direct the hauling in of the jugs of water. Many minutes later, she entered again, clad only in one of her functional chemises. She approached the bed, her thighs pressed against the frame.

"Did you lock the door after they left?" he inquired.

"Yes."

"Did you double-check?"

"Yes!" She was riled by his caution.

"Are you certain?"

"Michael!" She was regularly exasperated by his overt vigilance. Even after everything that had happened, she was too trusting. With Brigham routed, she declined to suppose that there were others who might have designs on her.

"Are you ready for your bath, milady?" he teased.

"The water is too hot, so it needs to cool." She batted her lashes. "How will we pass the time?"

"You minx! You'll be the death of me yet."

"I hope not. I have too many licentious plans for you." She chortled merrily, then abruptly halted as she discerned a hint of his underlying distress that should have been prudently hidden. "You're upset."

"Not really."

"Don't lie to me." She possessed an innate insight where he was concerned. "I can tell when you are."

"Maybe a tad," he averred.

"Is your mother all right?"

"As far as I know."

She shuddered with relief, as though his mother was an old friend about whom she habitually fretted as the older woman flaunted herself across the Continent on her honeymoon.

During the cloistered supper they'd enjoyed in his bedchamber, he'd opened these doors to his personal history, and she'd gladly stepped through, then wheedled him to divulge some of his reflections about Angela and Edward, about James and his new bride, too, though why he'd discussed such delicate, private topics was a mystery. She'd just been so determined to drag his family's misery into the open, convinced that airing their dirty laundry was the best method for coming to grips with what had transpired.

Between bouts of frantic loving, they'd chatted incessantly until she was well versed in his foibles and squabbles. He had always been a detached, solitary man, and he couldn't believe how extraordinary it had been to confide in someone for a change, and he was disturbed by how much he'd miss their verbal intimacy once he moved on.

"Sit." He patted the mattress, and she stretched out as if she'd done just that on a thousand prior occasions. Her body perfectly conformed to his, and he situated her so that he could peer into her green eyes. He intended to always recall how brightly they shimmered, how scrupulously they assessed.

"What is it?" she queried.

"I'm leaving in the morning."

He wasn't sure what he'd anticipated from her. Weeping? Pleading? Assorted female histrionics? Assuredly not this dreadful calm.

"I see," she finally stated. "Why?"

"Lady Carrington asked me to."

"Why?" she repeated.

Many answers would satisfy, but so far, he'd deftly skirted the issue of his association with her brother, and he didn't contrive to address it at this late date. Apparently, she'd never guessed that he and Hugh might be acquainted, and he'd like her to remain ignorant of their sordid alliance.

He grinned, trying to make light of the circumstances. "She claims I've abused her hospitality."

"I thought you two were friends."

"We are"—he shifted uncomfortably—"but even Pamela has her limits."

"Brigham?"

"Yes."

"Where will you go?"

"I haven't decided. I've a dozen invitations to other parties, but I might journey to my brother's country house. It's remote and secluded, and I could benefit from the solitude."

"Will you continue on to town?"

"Eventually." His job at the club was the only decent method he'd ever detected for keeping himself out of trouble.

"You should head for home," she scolded. "The sooner the better."

They'd rigorously debated his plight, and he knew she was correct, but he couldn't seem to turn toward London. Not yet, anyway.

"If you went to your brother's rural residence . . ." She paused, contemplating. "Would you like me to join you there? I could probably find a way."

His heart pounded, then generated an odd rumble, and he was quite certain it might be breaking. More than anything, he wished she could follow him to James's house. The discreet staff would provide an exclusive haven in which to romp and build permanent memories, but it simply couldn't be.

"No," he ultimately declared, even as he marveled as to how he'd located the fortitude to refuse her. "We must say *adieu* tonight."

Unblinking, not breathing, she casually absorbed the news. "Are you positive?"

"Aye." She didn't argue or disagree, but still, he felt inclined to add, "It's for the best."

"I'm sure that's true."

He sustained a vicious impulse to shake her out of her acquiescence. Why didn't she react? Why didn't she quibble? Would it be so easy, then, for her to walk away?

When he'd instigated this insane business, he'd never projected ahead to the wretched finale. If he had, he'd definitely have fantasized that *she* would be the one dissembling, not himself. He was too confident, too in control. He could fuck a woman forever without growing attached to her.

Couldn't he?

"I want to make love till dawn," he said.

"So do I."

Yet, he couldn't seem to begin. Instead, he exhaustively regarded her, chronicling every particular. Dozens of words were poised on the tip of his tongue, and oh, how anxious he was to expound! If he'd been brave enough, he'd have confessed how much he'd treasured meeting her, how he'd valued their brief interlude, and how he hoped she would find happiness and serenity in the future, but he said nothing.

What good would it do to babble a pile of fatuous sentimentality? If he professed how much he cared, she'd likely do the same, and there they'd be, ensnared in an impossible circle of yearning and affection from which there could be no retreat.

Better to keep silent.

"It will be hard to say farewell," was all he could manage.

"I know."

"I'll miss you." *Always,* he was avid to append.

"And I, you."

They stared, neither willing to volunteer more, and he was so relieved. He couldn't bear to hear her actual ruminations, so he pretended that her internal musings adequately matched his own, though he didn't fathom how they could. His fondness for her had completely consumed him, and the concept of carrying on without this chance for sharing at the close of the day was beyond imagining.

The stirring, pensive moment ended when their lips touched in a quiet embrace filled with all that couldn't be uttered aloud. She riffled her fingers through his hair, stroked his neck and shoulder, until her hand settled on the center of his chest, resting over his heart, massaging and affording solace. Her tongue united with his in a peaceful dance that was familiar and delectable.

He'd never been much of a one for kissing, but with her, he couldn't withstand the slow provocation. Their breath mingled, their pulses beat in a constant rhythm. The sheer rapture of having her so simply and sweetly overwhelmed him, and he could have lain there in perpetuity, doing nothing more than pressing his mouth to hers.

The languid exchange couldn't help but grow more heated. Before long, her robe was off, and he was tugging her nightgown up her legs. He cupped and caressed her, relishing how her hips set the tempo.

His unskilled virgin had blossomed! She knew how to tantalize and arouse, how to originate and seduce, but also how to receive what she craved.

He toyed until she was wet with desire, her nether lips swollen and stimulated, and he succumbed to the lure of implanting her scent on his tongue. Her sexual essence was a potent aphrodisiac; it inflamed him and chased away his common sense.

Licking and tasting, he drove her toward her peak, but the wench was so proficient at restraint, so attuned to her body and his, that she was a veritable master at prolonging her pleasure. Tracing a path up her body, he lingered at her navel, at the valley between her breasts. He pushed her nightgown higher, revealing the undersides of those two spectacular globes, then higher still so that the nipples were bared and screaming for attention. Like a hungry babe, he nursed, indulging his carnal whims while her smell and warmth furnished unremitting succor.

Unable to delay, he yanked the sleepwear over her head so that she was naked, and his greedy eyes feasted on her comeliness, on her trim waist and flared hips. The sight caused his manly blood to flow until his cock was demanding surcease.

He jerked at his shirt, then tore at the buttons of his trousers, barely sliding them off his hips. Needing to be free of confines, in her hand, in her mouth, he was so hard for her, and he manipulated his turgid length as she watched then enthusiastically took over the task. She scooted down, bringing him to those chaste, pristine lips, that he loved to defile.

As adept as any courtesan, her tongue flicked out, again and again at the sensitive tip, then she sucked him in. He gave her all she could handle and more, probing deep, his titillation increasing because she couldn't seem to get enough.

Quickly, he'd arrived at an irrepressible zenith, and he

extricated himself, his heartbeat ragged, sweat pooling on his brow, his cock beseeching.

"Come in my mouth," she implored.

During all their rough antics, he hadn't yet, for despite how often she entreated, he didn't think she was prepared for the extreme experience.

"No."

"Michael . . ."

She protested as he skimmed down her body, removing his querulous phallus from temptation. He stroked the crown along the soft skin of her abdomen.

Powerless to avoid torment, he delved into her pussy, just the slightest inch, letting her erotic juices dampen the flaring tip. That he could plunge inside! Just this once! That he could have her in the only way that truly counted!

When he balanced on his haunches, she raised her legs and draped them over his thighs, offering herself. He could see her pink center, see the hairs that were slick and glossy. Her core was a slippery, menacing refuge, and he couldn't understand why he perpetually denied himself such unrelenting gratification.

As though reading his mind—a tactic at which she excelled—she chided, "It's our last time. Take me."

"Oh, Sarah . . ." He moaned in misery, poised at the apex, wondering where his willpower to desist would come from. "I'm not a saint. Don't give me permission."

"How can it matter?" She was panting, strained, eager.

"We've been over this and over this." He rubbed along her cleft. "If I destroy your maidenhead, you can't ever erase the damage."

"I won't ever want to. I'll never marry." She clenched her leg muscles. "Do it!"

Glaring at the ceiling, he was vacillating, ambivalent, unable to tolerate how she was pleading with her eyes. His buttocks tensed, and he flexed. He was playing with fire, at the point where he couldn't stop.

"I want to be your first," he inevitably affirmed, dropping his gaze to hers. "I want it to be me, so that you'll always remember."

"As if I could ever forget!"

She widened further, the move bringing him nearer, and he abandoned the fight. No going back. He steadied her, establishing himself to take her in a single, smooth thrust.

"This will hurt."

"Badly?"

"Just a little."

Tremulously, she smiled and arched up, lifting her breasts. He fondled a nipple, then trailed a hand down her front, to her waist and lower. Guiding himself, he rubbed across her, extensively moistening the blunt crest until he was sufficiently lubricated.

"No regrets," he reminded her.

"Never."

With a deft lunge, he was sheathed to her womb. As he sensed the tear, she cried out, and he leaned forward, looming over her, craving the chance to shelter and protect.

"The pain will pass," he whispered.

"It already is."

"Hold me tight."

She made a sound, and it could have been a laugh or a sob. "I never believed you'd actually fit."

"Told you," he murmured, kissing her again, struggling for composure while she acclimated to his abnormal invasion. Her pussy convulsed, permeated as it was with her virgin's blood, and his cock floated in a scalding, writhing sea of ecstasy.

At the first sign of her body's capitulation, he fervidly commenced. He'd desired her too badly for too long—all his life it seemed now, though he hadn't known it—and they simply couldn't have a tame copulation. Her tight cleft milked him, spurred him on, and he was able to allow himself free rein to vent his building lust.

Her admiration was visibly manifest, her veneration shining, and for once, he didn't shield his own feelings. He let the masks fall away, and he showered her with his adoration, mutely imparting that this interval with her had been a boon he had never foreseen, a gift he would infinitely cherish.

She responded to his every ministration, her desire transporting her beyond the initial discomfort. At the edge, he tossed her over with a well-aimed swipe of his thumb, then he accompanied her, though his trajectory was a bit altered from its natural course.

At the very last, he withdrew, the blistering spew of his semen shooting across her belly, and he snuggled into the crook of her neck, resting there while the tremors shook him, then waned. Gradually, he relaxed, but he didn't raise up because, in reality, he was a coward, afraid to look her in the eye and see what truths were lurking.

With the light kiss on his forehead, he couldn't thwart the inevitable. He peeked at her, only to discover that she was engulfed by such a profound sadness that he couldn't figure out what to say or how to react. Of all the emotions he might have named as to how she'd survive her deflowering, he'd have never picked despondency. His heart lurched and missed several beats.

"What is it, love?"

"I didn't realize you would pull out."

"I had to," he explained. "We daren't make a babe."

"Could we have from just one time?"

"It's possible."

She stared at him a long while, then proclaimed, "I wish we had."

He was shocked and awestruck, his senses reeled. A babe! With her! How he yearned to plant his seed so deep that it took root and flourished.

Biting back a groan, he clamped his eyes shut, but unwelcome, beguiling images of young children waltzed across his field of vision: little auburn-haired cherubs with their mother's alluring ways and soothing countenance; rowdy blue-eyed boys, with his sass and attitude.

Desperately, he craved the excuse to sire a babe on Sarah; he wanted it more than he'd ever wanted anything.

Frantic to inject reality into his fantasizing, he struggled to speak but what emerged was, "Would a babe make you happy, Sarah?"

"I'd love to give you a son." She brushed the hair off his face. "I'd be so proud."

"I'm so sorry that we can't." Even as he said it, his body leapt to readiness. Though he'd just emptied himself, his cock swelled to a rude, vehement length, arranged to commit an almost predestined, irrevocable mistake.

The bathtub!

The phrase screamed out as a mode of rescue from the deviant course his anatomy was imploring him to trek. He required involvement in a less ardent endeavor, although why he would view washing her flawless torso as *safe* was a question he didn't stoop to meditate upon. His lurid reveries had to be instantly curbed before he did something reckless, something irreversible.

Hoping that space would allay his wanton urges, he stepped to the floor. He was covered with her blood, his phallus and crotch a red smear, evidence of the sin he'd committed against her, his semen a drying pile on her stomach and leg.

Grabbing a towel, he wiped her clean, then himself, and stuffed his irritated privates into his pants. Through it all, she observed his every move, and he liked how he felt revered and precious under her blatant scrutiny.

"Are you sore?"

Undecided, she shifted against the mattress, and her body emitted a wail of protest. "Ooh . . . yes."

"Then let's sit you in your bath for a soak." He helped her up. "The water will ease the tenderness, and wash away the blood."

"Am I injured?" She glanced down and scowled, not understanding the physical consequence.

"No, but you're no longer a maid." Insolently, he preened that he'd been the one to relieve her of her virtue.

"Will I bleed every time?"

"Just this once and"—he steered her toward the dressing

room—"when your lovely bottom is healed from tonight's
adventure, it won't hurt ever again, either."

"I feel as if you split me in half."

She glared at him over her shoulder, and she was a
charming vision, all shapely ass, long legs, and smooth,
naked skin.

"I'm a very big man." He shrugged, conspicuously overbearing, but like the cad he was, he couldn't resist gloating
over what he'd just purloined from her. He stole a kiss
before she could whirl around. "You make me wild with
passion. I couldn't be gentle."

"You are such an arrogant rogue. Maybe I won't tell
you how glad I am that it was you."

Her comment delved far into the spot where he was so
lonely and alone. They were at the edge of the tub, so he
bent down and tested the temperature of the water, finding
it to be warm and inviting.

Pretending a detachment he hardly felt, he casually mentioned, "Are you . . . glad . . . that it was me?"

"Very."

He met her gaze then, and she was smiling at him with
such an affectionate expression that he had to swallow three
times before he could communicate further.

"In you go." He stabilized her as she climbed in and slid
down.

"Aah . . . I'm a tad tender." Lowering herself, she winced
as her beleaguered pussy coped with the heat, but then she
rapidly acclimated, and she reposed, braced against the back,
her knees spread wide.

For a few minutes, her body mended in the mild broth,
and he knelt by her side, entranced by her loveliness and
disposition. She turned toward him, her forearms on the
rim, so that they were nose to nose, skin to skin, eye to
eye.

"Will you let me wash you?" she appealed.

"Absolutely."

"And will you make love to me again afterward?"

"All night long"—he took a cloth and swabbed her

breasts—"if you're not too sore." At the wicked wink she
flashed, he ducked under her chin and nibbled at her neck,
inducing her to squirm and giggle.

"I get to be on top."

"Lord have mercy," he grumbled.

Presently, a noise vaguely registered—a throat being
cleared—but it was so out of place that many moments
passed before he honed in on what it was. He hesitated,
then his focus went to the door that connected the dressing
room to her outer bedchamber.

"Well . . . well . . ." oozed a familiar, much-loathed
voice, "look what we have here."

"Bloody hell!" Michael cursed.

Sarah whipped around, gasped in dismay, and sank into
the water, striving to shield herself.

Hugh Compton and Rebecca Monroe studied them,
every decadent detail of their nude caper, and Rebecca's
mouth gaped open like a fish pitched onto a riverbank. The
four of them were a frozen quartet, then her brother had
the decency to shove Rebecca away, so that she couldn't
witness more of their lewd escapade.

Stationed by himself in the doorway, Hugh was framed
by the threshold.

"Hello, sister," Scarborough intoned with a mocking
bow. "And Stevens! How damned *interesting* to encounter
you with Sarah." He tsked. "And in such a disgraceful condition!"

Michael had never felt so vulnerable, had never been
caught so off guard. Warily, he vaulted to his feet. "What
the hell are you up to, Scarborough?"

"I might ask you the same."

Scarborough was leering, straining on tiptoe for a
glimpse of Sarah's breasts. The coarse attempt brought Michael's temper to a fast boil, and he sprang to action.

"Get out"—he jumped in front of the tub, so that Scarborough's glimpse was cut off—"or I'll kill you where you
stand."

"Bastard . . ." Scarborough ground out. "Of course, you realize what this means."

"Go!" Michael shouted with such authority that both Sarah and Scarborough flinched. "Now!"

Not cowed in the least, Hugh straightened to his full height, which didn't match Michael's own, but nonetheless, he appeared threatening. And gleeful. The churl was ecstatic, and Michael longed to clutch him by the throat and squeeze until there was no air left in his lungs.

How had he, Michael Stevens—the most cautious and circumspect of men—fallen into an ambush set by such a despicable swine?

His heart plummeted as a horrid supposition cropped up, one he could scarcely give credence to, but he couldn't silence it. He wrenched his angry glower from Scarborough to Sarah who was huddled down in the basin. As he speculated, and evaluated, old doubts and misgivings crept in, and he couldn't help suspecting the worst.

Had she orchestrated this debacle with her brother? Had her seemingly gracious esteem been feigned? Scarborough wasn't clever enough to initiate such a scheme, or to pull it off successfully. Neither was his cousin. But Sarah?

It must have been her.

There was no other explanation as to how shrewdly and effectively the trap had been baited and snapped shut, snaring him in a coil of his own creation.

Earlier, when she'd arrived in his bedchamber, he'd interrogated her as to whether she'd locked her door, and she'd adamantly said yes. He'd been so befuddled by her that he'd simply taken her word for it; he hadn't gone to verify as was his custom. The depth of his enamoration had provoked him to act out of character, to trust and assume.

Such foolishness! Such stupidity!

He jerked his gaze to Scarborough, once again, and the earl laughed and nodded, confirming his excruciating deduction.

"My compliments," Michael coldly declared. "Well done."

"Yes, it rather was, wasn't it? We've all worked so hard on this," Scarborough observed smugly. "I'll meet you down in the library. In fifteen minutes." He spun around to depart, then cast a scathing glance over his shoulder at Sarah. "Leave our little whore to her bath. I'll deal with her later."

Chapter Eighteen

Hugh waltzed out, his egress marked by a resounding slam of the door as he exited into the corridor. For a brief moment, Michael glared down at her, his countenance a medley of fury, regret, and disbelief that was swiftly masked. Without speaking, he marched to the outer room where she heard the lock turning, and a heavy piece of furniture being dragged as a barricade so that no one else could surprise them.

Did he suppose that she'd contrived this fiasco? That she was in league with Hugh? She cringed. Of course he would! The blackguard!

Abruptly feeling not just naked, but exposed, she was desperate to cover herself, and she scurried from the tub. Not bothering with the towel, she was just tying the belt of her robe when he stormed back in. His sapphire eyes blazed with fire, his body trembled with controlled rage. Then, he checked himself, exhibiting the icy composure he displayed to the world. He'd reerected the protective walls that kept him safe from those who would maltreat him, and evidently, he now included her in that number.

"You assured me that you'd locked your door," he reproached.

"I did!"

"Then, madam, how did your brother get in?"

"I have no idea."

"So you say—"

"Yes, I say!" she interrupted. "Don't you dare charge otherwise!"

They angrily stared at one another across a hopeless expanse, and she couldn't have him suspecting that she'd be-

trayed their relationship. Tendering her hand, begging him
to take it, she reached out, but he didn't so much as glance
at it.

"Michael," she beseeched, "don't let's fight. We must
figure out what to do."

"What to *do*?" He lurched away as if she'd admitted she
had the pox.

"Yes, we're intelligent people. We can devise a practical
solution. I'll talk to Hugh."

"You're very good at this"—he narrowed his eyes, scathingly assessing her—"and you play the innocent excel-
lently, but there's no reason to maintain the ruse. You've
snared me most effectively."

"You think I . . . that I . . ." She'd already deduced that
he suspected her of duplicity, but his indictment stirred a
surge of wrath. How could he distrust her! After they'd just
lain together! "You bastard!"

The approbation spurted out before she could chomp
down on it, and a dangerous, probing malice enveloped
him. "I've never claimed to be anything but—"

"I apologize. I didn't mean that," she injected, yet he
kept on, his voice brittle.

"—so why you would wish to tie your life to mine is a
mystery." He spun toward his room. "But I guess we'll both
have copious opportunity over the years to decide why you
would agree to such a reckless path."

He was nearly at the portal, and she was terrified that
he'd step through and disappear, that these pernicious, vehement declarations would be the last they ever uttered. She
hustled to his side and put her hand on his arm, stopping
him.

"Michael . . . wait. Let me explain." But as she'd had no
part in what had befallen them, she wasn't sure what her
explanation could be.

"You needn't justify your conduct"—his chilly façade
was frightening—"and I won't suffer through an accounting of your rationalization. Or your brother's."

"But that's just it. None of this was my doing."

"Lady Sarah," he frigidly intoned, and his use of her title cut her to the quick, "the time that I would believe you is long past. Now, if you will excuse me, I've an appointment belowstairs."

"Give me a minute to prepare myself. I'll accompany you."

"Milady, your presence is neither necessary nor required."

He bowed slightly, then shut the door in her face, and she was so dazed that, before she could react, he'd bolted it with a determined click. She pounded on the unyielding barrier, roaring, "Michael Stevens! Open up this instant!"

Her command was greeted with silence.

She beat on it again and again till her fists ached, but her attempt went unacknowledged, and she inevitably ceased, holding very still, putting her palm to the wood. On the other side, she could sense his movements as he dressed in his fastidious manner, readying to descend for the momentous showdown with Hugh.

How would they respond to one another? What would they say? Would Hugh call him out? She blocked the ghastly notion, unable to abide reflecting upon her brother and her great love dueling, perhaps to the death.

"Damn you, Michael," she muttered, certain that he was listening. "I won't let you walk away." No rejoinder. "Do you hear me?" She kicked the bottom of the door so solidly that her foot throbbed from the impact.

Limping to the bedchamber, she cast about for some clothes, but she couldn't don the dastardly garments on her own, and she declined to confront the two men unless she was completely contained and self-possessed.

Fuming, sucked into an inferno beyond her ken, she hurled her corset on the bed and rang for a maid, then paced by the clock, counting each agonizing second until the woman appeared. With a relief that bordered on madness, she seized the retainer and drew her inside, and the servant—prudently cognizant of acute distress—made no comment, but efficiently went about her task.

The final comb in her chignon was scarcely in place when Sarah grumbled an insincere platitude and hastened out. Though she vividly remembered Brigham and the perils of wandering the halls, she wasn't worried. In her current mood, just let some brigand try to accost her! She was fixated on getting downstairs, and Lord help the gentleman who sought to detain her!

She was irritated at Michael for his proceeding without her. So much time had elapsed! Would he and Hugh still be conferring? What would be the topics? How could Michael mitigate what Hugh had witnessed?

Better than anyone, she understood Hugh, his mind, his disposition, his short-fused temper. *She* was the one who should be dealing with him. Not rash, imperious, benumbed Michael. What a disaster, to have two such intractable men at odds over a situation that was exclusively her fault! She had to intervene with Hugh before they exchanged so many insults that neither could back down.

Maneuvering her way to the bottom floor, she didn't encounter anyone, and she looked a sight, but she didn't care. As she raced toward the library, activity was audible in the various salons, the guests immersed in evening merriment, but who occupied them, or what they were doing, was a blur.

The door was just ahead, and she hurried to it, geared to knock once, then fling it open, but her desire for a grand entrance was spoiled as Michael emerged. Larger than life, he bristled on espying her, and she slid to a halt lest she plow into him. Behind them, Hugh's grating laughter rang out.

"Come with me." His dictatorial tone irked her, and he squired her away from the library and the battle she'd planned with her brother. She dug in her heels.

"No"—she grappled against his tight grip—"I must confer with Hugh."

"That's not going to happen."

He continued hauling her toward the foyer as though she was a naughty youngster about to be disciplined. She contemplated loudly bellowing her displeasure, but there were people about so she couldn't cause a scene, though she was relieved to note that no one paid any attention to her passing. While she wasn't overly acquainted with any of them, she wasn't about to have others watching as she was towed along like an unruly child.

Crude jocularity drifted over a threshold, and she peeked back, afforded a fleeting glimpse before Michael whisked her on. A naked woman posed on a table while a half-naked man tarried before her, kissing her breasts. A thick, hazy smoke provided a grotesque, hallucinatory ambiance, obscuring the many spectators who were hovering in the corners.

As she flinched, Michael yanked her away so quickly that she wasn't positive she'd seen it at all. Could it have been real?

She shuddered with distaste.

Before she could gather her wits, they were through the main door of the manor and out into the quiet, fresh night air. She breathed deeply to shed the pall that had hung over the residence, but Michael ceded her no enjoyment of the brief serenity. He ushered her to a carriage, and questions flew—why were they leaving? what did this portend?—but mostly, she inanely concentrated on how the infuriating man had arranged for a carriage to be brought around so promptly.

In the past hour, too many outrageous catastrophes had arisen. Her thoughts were in chaos, her emotions in turmoil, and she was convinced that she shouldn't absent herself from the property, but Michael was even now hoisting her in, and she struggled to arrest his progress, managing to pitch back onto his chest.

"Get in, madam."

"I won't."

She whirled around, stomping her foot, and she imagined she resembled a petulant toddler, throwing a temper tantrum. Throughout her life, men had endeavored to manipulate her and force her to do their bidding, but she'd never acquiesced, and she wasn't about to start now. If Michael wanted something from her, all he had to do was ask. Manhandling her was not the way to go about it!

"You will. Now, or I shall lift you in bodily."

Indignant, she bit at her bottom lip, crossed her arms, and affected the mien that regularly set adult males to trembling. "I insist that you apprise me of your intentions, or I will raise such a ruckus that the entire household will come out to see what's transpiring."

He was unfazed by her threat, his eyes glittering menacingly, and if she hadn't been persuaded as to the type of man he was, she might have feared for her physical safety.

"As you obviously do not comprehend this about me"— he leaned close, articulating softly so that no one lingering nearby could perceive their quarrel—"I must advise you that I *never* prance about in public, engaging in discord where others might observe my personal squabbles. That said"—the presumptuous knave clasped her waist and tossed her in—"I will not loiter in the drive, arguing with you."

"Fine!" As incensed as he, she'd like nothing more than to whack that insolent smirk off his pretty face.

She moved to the far corner and huddled against the squab, as Michael delivered a few abbreviated commands to the coachmen. Then he climbed in behind her, his huge form blocking the small hatch so that she couldn't have vaulted out even if she'd considered it, which she hadn't. Crazy as it sounded, she was excited about the prospect of traipsing off with him. Whatever ensued, she intended to make the most of it.

He settled himself and rapped on the roof. The carriage clattered away at a brisk speed, and she clutched at the strap to keep from sliding off the seat. They cruised down the long lane toward the village, and then the road to London that lay beyond. He stared out the window, pretending he was the sole passenger, so she pulled back the curtain and peered outside, as well.

The moon was full, the countryside brilliantly illuminated, and she surveyed all for a quiescent, passion-charged interlude.

She'd meant to ignore him, but he simply pervaded the enclosed area, and she wasn't about to demurely submit to his carting her across England without having some idea of where they were bound or why.

"Where are we headed?"

The lengthy pause made her conclude that he wouldn't reply. Then ultimately, he focused his rabid gaze on her. "*You* are to stay at an inn."

"At this hour? How will we locate one?"

"We are near enough to town that there are several suitable choices."

"We couldn't have left in the morning? Like two normal, decent people?"

The word *decent* had him snorting derisively. "For over two weeks, I have been suggesting that you vacate the premises, and you would not heed me. Previously, I hadn't the authority to enforce your departure." His eyes constricted with an ominous venom. "Now, I do."

"Who made that decision?"

"Your brother"—he hesitated, striving for maximum effect—". . . and I."

The two cads! She wasn't some incapable young maiden. How dare they initiate a resolution without seeking her opinion!

"You might have permitted me to communicate my thank-you and good-bye to Lady Carrington."

"I'll offer your apologies."

"What about my belongings?"

"I'll have them packed and sent to you."

Ooh . . . and wouldn't she just like to shake him! This was how he'd acted when they'd first met, before they'd become lovers, and she abhorred this calculated indifference. She was wiser now as to his comportment, and she recognized that the hostile, flinty demeanor indicated he was hurting.

He presumed that she had schemed with Hugh, but after

all they'd shared, how could he be so willing to assume her complicity?

"What did Hugh say to you?"

He chortled. "As if you didn't know."

"Tell me!" she decreed.

"Be silent, woman! I don't propose to bicker with you all the way to the inn."

"We haven't begun to argue!"

"Don't push me!"

"You're behaving like a lunatic."

Seeming to deflate, he sank back and gaped out the window, once again. "Give it a rest, Lady Sarah."

"And quit addressing me by my title. It wounds me when you do."

Weary, he tipped his head toward the leather, and she longed to close the distance between them, to sit on his lap and guide them back to that special spot where they talked and loved so easily.

"I want to help," she murmured, but he had no retort. At a loss, she perused the outside landscape. Eventually, they slowed, and the driver urged the horses into the circular courtyard of an inn. Lamps were burning on the lower floor. Their conveyance rattled to a stop, and a postboy ran out from the stable to drop the step.

"Wait here," Michael exclaimed, springing out and banging the door behind.

She was half-tempted to pursue him just to have the satisfaction of disobeying his spurious mandate, but she wasn't about to meander into an unfamiliar establishment in the middle of the night without an escort. Reposing in the shadows, she scrutinized the surroundings, the only noises coming from the horses as they calmed themselves, the driver as he shifted about.

Many minutes later, Michael returned and assisted her to the ground. A serving girl held a lantern and, without debate, they followed her inside. Voices and revelry emanated from one of the common rooms, but Michael directed her past and up the stairs and, without incident, they ascended to a clean, tidy chamber at the end of the hall on the second floor.

She balanced on the edge of the bed while the girl lit a fire in the brazier. Michael guarded the door, a fierce, tempestuous sentinel who hovered over all while the girl finished her chores, then withdrew.

The stillness left in her wake was instantly oppressive, and Sarah stirred nervously, afraid to learn what was coming, just as afraid not to.

"Well . . . ?" When it seemed he'd never commence, she rose and listed his recent transgressions on the tips of her fingers. "You kidnapped me from Lady Carrington's estate. You won't divulge the contents of your conversation with my brother. You brought me to this strange inn. Explain yourself—immediately—or I guarantee that I shall hie myself downstairs, and find my way to Pamela's—if I have to hike every bloody mile through the dark to get there."

Without her being aware of it, she was essentially shouting, and someone in one of the adjoining apartments pounded on the thin wall and bellowed for her to "be quiet." Mortified, she lowered her volume to a harsh whisper. "I've had enough! This brooding, rude attitude may stand you in good stead with others, but I will not tolerate it. Now, speak to me like a sensible, civil grown man, or leave me be!"

"As you wish, milady." Apparently, he wasn't used to anyone remarking upon his ill humor, and he was jolted. Whispering as well, he informed, "Please break your fast and be dressed so that you are ready by eleven."

"What's occurring at eleven?"

"Why . . . we're off to the church." He gestured as though she was a simpleton. "To marry."

"We're to wed?" Naturally, that's what Hugh would demand. How stupid of her not to realize it! With how rapidly circumstances had escalated, she hadn't had two seconds to reach the inescapable conclusion. She'd simply been scared that they might grab for their pistols.

Her heart was suddenly thudding so fast that she felt it

might burst from under her ribs, and she eased down on the mattress, her legs unable to sustain her weight. Emotions warred: unconditional joy, fury, desolation.

To marry Michael Stevens! If the chance had been presented earlier in the evening, she'd have soared to the heavens, but not now. Not with him in such a snit. And most especially not when he and her brother had come to some sort of agreement without consulting her. She would not be bullied. Not by either of them.

She couldn't stop her flippant query: "Are you proposing?"

"No, because your answer is of absolutely no consequence."

Sighing heavily, she battled tears. How had her great fondness for him brought them to this hideous juncture? She blinked, then blinked again, recalling that she never cried—about anything—yet since he'd crashed into her staid, boring existence, she was constantly prone to weeping.

"What a coil . . ." Reduced to sniffling, she studied her lap, longing for solitude so that she could compose herself. As it was, a tear dribbled out and slipped down her cheek.

"There's no call for theatrics," Michael mentioned upon noticing. "Your display will produce no response from me."

Legs braced, hands secured behind his back, he was handsome, refined, aloof, and so very alone. This cold, hard stranger was no one she knew, no one she had ever known. The affection he'd harbored for her was totally lacking, and she couldn't bear its absence.

Their situation had revolved to where marriage was an option. While he brooded and stewed, her heart sang with the possibilities. She wouldn't view this calamity in negative terms.

He didn't love her; she appreciated that. In view of the type of man he was, and the world from which he'd evolved, perhaps he never would. But she loved him, and if he would just allow her to, she would spend the remainder of her days making him happy and, in the process, obtaining no meager amount of contentment for herself.

There had to be a method of chopping through his bulwark of animosity and suspicion. She simply wouldn't let him spurn her. Whatever it took to restore their unique relationship, she would gladly do—if it meant she had to grovel at his feet. This was no time to be timid, and she carefully tucked away her pride where it couldn't interfere.

"Don't growl at me," she entreated. "I hate that you're so upset, and I don't accept that this is a horrid turn of events. I'd be proud to be your wife. I love you."

"How extremely convenient."

His curt rejoinder was like a slap. She'd never uttered *love* to another soul, and it was painful and humiliating to have her attestation callously hurled back in her face. Resolved to prevail, she forged on.

"It's true, Michael. You know it is." She went to him and rested her fingers on the center of his chest, but touching him was like caressing a cool slab of marble. "I understand that you don't love me in return, but you hold me in some esteem."

"Don't flatter yourself." He removed her hand, then stepped away, creating space as he coarsely evaluated her breasts. "What I've felt for you is lust. Naught else."

Making him see the bright side would be much more difficult than she'd anticipated, but she wasn't about to capitulate. He could be stubborn, rigid, and headstrong, but she wasn't exactly a shrinking violet.

Refusing to be brushed off, she persevered. "You can bark and protest, but you'll never convince me that your feelings aren't genuine. As far as I'm concerned this is a marvelous predicament, and I can't fathom why you're so annoyed."

"Perchance, milady, it has something to do with the fact that your brother arrived with a fully prepared Special License."

"What?"

She couldn't have discerned his pronouncement correctly. A Special License would authorize an immediate wedding. It negated the necessity of calling the banns; any waiting period was void. Why would Hugh have one in his pocket?

An unwelcome pot of disturbing ruminations bubbled over, hinting at deception and betrayal, but the implications were so stunning that, after everything that had already unfolded, she couldn't begin to process them. Only through sheer force of will did she prevent herself from falling on the bed in a state of shock.

"You're not joking, are you?"

"It was signed by the archbishop, no less." He whipped out the paper and waved it under her nose.

"We were so discreet. How could Hugh have discovered what we were about?"

"How indeed?"

The lull that resulted was damning. What could Michael surmise but that she'd had a stake in this? Hugh had as much as said so. She was furious at Michael for accusing her of such deviousness, but she was more enraged at her idiotic, deceitful brother. What did Hugh hope to gain?

Just to scurry the absurd cabal Hugh had hatched, she had half a mind to reject the marriage, yet even as she mulled the sentiment, she knew she wouldn't. Hugh had positioned her on a collision course with Michael, and she wasn't sorry.

They would marry, and Michael would calm down. Time would pass, he would adapt, and they would build a solid life. They would have children, a family. She would support him in his business ventures, and he could recommend how she should restore the Scarborough estate after it was pillaged by Hugh's latest gambling nemesis.

Michael owned a gentleman's club. He might know the scoundrel who had bested Hugh. Once they were wed, he could approach the villain on her behalf, or he might have contacts who could plead her case.

She whirled with excitement. They belonged together. Down to the very marrow of her bones, she sensed that this was the proper route for both of them, and she wouldn't be dissuaded, no matter how he grouched and snapped.

"I'll be a good wife to you, Michael. I swear it."

"Well, bully for you, Lady Sarah, but I've never wanted a *wife*. And"—he stalked to the door—"if I had ever thought to select a bride, it would hardly be a conniving, duplicitous aristocrat such as yourself."

"Will marriage to me really be so terrible?"

"Milady, I can't conceive of anything worse." He departed without a backward glance.

Horribly afflicted, she sank onto the bed, wondering how she'd ever make this right.

Chapter Nineteen

Rebecca tiptoed down the hall toward Hugh's room. Her pulse tripping with excitement, she couldn't wait to hear the joyous news of what had occurred during his meeting with Michael Stevens.

A smile tugged at her lips as she recollected every delicious moment of Sarah's fall from grace. She was glad she'd accompanied Hugh so that she'd been able to witness it for herself. Though she'd only snatched a fleeting glimpse before Hugh had shoved her away, she'd seen enough to understand Sarah's impossible situation. The bathing tub, the nudity, their scandalous seclusion, the imbroglio couldn't have transpired more perfectly if Rebecca had staged it.

The fact that Sarah had humiliated herself so thoroughly was amazing. In her wildest fantasizing, Rebecca hadn't anticipated anything so decadently marvelous. When they'd decided to enter, she'd thought they might catch Mr. Stevens in Sarah's bedchamber, that the pair might be talking or even kissing. But to stumble upon them naked and washing each other!

The reality was simply too sweet.

Her ruse to ensnare Sarah in a matrimonial web had been risky, and she hadn't really been convinced that she'd prevail, but she'd been desperate to prove herself to Hugh. So often, he treated her as though she was of no value, that she was stupid or ineffectual, and his disregard stung.

For the past three years, she'd toiled to situate herself so he'd conclude that she'd be a wonderful countess. She'd minded his town house, administered his calendar, hosted his parties, warmed his bed. In every fashion, she'd ingratiated herself so that he'd see her as viable to his enduring happiness. While her duties—especially the intimate ones—hadn't always been pleasant, she'd performed them competently, confident that he'd note her proficiency, yet he was never satisfied. He reproached and ridiculed, and she wasn't sure why she persevered.

The sole incentive that made it worth the effort was envisioning herself as the future mistress at Scarborough. She would revel in the position as Sarah never had. The house and property amply restored, a skilled staff at her beck and call, dressed in luxurious gowns and exquisite jewels, she would be society's most notable, embraced hostess. With her exalted husband by her side, she would dine on the finest foods, drink the rarest vintage wines, throw lavish balls and parties, and be envied by all.

Thanks to Sarah and her lustful conduct, Rebecca's reveries were about to come true. Who would have imagined that levelheaded, proper Sarah would be so freely led down the carnal path? Of course, from the looks of Mr. Stevens, it was easy to see why even a saint might be tempted.

Nearly skipping with delight over how circumstances had unfolded, and deliriously exhilarated as to her involvement, she hurried the last few steps. Hugh would be so proud of her! So gratified! He would finally behold her as a driving force, as the woman he wanted forevermore. They could be married, as he'd been guaranteeing for so long. With Sarah provided for, there was no reason to delay.

"Rebecca Monroe Compton, the Countess of Scarborough," she practiced, liking how regal the title sounded.

Close to giggling, she reached the door to Hugh's suite and stealthily slid inside.

Hugh was in a plush chair in front of the fire, clearly foxed, a half-empty decanter of brandy in his hand. There was no glass in sight, but she wasn't about to castigate him. This was a night for celebrating. If he chose to crudely swill from the bottle, who was she to say nay?

"Is Sarah with you?" he testily inquired.

"Sorry, Hugh, but she's still not in her room."

"Damn! Where could she be?"

"I searched everywhere." One of the servants had left a supper tray, and she grabbed some cheese off it before going to sit on his lap. "Her belongings are still in the wardrobe."

"Indubitably. Why would they be gone?" He downed a swig of his libation. "How about Stevens? Was he lurking about?"

"No, he wasn't there, either."

"Do you suppose they went off together?" Disturbed by the possibility, he stared into the fire, then slammed his fist on the arm of the chair. "Blast! I need to discuss this with her before Stevens does."

"What's to discuss?" She snuggled her bottom in the manner he enjoyed, but he was too distracted to notice. Though imbibing heavily, he certainly didn't seem to be jubilant. Suddenly worried, she prudently queried, "Everything proceeded as planned, didn't it?"

"The blackguard refused to sign the contract I'd drafted."

"How could he?"

"He laughed in my face!"

Instantaneously, her euphoria evaporated. Would her scheming be for naught? "He'll marry her, though, won't he?"

"He said he'll need to *contemplate* whether his sense of *duty and honor* would require it."

"But what about the marriage settlement you demanded?"

"He wouldn't agree!"

Not recalling that she was perched on his thighs, he jumped to his feet and sent her sprawling, and she scrambled to latch onto a bedpost so she wouldn't land on the floor. "So . . . we're to get . . . nothing?"

"He swore he'd see me dead and buried before I received one farthing of his blessed fortune."

How dare Mr. Stevens spoil her hard-earned victory! Utterly flabbergasted by this unseen turn of events, she sank down onto the mattress, thinking she might be ill.

Pacing back and forth, clutching his accursed bottle of spirits as if it was a magic talisman, Hugh ranted and raved about Michael Stevens and his tyrannical procedures.

"What about Sarah?" she injected into his diatribe. "Could she convince him?"

"That's what I'm hoping. She absolutely must consent to speak with him."

"And if she won't?"

Hugh didn't reply or perhaps, in his overwrought condition, he simply wasn't paying attention. He resumed his march across the rug, while she pondered how quickly her dreams had dwindled to ashes.

She'd plotted down to the smallest detail: Whichever fellow eventually ended up compromising Sarah, he would be a gentleman who recognized Hugh's status and rank, and he'd feel obligated to rectify the slight he'd committed against Hugh's family. The unlucky bridegroom would apologize in the only mode that mattered—by tendering money. Lots and lots of money.

Who would have thought that her strategy would be subverted by the likes of Michael Stevens? The man didn't comprehend the rules of civilized behavior! He was so far below Sarah's exalted station; it was a privilege for him to have been granted the opportunity to wed her! Didn't he grasp that his actions constrained him to make amends?

Rebecca brooded, heartsick and distressed, listening to Hugh rail against fate, watching him stagger and fume.

She remembered Sarah, and the expression of joy she'd exhibited that odd afternoon on the lawn when she'd been in Michael Stevens's presence, and one truth became abundantly clear: Sarah would never solicit Mr. Stevens on Hugh's behalf. Never in a thousand years.

Their conspiracy had been to no avail, though Hugh didn't know it yet. He never could face the consequences of his acts, but then, for much of his life, he'd had his father to hide behind, then Sarah, then herself. Despite their divergent interests, she and Sarah had shielded him from himself, but this decisive fiasco had proved too great a folly. She wanted to weep for what was forfeit.

The town house, with its pretty furnishings and lovely view of the park, was gone. As was the jaunty carriage, with its high-stepping chestnuts, that Hugh drove when he was squiring her about town. So too her closets of fancy clothes and baubles.

Most painful to consider was her loss of Scarborough. What a charming vision she'd painted, and what a fool she'd been to assume that it might come to pass. For just a moment, she closed her eyes and pictured herself floating down the grand corridor on the main floor of the mansion, her skirts brushing the tiles, as she waltzed to the parlor and greeted a new group of guests who had stopped for a visit.

The illusion faded, and she focused on Hugh, once more. Much like a petulant child who'd been denied a treat, his tantrum was terminated, and he was reclined again by the hearth.

"We won't be able to marry, will we?" She knew the answer, but she had to hear it from his lips.

"What?" He glared at her as if she was mad.

"You promised that we'd marry once Sarah was established, but we can't now. Not without any blunt coming in."

"Honestly, Rebecca." As he stared her down, he didn't seem quite so handsome; just inebriated and obnoxious. "You actually expected that we would marry?"

"But you said . . ."

"Bah . . ." He gestured obscenely, dismissing her—and her hopes—with a single motion. "I could never marry *you*. The notion is ludicrous."

Frightened, she swallowed down a panicked breath. "The very first occasion when you coaxed me to your bed, you vowed that we would."

"How could I?" Heedlessly, he trembled with mirth. "God, you're my cousin! And you're a commoner. Are you *that* naïve? I'm a man; I was just trying to lift your skirts. Surely you realized that?"

"No, I didn't," she mouthed.

"It worked, too!" Guffawing, he slapped his leg as though he'd just pronounced a hilarious joke at her expense, and she sincerely felt her heart might quit beating.

"I believed everything you said."

She thought of his disgusting habits and temper, of his grumbling and fussing, his lewd bedroom antics. Because she so fiercely craved the future he could have rendered, she'd braved all.

"Gads, just last week, I offered for Tilsbury's daughter"—he was babbling, having forgotten she was there—"but he insisted that I reverse some of my debt predicament before he'd reflect upon it." He shook his head and studied the flames. "That deal's shot to hell."

The embers glowed, and his morose meditation continued while she meticulously evaluated him, an unvoiced rage at his betrayals brewing dramatically. Gradually, his eyelids fluttered shut, and he began to snore. The decanter fell and clanked on the floor, but the noise failed to stir him.

Quiet as a mouse, she rose and sneaked away, even as she was deliberating on how she would retaliate for everything he'd done.

"I now pronounce you man and wife," the vicar intoned. "You may kiss the bride."

A lengthy, uncomfortable silence ensued, and Michael gawked at him as though the man had snakes in his hair.

Taken aback by the virulent appraisal, the minister gulped then muttered something that sounded like ". . . or not . . ." and snapped his prayer book closed.

At the intentional slight of his new bride, Sarah stiffened and shifted away, unable to tolerate his boorish company.

Good, Michael mused. *Let her be wary.*

When he'd arrived at the inn to retrieve her shortly before eleven, she'd been eagerly awaiting him in one of the private parlors. Perplexingly, she'd primped and preened in preparation, as if the farce was a real ceremony. Wearing a simple gown, but with her hair curled and swept up on her head, she'd appeared cheerful and beautiful.

Any man in the kingdom would have deemed himself fortunate to wed her. Not Michael, for he knew that looks could be deceiving. Underneath that pale elegance and allure beat a black heart.

He was a cautious individual who'd been whisked up in a disaster. This was the type of wretched debacle more suited to James than himself, and if anyone had suggested that he might one day find himself repeating his vows as reparation for a moronic carnal misstep, he'd have laughed aloud. He'd always presumed that he was too astute, too smart, too calculating, to end up on the wrong side of a marital calamity.

Once he'd learned that she was Hugh Compton's sister, he should have resisted his attraction instead of being beguiled by a virtuous flare and a pair of emerald eyes. How they'd sparkled when she'd beseeched him to engage in an abbreviated tryst! How they'd glistened when she'd shed enchanting tears! How they'd intensified when she'd called his name and cried out in sexual ecstasy!

What had possessed him to be so reckless, so negligent? He took pride in his self-control and discipline, and he couldn't accept the depth of his idiocy where she was concerned.

Well, he had no one to blame but himself for this catastrophe. While he wanted to chastise Lady Sarah and her brother, they couldn't have succeeded if Michael hadn't been so atrociously gullible.

On principle, he should have declined to marry her, but he wasn't that kind of person. Even before he'd gone down to the library the previous night, he'd been aware that Scarborough would insist on matrimony, just as he'd acknowledged that he would acquiesce.

After all, he could hardly argue that he wasn't culpable.

Yes, Lady Sarah had begged for the affair, and yes, she'd placed herself in his way at every turn, but he was a mature, experienced man, who should have withstood her campaign.

He was *not* his father, and he wouldn't shirk his responsibilities, but that didn't mean he would play Scarborough's game, either. Scarborough had hit him up for money—big money—as Michael had predicted he would. Yet, as Lady Sarah and her conniving brother were about to discover, Michael's sense of accountableness only extended so far.

For his crime of ruining Lady Sarah, he was constrained to wed her. Regretfully, he would impart to her the respectability that came with being a married woman, but that was all. He would never offer them a single penny in reparation.

Hugh and Sarah Compton could choke on their poverty.

The country chapel, with its pews, dark walls, and stained glass, smelled of wax and polish, of travail and prayers, and it occurred to him that he hadn't set foot in a church in years. He was surprised that he hadn't been struck by lightning when he'd stepped through the doors. Bearing in mind the plight of his immortal soul, a fiery, celestial thunderbolt wouldn't have been unexpected.

"Are we finished?" he irritably inquired. The sooner this travesty was concluded, the better off they'd all be.

"Ah . . . yes . . ." The vicar was still flustered by Michael's unwillingness to kiss the bride, but he pulled himself together, adjusting his spectacles on his nose and leading them to a table at the rear. "We just need your endorsement on the registry. And the license."

The vicar's wife, an older, crafty-looking sort, was the only witness to the sorry business. She kept sizing him up, readily distinguishing him as a sinner. Michael signed his life away while she held a lamp, and she regarded him with such disdain that he was positive she would comment on his insufferable deportment. He stared her down, daring her to utter a word, and she ultimately glanced away as Sarah too inscribed her name on the appropriate lines.

She's left-handed, Michael absurdly noted, as she shakily gripped the pen, and the cheap gold band that he'd slipped on her finger was highly visible in the dim light, a jarring reminder of how she'd abused his trust and shattered his illusions.

The ring wasn't even authentic. There was no jeweler in the area, and he hadn't had time to have a genuine one delivered. Not that he would have. He'd purchased it from a serving girl in the taproom at the inn, and he almost wished he'd be around to observe when the Comptons tried to pawn it and found out it was worthless.

Sarah stood, the signatures completed. She clasped a meager bridal bouquet, a bundle plucked from a vase near the altar after the vicar's wife had ascertained that Sarah had no flowers. Slightly wilted, petals drooping, she clutched them to her chest as though they were the finest hothouse roses.

"You've been very kind," she murmured to the older woman, brimming with transparent bliss as she hugged her tightly, mangling the blossoms in between their bodies.

"You're welcome," the woman asserted, and she added a phrase that he couldn't decipher, but it sounded like "Be strong, dear."

They parted, and the vicar's wife cast him a scathing look, and he blanched under her irascible examination. Obviously, she'd bonded with Sarah in some incomprehensible, feminine show of support, and she erroneously conjectured that Sarah was a put-upon, downtrodden bride who needed a champion. If he'd cared in the least—which he didn't—he might have taken a second to set the woman straight.

No doubt, she and her husband were dying of curiosity. After all, it wasn't every day that a country vicar was presented with a Special License and asked to immediately marry two strangers who were so aggravated with each other that they weren't conversing. It was extremely apparent that they were involved in a serious, odious dilemma, yet Sarah managed to seem innocent and vulnerable.

What would the other woman think if he apprised her of Sarah's capacity for deceit and artifice?

Michael furnished the vicar with a heavy bag of coins, an amount sufficient to quell speculation or gossip. Without contributing any further remarks, he exited the chapel, the noonday sun temporarily blinding. By the time he'd regained his equilibrium, Sarah had joined him and, as he advanced down the narrow path, she matched his strides.

His carriage awaited, as well as a horse he'd borrowed from Pamela that was tethered to the boot. Beyond, a trio of people gathered under a shade tree. His driver and a coachman, who were also bodyguards, were huddled with a widow he'd employed as Sarah's companion for the next week. As he and Sarah approached, the group leapt to attention, but he waved them off so that he and the lady could have a private good-bye. The servants could ruminate forever about what was transpiring, but they'd get no confirmation from Michael.

He reached for the door, while she hovered, pressing her tiresome bouquet to her nose.

"That wasn't so bad, was it?" She smiled gaily, her evident rapture setting him on edge.

"Get in." He lowered the step, but she didn't move.

"Don't be such a grouch," she chided. "You look as if you've just been to the blacksmith and had a tooth pulled." Embarrassingly, she captured his hands and whirled herself around in a circle, swaying with gladness over what they'd just accomplished. "What a gorgeous day! The sun is bright, the sky is blue, and I am so happy! Thank you!"

He hadn't the faintest inkling why she would be grateful, but then, he'd secreted her away before she could talk with her brother, so she wasn't cognizant that their contrivance had been foiled. She was laboring under the mistaken impression that there were grounds to rejoice.

"You sourpuss!" she was saying merrily when he displayed no reaction. "I won't allow your bad temper to spoil my celebration."

Ere he could stop her, she rose up on tiptoe and stole a kiss. As he inhaled her familiar, beloved scent, his hands inched to her waist, and he just desisted before he perpetrated a reprehensible gaffe.

He *did* take hold of her, but only long enough to set her away.

"Come on, Michael. Cheer up!" She laughed and danced a little jig. "This is our wedding day; not the end of the world. How long do you intend to be angry?"

As long as it takes. He eyed her dispassionately, wondering how she could be so bloody ecstatic, how she could prance about, reveling in her purported good fortune while throwing her cunning in his face.

Had she no shame? No remorse? No conscience? Did she care—even the tiniest bit—that she had devastated him?

"Get in," he repeated and, with his sharp tone, she finally heeded his irate condition. She ceased her bobbling and prattling.

"Oh, all right, you sorehead." Stabilizing herself, she placed her foot on the step. "Where are we off to? Have you selected some totally decadent spot in which to spend our wedding night? I'll have you know that I prefer chocolates and champagne!"

What was causing her to suffer these outrageous flights of fancy? Why pretend this was anything other than a sham? "*We* aren't going anywhere. *You* are going home."

The abrupt news stunned her. Her eyes widened with astonishment and hurt, and he steeled himself against all the ways in which she was still capable of provoking a response in him.

"To Yorkshire?"

"Yes."

"But I thought . . ."

"Thought what, Lady Sarah?"

"Well . . . that we would . . . travel to London." She

scrutinized him fervently, carefully choosing her words, beginning to appreciate that no matter the comment, it would be inappropriate. "I'd hoped we'd visit your family."

"I have no desire for you to meet my family. Not now. Not ever."

"You don't mean that."

"Oh, but I do."

She paused, searching his eyes, dissecting his demeanor. Something tripped and cracked—perhaps it was the final piece of his heart fracturing—and he forced himself to remain unmoved as perception dawned on her.

"You don't consider this a real marriage, do you?"

"Hardly."

He might as well have slapped her. As though her bones had transformed to mush, she sank down, the carriage stair impeding her progress, and she balanced against it.

"But . . . but why? You care for me. We could make this work. We could turn it into something wonderful."

"Why would I want to?"

With each harsh utterance, she deflated a tad more, and he felt he'd evolved into someone else entirely, that he'd been inhabited by an alien being who was bent on tormenting her until she crumpled into a heap.

What a *fine* man he'd grown to be, the son Angela Ford had raised to be such a chivalrous fellow. Michael Stevens—the eminent despoiler and defiler of women! If his mother could witness him now, in all his wretched, miserable, scurrilous glory, she'd never forgive him.

How had he fallen to such a contemptible state that he would behave so despicably? The only plausible explanation was that his feelings for her had been so pure and sincere—as close to love as he might ever come—and he simply couldn't countenance how grievously she'd wounded him. He could only react by striking out. By keeping on and on—until she went away, as agonized as he.

"When will I see you again?"

"I have no idea."

With the admission, sadness engulfed him, and he

shoved it away. If she had any concept of the profundity of his regret over their acrimonious split, she'd have incredible power over him, so he couldn't let her deduce how much he'd miss her, or how long it would take him to inure himself to their horrid farewell.

"Where will you be?"

"I'm not sure."

"What if I need to reach you?"

"I can't fathom why you would."

God, but he felt he was kicking a puppy. With each retort, she shrank back as if he was physically striking her. He couldn't endure much more, nor could she, so he helped her to her feet and guided her into the coach. Thankfully, she didn't resist or argue.

The driver and others neared, ready to discharge their duties, and she peered out the opening, her brilliant green eyes silently begging.

"It doesn't have to be this way."

"Doesn't it?" he interrogated caustically. "Next time you talk with your brother, give him a message from me."

"What?"

"Our marriage makes no difference. His debt stands. The inventory of the Scarborough property was effectuated while you were here in Bedford. My men will be around to collect my chattels on the appointed date. Unless, of course, he can locate the cash he owes me before then."

For a lengthy interlude, she assessed him. Mute, confused, she seemed to have no clue as to what he referred. Was she daft? The purpose of her seduction had been a misguided attempt to coerce him into returning Hugh's markers, so why was she so baffled? Scarborough's gambling debt was the reason she'd started it all.

Wasn't it?

Her revolting brother had contended as much during their contentious meeting in the library.

Unease swamped him. Doubts—vexatious, persistent, unavoidable—crept in, inducing him to hesitate and falter.

"You!" she howled, and she was horrified. "You're the one!"

"Don't act dumb, Sarah. It doesn't become you."

"You're a gambler?" She articulated the term with such loathing that it sounded like the worst epithet.

"When the spirit moves me."

"But you claimed you own a gentlemen's club."

"I do." He frowned at her affront. "Wagering is our main source of income. It's how *gentlemen* entertain themselves."

"A gambler," she wailed. "I've married a gambler! After everything I've been through!" She was teeming with righteous indignation. "Why Hugh?"

"Why not?"

"Why not! That's all you have to say for yourself?" Her fury was growing with each exchange. "Tell me why!"

"Because he's an ass. He deserved it."

"Give it all back! The markers, the property! Whatever you won, I order you to refund it to him."

"No."

"I demand it of you!"

"No," he reiterated. "Your brother wrought exactly what he deserved."

"That may be true, but he gambled away *my* home and the clothes on *my* back. *My* retainers will have no food in their bellies or coal for their stoves this winter."

"It's Hugh's doing," he callously barked, "and none of my concern."

"Why am I not surprised by your impervious attitude?" Scornfully, she shook her head. "While you were making love to me here in Bedford, you had men in my house, counting the silverware! What kind of pitiless monster are you?"

The damning question hung in the air, but there was no adequate answer he could supply. How had it happened that it suddenly seemed *he* was in the wrong?

Her traveling companion had been prowling on the fringes of their quarrel, pretending to ignore the heated exchange, and Sarah beckoned her on and in, then pulled the door shut in his face. At the last, she leaned out the window, her shrewd gaze running up and down his broad frame, taking his measure and plainly finding him lacking.

"Don't ever contact me again," she declared.

The curtain fell back, and she impatiently rapped for the driver, signaling him to carry on. The man looked to Michael, seeking permission, and Michael untied his horse, then consented with a nod of his head.

He yearned to plead his case, to explain or justify the belligerent contest with Hugh, but he was caught off guard by how the tables of outrage had been so promptly turned, and he couldn't defend himself.

As the carriage jingled to life and rolled off, her arm shot out the window, and for a brief instant, he sustained a foolish, thrilling rush as he presumed she was waving good-bye. Then, he saw that she was only flinging out her bridal bouquet, unable to bear having it in the coach with her. The pitiful arrangement rippled to the dirt, a morose, poignant statement of her abhorrence. The *faux* wedding band followed.

Walking down the dusty lane, he scooped them up, crushing the petals in his fist as he watched her disappear in the distance. He should have been savoring some moment of satisfaction; he should have been shouting good riddance and *adieu,* but all he felt was alone again and very much like the young boy in that Paris flat, waiting . . . waiting . . . for the father who never arrived to fetch him home.

Chapter Twenty

Michael paused on the stoop of the London home where he had passed the prior decade of his life. The three-story row house was situated on a narrow, busy street, a few blocks from their gambling club, and a few more from the Chelsea Theater where his mother spent so much of her time.

They'd moved into it shortly after leaving Paris. He'd been seventeen, and for all intents and purposes, a Frenchman, having been whisked away to the exotic country at the age of three so that he had few memories of England or the world they'd left behind. He'd loved their Continental lifestyle and friends, the foods, the wines, and the pretty, generous French girls, and he'd greatly begrudged his mother her decision to return.

What a shock the change of cultures had been! In Paris, he had been the son of a renowned celebrity. In London, he was merely a scorned oddity, one of the dozens of bastard boys of the aristocracy, trying to find their place in a community that shunned them.

Luckily, he'd fared better than most, due in no small part to his father, Edward Stevens. Though he hated to admit it, he had to give the man credit. Edward had purchased their gaming establishment for them, presenting it to James as a gift after his first marriage when he was but a lad of twenty in the hopes that the guarantee of regular employment would curb some of his more wicked tendencies.

The ploy had worked. Overly proud, they'd refused to flounder in front of Edward's peers—especially when those exalted nobles were positive that he and James would never amount to anything. In a big way, they'd proved everyone wrong.

They had a knack for earning money, possessing an innate aptitude for gambling, and for commerce with the types of fools who were drawn to it. They knew how to amuse and divert even the most surly guest, and they'd lined their purses in the process.

Their effective management had gained them powerful prominence on the fringes of High Society where they were admired and despised in equal measure. Customers detested their success, but still they came to play, unable to avoid the lure of the club that was the best spot for a fashionable gentleman to be seen while in town.

From the wagering and their dubious side ventures, they had grown obscenely wealthy, and they'd used the profits wisely, investing for the future and caring for their mother. They'd bought her this residence, and she'd constantly adored it. The sturdy abode of brick and mortar had shielded them from the harsh glare of London's snobbery and contempt. Theirs was a high-profile existence that provided scant privacy, and they'd been safe and carefree behind the closed front door.

He'd loved its spacious salons, comfortable furnishings, and efficient staff. A peaceful haven from his hectic hours at the club, the rooms were warm and cozy and, whenever he'd arrived home after a long night, he'd been soothed by shedding his cloak in the foyer as the aroma of James's American-style coffee wafted down the stairs, as his mother's laughter rang through the halls.

Tarrying for a moment, he relished the memories before he stuck his key in the lock.

Would it still fit?

With James's wife shaping her own domestic arrangements, he had very likely forfeited his freedom to come and go and, though he wasn't personally acquainted with the new Mrs. Stevens, he was quite sure that the ambiance created by his flamboyant mother would be a tad too extravagant for the composed noblewoman. He couldn't help pondering how much reorganization he'd confront and how he would deal with it. While he desperately needed the solace of hearth and family, the traditional might have vanished.

Surprisingly, the door opened, but as he stepped through, he vividly recalled the last time he'd entered. He'd just rescued James from a pub where he'd been drinking and carousing and suffering from the aftermath of his burgeoning love affair with the woman—Abigail Weston—who would become his wife.

Distraught, afraid for his brother, Michael had wearily trudged home, only to walk in on his parents and the tidings that they were lovers, that they were finally destined to marry. The scene that followed had been dreadful, and every word Angela had uttered in Edward's defense had stabbed like the sharpest blade.

After all the ways Edward had dishonored her, she'd fallen for him like an infatuated girl. Her decision had seemed abhorrent and crazy, disgraceful, and he still couldn't comprehend why his proud, strong mother had been so willing to debase herself over an aging reprobate who'd never given her anything but heartache.

Affronted and dazed, he'd left London that day, filled with exasperation and rage, and he truly hadn't known if he'd ever return. He'd simply had it—with his mother, his brother, his father—but his pique had ultimately faded, so there was no reason to have stayed away so long, yet he hadn't been able to make his way back.

His mother had wed, and Michael wished her happy. He really, really did, for he loved her very much, and he could never send her a bad thought. But if Edward hurt her again . . .

Michael repressed a shudder. If Edward hurt her, Michael couldn't imagine what his response might be.

He stood in the silent anteroom, feeling a bit lost. Recollection swamped him: the marvelous years with James and Angela, the terrible conclusion wrought by Edward. His father was a bane, like a cloud of poisonous gas hovering over Michael so oppressively that he couldn't shed the onerous cargo.

Edward's treachery when Michael was but a child had made him permanently wary, unequivocally cautious, and he had never let his guard down until Sarah Compton had ripped through the fabric of his staid environment, inducing him to yearn for things he couldn't have, encouraging him to dream, to speculate over what *could* be instead of settling for what *was*.

The burden of relinquishing Sarah—before he'd ever had her—was more than he could bear. When he'd lingered in that rural churchyard, and his carriage had lumbered away with her inside, he hadn't known where else to go but to London. *Home* had been the only option.

After their sham of a marriage ceremony, and the brutal comments they'd exchanged, he'd been perplexed and rankled. He was an excellent judge of people and their veracity, and on learning that he was a gambler, Sarah had been aghast and outraged that he was the individual who'd destroyed Hugh Compton.

Had Sarah been innocent? Had she been a pawn to Hugh's manipulations—just as Michael had been? Hugh insisted that she was culpable, but her categorical pleasure over their marriage had been authentic. If she'd acquiesced solely to placate Hugh, why feign such joy and affection?

If she was guiltless, he'd treated her abominably, and he couldn't face the notion that he'd erred, that he'd jumped to a faulty verdict. He'd just been so bewildered and angry that he couldn't think straight, and he'd craved a stable destination, a refuge where he could rest and regroup. So London had beckoned.

But now . . .

This was a mistake. I don't belong here anymore.

The concept spiraled through his head, and he couldn't remain. He turned to depart, but before he could escape, Abigail Weston strolled into the corridor. Completely absorbed, she was reading a letter, so she didn't notice him, and he furtively studied her. She was slender and petite,

with pale creamy skin and eyes as green as Sarah's. Her
hair was long and blond, and though it was the middle of
the afternoon, she wore it down and tied with a ribbon as
a young girl might.

He'd always been aware of who she was, because he
made it a habit to investigate the family members of their
clientele, but he'd never been this near to her before, had
never judged her comeliness.

No wonder James couldn't resist, he petulantly conceded. She was a raving beauty, but then, his brother would
have settled for nothing less.

Sensing his presence, she glanced up, and her brow furrowed, as she searched to deduce his identity.

"Michael . . . ?" she asked haltingly. The letter dropped
and fluttered to the floor.

He tipped his head and acknowledged her in French,
though he had no idea why he would. *"Bonjour."*

"I'm Abigail Ste—"

"Yes, I know." He cut her off. "I stopped by to pick up
my belongings, but I'll try later when I won't be a bother."

"No, no, it's not a problem." She acted as if he were a
frightened dog that might scurry off if he moved too rapidly.

An accurate description, he mused, for that was exactly
how he felt, as if he'd been stranded on a desert island and
no longer understood the rudiments of speech or civilized
behavior.

"Please, won't you come in?" She gestured toward the
receiving parlor, but he couldn't compel himself to meander
in the direction she'd indicated. "We've been distressed by
your absence," she said quietly, "and James will be so relieved that you're here."

He'd meant to speak his good-byes, but her overt concern had him dawdling like a mute imbecile.

More footsteps reverberated down the hall, and a new
maid approached. Lady Abigail shifted toward the girl, but
her focus was fixed on Michael, apparently afraid he'd
evaporate into thin air.

"Would you fetch my husband?" she advised the servant. "Fast as you can?"

The maid hustled up the stairs, and momentarily, James hastened toward them. He skidded to a halt at the top step, his trousers scarcely on, his feet and chest bare.

His wife beamed up at him as if he controlled the moon and the stars. "Look who's here."

"Michael . . ." The appellation spewed out in a rush.

"Hello, James." He replied casually, pretending that his arrival was perfectly normal, and he was pleased at how unemotional he seemed. There was no tremor in his voice, and none of his anguish poked through.

James froze, anxious, then he took the stairs two at a time, racing down until they were face-to-face. "You bastard!" he crudely exclaimed, totally forgetting himself in front of his wife. "It's been three months! You had me frantic with worry!"

"You shouldn't have fretted," Michael asserted. "I told you I'd be all right."

"Liar! You look like death warmed over. What's happened to you?"

He grabbed Michael and crushed him in a fierce hug that continued on and on. Michael didn't reciprocate, but endured the reception like a statue, though he did close his eyes and inhale James's pacifying scent. James ended the embrace, but he kept touching, running his hands up and down Michael's torso and limbs, checking for injuries, or perhaps, verifying that Michael was real and not an apparition.

Locking an arm around Michael's neck, James pressed their foreheads together, whispering, "Don't ever scare me like that again!"

"I'm sorry."

"I'm just so glad you're here." He pulled away, once more, but not before bestowing another tight squeeze, and Michael garnered the distinct impression that James was cushioning him for a blow.

James said, "Many events have occurred while you were away. Mother married."

"I know."

"So did I."

"I heard."

"Abby, come."

James motioned to his bride who was across the foyer. Nervous, she didn't step toward them, so James went to her, and the manner in which he smiled at her caused Michael's heart to reel in his chest.

Clearly, this was not a marriage of convenience, not a misdeed James had righted by offering his name. There was steadfast devotion between them, stalwart emotion. James appeared exhilarated and smitten, and Michael was stunned to discern that his brother was terribly in love.

From the genuine regard mirrored by Lady Abigail, it was obvious that she loved him, too. Their open, irrefutable affinity afforded glaring evidence of how reality had been transformed while he'd been away. His worst suspicions were confirmed: The house was no longer his home. James now shared it with another, and though James would never say as much, he would need abundant private opportunity to establish himself in his new life with his wife.

While Michael wanted to castigate his sister-in-law for instigating the modifications, he couldn't. Yes, she'd thrust herself at James, and her tenacity had been the catalyst that had brought the disasters crashing down, so Michael longed to condemn her, or at least dislike her but, on discovering how fond she was of James, it was difficult to maintain any aggravation.

James had encountered little tenderness in his thirty years; few people had truly cared for him, and Michael was heartened to see Lady Abigail displaying such warm, visible sentiment.

"Abby," James proclaimed, "this is my wayward brother, Michael."

"Hello, Michael." She gifted him with a dazzling smile. "It's splendid to meet you."

"How do you do, Lady Abigail."

"Please call me Abigail."

"I will."

"We were just about to eat so that James can be off to work. Won't you join us?"

"You must!" James asserted. "We'll catch up on your travels, and then we'll go to the club. The staff will be so excited to have you back."

Bright, expectant, they stared at him, a paired unit of like disposition and purpose, eagerly anticipating the dissection of his adventures over a leisurely meal.

On innumerable occasions, he and James had come home at dawn, intending to sleep the day away, but before they took to their beds, they'd relaxed in the dining room, replaying the hours of vice and sin they'd experienced. Their mother was usually with them, adding her pithy observations and insights.

He missed those times and, while he ached to participate in the modest ritual, he recognized that he dare not. They would quiz him as to where he'd been, what he'd been doing. How could he possibly explain? He didn't understand it, himself, so he could hardly render an accounting to others.

James wouldn't bat an eye over his antics, but there was very little he could speak about to Lady Abigail, and any explication would lead to the end and Pamela's party. How could he describe what had transpired? He would have to relate the details about Sarah. About loving her and hating her.

He couldn't think about her; he couldn't talk about her. He simply could *not*. Not now. Perhaps not ever. He could only carry on.

"No, but I thank you." At his rejection of their hospitality, they deflated. Doubtless, James hoped he'd befriend Lady Abigail, and he would eventually. But at present, he couldn't stand viewing James's palpable bliss, not when his own life was such a mess. "I have a thousand errands to run."

"Will you at least visit the club?" James inquired hesitantly.

"Yes." He nodded, deciding as he went along. "In fact, for the time being, I'll take a room there."

"No!" Abigail announced. "We insist that you stay with us. Don't we, James?"

"Absolutely." James laid a hand on Michael's shoulder. "This is still your home, Michael. Nothing's different."

Did James really believe as much? Probably. His older sibling could be horribly oblivious.

"It's best if I go." He forced cordiality into his tone as he politely bowed over Lady Abigail's hand. "It was a pleasure, Abigail." But the informal mode of address seemed foreign on his tongue. Then, before James could detain him, he spun and walked outside.

Needing to be away, but not sure of his destination, he hurried off. Though he felt he was wandering aimlessly, he gradually perceived that his feet were reflexively leading him to their gambling hall.

He'd perpetually enjoyed his position there; the crowds, the pace, the action, the money. Employment had kept him out of mischief and off the streets and, in his prevailing disordered state, he definitely required the steady diversion and stabilizing influence. Increasing his stride, he realized that he'd forgotten how attached he was to their business, and now more than ever, his job would keep him occupied so that he'd have no chance for reflection or deliberation.

Work . . . that's what he craved. He would immerse himself so thoroughly that there wouldn't be a single, idle moment when Sarah might cross his mind.

Rebecca scowled down at Hugh Compton, unable to conceal her contempt. He was unconscious on his bed, his breathing ragged, his odor foul. Liquor bottles were scattered about, his pipe tipped over. Like a helpless infant, he'd wet himself but, in his intoxicated condition, he wasn't cognizant of anything.

"Some fancy *lord* you are now, my Hugh." She glanced around at the disgusting chamber, part of the three-room flat she'd located after Michael Stevens had foreclosed on the town house. She'd convinced Hugh to vacate before the embarrassing date, declining to grant Stevens the satisfaction of tossing them into the street like a couple of beggars so, as his men had carted away the last of the furniture, she hadn't had to watch.

What a low level she'd reached by allying herself with Hugh!

When her parents had died four years earlier, and she'd accepted Sarah's invitation to live at Scarborough, she hadn't expected much. A roof over her head, food, companionship. But after she'd ingratiated herself, the possibilities for more had seemed so distinct and so easy to achieve. Especially after her initial excursion to London with Hugh.

Rebecca had been captivated by the gay parties, the jovial people, and she'd quickly determined that she belonged in the city, at the center of the merriment. She'd analyzed and plotted, then she'd promptly set her cap for Hugh.

In the beginning, she'd liked him well enough and had been content hosting his entertainments, supervising his household and social calendar. If he wasn't drinking and carousing, he could be pleasant, but his addiction to his precious Chinese herbs had weakened him until he'd grown surly, impetuous, and, at times, downright dangerous.

Rubbing her side, she felt the bruising from where he'd punched her the prior evening. How had her circumstances been reduced to this? To surviving in a hovel, with a cruel, vicious man who'd double-crossed her at every juncture?

She deserved so much more.

Of course, Hugh charged her with the entire debacle. He never thought anything was his own fault. Having failed in their attempt to bring down Michael Stevens, Hugh had incessantly railed over how she'd misread the outcome.

Sarah had scurried back to Yorkshire—how she'd accomplished the feat was still a mystery—before they could parlay with her. Michael Stevens had returned to town, bold as brass, and proceeded about his business as though he'd done nothing improper.

Rebecca and Hugh had been left standing with their hats in their hands, like witless fools, and Rebecca was compelled to confirm a lone mistake in her careful planning: Only she and Hugh had witnessed Sarah's disgrace; they hadn't brought along any spectators. With Hugh's word against Stevens's, and considering their history, who would believe Hugh?

Stevens had deftly rebuffed Hugh's financial stipulations, leaving Hugh with a duel as his sole means of redress, but Hugh would never have challenged Michael Stevens. Stevens was a master at pistols and swords. Fists, too. Cowardly Hugh, with his shaky, meager physique, couldn't have acquired an agreeable result through threat of violence.

They'd been so assured that Stevens would capitulate, but they hadn't comprehended that he had no sense of honor, so he had successfully outmaneuvered them both. Nary a whiff of scandal had affixed to himself or to Sarah who was, once again, ensconced as the mistress of Scarborough, persevering as if naught untoward had occurred.

At Rebecca's insistence, Hugh had made a single trip to the estate, demanding information and assistance, and the scene between brother and sister had been appalling. Sarah was furious over Hugh's machinations, and she'd rejected every proposal and ultimatum, firmly declaring that she never intended to set eyes upon Michael Stevens again.

The actual particulars as to what had happened between the two lovers was unclear. Sarah wouldn't say, so Rebecca didn't know how her cousin had readily moved from a romantic, naked bath frolic to a heightened case of loathing. Sarah wasn't about to confess that Michael Stevens had compromised her, and she'd vociferously avowed that if Hugh so much as hinted of the scandal to others, she would deny it to her dying breath.

Hugh blamed Sarah for all—when he wasn't blaming

Rebecca. In the wake of the fiasco, he'd selected his usual route for tackling a catastrophe: over-imbibing, smoking herbs, and decrying his fate. When she'd wearied of his diatribe, and had pointed out his specific liability, she'd procured a few hard punches to her rib cage.

"Well, dear Hugh," she murmured, "nobody hits Rebecca and gets away with it."

And nobody breaks a promise, either.

She frowned at the message that had just been delivered. It was from the father of a rich girl he'd been secretly courting. The wealthy merchant had politely and wisely spurned Hugh's offer of marriage, and if Rebecca hadn't been so enraged over Hugh's duplicity, she might have laughed aloud.

The precious heiresses wouldn't have him! Not even to buy the title of countess!

Walking over to him, she held her fingers over his face. The special concoction she'd mixed in his brandy was rapidly taking its toll. He was barely respiring, and it would likely be just a matter of minutes before he ceased altogether, so time was of the essence.

He didn't eat much anymore, so he'd lost weight, and his last ring slid off smoothly. She pocketed it, along with the gold buttons from his coat.

While she'd pinned many hopes on Hugh, and the largess he might eventually supply, she was no fool, either. Her mother's daughter, she'd covertly squirreled away a nest egg, so she'd get by. Not in the lavish mode to which Hugh was accustomed, or in any manner he would have deemed acceptable. But she had enough to buy a small house, and she'd have an income, though insignificant, that would keep her from the poorhouse.

Her only other option was to hie herself off to Scarborough, to dawdle about in the empty mansion with Sarah while her cousin tried to salvage the remnants, which Rebecca wouldn't do. She abhorred the country and thrived in the city, and without Hugh to ruin her prospects, she imagined she'd find ample serenity.

Through her contacts with Hugh, she'd met many gentlemen who delighted in her company. If she calculated correctly, she might still make an advantageous marriage. In the meantime, she'd become friends with a widow who needed lodging. They were compatible and sharing a domicile would decrease expenses. Rebecca would have her own home, where she would look after herself, and she wouldn't have to rely on a lush like Hugh Compton for her daily security.

In the wardrobe, she rifled through in a final search, ferreting out several pound notes, an ivory cigar case, his silver flask. She critically surveyed the rest of the apartment, stumbling on other incidentals that, in her initial haste, she'd omitted. Stuffing all in a drawer, she retired to her cot and snuggled down under the single blanket.

The night passed with agonizing slowness, and she steeled her emotions so that she could manage to appear shocked and overwrought when the serving woman arrived in the morning and found Hugh dead in his bed.

Chapter Twenty-one

Sarah stood in the silent mansion, peeking out the window as a small, black carriage plodded up the drive. The instant it had turned off the main road, she'd noticed it, and the sight filled her with unease, because she couldn't fathom who it might be.

No one visited Scarborough anymore. Between Michael Stevens's despicable avarice, and Hugh's untimely death after a squalid episode in town, she'd become a pariah. Neighbors had been rabid to gossip, chewing over her wretched plight like dogs over a bone, and they'd abandoned her to her fate. She was the talk of the countryside, so she never ventured out, because she couldn't abide the pitying looks, subtle remarks, or false sympathies of those acrimonious people whose welfare she'd valiantly fought to sustain.

In the village, they blamed her for what had transpired at the estate, for the foiled commerce and trade that had unmercifully affected their connected livelihoods, so she stayed at home with the elderly retainers who'd kept working for her merely because they had nowhere else to go.

With Hugh's demise, merchants now made no pretense of denying assistance. Without monetary resources to back up her petitions for coal or edibles, she'd had to survive on what she could scrounge from the gardens, or the pittance of animals that had escaped Michael's notice.

"Wait until we hear from the new earl. We'll decide then," was the standard response to her entreaties.

The sentiment had been expressed on copious occasions, until she'd ultimately realized that it was fruitless to reason with any of them. They were aware that she was at the end of her financial rope. No money would be forthcoming in payment, and if they offered her items on account, they'd never collect.

They were irrationally optimistic, presuming that the unknown earl would fix what she'd broken, and she shook her head at the ludicrousness of their misguided expectations of rescue.

Hugh had died without an heir, and his successor was a distant cousin whom she'd never met and who supposedly resided in Virginia. She'd sent a letter, but with the impeded speed of ocean crossings, it wouldn't reach its destination for weeks, and then several months would pass before she received a reply. And that was *if* she had the correct address and *if* the man was still alive.

She knew nothing of his fiscal assets. If he was a gentleman of modest capital, and he took over the reins of Scarborough, how could he succeed? Very little land came with the inheritance—the unentailed acreage had been sold off long ago—so he couldn't revive the estate through farming, yet the villagers absurdly hoped for an impossible miracle.

Clearly, however, they were no more foolish than she, sitting as she was in the cold, bleak mansion, cursing her fate, and waiting for something—anything—to happen.

What was she going to do? The American earl might not wish to support her, or if a wife accompanied him, the other woman might not care to have Sarah hovering about and interfering. Sarah would have to make her own way, but how and where?

She'd never resided anywhere but Scarborough, had never imagined any other life. With no skills, or the funds with which to alter her fortunes, she had no choices. She was too independent and proud to hire herself out as a maid or governess to an affluent family. The only other option that presented itself was to head for London, to demand her rightful place by her husband's side, but she couldn't debase herself so completely.

Whenever she recalled how he'd exploited her, how he'd

lured her into the mess with Hugh, how he'd swindled Hugh then refused to back down, she saw red.

A gambler! After all she'd endured, she'd cast her lot with a capricious bounder, and she passed her days—when she wasn't fretting about where she'd find food for supper—worrying that he'd publicize their marriage, that he'd forfeit his last farthing in a card game, and then *his* creditors would start pounding on her door.

If that moment ever arrived, she'd journey to town and shoot him right in the middle of his black heart. She didn't own a gun anymore—his henchmen had snared her remaining pistol—but she'd obtain another somehow, and she derived incredible satisfaction from reflecting upon how loud the bang would be, how shocked he'd appear when he fell dead at her feet.

Ooh, she could conceive of it so vividly!

The dark conveyance approached, stark against the white snow that littered the yard and sparkled like brilliant diamonds in the winter sunshine. Eventually, it halted out front. The coachman was bundled in a greatcoat, a cap pulled low. His skin was ruddy, and his breath swirled about his head in a cloud.

"Who could it be?" she pondered aloud, her voice jarring in the empty salon. But for a writing desk and two dilapidated chairs, the furniture was gone, her husband having carried out his threat to call in his markers.

Three weeks after she'd returned from her disastrous visit to Pamela Blair's party, several dozen men had shown up with large freight wagons and pages of lists that enumerated the household items. They'd seized the lot, down to the inkwells and stirring spoons, all those insignificant belongings that her father and Hugh hadn't previously squandered simply because they were so trifling that their value was negligible to any gambler of means.

Apparently, her absent spouse wasn't included in that group. No trinket was too minor to escape Michael Stevens's penurious revenge.

They'd loaded their carts, then departed, weighted down with the scraps of what had been her world.

How could Michael have done this to her? How could he shame her so terribly? She couldn't begin to theorize as to what he wanted with the last of her things, or why he would care about them so vehemently and, when she was extremely vexed, she'd wonder where he had taken them.

Infrequently, she'd foresee packed boxes, covered with cloths in a sterile warehouse, drawing dust and mice. Other times, she'd envision him selling everything at a fair, and some other faceless, impoverished woman buying all, then relaxing on what had been her sofa, or seating herself at the table that had once filled the breakfast parlor.

Given the rundown condition of most of it, perhaps he'd just dumped it in a pile and burned it. Those ancient beds and chests of drawers would have burst into a ball of flames, quickly devouring the evidence of how hard she'd tried to preserve a heritage that the men of her family had never respected.

"Bastard . . ." she muttered crudely, though she wasn't sure to which man she referred.

Unquestionably, her spouse—with his irascible will and irrational disposition—fit the bill, but the epithet could also apply to her irresponsible brother who'd had the audacity to die prematurely at age thirty-two without a cent to his name.

Sarah's only link to the event had been her receipt of a disconcerting message from Rebecca, informing her of the sordid details. Another had come from Hugh's solicitor, with a polite request as to when Hugh's account might be squared. The third was from the undertaker, outlining miscellaneous burial costs, but she hadn't had the money for his London funeral, let alone the quantity required to transport his body to the estate for interment.

Between the two of them, Michael Stevens and Hugh Compton, and the despicable level to which they'd reduced her state of affairs, her mind was so disordered, so disjointed and rambling, that she couldn't adequately grasp what had occurred, nor could she forge a plan for the future. She was bogged down, powerless to advance out of her current doldrums, because she couldn't move beyond her ruminations over their mutual duplicity.

Michael had known Hugh long before she'd ever crossed his path. Their tainted history had crashed into her, running her over like a runaway coach. She'd had the misfortune to be swept up in the catastrophe the pair had instituted, and she wasn't even sure why she'd been at the center.

What had they both been trying to accomplish? Michael, especially. Why had he corrupted her?

On her end, she'd desired him with an uncontrollable, stubborn passion and, because of it, she'd been determined to instigate a liaison and damn the consequences.

But what was his excuse? How did he justify his misdeeds? Was her seduction simply a cruel attempt to further *take* something from Hugh? Was she just one more chattel of Hugh's that Michael wanted to confiscate in order to prove whatever point he'd been so adamant about making?

If she was naught but a pawn in his machinations, then he'd not been fond of her in the slightest. The idea hurt unbearably, for though she was loath to admit it, she'd tossed and turned many a long night, reliving those glorious assignations where they'd learned to love fully, thoroughly, and without reservation.

The loss of that closeness, of the joy and passion they'd shared, was too painful to acknowledge, so she didn't. She declined to ponder why he'd married her, why he'd sent her away immediately after, why she hadn't heard from him since. She wouldn't torture herself with what-ifs and what-might-have-beens, or chastise herself over how she might have handled that final, dreadful day any differently.

Despite the awful factors that had brought them together, she'd been deliriously ecstatic at their wedding, elated over her destiny, only to discover that he considered marriage to her an embarrassment or worse.

Shuddering, she recoiled from the opportunity to wander farther down the road of personal recrimination. She absolutely would not mourn Michael Stevens another second!

The driver hopped down and lowered the step for her visitor, and Sarah was stunned to see Rebecca descending. She was snug in a plush, black cloak, with a matching fur muff and hat. Her china-blue eyes were bright, her cheeks rosy. She looked pretty and flourishing and, by comparison, Sarah felt dowdy in her brown wool gown and heavy boots, her knitted mittens with the fingertips cut out so that she could work on her correspondence, her thick shawl wrapped tight against the chilly temperature.

She hadn't seen Rebecca since that hideous encounter when Hugh had traveled to Yorkshire for the sole purpose of convincing Sarah to seek reparation from Michael. Rebecca had joined with Hugh in spewing outrage over Michael's behavior, but their concern for her welfare had rung false, and she'd ignored their interrogation as to Michael and what had transpired in Bedford. Something—arrogance? stupidity?—had prevented her from confessing that she'd married the blighter, though she couldn't have explained why.

Perhaps it was Hugh's firm resolve to compel Michael to pay for sins that Sarah believed were her own. Or perhaps it was the way Rebecca had gleamed as she'd cajoled over what they could *get* from Michael Stevens.

Sarah wasn't about to help them wheedle their way into Michael Stevens's pocketbook, because she wouldn't humiliate herself by confronting him again when he so obviously despised her. His disregard would have killed her, so she'd denied all and, as far as she knew, no one had a clue that she was wed to the notorious London gambler, the man who'd broken her heart by spurning her on her wedding day. And if she had anything to say about it, no one would, either. She'd cut out her tongue before she'd ever confirm their union.

Rebecca entered on a rush of frigid air, definitely fine, in spite of her ordeals in the large metropolis. She was plump and healthy, plainly not worried about where her next meal was coming from. Her black mourning outfit was beautifully tailored and sewn in a quality fabric.

Sarah had no black attire to wear in order to grieve for her unlamented brother. She'd outgrown the garments she'd donned at her father's passing, and she couldn't employ a seamstress for any excessive alterations. As her cousin walked into the foyer, cocky as a rooster on a summer morning, the very image of perfectly coifed English gentility, Sarah caught herself jealously staring, speculating as to how Rebecca had managed so well.

This isn't fair! she thought irritably, and she didn't even try to quash the petty opinion. Too much had happened in the past six months for her to be feeling charitable.

Since Hugh's death, she and Rebecca had exchanged intermittent letters. Rebecca had purchased a modest residence, had a roommate, and sufficient funds to engage a cook. While she didn't move among the highest echelons of society, she wasn't lacking for entertainment. She attended the theater, various musicales and poetry readings, balls and soirees. Where she'd gotten the money for her new lifestyle was a mystery Sarah didn't prefer to explore.

In her missives, she always urged Sarah to forsake Scarborough and come to town. Sarah regularly declined, and she had the sneaking suspicion that Rebecca tendered the recurrent invitation simply because she was so positive that Sarah would never accept.

Rebecca huddled in her fancy cloak as she scrutinized the vacant space, the bare walls and floors. Sarah had been explicit in her written descriptions, but still, she supposed the changes were difficult to visualize. Rebecca evinced such pity for Sarah's diminished circumstances that Sarah was overcome by a strong desire to slap her.

She didn't want or need this woman's sympathy. She needed cash and time and alternatives, but—heaven forbid—not empathy and certainly not compassion.

"Hello, Rebecca."

They embraced halfheartedly, and her cousin brushed at a few flakes of snow, and Sarah could only peevishly note that the hat, by itself, had probably cost more than she had spent on food in a year.

"My, my, Sarah"—Rebecca disdainfully assessed her surroundings—"you endeavored to elucidate, but I didn't appreciate your desperate predicament until now."

"It could have been worse."

"I don't see how."

"Well, Stevens's men could have set a torch to the house on their way out."

Sarah led her to the parlor, the only room that had a fire going and two chairs to drag next to it. Luckily, the adjoining salon was closed off so Rebecca wouldn't detect that Sarah had made a bedchamber out of it. There wasn't fuel for the elevated floors, so she slept downstairs, heating just the two rooms. Not that the discontinued use of the upper chambers mattered; they contained no furnishings.

"What are you doing such a distance from London?" Her pitiful situation precluded chitchat, and she was glad. She couldn't comprehend why Rebecca had come to call, and she wanted her gone.

"I'm off to a Christmas house party near Middlesbrough, but I couldn't pass so close without stopping."

She then regaled Sarah with boring anecdotes about her fashionable friends, and about her roommate who was awaiting her at the coaching inn in the village, and Sarah was relieved that Rebecca hadn't brought her associate along to witness how far Sarah had fallen.

Sarah was polite and commented where it seemed appropriate, but she couldn't quite enjoy their odd conversation. Rebecca appeared so happy and contented, while Sarah viewed herself as doomed and devastated. The contrasts in their personalities had never been more glaring, and Sarah resentfully discerned that she envied her cousin for her freedom and adaptability.

"I've been thinking about Hugh's body," Rebecca said.

Her bizarre pronouncement terminated Sarah's shallow reverie. "What about it?"

"He needs a proper burial."

"Wouldn't that be nice," Sarah responded sarcastically. "How could I afford it?"

"Well, I understand that you don't like to talk about Mr. Stevens"—her mention of Michael had Sarah fuming—"but he was overly fond of you once, and I was simply curious as to whether you might prevail upon him to have Hugh shipped home. Hugh would have liked to be entombed with some fuss and pomp in the crypt here at Scarborough, and it's a tragedy about his grave in London. Why ... there isn't even a stone."

"I couldn't pay for one," Sarah testily replied.

"That's just my point, dear." Rebecca leaned over and condescendingly patted Sarah's arm. "My roommate slipped on some ice and injured herself, so we've had unanticipated expenses. I went to Mr. Stevens, myself, just two weeks ago, and appealed for a few pounds to tide us over."

Sarah was murderously calm; her ears must be deceiving her. Battling to maintain an unaffected smile, she blandly declared, "You asked Michael Stevens for money?"

"Yes."

"What did he say?"

"He was exceptionally generous, and he donated much more than I'd solicited."

"How did you dare?"

"I felt he owed us some recompense. After all"—she shifted, her plush skirt swishing at her legs—"you and I weren't involved in his quarrel with Hugh, but look where it left us."

Where it left us, indeed, Sarah thought acridly, gazing around the barren chamber and adjusting her bulky clothes against the cold.

Rebecca preened as though her contacting Michael Stevens was eminently suitable, and Sarah resisted the impulse to scream with frustration.

How could Rebecca communicate with Michael! How could she degrade herself like a common beggar! Didn't she have any pride? Didn't she recognize Michael Stevens for the scoundrel he was?

"I'm surprised he had any blunt to bestow," Sarah stated with more bitterness than she'd intended to show.

"Whatever do you mean?"

"Well, with his being a gambler, I can't believe he has two pennies to rub together."

"Michael Stevens?" Rebecca laughed gaily. "Oh, Sarah, the man is richer than Croesus."

"From gambling?"

"No, silly, from the club he owns with his brother. It's the most popular spot in the city for a gentleman to pass his leisure time."

"But I thought he survived from game to game."

"That he gambled to earn his income? No," Rebecca clarified. "And when he plays for any kind of stakes, it's only with fools."

Like Hugh, was the unuttered reproach.

"But if he's so wealthy . . ." Sarah couldn't say the rest: Why did he do this to me? Why did he leave me like this?

"Why did he take everything?" Rebecca finished for her. "Sarah, his and Hugh's dispute was protracted and bitter. You don't know what Hugh was like in town."

"No, I don't." But she had a fairly good notion. She'd observed Hugh at his worst many, many times. He'd been insufferable.

"While I'm not definite on the particulars of his game with Mr. Stevens, there have been stories. I hate to tell you this, but Hugh probably deserved what he got; he was a total ass, and you must remember that Mr. Stevens's animosity was provoked over a lengthy period of numerous insults."

"Possibly," Sarah mused.

Her mind was reeling, but she could only focus on one, novel fragment of what Rebecca had imparted: Her husband was wealthy. He was economically settled, so much so that he would graciously lavish several pounds on a woman with whom he wasn't acquainted simply because she had the gall to inquire.

Slowly, her temper ignited. For months, she'd been struggling to recover from being captured in the whirlwind that had enveloped Michael. She'd been languishing from terrible bouts of melancholia, incapable of dealing with how Michael had burst into her life, then vanished like a magician in a puff of smoke.

She was enraged. About how he'd failed to trust her. About how he'd manipulated and abused her. About how he'd abandoned her to flounder and wallow in the poverty he'd inflicted.

While Rebecca was smartly dressed and on her way to Christmas festivities, Sarah was scrounging for the barest necessities, grappling with debt collectors, searching for pen and foolscap so that she could draft her daily rationales as to why they must continue to wait for compensation.

Fury burst upon her in a wave of unrelenting ire. How could he treat her so shabbily? And why had she allowed it?

He'd sent her to Yorkshire like a naughty child, and she'd scurried home, with nary a complaint or thought as to whether his decision was correct.

His conflict had been with Hugh, not her, and she was tired of being painted the villain. Hugh was dead, interred in a pauper's grave, and Sarah was Michael's wife. The man had responsibilities to her. No one had forced him into marriage; he'd done so freely, albeit reluctantly, and it was past time he honored his vows.

Suddenly sensing that she'd overstayed her welcome, Rebecca rose and prepared to depart, prattling on as to how her companion would be getting anxious.

"Don't let me keep you," Sarah advised, sounding horridly uncivil.

"I wish you'd come to London." Rebecca repeated her overture. "I hate to see your dire straits, so please say yes. We've an extra room that could be yours. Would you like me to stop by on the return trip? You could ride with us. We'd have space for a bag or two."

"No, Rebecca, but thank you."

Then and there, she decided she'd make her way to town, but not for any of the reasons Rebecca might conjure up. She had words—a few nasty, indelicate, rude words—that she planned to speak to her *husband*. And by God, he was going to listen to every one of them, if she had to tie him down while she said her piece!

"At least, let me give you this." Rebecca held out a bag of coins, and Sarah didn't hesitate to grab it. "It's some of what Mr. Stevens dispensed."

"How wonderful!" She derived perverse pleasure from knowing that she would pay for her excursion with the cad's very own money.

Rebecca strolled out, and the carriage whisked her away. Sarah watched until it was just a dot on the horizon, then she marched to her lonely, desolate parlor, delighted that Rebecca had visited, relieved that the woman's disclosures had spurred her to action.

"Well, Mr. Stevens," she announced to the dying fire, "I'm off to London. What do you think of that?"

Pitching the bag from hand to hand, she relished the coins clinking together as she pictured how astonished he'd be when he opened his door to discover her on his stoop.

Was he in for it! Very likely, his ears were already ringing.

Chapter Twenty-two

Abigail Weston Stevens was walking down the stairs when she heard a knock on the front door. Previously, she might have ignored it, anticipating that the butler would take on the mundane chore that she would have deemed beneath her station but, in the past year, her life had been transformed. For the better.

She wasn't in her brother's grand mansion, filled with dozens of servants, but in James's small house that was truly a home. Fondly, she tended to, and oversaw, the cheery abode in her recurrent efforts to instill the sense of serenity and closeness that James had missed out on while growing up.

Marriage had definitely generated changes! By allying herself with the nefarious rake, she'd been altered in more ways than she could count. Lovingly, she traced a hand along the swelling in her abdomen, the babe he'd so lustily planted just beginning to show.

As always happened when she thought of her robust, vital husband, butterflies swarmed through her stomach. She was so appallingly happy! Each day was superior to the last, just as she'd surmised they would be when she'd begged him to make her his bride.

Since they'd been together, James had calmed and matured, delighting in the simple pleasures. They were a family, and with the approach of summer, their number would increase by one more when she gifted him with a beautiful son or daughter. A wave of tender sentiment brought tears that moistened her eyes. With her pregnancy in full bloom, she cried about everything and nothing, and she tried to quell the surge of emotion but, as she sauntered over to greet her visitor, she could barely contain her joy.

She turned the knob, and she wasn't really thinking about who she might encounter—perhaps one of James's business associates or one of his employees—but the pretty woman lingering on the stoop had her snapping to attention. Her comely face and unique auburn hair were mostly shielded from view by her dark cloak, and Abigail suffered a moment of uncanny compassion as she recalled her own furtive trip the prior spring to see James's mother, Angela Ford, and her beseeching Angela to aid in convincing James to wed.

"May I help you?" Her curiosity was thoroughly piqued.

"I hope so. I realize this is terribly forward of me." The woman blushed becomingly, and nervously glanced about, checking that she had the correct address, then she braced herself. "I was advised that this is the residence of Michael Stevens, and I must speak with him."

"And you are . . . ?"

"Sarah . . ." Nodding authoritatively, she added, "Sarah Compton . . . Stevens." She pronounced *Stevens* as though it didn't fit on her tongue.

"I'm Abigail Stevens. I'm married to James. Are we related?"

"Yes." The woman studied her carefully. "Michael is my husband."

"Your what?"

"My husband," she repeated, daring Abigail to dispute her allegation.

"Oh, my . . ." Abigail was totally flustered. Could it be true? With Michael and his bizarre mode of carrying on, she supposed anything was conceivable. Even an unknown wife! "When . . . ?" she managed.

"In June."

"But that was six months ago!"

Just about the time his excursion to the country had ended, and he'd stumbled into London, so lost and forlorn. Little had varied since then. He was reclusive, morose, incomprehensible in his conduct and methods. Abigail had struggled to befriend him, but he was an elusive thorn in her side, rebuffing her and James's attempts at reconciliation—when she wasn't positive what they needed to *reconcile.*

"Forgive me," she said, as she recalled her manners and gestured. "Come in, come in."

"Thank you."

Abigail ushered Sarah into the foyer and, as the butler retrieved her cloak, Abigail quietly counseled a footman to dismiss Sarah's rented hack. Their pending discussion would last more than a few minutes, so the driver needn't tarry.

They entered the parlor, and Abigail noticed that Sarah was chilled to the bone and, as Abigail ordered snacks and tea, she wondered how far the woman had traveled—and how dreadful had been her journey!

She was brave to show up unannounced, but Abigail was tickled that she had. Whatever hideous misery was gnawing at Michael, perhaps the basis was about to be revealed, which was an immense relief. There was a mystery here, and she was determined to get to the bottom of it.

Michael had undergone numerous modifications in his personality that had reshaped his relationship with James, and James was bewildered by the loss of their friendship. He couldn't mend the rift that had developed, and it was tormenting him.

Introspective, pensive, covert, Michael had always been somewhat reserved, but now, he was taciturn to the point of absurdity. James swore that something was terribly wrong, that an egregious incident had occurred while he'd been away. Michael wouldn't—or couldn't—talk about it, and James couldn't break through Michael's melancholy.

His younger brother lived by himself, in a house James owned a few blocks down the street. Michael worked, he ate, he slept, but he was like a person who was dead inside. There was no enjoyment or satisfaction as he went about his responsibilities. The contentment James assured her had once been there was gone.

Had this woman been the root of his affliction? If so, would she be the cure?

Optimistic, she sat forward. "We're sisters-in-law."

"You believe me, then?"

Sarah was so clearly relieved that Abigail could only smile. "Of course I believe you." Who would lie about being married to Michael? While the man was as good-looking and intriguing as her husband, he was so enigmatic that he frightened her. "Why wouldn't I?"

"Well, my impromptu visit is rather odd."

No more *odd* than when Abigail had confronted Angela Ford, but she didn't mention it. "What shall I call you? Since we're both *Mrs.* Stevens, the formality is a bit ridiculous."

"Sarah."

"And I'm Abigail."

From Sarah's comportment and demeanor, Abigail discerned her to be of the Quality. "Who is your family, Sarah? Did you say Compton?"

"Yes."

"Are you, by chance, related to the recently deceased Hugh Compton, Earl of Scarborough?"

"He was my brother."

An earl's daughter! An earl's sister! Abigail was stunned. Michael had privately and clandestinely married into the aristocracy, and he'd kept it a grand secret. Why?

The shocking gossip about Hugh Compton rushed back. While he'd been alive and provoking mischief, it had been impossible to avoid the sordid stories. James, who was a constant fount of discourse on the rich and infamous, had imparted his portion of them, but no one had ever hinted at this information.

Michael had surreptitiously married Scarborough's sister, and neither Hugh nor Michael had ever whispered a word about it. Had Hugh Compton even known? What did it all mean?

Abigail relaxed on the sofa, the preposterous revelation sinking in. She almost couldn't credit the woman's statement, yet she did. A deep wound had been haunting Michael, plaguing him heart and soul, but in their ruminating over the probable cause of his injury, they'd never conjured up an explanation like this!

"Sarah, I imagine you have a very fascinating tale to relate. Would you mind waiting for my husband? He'll be interested in your comments." At the reference to James, Sarah appeared ready to bolt, and Abigail laid a consoling hand on her arm. "Whatever it is, he'll be an incredible help to you."

"Are you sure?"

"He has an extraordinary knack for sorting out problems and devising solutions."

Abigail walked to the hall and conferred with their majordomo Arthur, who efficiently hovered nearby. His brows flew up in amazement as he learned of their guest's identity and, with no further urging, he hurried off to roust James out of bed.

A maid brought refreshments, and Abigail was offered a reprieve from conversation while Sarah wrapped her fingers around a hot cup of tea and absorbed its warmth. From how she gobbled down the slices of meat, cheese, and bread, it was obvious that she was famished.

When did you last have a decent meal?

Abigail was saved from posing the indelicate question aloud because, just then, James hustled in.

Considering how rapidly he'd been awakened, he was flawlessly dressed, and intent on beholding Sarah Compton Stevens with his own two eyes.

"James"—Abigail rose placidly and went to him, silently begging for calm—"I'm so glad you're here. The most marvelous guest has stopped by."

"Yes, Arthur informed me." He stomped across the floor until he was directly in front of Sarah. "Excuse my abruptness. I'm James, Michael's brother."

"No apology is necessary," Sarah graciously indicated. "My arrival was unforeseen, but I was so eager to meet with Michael. I came here straightaway."

Abigail conceded, "And we're delighted that you did." James made no signal of agreement, so Abigail poked him in the ribs. "Aren't we?"

"Yes," he then replied emphatically, "we certainly are."

Sarah stood, and they scrutinized one another like predators circling before combat. Seeming astonished that two such attractive, potent men could exist simultaneously, she eventually noted, "You look just like him."

"No"—James's smile heated the room—"you're mistaken. I'm *much* more handsome."

"Oh, James," Abigail chastised, but his stab at humor was successful. Sarah's tension eased as she finally comprehended that she was safe and wouldn't be sent packing. "Let's sit, shall we? I gather we're in for a lengthy and engaging narration."

"And I for one," James retorted, "can't wait to hear the details."

They adjusted themselves on the furniture, facing one another, and Abigail discreetly pressed food on Sarah while the woman regaled them about her adversity with Michael. Although she omitted the juiciest parts, they concluded that Michael had compromised her and married her because of it.

But as her recital continued, as she depicted how he'd sent her home to fend for herself, as she described the autumn and the seizure Michael had accomplished of all Hugh's belongings, as she itemized the poverty and hardship she'd been constrained to endure, they stiffened with outrage. James, especially, was disturbed by how badly Michael had behaved.

As she reached her summation, explicating how she'd decided to head for London, Sarah's ire equaled their own, her temper rekindled by her accounting.

James was irate, unable to be still, pacing behind the couch, and Abigail received the distinct impression that Michael was lucky he was absent. Her husband and sister-in-law had allied against him, and they were dangerously bent on getting answers from the unsuspecting man. Abigail would have felt sorry for him had he not acted the categorical bounder toward Sarah.

"What now?" she asked into the deafening silence that ensued once Sarah finished her chronicle.

James summoned Arthur to fetch his coat. "It's high time my brother and I had a chat."

"Do you know where he is?" Sarah queried.

"I might." His response was intentionally ambiguous.

"I'll go with you." Sarah crossed the room, prepared to join in the search.

"Perhaps it would be best if you stayed here with Abigail." He stared at Abigail, seeking her intervention. "I'll be back shortly."

"I've planned this moment for six months," Sarah asserted, "and I won't delay another second. I'm going!"

She proclaimed it with such finality that Abigail couldn't see how James would dissuade her. Nevertheless, he visually spurred Abigail to intercede as he implored, "I really don't think that's wise."

James was outright pleading now, and suddenly, Abigail got his message. "Oh, dear . . ." she grumbled, not meaning to grouse audibly.

"What is it?" Sarah asked.

Abigail sighed. Poor Sarah had been through so much; she didn't need any grave tidings. "James is right," Abigail gently cautioned, "perhaps you should remain behind."

"I'm not a child." Sarah glared testily at both of them. "I demand the truth."

James flashed Abigail a tortured look, in typically male fashion, incompetent to elucidate, forcing her to do the dirty deed. "Michael probably isn't alone."

"With whom would he be?"

Abigail yearned to soften the blow but couldn't decipher how to make it sound less damaging than it was. "Presumably, he's with Pamela."

"Pamela . . . Pamela Blair?"

"Yes." Abigail drew near to her. "He's been cavorting quite shamelessly with her since last summer."

"There've been rampant rumors they might marry," James felt obliged to append.

"James!" Abigail scolded, and he reddened at how his disclosure affected Sarah.

Her legs had ceased to support her, and she sank onto the sofa. "But she's my friend."

"I'd bet my last pound that she doesn't know about the two of you," James inappropriately interjected. "Michael hasn't confided in anyone."

Abigail was exasperated with James. His remarks were cutting like a knife. Obtuse creature! In light of his employment and the uproars in which he typically became embroiled, he was usually adept at handling the most difficult situations. The fact that he was stumbling only underscored how rattled he was by Michael's deportment, so she couldn't be too aggravated.

She sat with Sarah and held her hand. "What James is clumsily saying"—she optically threatened him with dismemberment—"is that we don't understand Michael anymore or what's troubling him. He's been so contrary that we hardly know him."

"Exactly," James put in. "He's so strange, and he's been so uncommunicative, that he and I scarcely converse. I've always assumed that he endured a trauma while he was away, but I've never ascertained what it was."

"He seems heartbroken to me. Very sad," Abigail volunteered. "He's grieving." Encouragingly, she suggested, "Perchance, he's hurting over what transpired, and he can't figure out how to mend your differences."

"Carrying on with Pamela . . ." Sarah muttered to herself. "I will *absolutely* wring his pitiful neck!" Blatantly furious, she marched over to James, fists clenched, eyes sparking with rage. "Take me to him immediately!"

James appealed to Abigail for guidance, but she merely shrugged. "Maybe you should." She brightened. "We'll all go."

"*We* will not!" James declared, then cleared his throat. "I mean . . . I want to keep you out of it."

"Why? Sarah may need me."

"Abby . . ."

She bristled over his reticence. He was, once again, treating her like some wilting noblewoman, and she hated it. "You're embarrassed to introduce me to Michael's"— she almost said *mistress* but couldn't utter the despicable term in front of Sarah, so she switched to—"companion. Honestly, James, I won't expire."

"This might not be pretty, and I won't have you involved." Disconcerted, he reminded her, "The babe's been making you ill all morning."

"But I'm fine now."

Not wishing to induce dissension, Sarah interposed, "James is prudent to fret over you, Abigail. Michael and I both have tempers, so what I have to say to the cad won't be pleasant."

"Please?" James sweetly requested. "For me?"

"All right," she griped, powerless to refuse him anything. "But you must promise that you'll relay all the gory particulars; you can't leave anything out! And Sarah . . ."— she went to her newfound sister-in-law and enveloped her in a tight hug—"if your meeting with him is overly wretched, return here at once. You're family; we'll help you."

"You're very kind, Abigail."

They departed together; James guided Sarah into his carriage, then he scrambled in behind, and Abigail watched, feeling left out.

"Come for supper," she called at the last, "and bring Michael with you—if you can!"

Sarah waved her confirmation, as James pulled the door closed and motioned to the driver. Abigail lingered until they disappeared around the corner.

Sarah loitered in Michael's bedchamber and critically surveyed her surroundings. There had been a few signs of Pamela's occupancy, but after James had acquainted her with the staff, they had readily complied in assisting her to erase any evidence of the other woman. The handful of combs, the red silk petticoat, and the slinky peignoir she'd located were currently being delivered to Pamela's own domicile.

Satisfied with her afternoon's endeavors, she descended the stairs to sit with James in the parlor where he was patiently sipping on a brandy while awaiting his brother.

Michael's house was a charming place that James had purchased years earlier for his first wife and, from the moment they'd arrived, James had acutely enjoyed himself as Sarah had stormed about. Her fury had escalated as she'd proceeded from room to room, witnessing how comfortable Michael had been while she'd been scrimping and freezing in the country.

The three-story row house was nearly identical to the one where James and Abigail lived. On a busy, affable lane, it was cozy and plushly decorated with a welcoming ambiance. There was a feminine flavor to the decor that she liked, and she couldn't move beyond the despicable, petty notion that this warm, snug abode could have been hers— had she not been a coward and let Michael contend that their marriage was a fraud.

When they'd shown up at his door, Michael had been out, but the servants had insisted he'd be back soon, so they'd bided their time rather than track him all over London. Yet, once they'd settled in, Sarah couldn't abide the dawdling. She'd begun exploring, and though Michael's personal mark was scarcely apparent, his clothes were in an upstairs bedchamber—along with some of Pamela's. If Sarah hadn't been so angry, she might have been shattered.

While they'd been separated, she'd convinced herself that she had no feelings for her husband. During those long, lonely months at Scarborough, she'd persuaded herself that their brief affair had been an aberration, that she hadn't loved him madly and passionately but, as she'd fingered his apparel and shaving equipment, as she'd rifled through his dresser—just as she'd loved to do when they were together in Bedford—the sorry truth had crashed down on her. His presence had been so strong that she'd been impelled to admit how much she still cared.

How could he have set her aside so easily?

From what James had imparted, she was aware that Michael had come back to the city, then started up with Pamela shortly after. He'd hardly blinked between taking a wife and taking a mistress.

What was she to make of such disrespect?

She appreciated that he was overly virile and had an unrelenting sexual drive, that he regularly assuaged it with any woman who acted the least bit interested, so she harbored no illusions about his carnal attributes. Yet, she was stunned that he'd so hastily turned to another lover.

Oh, how it distressed her to acknowledge that she hadn't mattered to him! That she very likely hadn't crossed his mind after he'd walked away from the small church where they'd wed.

Well, Michael Stevens was in for a surprise. Sarah had had plenty of opportunity to reflect during the laborious, frigid trek to London. She craved a valid marriage, and she wanted a house full of boisterous children, with Michael as their father.

With the exception of the unfathomable Rebecca, her own family was nonexistent. Her father and mother were dead, and Hugh—pitiful Hugh, whom she didn't mourn or miss—the last of their line. The Scarborough estate she'd fought so valiantly to protect wasn't hers. She belonged nowhere and felt as if she had no past or future, and the single component that connected her to the rest of the world was that she had a spouse; a husband who didn't fancy her, but that was about to change.

If the trying killed her, they would come to terms with what had transpired. Michael Stevens hadn't discovered what her father and Hugh had always known: She was stubborn and determined. She didn't quit, she didn't surrender, and she never capitulated until she'd achieved her goal.

From her perspective, conditions looked desperate; she

was out of options, and she wouldn't desist until she had, once again, broken through Michael's wall of reserve. She hadn't forgotten what it was like to have his undivided attention, to bask in his admiration, to win his regard. There was nothing quite so fine as holding him close while knowing that she was the sole person who had ever loved him. He was no match for her in resolve or persistence.

She stepped into the parlor just as a key clicked in the lock. Her heart skipped several beats, her step faltered, but she regrouped, ready for battle.

"Are you up to this?" James asked.

"Yes."

"Abigail and I are here for you."

She smiled at the man who was already a good friend. "I'm grateful."

"If he tosses us out on our ear . . ."

"I won't permit it," she scoffed. "Your brother's days of bossing me around have ended."

"I can see that." James chuckled at her pluck and tucked her arm in his. "But in case you've miscalculated, you can stay with us for as long as you like."

What amenable news! To be granted shelter! Somewhere clean and safe, where people cared about her! Until that precise moment, she hadn't truly believed that she could escape her seriously dire straits.

"Your hospitality won't be necessary. Michael will be thrilled to see me." They walked out to the foyer. "It just might take him a while to realize it."

They halted in front of the door, and Michael strolled in—with Pamela by his side. She was lovely as ever, fashionable in a dark fur cloak and hat, with red feathers dangling over her shoulder. Her nose and cheeks rosy-red, she was laughing over something Michael had just said.

It had commenced snowing, and a flurry of huge, white flakes cascaded in behind them. Michael stamped his feet against the cold, then spun around and espied them huddled, critical and condemning, but as was his habit, he displayed no outward sign of consternation or recognition.

Sarah might have been crushed by his seeming lack of reaction, but she wouldn't allow herself to grapple with pity or regret. She simply stared, then stared some more.

He was more handsome than she remembered, and her heart ached at observing his masculine beauty up close. She had never been able to gaze upon him without being moved. He was too dynamic, too commanding, and her pulse wasn't steady.

With the snow dusting his hair and shoulders, his blue eyes aloof and withdrawn, he appeared distant, unapproachable, unattainable, and she steeled herself to the daunting task that lay before her. She would not fail in claiming him for her own!

"James . . ." Michael nodded. "Sarah . . ." he adjoined cautiously.

"Why, Sarah Compton," Pamela gushed merrily. "How wonderful that you're in London! You're the very last individual I expected to see in town today!"

"I'll bet," Sarah responded miserably, reining in her resentment. Pamela wasn't cognizant of the circumstances; the blackguard had never told her!

Pamela clutched Sarah's hands and gave her an affectionate kiss on the cheek. "How have you been?"

"Fine," Sarah lied.

"In June, you abandoned my party so fast that we never even said good-bye!"

"I'm sorry." Sarah threw Michael a quelling glare that he coolly mirrored. "Michael promised he'd make my apologies."

"Oh, he did, but you know men!" Pamela gestured gaily, flinging them all off as unreliable. "He wouldn't say why you'd gone. I hope you weren't upset about anything . . . ?"

There was a question posed in her remark, and Sarah's wrath intensified. How dare Michael do this to Pamela! How dare he put Sarah in such an awkward position!

Tired of the ruse, wishing the acrimony over, she barked at Michael. "Tell her."

"Tell me what?" Pamela innocently grinned up at Michael who was wholly unaffected.

"Tell her!" Sarah repeated sharply.

"Sarah and I married," Michael acclaimed, calm as all get out.

"When?" Pamela choked, instantly looking sick.

"That last day in Bedford."

Pamela's mouth fell open. "All this time . . . you were . . ." She couldn't complete her sentence, and her expression was so full of indignation that Sarah was somewhat appeased. "Oh, you unmitigated rogue! How could you!"

"That's what I've been dying to know," James accused, tensing with virulent menace. "I'd love to have your answer, brother—if you think you could possibly provide one that I would tolerate."

Michael was firmly, doggedly silent, though his eyes glittered with a peculiar fire. A thousand words were poised on the tip of his tongue, but Sarah knew him well. He'd never speak up in the middle of this vile scene.

"Sarah," Pamela interrupted, "forgive me! I had no idea!"

"I believe you."

"You're my friend. I would never . . ." She cast Michael another scathing look. "I am so mortified! I should go . . ."

But she didn't depart, and an awkward interlude developed, so Sarah said, "I'm going upstairs to dress for supper. You have five minutes to make your farewells. Then, I don't want you over here again."

"No, I won't come by," Pamela vowed, shaking her head in dismay, "but would you . . . would you visit me later? After everything is more settled?"

"We'll see," Sarah blandly acquiesced.

Sarah turned to James. "I won't be having supper with Abigail this evening. I'm dining in—with my husband. I'll send a note to her on the morrow."

"No need." James expressed. He leaned near and whispered, "If it turns out that you can't bear to stay, send one of the servants to my club. They'll know where. I'll come and get you. Despite the hour."

"I won't require any assistance." Climbing the first two steps, she spun around, then glared down at Michael and Pamela. Michael still exhibited no emotion, while Pamela looked as though she yearned to shrivel into a ball and die. "Pamela, I'm sure you didn't mean any harm, but I intend to keep my husband. If I catch you sniffing around him again, I'll break both your legs. I swear it!"

"Oh, God . . ." Pamela blushed furiously.

"Even if he begs, don't meet with him ever again. Don't make this any worse than it already is."

"No, I won't, Sarah. I promise you!"

"And do me a favor?"

"Anything."

"Spread the word to his other paramours: I won't have him philandering. He's mine. And I'm not sharing!"

As she hurled the challenge, she met Michael's gaze, and something dangerous and unreadable flickered in his eyes, then vanished. She stormed up the stairs, not glancing back.

Chapter Twenty-three

Michael frowned at Sarah's pretty backside as she marched up the stairs. She was a sight, with all that wifely affront directed at himself and Pamela. With her proprietary disposition, and that affectation of umbrage and offense, it almost seemed as though she was truly perturbed, but then, she was a terrific actress. She could have made a name for herself on the stage alongside his mother.

Once the sound of her wrathful retreat had faded, he stirred uncomfortably, sequestered as he was with Pamela and James. Their joint censure was tangible, their anger explicit, their dismay substantial.

"I could wring your bloody neck." Pamela seethed with righteous indignation, and he couldn't blame her.

He'd longed to confide in her, but he couldn't discuss the anguish and disappointment he'd suffered at Sarah's hands. Pamela would have listened and advised, but Michael couldn't bring himself to confess.

Straining, he tried to decipher where Sarah's footsteps had led her, and he surmised that she was in his bedchamber. Sighing, he pondered why she'd feel free to rummage around in his personal apartment. She couldn't be moving in and making herself at home! They weren't destined to cohabitate, and he was curious as to why she'd finally come slinking to town.

What was she doing here? Why now? What sort of disaster did her presence portend?

On dozens of occasions, he'd picked up a pen, aspiring to write and inquire after her circumstances—especially after Hugh had died—but he hadn't been able to put ink to parchment.

When her cousin had solicited money, which he'd supplied with nary a thought, he'd been hard-pressed to keep from plying her for details as to how Sarah was faring. After Miss Monroe's departure, he'd stewed for hours, searching for some method of mending their predicament, but he'd generated no ideas, and he'd ultimately determined that any communication would have been pointless. If he'd contacted her, what would he have said?

That he was sorry? He wasn't.

That he missed her? He didn't.

That he apologized? He wouldn't.

That he wished things had ended differently? Now, that was a question worth considering.

Whenever he closed his eyes, he envisioned her dancing out of the church after their wedding ceremony, clutching her pathetic bouquet and smiling joyfully. Her emotion had seemed so real, as though she'd developed a genuine *tendre* for him that had nothing to do with Hugh or his scheming.

How she'd feigned such valid sentiment was a mystery. *Why* she would pretend such extreme affection had kept him up many nights since they'd separated. On that fateful, hideous wedding day, he'd been so angry, and she'd been so happy, and there hadn't been a way for those two human conditions to meld.

Since then, there'd been no suitable opportunity for reconciliation, though he couldn't fathom what needed to be resolved. She and her dubious brother had endeavored to blackmail him into a financial rescue that he would never undertake. He and Sarah were strangers, from opposite worlds, and she was Scarborough's sister, by Hugh's own admission, as fully capable of deceit as Hugh had ever been. They had no common ground, or mutual foundation of trust, so why had he married her?

He'd asked himself as much a thousand times and still hadn't marshaled a viable answer. During the fiasco, he'd just been so shocked and overwhelmed. Her chicanery and betrayal had wounded him, and he'd needed to ruthlessly react, so marrying her had seemed a sufficient punishment.

Since meeting her, he'd become a fool. Where Sarah Compton—*Stevens* a tiny voice added—was concerned, he couldn't locate solid ground. The earth kept shifting under his feet, inducing him to sway and vacillate from one bad decision to the next. He'd wed her in a fit of pique, he'd sowed the oats of his wretched future, and she was his now, whether he wanted her or not.

She'd arrived, demanding respect, recognition, most likely money, and he couldn't begin to guess what else.

What a tangle!

Pamela stepped in front of him. "You'd better hie yourself up those stairs and do some fast talking. Tell her the truth, or I'll never forgive you." Snapping the clasp on her cloak, she huffed to the door. "I may not forgive you anyway!"

"If you can wait just a bit, Pam," James injected, "I'll see you home."

"My carriage is parked out front," she said, and she paused, not quite geared for farewell. Squeezing Michael's fingers, she entreated, "Don't call on me, darling. I'm not interested in your justifications, and I'd die if she learned that you'd stopped by!" In parting, she stole a quick kiss. "I don't understand any of this, but you need to work it out with her. You won't regret it."

As she walked out into the cold afternoon, he made no *au revoir*. In a smattering of minutes, he'd gained a wife he didn't want and lost a friend he'd truly miss. The day had gone to hell, and it wasn't even four o'clock. He leaned against the door, physically bracing himself for whatever James was about to say.

Through the awkward silence that followed, he couldn't look at his brother, so he stared at his feet instead, remembering all the prior occasions when they'd had a good row, when they'd argued and fought, counseled and coerced, consoled and constrained. How he had always loved James! But just now, he couldn't bear to hear the questionable words of wisdom his older brother might choose to impart.

"What happened?" James queried with much more calm than Michael had predicted.

"You're aware of the card game Scarborough and I played last spring."

"Yes."

"So, you know how he was acting. His derogatory remarks. I couldn't back down."

"I'm surprised you didn't call him out. I would have."

"I judged it more gratifying to have him alive and paying through the nose." His blasted pride never ceased to get him into trouble. Why had he let Hugh goad him to such absurdity?

"What about *her*?" James referred to Sarah.

"She was at Pamela's party."

"Did you debauch her to retaliate against Hugh?"

"No . . . yes . . ." He dug the heels of his hands into his eyes. "Maybe. I'm not sure. She was staying in the room next to mine. I couldn't resist." Brimming with memories, recollecting all, he reminisced over how sweet it had been, and his heart constricted and ached. "I wanted her," he inevitably affirmed, "and it didn't have anything to do with her brother."

"I never suspected it had. She's quite stunning."

"Aye."

"So . . . you seduced her?"

"Yes, but she was simply plotting with Hugh, working us into a compromising situation so they could extort money—and compel the cancellation of his markers."

James bristled. "Who told you that?"

"Scarborough, himself."

"You believed him?"

"Why wouldn't I?" Michael's sizzling gaze locked on James's, and he encountered conspicuous skepticism. "She left the door unlocked."

"Are you positive?"

No, he yearned to shout, but he was no longer certain. "Hugh insisted that they'd concocted it together. That she'd been involved every step of the way."

"If you buy that nonsense"—James advanced until they were toe to toe—"why did you marry her?"

He gulped, struggling to breathe. "Because I didn't want anyone to think I'm like our father."

James laid a hand on his shoulder, and for once, Michael didn't shake it off. "Hugh was lying to you. About her. About her participation."

"How can you be so confident?"

"I quizzed her extensively. She was caught up—just as you were."

"What if you're mistaken?"

"I'm not," he said evenly. "Promise me you'll let her explain her side of it. And get a few things off her chest. She's fairly vexed with you."

"As I am with her."

"She's had a difficult few months."

"So have I," Michael irascibly contended.

"And with Scarborough dead"—James wouldn't argue when Michael would have loved nothing more than an enthusiastic spat—"she has nowhere to go, and no visible means of support. She needs your protection."

The information made him hesitate. Many a night he'd tossed and turned in his lonely bed, wondering what would befall her, but he'd refused to fret. His cup overflowed with recrimination, but immature as it sounded, his vanity wouldn't allow him to grovel before her, offering unwanted aid that he was convinced she'd throw in his face.

"What would you have me do? Beg her to take advantage of me? To rifle through my pockets so she can pilfer the last of my coins?"

"The solution is up to you," James stated, "but you're going to have to *do* something. She's here, she's your wife, and, from what she told Abigail and me, she won't be leaving anytime soon." His grin was full of mischief. "I hauled her trunk upstairs. She's already unpacked."

"Why, thank you, brother," he remarked sarcastically, gnashing his teeth.

"Glad to help." James chuckled and bowed mockingly,

and strangely, the silly display made Michael feel better than he had in a long while, and he realized that they hadn't joked in ages.

"God, what a mess," he mused.

"Look . . . she came to you," James indicated. "She took the first step. Can't you meet her somewhere in the middle?"

"Count on you to say something thoroughly idiotic."

"Now . . . now . . ."—James lectured like a seasoned old man—"being married is *not* the end of the world. If you give it a try, you might even grow to like it."

Michael looked at his brother, *really* looked for a change. He was contented as he never had been before. The rough edges of dissatisfaction and disappointment that had shadowed his character, and driven his reckless behavior, had vanished, replaced by a disgusting veneer of blissfulness that only the newly married could ever manifest.

"Go home, James." He was eager to be spared this novel glimpse of his brother. Besides, it was time to confront his wife, so he opened the door and pushed James out.

"For once in your life," James admonished, "do the right thing, will you?"

"I don't know what the *right* thing is," he rejoined truthfully.

"Yes you do," James asserted with smug confidence. "If you need me, send a message. I'll come back immediately."

"As if I could stomach more of your bloody assistance," he grumbled as he shut the door, his final view of James, his complacent, irritating grin.

The silence of the house enveloped him. His handful of well-trained servants were politely absent, leaving him to his bitter introspection. Then, the inevitable couldn't be avoided, and he mounted the stairs, his tread heavy, like a condemned man to the gallows.

Where she was concerned, he'd developed a second sense, so his intuition easily guided him to her. From the threshold to his bedchamber, he could distinguish her movements in the adjacent room where she was boldly preparing to take a bath. As was her habit, she'd added rose oil to the water. The smell permeated the air and tickled his nostrils.

The sleeping arrangements were very much as they had been in the country: two bedchambers divided by a communal dressing room. For a brief instant, he presumed that she'd moved into the adjoining salon, but then he saw her combs on his dresser, her corset draped over a chair. He stalked to the wardrobe and peeked in. Three of her dresses were hanging next to his shirts.

Did she propose that they would share a bed as man and wife? They wouldn't spend any time sleeping! Surely, the insane woman realized that fact! His physical fascination with her hadn't waned in the slightest. Just the thought of her readying to bathe sent the blood surging to his loins.

His temper flared. Six months had passed, and without notice or warning, she had the audacity to show up and insinuate herself into his house and his bed. How was a man to cope rationally with such a contingency? Did she hope for a platonic accord? Or did she fancy they would carry on as lovers?

At the notion, his cock distended brutally, and he resolved not to give her a choice. She'd foolishly inserted herself into his life, so she would suffer the consequences— although *suffer* was probably not the correct term. After he'd initiated her into the sexual arts, she'd developed into an adept, proficient lover so the *suffering,* such as it was, would be magnificent, and he would wallow in every erotic, disturbing minute of it.

He approached the dressing room and, through the crack in the door, he could see her. She was undressing, and he stealthily and inappropriately spied. Had she decided to use a flash of bare skin in order to entice him to commit acts he didn't intend?

Well, whatever her game, she'd miscalculated. If she was careless enough to imprudently disrobe before his very eyes, she would pay whatever price he extracted.

Poised on the brink, cognizant that he should announce

his presence, he couldn't impel himself to stop her. Like a practiced courtesan, she'd undone the buttons and ties on her gown and was slowly tugging it to her waist, past her hips, until it pooled on the floor.

She lifted her foot onto a stool, furnishing him with a wide expanse of naked thigh as she removed one shoe and the other, pitching them with an unceremonious clump. In a smooth motion, her chemise was off, and momentarily, she wore only a pair of her sheer French drawers, stockings, and garters.

A gentleman with even the smallest measure of civility would have departed, but like a perverted voyeur, he wrongly watched her stripping. Irreverent as always, he didn't care as to her opinion of his conduct. She appreciated the sort of scoundrel he was, yet she'd come to him anyway, and he wasn't about to deny himself such outlandish carnal pleasure. Morals and manners be damned!

She faced him then, and she did nothing to conceal herself. Her flawless breasts, nipples peaked, invited his crude investigation. The two mounds were ungodly in their perfection. No mortal man could gaze upon them and behave himself, and he wasn't about to. She'd disrobed in his bedchamber, so whatever transpired was no more than she deserved.

Once again, she placed her dainty foot on the stool, bending over to untie her garters and roll down her stockings, then she stood, her hand pulling at the bow that laced her drawers, and she conducted them over her hips, her legs, until she was exquisitely, sinfully naked. At ease now, with her body, with her nudity, she stretched her arms high, flexing her muscles and arching her back.

Her hair was piled on her head, so none of her charms was hidden. Observing all—the wide shoulders, the nipped waist, the flared hips—his brow creased with anxiety as he noted that she'd lost weight. He was intimately familiar with every inch of her torso, his tongue having traced over curve and valley. She was slimmer, but from what?

Shaking off the disturbing insight, he focused instead on

the crimson hair shielding her pussy. Its dangerous lure impelled him to the door just as she moved to the tub.

She perceived his presence and halted in mid-stride, her foot balanced on the rim, the pink of her cleft winking at him from between her legs. He fought down the impulse to rush to her, to touch her there, to kiss her there.

"You can't expect to watch," she complained.

"Absolutely."

"I don't want you in here."

"Milady, we are far past the time when what you *want* matters to me at all."

Her emerald eyes sparked with ire, and she held his gaze, set to engage in verbal fisticuffs, but the warm water beckoned, and she turned away.

"Why am I never surprised when you act like an ass?" Then, she proceeded to ignore him, testing the temperature with her toe. Deeming it adequate, she slipped in, a moan of delight bubbling from her ruby lips. "Aah . . . I haven't had a hot bath in an eternity."

He declined to examine the statement too closely, wouldn't ask: how come? Instead, he concentrated solely on the sensual illustration, rejecting the chance to discern more than he dared.

There was a mirror behind the tub, so he could rudely analyze her antics. He'd always relished seeing her at her bath; she lowered her guard, cherishing the occurrence like a sailor; maidenly modesty forsaken.

Relaxing, she widened her legs. Her thighs were spread, and he could conceive of her pussy below the water, wet and swollen from the heat. He neared to obtain a better view, and her breasts floated on the surface.

"Is your mistress gone?" She stared at their posed reflections in the glass.

"I have no mistress."

She scoffed. "I meant what I said."

"What was that?"

"If I catch her panting after you again, I'll kill her"— her rabid regard dropped to his crotch where his overblown phallus prodded blatantly against the placard of his trousers—"then I'll castrate you."

He marveled at the threat. She was so bloody enticing when she was exhibiting her true character, and he grappled with the significance of her caveat. Did she consider him worth having? Worth keeping? Worth fighting for? She seemed to be jealous of his alleged indiscretions with Pamela, which could only arise from her harboring valid emotion.

His confusion increased.

"You have a wicked tongue, madam."

"Mrs. Stevens to you," she proclaimed caustically. "Have the decency to acknowledge who I am."

At the reminder, he flushed, two bright marks of red staining his cheeks. "Dear *wife*," he emphasized, "you've only just arrived. Don't command me about."

"You'll seek me out"—she raised a defiant brow—"whenever you have need of a woman's services. You'll not embarrass me by cavorting with every whore in London."

"Pamela is not a whore," he felt obliged to relate.

"I never said she was," Sarah conceded, "but you won't dally with her again. I'm afraid my mind's made up, and the subject is not debatable."

So . . . she thought to employ her corporeal wiles to keep him on a tether. An excellent ploy. In light of how attracted he was to her, how captivated he'd always been, the concept of having her regularly was acutely tempting.

Did she assume that she was imposing an untenable burden? He had no qualms about slaking his lust with her. If she was heedlessly volunteering, he'd promptly assent.

Weeks—nay months—of lewd excess stretched ahead, and he tried to calculate why he'd denied himself. She was his wife, he'd seen to that by speaking the vows, but he'd only perceived the onus brought on by allying himself with her. Not the incomparable satisfaction.

His body had never known such outrageous luxury and, at that very moment, it was pleading to be assuaged. Why not submit? What reason could possibly justify restraint?

He toed off one boot, then the other. Only when he drew off his jacket and dislodged his cravat did he garner any undue scrutiny from her. She came up on her knees, glaring at him over her shoulder.

"What are you doing?"

"What does it look like?"

"You're removing your clothing!"

"An accurate assessment."

"To what purpose?"

"I'm joining you."

"After all your misdeeds! You're mad if you suppose you can saunter in here, snap your fingers, and require me to fornicate!" In a snit, she shook an accusing finger at him. "You thought I contrived against you with Hugh. You didn't trust me. You didn't believe in me." She paused, swallowed hard. "I'll do whatever you ask," she said, "but first, you must admit that you were wrong about me. Tell me you're sorry."

"I'm not."

Gad, those eyes! They tortured him! They delved to his core, exposing how much he'd missed her without his even knowing he had.

"Well, *I'm* sorry," she quietly professed, "for everything. For doubting you, and maligning you. For letting you chase me home to Scarborough. I should have stayed with you. There's a fine connection between us, and I'm willing to put our differences aside. To start over."

Her gracious expression of remorse felt like a noose around his neck, strangling him and, consummate villain that he was, he couldn't reply. While she was disposed to mend and heal, he was hurting too much to make concessions, not even something as simple as the apology she craved. He had to protect himself—at all costs!

She waited in vain, until she understood that he wouldn't beg her pardon, and she sagged in defeat as he plucked at the front of his pants, the top button popping free.

"Didn't you hear anything I just said?"

"I'm aroused." Another button flipped from its enclosure. "I've tolerated a lengthy period of sexual abstinence."

"I'm to infer that you and Pamela have merely been attending the opera?"

"Exactly."

"I discovered some of her clothes. In this very room."

"She frequently overimbibes"—he shrugged away the untoward rumors—"and has spent the night."

"You must conclude that I'm appallingly gullible."

She tried to exit the tub, but he rested a restrictive hand on her shoulder, adding tension, impeding escape. He was being cruel, but he simply couldn't let her wheedle herself under his skin again. If he opened his heart even a minute amount, she'd barge in, and he was terrified by the prospect.

"Have you had any lovers?" he boorishly inquired, and it dawned on him that her answer had better be *no*. An alien torrent of jealousy coursed through him; he'd very likely have to slay any man who'd had the audacity.

"No." She was emphatic, insulted. "How about yourself, my dear and *faithful* husband? Can you make the same vow?"

"Yes." He was just as definite. "Now that the issue is settled, I plan to indulge."

"Not until we hash this out."

"I've no intention of talking this to death. You're here, and you're naked in my bath. You'll do what I say, and you'll do it gladly."

"And *you* are a dreamer." But she continued to avidly peruse him as he shed his trousers.

Languidly, prolonging the ecstasy, he dragged them down his legs and kicked them away, then he rose beside her. Naked and hard, his cock an offensive size, he gripped it in his fist, easing some of the urgency. His phallus was mere inches from her plush, alluring mouth. He stroked himself, revealing the tip, knowing how fabulous it would feel to be inside that moist haven, to have her kneeling before him and sucking at him until he was imploring her to stop.

"Touch me," he commanded.

"No." But he wasn't about to be denied.

Before she could react, he slid into the tub and sank down behind her. They were wedged in the narrow space, her backside pressed to his front, his thighs mashed to hers, their calves and feet overlapping. Slippery and smooth, she smelled like sex, and woman, and roses, and he centered his cock on the cleft of her ass, his hands gripping her waist.

Her bounteous hair pricked his nose, and he yanked at the combs. It swung down in a cascade, the ends dangling on the water, and he shoved the heavy mass aside, then leaned forward and bit against her nape, causing her to writhe and squirm.

Insolently taunting, he held her firmly against him. "Have you been pining away for me?"

"Not for a second."

His fingers slipped down her stomach, kneading through the springy red curls, dipping into her, and she tensed at his unexpected invasion. Her pussy had only previously endured his unrefined style of penetration, and at the vain realization, his cock inflated further.

"I hate you," she charged but without conviction.

"Then why have you come?" He kissed up her neck, nuzzled her hair, and was pleased to detect goose bumps.

"So that I could tell you—to your face—what a wretch I think you are." Jostling him with her elbow, her blow glanced off, the only tangible result being that she inadvertently rubbed her shapely ass across his erection.

"Ooh . . . do that again." He bit at the lobe of her ear, and raucously grasped her nipples, as he studied their joint reflection in the mirror. Her abundant breasts and lush pussy were discernible. He lurked behind her, a dark, looming menace who boded ill.

"Look at us, Mrs. Stevens."

His cajoling dragged her attention to the mirror. With a

strained intensity, she evaluated the placement of their bodies, of his lips at her cheek, of his fingers at her nipples.
As lovers, they were impeccable together; they always had
been.

"Do you remember the first time I visited your bedchamber at Pamela's country house? I fondled you like this,
and you watched in the mirror. You were so hot, so beautiful. Just for me."

"Your conceit knows no bounds," she mutinously main-
tained. "I was bored and lonely; I might have welcomed
any man stupid enough to enter."

"I was the one. The *only* one."

"You flatter yourself."

With one hand, he manipulated her breast, while the
other fell to her pussy. Palpating her vigilantly, he probed
and explored, and eventually, he secured what he'd been
seeking: a scant response from her hips. He pressed against
her mound, eliciting a groan she didn't want him to discern.

"You are so ready for me."

"Arrogant beast!"

Like a scientist with a new invention, he found her clit
and began to play, working, toying, and teasing her. Her
hips succumbed, more brazenly adopting his rhythm.

He'd forgotten how much he treasured her sexual predilection, how he was attuned to her every need, how his
spirit soared at her prurient nature. Bending down, he
doused his cock, wetting the erect member. "Take me inside you."

"I won't," she argued. "I haven't forgiven you."

"I don't care."

He inserted the blunt tip, gave her a tad more. Her eyes
widened, as if she didn't recall how big he was, and he
could barely stifle a moan of pleasure at having her, once
again. "I love fucking you," he indelicately mentioned. "I
always have."

As he intruded slowly, meticulously, their gazes linked
in the mirror. Cautiously, she reached behind her head, tracing along his neck, his face, his lips, and he kissed her

palm, awed by the emotion that blazed from the simple gesture.

He couldn't stand this effect she so easily managed!

The only thing he wanted from her was spicy, tempestuous sex. Nothing more. Clutching her hips, he attempted to ardently thrust, but the tub was too cramped, and he couldn't exert the pressure he longed to wield, but apparently, excessive endeavor wasn't necessary. After minimal effort, he was at the sharp edge of release.

Almost without warning, he started to come, and he frantically grabbed for her, striving to withdraw so that he could disgorge his seed across her back and keep it away from her womb, but she'd been anticipating the maneuver. She ground her buttocks into him, their awkward poses propelling him against the rim of the tub and blocking his egress. Her cleft milked him with its severe stimulation, and his body arced, his cock throbbed, his seed shooting into her body in a sizzling river.

He couldn't recollect when he'd last spilled himself inside a woman. The wrongness of it, the folly, the impropriety, produced a bizarre thrill that billowed through his loins as he primally delighted in his ultimate possession.

She was *his.*

With a decisive, possessive plunge, he buried his forehead in her hair, treasuring the sensation of having her so completely, a feeling of rightness flooding over him, then gradually, sanity was restored, and he pulled away as much as he could, alarmed by what he'd just accomplished.

How did she so freely overwhelm him? He'd come like an untried lad of thirteen, ejaculating inside her as though it was a normal course of events. How could he defend his negligent incursion?

Wary of what he would discover, he met her gaze in the mirror, once again. A strong emotion flickered in her green eyes, but he couldn't decipher it.

"I'm sorry for my lack of control—" he commenced falteringly, but she cut him off.

"If you've decided to apologize for something," she replied scathingly, "don't you dare let it be for coming inside me. I do believe I might strangle you before I'd listen."

She huffed out, water splashing onto the floor with her departure. In a temper, she snatched her robe and stomped away, silence left in her wake. Pondering the perplexity of females, how incomprehensible they were, how mysterious, how irksome, he sank down in the tub.

His knees weak from the potency of his orgasm, he rested his arms on the edge of the basin as he took a cloth and scrubbed himself, recovering from the vigor of their copulation. Incrementally, he calmed enough to dry himself, then don his trousers.

When she'd stormed out, he hadn't nettled over where she'd gone, postulating that she'd run downstairs, or fled to one of the other bedrooms to fume and seethe.

To his dismay, she was lying on his bed, her head on his pillow, her body curled into a ball and covered with a knitted throw. Facing away from him, she appeared petite and vulnerable, and he knew with a glaring certitude that his bed would never be his own again. From that moment on, no matter when or how he looked at it, he'd always picture her there, seeming to have staked out her spot with no intent of relinquishing it.

Baffled, abashed, he huddled in the doorway, not sure what to say or how to say it. He could never find his balance with her.

"Where are my things?" Her question was so quietly voiced that he wasn't sure she'd spoken.

"What things?" he inquired.

"The furniture and possessions that belong at Scarborough."

"They're stored in a warehouse. Why?"

"I want everything sent back."

"All of it is mine," he couldn't stop himself from peevishly pointing out. "Your brother—"

"Hugh is dead," she tersely interjected. "Whatever happened between the two of you, it's not important anymore. The new earl is on his way. From America. He's a distant cousin whom I've never met, and I won't permit you to shame me by having the manor in a shambles when he arrives."

It was easier to relent than he'd imagined. He'd never wanted the blasted chattels in the first place. The entire cargo had been nothing but a daily, constant reminder of his mistakes. "I'll see to it."

"I have some elderly retainers who need to be pensioned off, but I've never had any money to help them."

"Done."

Trembling, she breathed deep, then exhaled, and he watched the rise and fall of her rib cage. "And I want Hugh's body shipped home so that he can have a proper burial." She gave a soft laugh that sounded very close to a sob. "His grave is here in London, and I don't even know where."

His initial inclination was to deny the modest request, but he couldn't. What did he care where Hugh Compton was buried? He acceded again, even as he marveled that he was being so accursedly cooperative. Next, she'd demand the shirt off his back, and he'd be jerking it over his head and presenting it to her on a silver platter.

"I have a secretary who works for me at the club," he said. "He'll visit you tomorrow. Tell him what you need; he'll handle it."

"Thank you." There was a protracted pause, then she forged on. "I'm prevailing on you horridly, but there's one thing more."

She was still staring at the wall, and it annoyed him that she wouldn't roll over. Usually, she was stubborn enough to confront any obstacle, to slave through any disagreement, and he recognized that he'd succeeded in pushing her past her limits.

"You're my wife." As he acknowledged her, he experienced an extraordinary rush of pride at claiming her. "I'll render to you whatever I have the means to provide."

"Then . . . I ask that you put some money in a trust for me. Not very much," she hastened on, lest he rebuff her.

"Just enough so that if you gamble away what we have, I will have some funds to tide me over. That way, I won't be cold, or hungry, or scared ever again."

His heart flipped over in his chest. What had he done? While he'd inflicted a terrible price on Hugh Compton, he'd avoided estimating the probable repercussions to her.

"Oh, Sarah . . ." Like a blind man, he stumbled toward the bed and glided down onto the mattress, resting a hand on her back, massaging in soothing circles. "I'm not a gambler," he declared. "I wager on occasion, but rarely, and only for meager amounts. I'm not obsessed like your father was. Or your brother."

"Swear it."

"I swear it to you," he reassured her. "You'll never go without."

Her body shuddered, then she nodded, accepting his pledge, and he caressed across her hair as though she was a young child in need of comfort. Her tension dissolved, and he turned her onto her back. Tears streaked her cheeks, and his heart lurched once more. He couldn't bear to have her unhappy.

"Don't cry, love." He swiped at the residue with his thumb.

"I didn't plot with Hugh," she fervently attested.

He examined her, scanning for deceit or cunning, but there was no sign of duplicity and likely never had been. Hugh's treachery had instigated an anger that had burned furiously, but it was rapidly waning. She was wiser than he, pursuing a new beginning, and his initial step toward her had to commence with a speck of trust. Of her, and her motives.

"I believe you."

Chastely, he kissed her, with the simple embrace, tendering apology and receiving pardon. When he tried to move away, she held him just there against her mouth. She opened for him, and the tranquil kiss became something more, something profound and poignant that brushed his very soul.

As their lips parted, she was beholding him with a clear, abiding affection, and he earnestly stated, "I haven't been with Pamela. After you . . . after we . . ." How to divulge this? His chagrin was excruciating. "I went to her bed once, and I couldn't go through with it."

"I believe you," she said, as well.

"I kept thinking about you"—he hated to disclose that she was his greatest—his only—weakness—"and about how much it would hurt you if you knew."

"I'm glad."

"So am I."

There was so much more he yearned to say, but powerful sentiment rocked him, and he was frightened by its strength. Suddenly out of his element, he extended himself next to her, burrowing himself in the crook of her neck, tasting the salt of her skin, inhaling the musk that was her very essence.

He snuggled down to her chest, where her pert nipple poked at his cheek, and he sucked at it, nursing at her breast, easing his woes and consternation. But when she was near, his need for succor transformed, and he grew hard with wanting her, the force of it never ceasing to amaze. He positioned himself, bracing his weight on his arms, and he gazed down at her with what could only be unbridled joy.

Flexing his hips, he dallied until he was fully sheathed, snug in her succulent haven, and his cock expanded as her muscles clenched around him.

"Let's make a babe, Michael." She smiled up at him, welcoming him home. "Give me someone to love besides you, you miserable oaf."

She loved him! Pulse racing with excitement, he was desperate to repeat the sentiment, but the words—never uttered to another—were lodged in his throat, and he couldn't push them out.

His dread of abandonment reared up. It had ruled his life, ever since the day when he was three and his father had forsaken him, and he was overcome by his dormant, destructive fears.

"I can't get you with child!" He was almost wailing. "I'll grant you anything but that!"

"Why?"

"I couldn't bear it."

"Michael . . ."—her exasperation with him was evident—"we're going to have beautiful children. Many, many of them."

"But if you left me, or if something happened . . ."

"I promise you"—she laid her palm on his cheek—"that I will never leave. No matter what." She grinned wickedly. "Despite how obnoxious you are, or how horridly you try my patience, I'll always remain by your side."

He felt driven to explain his anguish, but he wasn't sure he could. After the upheavals of his childhood, he'd survived by becoming a creature of habit, needing regularity and normal routine. He loathed change; it was too painful.

Candidly, he admitted, "I don't know where I belong anymore."

"That's easy. You belong with me. You always have."

He filled her then, entering and retreating, slowly, mindfully, basking in the delectation, but he couldn't restrain himself for long. His hunger ran fierce as ever, and he was frantic and precise, taking them both beyond space and time to where they could soar as one.

When she called his name, he captured her rapturous cry on his lips, cherishing the exquisite and total wantonness with which she let herself go. United with her, his body quivered and, at the last, when he would have pulled away, something mighty—his love for her—prevented him from disengaging.

He longed to gift her with her heart's desire. In a fiery torrent, he emptied himself against her womb, flooding her, and he whispered a prayer that his seed would take root, that he could give her the child she craved.

They floated back to reality, and he was safely cradled in her arms. He kissed her hair, her cheek, her mouth, and his fondness for her wrenched the avowal from his very core.

"I love you," he choked out on a hitched breath.

"Yes, you do," she said, "and I love you, too."

"Will you marry me?" She was confused, so he clarified, "Again? So everyone will know that you are mine?"

She assessed him, checking for cowardice or indecision, but saw neither. "I'd like that very much."

In accord, he nodded, and she nodded, too. Then, he kissed the middle of her hand and laid it on his chest, directly over his heart so that she could feel it beating in a tempo with her own.

He was sated, assuaged, reposed, and as sleep took him, he rested peacefully, aware that when he awoke, she would still be there. That she would be there forever.

Chapter Twenty-four

Sarah dallied in her bedchamber, admiring the beautiful emerald band that Michael had placed on her ring finger, and listening to how quiet the house had grown. With the exception of James and Abigail, the wedding guests had departed, and she was relieved by the pending solitude. Although the occasion had been happy and jubilant, she was impatient to have her husband all to herself.

Day was rapidly turning to evening, and Michael's efficient staff—with a few female members added for her comfort—had the fire burning, candles lit, and a bath laid out in the dressing room.

Iced bottles of French champagne, and an assortment of delectable chocolates, were arranged on a table in the corner, and she couldn't help but be warmed by the sight. On her *first* wedding day, that horrid event at the chapel in Bedford, when she'd erroneously presumed they would have a wedding night in which to partake of them, she'd impishly demanded the treats of Michael.

To her delight, he'd remembered her request, and the humble gesture seemed to be another quiet apology for the things he'd done. In every feasible manner, he continually let her know he was sorry, and she was consistently touched and moved.

Michael had even offered to suffer through the grandest nuptials London had ever seen—if that's what she'd fancied—but he'd have been miserable with an elaborate fete, and opulence had never been her style, either, so she'd opted for an unpretentious affair, one that could be effortlessly planned and hastily thrown together.

With Rebecca still visiting in the country, Sarah hadn't

had any guests to invite, so they'd filled the list with Michael's handful of friends, the senior staff from the club, and a few of his and James's more prominent business associates. They were an engaging, entertaining group of people, their wives amicable and accepting, and the celebration had been extremely merry.

The group was cordial, and they'd appeared sincerely pleased to have Michael married and settled. Any fears she'd harbored about fitting in had vanished. With ease, she could envision herself established in his world. What a blessing that she'd finally escaped her doldrums and traveled to town!

At the window, she stared down into Michael's backyard. *Her* yard, too, she reminded herself, amazed at how she'd barged into his life, at how quickly she'd begun to think of the property as her own. With no trouble at all, she'd made herself at home.

The modest, neatly groomed garden appeared forlorn and dilapidated in the cold of the late December afternoon, and she could just picture how pretty it would be in the spring, when the trees started to bud and the flowers to bloom.

James and Michael were huddled in the center, their heads pressed close, their breath mingling and swirling in a white cloud. The grays and blacks of their formal wedding attire blended with the decaying foliage, but clothing couldn't dull their appeal. They shone brightly, too intrepid, too bold, like exotic birds who'd been dropped from the sky into an alien habitat.

She raised her hand to the pane, feeling the cool glass against her fingertips, as she furtively watched them and wondered what they were discussing. Their relationship had realigned to the steady, firm condition they'd previously enjoyed, their bond devoted and true as it had been before Michael had fled to the country.

Although she wasn't cognizant of what had transpired to resolve their tensions, she supposed that they were simply too attached to be at odds for long. They were different, yet so alike—two peas in a pod, as the saying went—and it was fascinating to be in their company. Their minds worked in similar patterns, their thoughts so attuned that they frequently finished one another's sentences.

James uttered a remark that made Michael laugh aloud and vigorously shake his head, and she couldn't stop smiling. She loved the sound of his joy.

Though she'd only been in residence for two weeks, he'd been transformed, and she liked to secretly postulate that her presence had brought about the striking, welcome changes.

Now, if she could just figure out how to convince him to emit even a fraction of the same openness and solicitude for his parents when they returned from their honeymoon on the Continent, she'd consider herself to have accomplished a major feat.

Sensing her presence, he focused on the upper floors, searching the windows. His blue eyes locked on her, glittering with approval, roving over her form in a languid, sensual perusal. Her nipples were instantaneously alert, her corset laced too tightly, and she was boorishly anxious for James to leave, for her wedding night to commence.

Behind her, footsteps resonated in the hall, and she glanced over her shoulder as Abigail entered the room. With her own family gone, Sarah had every intention of replacing it with Michael's, so she called upon Abigail at every opportunity. In a smattering of days, their relationship had evolved to where it seemed they'd been companions since childhood, that Abigail was the sister she'd never had.

"May I come in?" Abigail asked, her demeanor disheveled and a bit bewildered.

"Please do."

With her pregnancy playing tricks, Abigail had dozed off on a couch during the noisy, boisterous reveling that ensued after the ceremony and, without the woman stirring, James had affectionately carried her upstairs and tucked her in bed for a nap.

"I fell asleep."

"Yes."

"For how long?"

"Only about two hours."

"Aren't I interesting company! How embarrassing."

"Don't worry. No one noticed."

Actually, everyone had, but they'd discreetly watched how sweetly and tenderly James had seen to her welfare. Apparently, James's circle of acquaintances was amazed by the modifications that matrimony had contributed to his character, and the variations were a perpetual topic of gossip by all.

"I was never informed that a woman underwent so many bodily alterations when she was increasing." Abigail moved to Sarah's side. "Just wait till it happens to you."

Sarah absently ran a hand across her abdomen, speculating as to whether it might have already occurred. As though he'd stored up months of lust, Michael couldn't get enough of her. Evidently, he'd merely been biding his time until he could show her how much he needed and wanted her, and now that he could unleash his desire, there was no reining him in.

Since the afternoon of her arrival, they'd rarely left their bed. They couldn't make it down to the parlor, or sit through an entire meal, without rushing back to the bedchamber for another experiment with passion. When they'd been in Bedford, Michael had taught her much, but the brief stint had provided her with only an inkling of the vast array of rapture that was available under his tutelage.

Abigail sidled nearer in order to see what had Sarah so preoccupied. On perceiving the two men, she murmured, "What a dashing pair of rogues they are."

"It ought to be a sin to look so splendid."

"I've always thought so."

Abigail sounded almost petulant about it, and Sarah laughed as they surreptitiously spied on their husbands. Eventually, the duo concluded whatever conversation had them so engrossed. James wrapped an arm across Michael's shoulder—very much the elder, wiser sibling—and they vanished into the house.

For several lengthy moments after they'd disappeared, the two women peered at the spot where they'd been, then the observation burst from Sarah: "Lord, but we're fortunate, aren't we?"

"For a couple of girls from the country," Abigail concurred, "we didn't do too badly for ourselves."

"We certainly didn't."

Downstairs, the men were moving about, the soft hum of their voices drifting up, and Sarah concluded that they were in the parlor, having a last whisky.

She and Abigail shifted away from the window, causing Abigail to heed the candlelight, the covers that had been turned down on the bed, the rose petals strewn about, and Sarah hoped her zeal to be secluded with her husband wasn't too manifest. While she liked Abigail very much, she was ready for some privacy.

"I should be going," Abigail judiciously pronounced, but then she didn't budge. A tad flustered, she ultimately said, "Ah . . . I have something for you."

"Really?" Abigail had planned and hosted the reception, so Sarah had insisted on no other wedding gift from her. They'd agreed, so she couldn't conceive of what it might be, and her curiosity flared when she noted that Abigail was clutching a small leather satchel.

"A few weeks ago," Abigail explained, "I found these pictures of Michael in an old trunk in the attic, and I . . . I . . . didn't imagine they should just be lying about. I thought you might like to have them."

Unable—for some reason—to meet Sarah's gaze, Abigail proffered the portfolio. Sarah opened the flap and pulled out a dozen pen-and-ink drawings. Of her husband. Outrageously handsome. A decade younger. And naked. Very, very naked and disturbingly sexy in each one.

"What the devil . . ." Sarah briskly skimmed through the stack.

"You're aware that they grew up in Paris, aren't you?"

"Yes."

"Well, in their teen years, they had a friend," Abigail clarified. "An artist, who painted this sort of thing for money."

"You have some of James?"

"Three sets," she admitted, blushing a bright scarlet. "It's a long story," was all she added by way of elucidation. "Until I stumbled upon these, I hadn't realized that Michael posed, too."

As she persevered with her chatter, Sarah was energetically thumbing through the pile. From every angle and perspective, Michael was graphically, diligently depicted. He was etched with great care; front, back, side, no position remained unportrayed, and the artist was clearly a master at detailing the human form.

Michael was sumptuous, smug, vainglorious and, while much of his torso was narrower—his muscles and bones not thoroughly matured into the manly physique he would ultimately acquire—other parts of his anatomy were painstakingly delineated, and she couldn't quit gawking.

Even at such a tender age, his *best* attribute had been fully developed.

"Oh, my . . ." She used one of the drawings to fan her face against the sudden temperature of the room. "Did you peek at these?"

"I told James I hadn't, but"—a wicked and naughty disposition glimmered in Abigail's eye—"I especially like number six."

"You brazen hussy!" Sarah giggled like a schoolgirl as she swiftly hastened to the sixth picture. Michael was a negligent model, with an arm leaned against a window frame as he insolently pouted over his shoulder at the artist. The posture was provocative, arousing, his hind legs tight and defined. And his bare posterior was so damned cute.

"Number *six* is definitely entertaining," she promptly assented.

"Anyway"—Abigail was almost stammering—"you might have fun with them. Tonight and whenever . . ." Her cheeks colored to a blazing shade of crimson, and she clasped her hands over them, trying to ward off the flash of heat. "Oh, mercy me! I'd better be off."

They made their good-byes, with Abigail contending that Sarah needn't accompany her downstairs, and Sarah was glad. With only James and Abigail still in attendance, there wouldn't be much time before Michael joined her, and she needed every second to prepare. Now that she was in possession of Abigail's marvelous gift, she required a few moments to deduce how to utilize it to premium advantage.

Abigail started out, then halted in the doorway. "Don't you dare tell James I snooped at those pictures!"

"I won't," Sarah vowed, chuckling as Abigail scuttled away.

Immediately after Abigail's exit, one of the maids conveniently popped in. Sarah flung her pouch of illustrations on the bed, then mellowed as she was stripped of her clothes, her hair brushed out, but she declined the other woman's offer to apply lotions or perfumes.

Dismissing her, Sarah instructed that they not be disturbed till the morn, then she proceeded to her bath, sinking into the hot water and attempting to relax while she waited for her husband.

Her husband! The luscious concept tickled her stomach and ignited her anxiety. He would arrive anon, animated, domineering, urgent for her and what she could give him, and she couldn't stand the anticipation, so she strove to contemplate some other topic, but diversion was impossible.

Her ears perked, detecting the faint noises of James's and Abigail's farewells, which meant Michael would enter directly. She slumped down in the tub, immersing her breasts, her shoulders, aiming for every inch of her body to be wet and slippery.

Presently, he was ascending the stairs, then advancing down the hall. She paused until he was in the outer bedchamber, then she clambered to her knees, lazily stretching her arms, showing him her backside. Knowing he was at the door, she pretended she hadn't noticed, but she could sense him behind her, prowling like a caged animal.

Coming up on her feet, she stepped onto the rug, whirling about just as he moved into the room.

"Good evening, Mrs. Stevens." He formally greeted her, tipping his head in acknowledgment, and her heart did a colossal flip-flop at his mode of address.

"Mr. Stevens," she answered just as precisely.

His sapphire eyes shimmered with desire and something more, something she wouldn't even try to name. The cooler air had hoisted goose bumps on her skin, her nipples constricted, and he reached out and stroked an erect nub. "Always a pleasure to find you at your bath."

"Would you like to take one, too?"

"Momentarily. First, let's share a glass of champagne."

Remarkably, he wasn't his customary poised, confident self, and it was odd that, after their lewd frolicking of the past days, he could be nervous. Then, she recognized that she was tense, too. Assuredly, speaking those binding vows could unsettle a person; it hadn't been any less austere the second time around.

"I'd like that." The delay would be appreciated; the libation would calm them both. "It's a tad chilly in here. Would you dry me?"

Retrieving a towel off the vanity, he rubbed it up and down her back, front, bottom, legs, then he enfolded her in the large cloth, tucking the flap at her cleavage to secure it in place. His arms went around her, and he pulled her close.

"How was your wedding, madam?"

The query was lightly hurled, but his wasn't an idle question. With him, they never were. There was a lost little boy lurking at his core who desperately sought approval, though she'd never disclose that she pictured him as being so vulnerable.

"Everything I'd hoped for and more," she responded honestly. She lifted up on her tiptoes and kissed him on the mouth. "Thank you."

"You're welcome."

"I like your friends."

"I don't have many," he broached as though it was a crime.

"You're just choosy."

"No. I admit it's the beast in me. I scare people off."

"Without a doubt," she chuckled, "but not me."

"Aren't I the lucky one?" The opinion was voiced with much more sentiment than he'd meant to show.

"Yes, you are," she admonished, and she intended to regularly remind him just how fortunate he was. "Is everyone gone?" she inquired, though she knew they were.

"Yes, praise be." Breathtaking and magnificent, he smiled down at her. "I thought I'd never get you alone."

"Poor baby," she crooned. "Were you pining away?"

"All day."

The gentle admission incited profound emotion. How she loved this man and always would! Since he could be rude, overbearing, and pushy, there was no accounting for it, but who could ever rationalize why two people belonged together?

Occasionally, they discussed their novel connection in the dark of night, when shadows made it comfortable for Michael to confess what was in his heart. Why had they met? From where did this impression of abiding affinity emanate? Early on, she'd sensed it, and since her arrival in London, it had flourished anew.

How would it burgeon as time progressed? What would they feel in a month? In six?

She looked down the road, through their middle years and beyond, and she could behold him by her side, the radiant center of her life. The notion brought such exultation and contentment that a few blasted tears sprang to her eyes, and she tamped them down, refusing to exhibit an uncontrollable, maudlin rush that would likely leave her foolishly blubbering.

"I'm ready to drink that champagne now." She clasped his hand and led him into the bedchamber.

"Will you be naked while we are?"

"Is that how you'd like me to be?"

"Eternally."

"You're insatiable."

"Only since you stumbled into my life."

"Liar." She laughed, proceeding to the table laden with food and drink. "I saw how you misbehaved before I came along."

"And you'll never let me forget, will you?"

"Maybe in forty or fifty years."

While she tracked his every move, he opened the champagne and filled one glass, then toasted her. "Here's hoping it'll be that long. Or even longer."

"Here's hoping," she echoed.

"I love you."

Not a man to bandy about the word *love,* it was only the second instance he'd proclaimed himself, and her heart skidded with felicity and bliss. "I love you, too. I always will."

He tendered the glass so she could take a sip, and he twisted it so he could drink from the same spot on the rim. Then, startling her, he gripped an arm around her waist, and hauled her next to him. Using the stem of the goblet, he pushed down her towel, baring a breast, and she hitched a breath as he dribbled cold champagne across the extended tip, inducing it to pucker even further.

Leaning down, he laved it clean with his tongue, soaked it again, then dropped to his knees and indulged, slowly and exhaustively sucking at her. She adored how his lips toiled, how he dabbled and played. Her womb stirred, her thighs flexed; between her legs, she was moist and inclined to dally.

Sifting her fingers through his hair, she let it fall across her chest. Huddled there over her bosom, he looked sublime, and she rested her hand on his neck, imploring him, urging him on.

Inevitably, he pulled away, and he peered up at her, more wicked and dangerous than usual. He grabbed her buttocks and spurred her nearer, burying his face in her stomach, inhaling her essence. "You make me so hard."

"Good."

"I better have that bath. Or I'll never get it done."

"Would you like me to wash you?"

"Wench!" he chided, grinning, but he abruptly sobered. "Actually, I don't think so. I need a few minutes to myself." Mystified, confused, he asked, "Am I crazy?"

"No. It's been quite a day."

"Yes, it has." Briefly, it appeared that he might expound, but as she'd discovered, his revelations were saved for the wee hours. "You don't mind?" he probed.

"Go on." She assisted him to his feet and waved him toward the door, snatching a kiss as he passed by.

As he went about his business, she tended to her own, slipping into black stockings and mules, a sheer black robe. Checking her reflection in the mirror, she liked what she saw and decided to don nothing more. A hint of her nipples was defined through the thin fabric, and the middle of her torso was visible, showing her cushion of woman's hair, and a flash of smooth thigh, that added highlight and intrigue to the seductiveness.

On their bed, she fluffed the pillows, then reclined. The door to the dressing room was ajar, and she caught sporadic glimpses of Michael leaned back, his arms balanced on the edges of the tub. The familiarity of his motions should have been soothing—the water lapping, the washcloth rubbing over his skin—and she shut her eyes but couldn't calm herself.

Craving distraction, she picked up the portfolio of illustrations Abigail had given her. Avidly, she perused each picture, lingering over his various nude positions, assessing the width of his shoulders, the tuck of his waist, the curve of his rear. The representations were so lifelike; she felt she could jump into the drawings and tarry with him at will.

One, in particular, was mesmerizing. Spread out on a daybed, an arm casually bent behind his head, he was aroused, his phallus elongated and potent, and his fist was loosely clutched around it. Arrogant, imperious, intent on gratification, he focused resolutely, his body strained, as though he was expecting a lover who would eagerly service him in any fashion he demanded.

Had a woman been present when the picture was sketched? The notion had her recalling the other instances when she'd seen him engaged in ribald behavior, and she couldn't refrain from recollecting how riveting they had been. How improper. How utterly thrilling and wanton. Perfect musings, for the perfect wedding night.

Michael was climbing out of the tub, drying himself. "You're awfully quiet in there," he mentioned. "Are you all right?"

She couldn't help smiling. "I'm just doing a little light reading."

"I've got plans for you, so don't become too engrossed."

"Too late." She ran the tip of her finger across the shape of his cock. It was an odd tactile sensation, as if she was really touching him, and it made her completely wild to experience the genuine article.

What was it about nudity, about indecency and vice, that had such a stunning effect on her character? There was something so marvelously inappropriate about studying displays that she oughtn't to witness, or espying scenes she was never meant to view. Once she encountered a licentious spectacle, she couldn't prevent herself from wanting to see more.

"My goodness . . ." Just as he set foot in the room, she flipped to the next portrait—a bodily profile that flawlessly outlined his jutting cock. "I'd always heard that things like this went on in Paris, but I never believed any of the stories."

"What about Paris?" He filled another glass of champagne, then approached the bed, savoring the sparkling liquid. "I grew up there, remember?"

"Oh, yes. I remember."

"I'd like to take you visiting sometime, when the national upset is ended."

Garbed only in a towel, swathed at the waist, his eyes were tinted to a more absorbing shade. Smelling clean and manly, like soap and heat, his skin was damp, the tips of his hair curly from the steamy water. His crotch bulging deliciously, he was sin and iniquity swaddled in a dark blue package.

"What do you have there?" he inquired.

"A belated wedding gift from Abigail." She examined him carefully. "Turn sideways, would you?"

Unsuspecting, he complied without pondering her request.

"Drop your towel."

He started to, then stopped, the peculiarity sinking in. "Why?"

Endeavoring to keep a straight face, she glanced at the drawing, then dragged her torrid attention to those private parts that never ceased to intrigue and captivate her. "You've matured well over the past decade, but I want to compare."

"What are you talking about?"

Just then, he detected her treasure, and she prankishly shoved the stack under her hip, striving to hide it but not succeeding. Giggling, she scooted across the bed, but he leapt onto the mattress and pinned her down before she could escape. His hips pressed into her, his cock swelling ample and solid against her leg.

"Let me see!"

"No."

Playfully, he wrestled her prize into the open and, when he yanked it from her, there was no doubt that he recognized it for what it was. For once, he was rendered speechless. Mortified, too. A red flush initiated down low and swept up his chest and onto his cheeks.

He was aghast. "Where did you get these?"

"From Abigail."

Issuing a strangled groan, he rolled off her and onto his back, throwing an arm over his face. Chagrined, he stared toward the ceiling for a lengthy interval, then his elbow rose, and he peeked out at her. "Did she look at them?"

"Only number six." Snuggling over his chest, she hauled his arm away, and kissed him. "She thinks you have a cute bottom."

That strangled wail recurred. "James will murder me if he finds out. You'll be a widow."

"So I gather." She winked. "Your unique male beauty will remain Abigail's and my special secret."

"I'll never be able to go to supper at their house again. She'll constantly be assessing my rear."

"Probably." Considering his recurrent, dubious antics with women, it was charming that he could be so easily embarrassed. "You're very sexy in these. Young, too. You realize that we *older* women are extremely fascinated by younger men, don't you?"

"I've created a monster." As this was not the initial circumstance in which he'd made the point, he sighed. Resigned, he spun on top of her, trapping her to the mattress once more. "What will you do with them?"

"I guess I'll have them framed and hung in my boudoir, so I can gaze at them whenever I'm in the mood."

"Jezebel." He dipped under her chin and nipped at her nape. "Strumpet."

"You know how much I like to watch." She batted her lashes. "I learned from the master."

"And I suppose that's another topic of which I'll never hear the end."

"Maybe in forty or fifty years," she repeated.

"How wonderful"—he smiled at her, the power of it dazzling to behold—"to have you whispering in my ear all that time."

He took the collection and laid it on the stand next to the bed. Then, he rotated across the mattress, bringing her with him until she was on top. Her sex hovering eagerly over his, she braced herself on one arm, staring down at him as he sprawled against the white bedcoverings.

His mat of alluring chest hair begged to be stroked, causing her nerves to quiver and tingle. His tempting mouth—

that had simply been made for kissing—enticed her to sample. During their wrestling, his towel had come free, and his nether regions were exposed, cajoling her to look, to taste, to touch.

"Who needs to watch," he indicated, "when you can enjoy the real thing for yourself?" Taking her hand, he stroked it across the pebbled bump of his nipple.

"My thoughts exactly."

Stretching and purring like a contented cat, she splayed her fingers and rubbed in slow circles, feeling his heart thundering beneath her palm.

Suddenly ablaze, expectant, and wild with her desire for him, she tugged off her robe and tossed it on the floor.